I0762536

All Carry

ALSO BY GENE WOJCIECHOWSKI

Pond Scum and Vultures

You've Got to Have Balls to Make It in This League (with Pam Postema)

Nothing but Net (with Bill Walton)

I Love Being the Enemy (with Reggie Miller)

My Life on a Napkin (with Rick Majerus)

About 80 Percent Luck

Cubs Nation

The Bus (with Jerome Bettis)

The Last Great Game

My Conference Can Beat Your Conference (with Paul Finebaum)

No Excuses (with Bob Stoops)

Out of the Pocket (with Kirk Herbstreit)

All Carry

A Novel

GENE WOJCIECHOWSKI

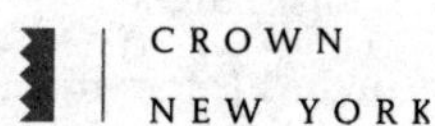

CROWN
NEW YORK

Crown
An imprint of the Crown Publishing Group
A division of Penguin Random House LLC
1745 Broadway
New York, NY 10019
crownpublishing.com
penguinrandomhouse.com

Library of Congress Cataloging-in-Publication Data
Names: Wojciechowski, Gene author
Title: All carry: a novel / Gene Wojciechowski.
Description: First edition. | New York: Crown, 2026.
Identifiers: LCCN 2025030110 | ISBN 9798217085828 hardcover | ISBN 9798217085842 trade paperback | ISBN 9798217085835 ebook
Subjects: LCGFT: Novels | Fiction
Classification: LCC PS3623.O53 A66 2026
LC record available at https://lccn.loc.gov/2025030110

Hardcover ISBN 979-8-217-08582-8
Ebook ISBN 979-8-217-08583-5

Editor: Amy Einhorn
Associate editor: Lori Kusatzky
Production editor: Liana Parry Faughnan
Text designer: Amani Shakrah
Production: Chris Andrus
Copy editor: Sibylle Kazeroid
Proofreaders: Vicki Fischer and Barbara Greenberg
Publicist: Elora Weil
Marketer: Hannah Perrin

Manufactured in the United States of America

1st Printing

First Edition

The authorized representative in the EU for product safety and compliance is Penguin Random House Ireland, Morrison Chambers, 32 Nassau Street, Dublin D02 YH68, Ireland, https://eu-contact.penguin.ie.

To my dad, Chet, who put the first club in my hand

All Carry

CHAPTER ONE

A Large Bucket

It was a dump.

The best thing you could say about the driving range was that it had a nice view of the commuter trains as they caromed back and forth from Chicago on the Union Pacific West Line. And that only three of the fifteen ancient and threadbare artificial grass mats had been stolen in the past month.

But it was Max "Hard Way" Mitchell's dump—or it would be in 109 more monthly payments. Located near an industrial park about twelve minutes west of his hometown of Wheaton, Illinois, the driving range covered seventeen acres. He had bought it on a whim after the commercial real estate agent convinced him that it would be a smart investment property. Back then, Hard Way was making solid money on the PGA Tour as a caddie. He could afford to take a financial flyer. Of course, that was before "The Incident."

Now he was eating cold Beefaroni out of the can for lunch and living in a converted storage room in the driving range office shack. He had a TV, a bed, a hot plate, and a toaster oven. He did his dishes in the office's bathroom sink. Even after giving up his apartment, he was struggling to pay his utilities, his grocery bills, and the monthly nut on the driving range. His checking account needed CPR, his savings account was a myth, and his pickup truck was approaching beater status. Marching bands made less noise.

Hard Way had purchased the property in the dead of winter, when snow masked the width and breadth of the landfill, and the hawk wind blew the smell of the methane gases away from the former cornfield. But it was summer now, and there was no mistaking that ever-growing garbage pile as it sat like a raised mole on the flat skin of western DuPage County. No amount of technology or venting pipes could eliminate the stench. And yet, Hard Way had grown to love his scruffy property.

It was late Tuesday afternoon. Other than the adjunct professor from the DePaul extension campus who had snuck over before his first class that morning, and the elderly couple who had split a small bucket during lunchtime, nobody had been there all day. A new SmashGolf facility only three miles away had stabbed his business in the heart. Everyone wanted to be entertained: electronic scoring, circle targets, animation, data monitors, a waitstaff, queso and chips. Whatever happened to finding your swing in the dirt, like Hogan did?

Hard Way's place, whimsically named To the Linksland (in honor of one of his favorite golf books), did have one thing that SmashGolf didn't: real grass. It wasn't much, but it was actual bentgrass, which was lovingly cared for by Hard Way and was the exact same variety found on Chicago Golf Club's fairways. He had seeded the area at the far end of the artificial mats, where there was enough room to rotate the hitting areas so the grass could recover from use—not that To the Linksland got much use these days. But the bentgrass was his baby, which he push-mowed and hand-watered on a regular schedule.

Hard Way was laboring through the *New York Times* crossword puzzle when he heard the screen door to the range shack open and close. He didn't bother looking up.

"How much for a bucket?" said the man's voice.

"Eight bucks for a large, five for a small," Hard Way said. "An extra two bucks for either if you hit off the grass patch instead of the mats."

"Thanks," the voice said. "Left you a ten."

Hard Way was only half listening as he scrolled down the row of crossword clues. As the door banged shut, he looked up just in time to see the back of the man through the screen, the green plastic bucket in his right hand, a Sunday bag slung over his left shoulder. "Hey! What's a ten-letter golf saying that dates back to 1681?" Hard Way shouted.

In the distance, Hard Way heard the voice.

"Try 'Far and Sure'!"

Hard Way filled out 31-Across.

"I'll be damned."

Hard Way spent the next hour finishing the puzzle (with some help from Google) and then worked his way through his monthly bills. As usual, more was going out than coming in. No amount of cooking the books was going to save this balance sheet.

At 6:30 P.M., Hard Way turned off the green neon OPEN sign in the shack's window and then fired up the ancient John Deere tractor equipped with an even older range ball picker. Gathering up three buckets of balls—that was the extent of the day's business—would take five minutes, tops.

Hard Way immediately spotted what he assumed to be the elderly couple's shots, most of them well short of the 100-yard marker. The picker scooped up the black-striped yellow balls in no time at all. Next, he weaved back and forth to pick up the professor's drives, some of which had almost reached the 225-yard sign. Hard Way had worked with him on his swing that morning. The professor was getting better.

But where were the other balls? He was still missing a large bucket's worth.

Hard Way steered the Deere toward the right edge of the range to check for banana slices, and then to the left edge to look for snap hooks. Nothing.

He put the tractor in neutral and scanned the acreage with his range finder. That's when he saw something in the distance.

"Nah," he said as he jammed the shifter into gear. "Can't be."

Hard Way drove past the 250-yard sign and then the 275-yard marker. When he bought the place, he had added a 300-yard sign that read HIT IT HERE, GET A FREE BUCKET. Nobody ever came close. And just for fun, he had erected a 400-yard marker with a painted bull's-eye and message on it: HIT IT HERE, GET A MASTERS INVITATION. You needed binoculars to read it from the range mats.

But there, at the 400-yard sign, were what looked to be seventy-five or so golf balls: the approximate number that fit into a large bucket. Hard Way turned off the engine, opened the pockmarked metal mesh door to the tractor cage, and walked toward the marker.

The balls were in three areas, as if they were separate herds grazing on the weeds and grass of the range. There were about twenty-five balls just beyond and to the left of the marker. Hard Way walked it off: 413 yards. Another twenty-five or so balls were a yard or two in front and slightly to the left of the sign. The remaining balls were gathered to the right and just past the sign—404 yards, in this case. If Hard Way hadn't known better, he'd have sworn someone had been working on their draw, baby draw, and power fade. The last time he'd seen a player do something like this, it was Tiger Woods. Nobody shaped shots like he did. But this was farther than Tiger ever hit his driver. It looked like a precision bombing exercise. Rory McIlroy and Ludvig Åberg could bomb it. So could Bryson DeChambeau, especially during his distended-stomach experiment phase, when he treated every day as if he were Joey Chestnut at Nathan's, but not like this. This was supernatural.

Hard Way checked the trees lining the right side of the fairway. The branches were barely stirring, and what wind there was had a hurty feel to it. As for roll, forget it; it had rained a day earlier. The ground was soft, the grass high and unmowed.

This was impossible. Nobody could hit a ball this far, especially not one of Hard Way's battered one-piece, rubber-core, Surlyn-covered range balls bought thirdhand. It was like hitting a walnut shell.

Hard Way made another sweep of the rear of the range. Maybe some of his buddies were having a laugh at his expense. But no, nothing.

Then Hard Way remembered.

"Far and Sure, my ass," he muttered. "Who the hell *was* that guy?"

CHAPTER TWO

Three Months Earlier, on a Friday . . .

"Jesus, Mary, and Joseph, not another garage sale, Mom."

Laurel Riley spun around from the worn bucket seat of her very used white Odyssey minivan and glared at her eight-year-old son, who glared defiantly back from his perch on his plastic booster seat in the second row. As an elementary school teacher, she was accustomed to precocious kids. But her younger son was in a class by himself.

"Chet, if I could sell you at a garage sale, I'd do it," she said. "But nobody would want you."

"Maybe we can try this morning," Chet said, now staring down at his iPad. "Mrs. Sievers says my diagnostic testing puts me in the top 1 percent. I'd make someone very happy."

Chet glanced up in time to see his mom shaking her head in the rearview mirror.

"Keep talking and I'll turn this car around right now," she said.

"Promise?" Chet said.

"You know, I'm going to make that DNA testing appointment after all," Laurel answered. "You can't be mine. There must have been a mistake at the hospital."

"Was it a secondhand hospital?"

This time Laurel smiled.

"Well played, my little dude."

"Thanks, Mom."

"But he's right, Mom," Chet's older brother, Buddy, said. "This is such a mid way to spend a Friday morning."

"I don't know what that means—'mid,'" she said as she drove slowly through the Arrowhead subdivision in search of driveway bargains. "Translation, please."

Buddy sighed in exasperation. He had just gotten home from Madison three days earlier, his sophomore year at Wisconsin now in the books. His only plans were to sleep late, work little, and party much before his summer internship began the following week. Getting roll-called out of bed by his mom at seven-thirty on a Saturday morning was a nightmare scenario.

"'Mid' means average, below average," he said, slouched in the front seat of the minivan. "And this is so below average. I can't believe you woke me up for this."

"You can sleep in tomorrow," she said. "But I wanted to get out and about before everything got picked over. This is prime early-bird shopping time."

"Great," Buddy said. "You can never have too many salt and pepper shakers, or puzzles of the Grand Canyon."

"Oh, c'mon," she said. "I bet you loved that puzzle we sent in the care package."

"I almost had to switch frat houses, Mom. Kittens dressed as U.S. presidents? Do you know how humiliating that was? It was—"

"Mid?" she said.

"Negative-integer mid."

"And yet you survived. Now you're helping the woman who bore you. Life's full of trade-offs."

"Seriously, Mom. You're like a thrift-shop addict. You know, they have actual stores where they sell furniture and clothes and books and albums and pepper shakers that no one has ever used."

"Oh, look," she said, ignoring him as she parked the minivan in front of a house with a promising display of merchandise. "Is that an Amish accent table?"

She was out the door and in the driveway before Buddy and Chet could unfasten their seat belts. Buddy pulled out his cell phone and began checking his texts. Nothing. Of course not—everyone he knew was still asleep.

"Buddy!" his mom yelled from the driveway. "Come here and bring me my purse."

Buddy grabbed the worn and weary brown leather bag from the back seat and took it to her. Chet found a place on the front stoop and returned to his video.

As his mom haggled with a young woman over the price of the accent table, Buddy walked into the garage and looked at the items lined up neatly on folding tables. There were American Girl dolls missing assorted limbs, a Chicago Monopoly game, a CD player, a row of Cubs baseball cards in plastic sleeves, a frayed Michael Jordan poster, a Crock-Pot, and an Old Style neon sign. On another table were rows of DVD movies. It was Relicpalooza.

Behind the tables and leaning against the interior wall of the garage were four golf bags, each one in worse condition than the next. An orange Powerbilt bag featured a battered metal driver and a handful of irons covered in dust and spiderwebs. There were several Adams fairway woods in the blue canvas bag next to it. A Top Flite bag with tags from the nearby Arrowhead Golf Club contained nothing more than a sand wedge and a pitching wedge, both gouged and battered to the point of uselessness. Buddy didn't bother with the fourth bag, a strapless white leather MacGregor bag featuring a tear that ran from the top lip to the bottom. There were woods, but each one was covered with an old athletic sock. And the irons had worn plastic covers on them.

Buddy, bored by it all, began to search for his mom. There she was, a floor lamp in one hand, a pepper shaker in the other. He started to walk out of the garage.

"You a golfer?"

Buddy was startled by the voice. He turned, and there in the shadows of the garage doorway leading into the house was an old man sitting in a wheelchair.

"Geezus," Buddy said. "I didn't see you there."

"I saw you," said the old man, who wore a USS *Higbee* DD-806 baseball cap. "You a golfer?"

"Not really."

"You were looking at those clubs like you were a golfer."

"My dad likes to play."

"You don't?"

"Used to, but I sort of gave up the game."

"Were you any good?"

"Decent. Better than my dad."

"Maybe he needs an equipment change, eh?" the old man said, gesturing toward the strapless bag. "You didn't look in that one."

"Yeah, that's OK. The others were kinda outdated."

"Hell, so am I," the old man said as he removed his cap and wiped his forehead with his forearm.

"What's a *Higbee* DD-806?" Buddy said, pointing at the cap.

The old man examined the ship silhouette above its bill.

"You know anything about the U.S. Navy?" he said.

"Not really."

He tossed the cap to Buddy.

"I was a machinist's mate on the *Higbee* during my tour in Vietnam. The DD is navy language for a destroyer. The 806 was its hull number. She was the first warship in the U.S. Navy to ever be named for a woman, a chief nurse named Lenah Higbee."

"My granddad flew fighters in Vietnam," Buddy said.

"He returned home safely?" the old man said.

"He did. My dad said he never talked about the war."

"That isn't unusual."

"He died of a heart attack a couple of years after I was born. I never had a chance to know him."

"Well, you know of his bravery."

"I guess I do. You survived, too."

"It was a war conceived by fools. I had friends who never returned. I was fortunate, as was your grandfather."

Buddy ran his finger across the raised emblem on the back of the hat, which featured a woman holding a trident and bow and with a quiver full of arrows strapped to her side. "What's this about?"

"You need to learn your Greek mythology," the old man said.

"I'm a business major," Buddy said. "Greek mythology doesn't come up much."

"That was the *Higbee*'s logo: 'Goddess of the Hunt.' If you studied the classics, you'd know that was taken from the Greek goddess Artemis. The *Higbee* saw service in World War II, Korea, Vietnam. She was decommissioned in '79, sunk as a target in '86. She had a helluva run."

"That's cool," Buddy said. "I mean, not the sinking part, but everything else." He handed back the cap.

"She was a damn good ship," the old man said. Then he pointed toward the fourth golf bag again. "And those are damn good clubs. You'd be wise to give them a look."

"Yeah, OK," Buddy said, hoping to humor the old man and then move on. He pulled a sock off the largest of the woods, expecting to see another dinged-up, second-generation, infomercial-quality metal driver. It was a driver, but it wasn't metal. In fact, it was unlike anything Buddy had ever seen.

"It's all wood," a surprised Buddy said, carefully removing the club from the bag. "This is a driver?"

"It is," the old man said. "A very special driver."

Buddy, suddenly reverent, turned the clubhead upside down and read from the metal plate screwed flush into its back.

"MacGregor Tommy Armour 945W driver," he said. He looked up at the old man. "It looks like it's never been hit."

"It hasn't. Well, that's not exactly true. There was one time . . ." His voice trailed off.

"The wood is—"

"Persimmon," the old man said. "It's one of the strongest, hardest common woods you can find. Only hickory is stronger. Look at the insert on the face of the club: the original MacGregor red and white. It has a mahogany finish. This was made by an engineer who was also a craftsman."

"You?" Buddy said.

"No, it was only a hobby to me. But I knew the man who designed these clubs. His name was Jack Wullkotte. Ever heard of him?"

"Should I have?"

"I suppose not. Long before your time. He was ninety-two years old and still tinkering with clubs when he died in 2022. Now look at the grip."

Buddy twirled the club like a baton until the grip rested in his left hand. He wedged the pinky of his right hand with his left.

"It's not very soft," said Buddy.

The old man noticed how comfortable Buddy's grip looked on the club. The lead hand and trail hand were positioned perfectly, the clubhead square. It was the grip of someone who had been taught well.

"It's wrapped in Lamkin leather grips with paper underlisting, 1/64th of an inch over standard size; it's not supposed to be soft. And in the butt end of the grip is a small weight."

"Why?"

"Because the man who played these clubs liked it that way. Wullkotte would make a $^{3}/_{8}$-ounce wooden dowel with lead in it, and then put the dowel at the end of the grip."

"You lost me," Buddy said.

"A club is all about balance, swing weight . . . *feel*. That clubhead is a D6 swing weight, but the player wanted D3. So instead of drilling any weight out of the clubhead—that would change how the club felt; it would reduce the mass of the clubhead—Wullkotte used the dowel as a counterweight. He did this with the 3-wood and the 5-wood too. You follow?"

"Sort of," Buddy said. "But wooden drivers don't go very far, right? That's why everyone uses metal woods. This clubhead is so small compared to my dad's."

"The man who played these clubs could hit this driver 341 yards, and that's with those liquid-core MacGregor Tourney balls, which were notoriously awful. With the balls they're using these days, he could have hit it 380 . . . 390, easy, in his prime."

"Uh-huh," Buddy said, not believing any of it.

"You're skeptical."

"I'm just saying that if wood—"

"Persimmon," the old man said, correcting him.

"If persimmon is so amazing, why aren't they still using it?"

"Because there's no artistry anymore. Drivers look like they're eight months pregnant. That club you're holding is a work of art: 43½ inches long, 9½ degrees of loft. It took Wullkotte 125 different steps to make *one* driver. He would make twenty-five drivers and maybe, just maybe, the player would like one of them."

"That Wullkotte guy sounds like he had a perfection problem," Buddy said.

"Perfection isn't a problem," the old man said. "It's an aspiration. To him, each driver had its own personality. He was the Antonio Stradivari of golf clubs."

"Who's that?"

"Don't they teach you anything in school? Stradivari built the finest violins ever made."

"Like I said—"

"I know, you're a business major."

"They *are* beautiful clubs," Buddy said. "Can I look at the rest of them?"

"I'd be disappointed if you didn't," the old man said.

Buddy carried the bag to the doorway. He removed the socks from the rest of the woods and then took the plastic covers off the irons. The grooves were in pristine condition. Virgins, it seemed.

"Forged MacGregor Limited Editions based on the Pro-81 template," the old man said. "The shafts are Dynamic Gold X100s with 5-inch tapered wooden dowels that were air hammered in at the tips. The grinds were done to perfection by Don White: flat sole, standard toe, straight leading edge, not much of a heel-to-toe radius, a topline that was thin but not too thin. White was the only person that Wullkotte ever trusted to grind Jack's irons."

"Man, you know a lot about clubs," Buddy said. "You sound like my dad. He's totally into the history of the game."

"Then he's a man I would be proud to know. You say he's not a very good player?"

"He tries. He used to be a caddie when he was my age, so you'd think he'd be better."

"A caddie? A noble endeavor. Here in town?"

"Over at Chicago Golf. He was an Evans Scholar."

The old man was impressed. The Evans Scholars program was named after the legendary Chick Evans, who grew up in Chicago and won two U.S. Amateurs and the 1916 U.S. Open as an amateur. The four-year scholarships were awarded to high-school-aged caddies with academic chops and financial needs. More than twelve thousand caddies had gone to college thanks to the Evans Scholars Foundation.

No local club was more invested in the program than Chicago Golf Club, the country's oldest eighteen-hole layout and perennially ranked among the top fifteen courses in the country. Chicago Golf, as it was known, was less than a mile from the old man's house in Wheaton. It bordered St. Michael's Cemetery to the north, Plamondon Road to the west, and a smattering of houses (all carefully hidden by trees) to the south and east. The club's entrance sign was the size of a license plate and surrounded by evergreens. Chicago Golf prided itself on its discretion and privacy. Its membership was small (for years, only 125 or so) but diverse and often distinguished (Masters champion Ben Crenshaw and noted course developer Mike Keiser, among others). The membership process was rigorous, often lengthy, and by invitation only. You didn't choose Chicago Golf; it chose you. Wealth and standing weren't a prerequisite, but patience and humility were. You couldn't buy your way into Chicago Golf, and if you tried, your hopes never made it past the evergreens at road's edge.

Chicago Golf treasured its caddies. Among the club's finest traditions was allowing any caddie who had done at least three loops (a "loop" was caddie-speak for carrying a member's bag for a round) the previous week to play the course on Mondays. Some of those same teenage caddies had returned years later as members of the club.

"What college did he attend?" the old man said.

"Wisconsin," Buddy said. "That's where I go."

"So he worked his way through high school and college—that tells me something about the man. And to caddie at the masterpiece that is Chicago Golf. You realize it was one of the five founding clubs in this country, that the United States Golf Association says no accurate history of golf in this country can be written without including Chicago Golf. In fact, the USGA might not exist without that club."

"If you say so," Buddy said.

"You don't share your father's passion for the game?"

The question caught Buddy off guard. It instantly took him to a place that both he and his father had pushed just below the surface of their relationship. Buddy weighed his response.

Was it worth telling the old man that he once had been a promising junior player, at one point ranked nationally in the top 300? That he had reported to Chicago Golf for caddie training during the summer before his freshman year in high school, just as his own dad had done decades earlier? That during his caddie debut, he had been assigned to a prospective member who had handed Buddy a sleeve of extra golf balls before arriving at the first tee and had said under his breath, "I need to impress these guys, so if I lose one in the rough, pretend you found it with one of these"? That when Buddy hesitated, the guest, a C-suite type who was used to getting his way, had said, "You're a caddie, not a conscience. Just do what I say, kid"? That Buddy had put the identically numbered and marked balls in his back pocket, and when so ordered by the guest, had miraculously "found" several of his player's errant shots in the thick, shin-high fescue? That one of the other caddies had spotted Buddy reach into his back pocket during a group search for a lost ball on the 18th hole and had told one of the Chicago Golf members, who then had confronted the guest? That the guest had expressed outrage at Buddy's actions, had dismissed him on the spot, and, in a final act of audacity, had lectured the members on the need to better vet their caddies?

No, Buddy decided, he would keep those humiliating memories to himself. He had been caught in the act of cheating and had deserved to be tossed from the course and the caddie program. He was ashamed that he had let the guest intimidate him, ashamed that he had knowingly done the wrong thing.

Of course, he had had to wait a week until he could tell his dad in person. Joe Riley had been out of town at the U.S. Open—what else was new? He was always gone, it seemed. The irony was that the final round of the U.S. Open was always played on Father's Day. Buddy had become resentful of his dad's absences. The day had lost its meaning to him. He didn't even bother buying his dad a card.

When his dad did return home, the confession had quickly devolved into an argument and then a shouting match. Buddy had tried to explain how the guest had bullied him into cheating, how he had felt helpless as a first-time caddie, how sorry he was that he hadn't acted differently and more honorably.

But he received no sympathy from his dad. Riley had repeated the maxim preached to him by his own father: "If you're going to do something, then do it right." In Riley's view, Buddy had failed on every level that day. "I taught you better than that," Riley had said. "We're going back to Chicago Golf, and you're going to apologize to the other caddies, and to the members who were in that group. Maybe they'll give you another chance."

A defensive, wounded Buddy had lashed back: "It's hard to teach me anything when you're never here."

Before the argument had ended, a defiant Buddy had vowed never to caddie or play again. He could see the hurt in his dad's face as he made the promise. True to his word, though, the stubborn Buddy had never carried another golf bag or swung a club in the six years since the incident. The equally stubborn Riley (like father, like son) had never tried to talk Buddy out of his decision. From that day forward, their relationship had a thick coat of tension covering it. Golf had been their common denominator. Now it separated them.

"Have I lost you?" It was the old man.

"I'm sorry," Buddy said. "I sort of checked out for a few moments, didn't I?"

"You seemed deep in thought. I was asking you about sharing your father's passion for the game."

"Uh, me and my dad don't always see eye to eye. I disappointed him."

"I doubt that."

"Yeah, you don't know my dad."

"I know that dads always love their sons. So whatever is broken between the two of you can be fixed."

"Well, he wanted me to play golf—and I don't. He wanted me to caddie at Chicago Golf—and I don't."

"Hmmm. Then maybe you can impress him with your knowledge of golf's history."

"Doubtful."

"Then let's begin your education. Certainly you know that the man who did the original design of the course was of Scottish descent and played handmade clubs from Old Tom Morris's shop in St. Andrews, that he *knew* Old Tom, that he played against the legendary Young Tom Morris during his time there."

Buddy sighed, thought, *The old man is persistent, isn't he?*

"Uh, Charles something? And I thought he was born in Canada? That's what my dad said."

"Charles Blair Macdonald, an imposing, demanding, pugnacious man who created more than just a golf course on those two hundred acres of the old Patrick Farm," the old man said, sounding much like one of Buddy's professors at Madison. "Yes, he was officially a Canadian, but his father was Scottish and sent him to St. Andrew's University as a teenager. He helped bring the Scottish golf heritage to this country. Consider this: The first full season of play at his Wheaton design was 1895."

"Is he the guy with the big mustache?" Buddy said.

"Yes! The big mustache! Big everything! That course has big green complexes, often as large as 10,000 square feet, and many of them with squared-off edges. He was larger-than-life, and so were his designs."

"My dad has a framed photo of him above his desk."

"Is he a member there?"

"No, but that was always his dream."

"I'm sure he's told you there is a framed painting of Macdonald in the Chicago Golf clubhouse. Abraham Lincoln's oldest son, Robert

Todd, was a member there. So was railroad magnate George Pullman. Members of the McCormick family. Marshall Field. Does this mean anything to you? They were American royalty."

"My mom has a photo of her holding me as a baby in front of the Christmas windows at the downtown Marshall Field's. Same guy?"

"Yes, he founded that empire. When he died in 1906, *The New York Times* said he was the world's richest merchant, the largest individual taxpayer in the country, and the third-wealthiest person in the United States. What kind of business school do you attend that the domain of Field isn't studied?"

Buddy shrugged his shoulders. "But he played at Chicago Golf?"

"Not only did he play there, young man, but his final round at Chicago Golf cost him his life."

"Really?" Buddy said, suddenly interested.

"He caught a cold while playing there on New Year's Day. The cold became bronchitis, which became pneumonia, which, in those days, became a death sentence. He died in New York about two weeks later. His wife died years later of the same condition."

"My mom calls those 'quinkydinks.'"

"The language of Chicago. It always falls gently on my ears. I assume she's a South Sider?"

"Beverly."

"There's a very fine course there—the Beverly Country Club—where Donald Ross did masterful work in his renovation of the original layout. Of course, you're aware of Seth Raynor's work at Chicago Golf?"

Buddy's face remained blank.

"Seth Raynor was Macdonald's personal choice to do the redesign, which was finished in 1923 and cost exactly $253,185," the old man said. "I've seen a copy of the club ledger. Augusta National spends that much on cocktail napkins. Would you like to guess how much Raynor received for his services?"

"No idea. A hundred thousand?"

"A mere $6,781.13. A bargain for a golf genius! They spent more on buying and shipping manure to the site—about $8,000—than they did on Raynor. Nowadays, the top golf architects are paid six- and seven-figure fees. What has your dad told you about the course?"

"I've never really asked."

The old man shook his head, exasperated by the indifference.

"What is your name?"

"Buddy."

"OK, Buddy. You can call me Gordo. But you can't live in this town and not know something about Chicago Golf. Every hole is so nuanced, so considered. I'm sure your father has told you about the par-3 seventh hole—the Redan hole, patterned after the 15th hole at North Berwick. Raynor and Macdonald often included Redans in their course designs. But my favorite is the par-4 12th, and if you polled the membership, I think it would agree."

"That *is* a cool hole," Buddy said, thinking back to the yardage book he had so painstakingly prepared for his first—and last—round as a caddie there. "I wish I could have played the whole thing. It's so perf. Guess I blew that chance."

"So you *do* care about the game?"

"Used to," Buddy said quickly. "What about you? Ever play there?"

The old man said nothing at first. Buddy noticed the hint of a bittersweet smile on his face.

"Yes," the old man said softly. "I suppose I did play there once. In a way."

"Whattya mean?"

"Let's just say it was the best and worst day of my life, and we'll leave it at that."

"That's not fair."

"I'll tell you my story when you tell me yours. For now, we'll keep our respective secrets."

The old man coughed and seemed in discomfort as he did so.

"You OK?" Buddy said.

"Oh, I'm fine," he said as he dabbed at the corners of his mouth with a handkerchief.

"For what it's worth, my dad still has his red CGC caddie bib,"

Buddy said. "He keeps everything. The funny part about it? He covers golf for AGN. He's around those pros all the time, and he still stinks."

"AGN?"

"The All Golf Network. He's a TV reporter."

"I watch that channel. I watch everything these days," the old man said, patting the armrest of his wheelchair. "What's his name?"

"Joe Riley."

"I've seen him! He does fine work."

"I guess."

"You don't watch your own father on TV?"

"Sometimes. But he's just sort of my dad. It's not like he's a big star."

Buddy pulled out the putter.

"Did this come with the set?"

"Wullkotte didn't make putters. If you must know, that putter has no real golf lineage. I bought it for a dollar, maybe less, a long time ago at a garage sale much like this one. I painted it white as an homage to the putter Nicklaus used to win the 1967 U.S. Open. It has sentimental value, but nothing more."

"Why white?"

"Nicklaus borrowed the original putter from a friend of a friend. It was a Bulls Eye model painted white to soften the reflection from the sun. They nicknamed it White Fang."

"I had no idea how much thought went into clubs."

"As I said, the putter is all but worthless. However, the woods and irons are invaluable."

"Where did you get them?"

"That's another story for another time."

Chet wandered into the garage.

"There you are," Chet said. "Mom needs you to help load that table into the van. Hurry up before she buys something else."

"I'll be right there," Buddy said.

Buddy shook the old man's hand. "This might be the first garage sale where I had a good time," he said.

"Tell your mom that she has a fine eye for furniture. That table is a keepsake."

"This is all yours?"

"I'm downsizing. My granddaughter organized the garage sale."

"Well, nice meeting you, sir."

"It was a pleasure. And remember, Buddy, life is too short to hold grudges for too long."

Buddy nodded and walked to the front yard, where he and his mom wrapped the table in a blanket and placed it in the flattened third row of the minivan. The lamp lay next to it, along with a pepper shaker.

"Who were you talking to in there?" Laurel asked.

"The guy who owns the house."

"Chet said you were looking at golf clubs? See anything you liked?" Her tone was hopeful. It had been Laurel who had often taken Buddy to his junior golf tournaments, who had seen the joy on his face after a match, who had noticed that when her older son watched a major on TV, he took careful notes not on the players but on the caddies. And it was Laurel who had tried to broker a peace between father and son. In this, she had half succeeded. There was a fragile peace, but no resolution.

Buddy shot Chet a sideways glance.

"The woman controls my weekly allowance," Chet said without apology. "I caved."

"Mom?" Buddy said.

"Your brother exaggerates," she said.

"Your brother tells the truth," said Chet, who had requested a *Wall Street Journal* subscription for his last birthday. "Money is my motivator."

"Well, you can't blame me for being a tiny bit curious," she said.

"It was nothing. Gordo—that's his name—was showing me some old-time clubs," Buddy said.

"And?"

"And they were cool."

"You know, it's your father's birthday on Sunday. You could surprise him with something before he leaves the next day for Columbus."

"Shocker," Buddy said. "He's leaving again."

"He's covering a golf tournament. That's his job."

Buddy didn't respond. Rather than press the point, Laurel closed the liftgate, made sure Chet was buckled in, and began to pull away from the curb. They were halfway down the block when Buddy suddenly said, "Mom, hold on a sec."

"No!" Chet said from the back seat. "We were almost out of here."

Buddy unbuckled his seat belt and ran back to the garage. The old man was gone. He approached the granddaughter, who was picking up coats and shirts that had fallen from a makeshift clothes rack.

"I'm sorry to interrupt," Buddy said.

"Can you believe these people?" she said, without looking up. "They're like locusts."

"I was just talking to your granddad."

"Whatever price he gave you, take 50 percent off and put the money in the jar. I need to move product."

"What about the clubs in the garage?" Buddy pointed to the white bag in the corner.

She squinted before locating them. "Oh, those? I'm sorry, they're not for sale," she said. "You can have the others for free, though. Otherwise, they're going in the garbage can."

"I really wanted to buy the clubs in the white bag."

"If it were up to me, I'd get rid of them all," she said, glancing briefly at Buddy before returning to her work on the clothes rack.

Buddy took one last look at the bag and began to walk toward the minivan.

"Young man!"

Buddy turned to the sound of the voice. There at the front door of the house was the old man. Buddy walked over.

"Forget something?" the old man said.

"More like remembered something," Buddy said. "Your granddaughter said the clubs in the white bag weren't part of the garage sale, but would you consider selling them?"

A horn honked. Laurel had circled back to the front of the house. Buddy held up a forefinger to buy some extra time.

"I thought you'd never ask," the old man said. "But why would you want them? You said you don't play. And even if you did, these are ancient artifacts."

"You and my mom got me thinking. I want to get them for my dad. It's his birthday. I think he'd appreciate what they are. He'd appreciate . . . the artistry, the history."

The old man leaned forward in his creaky chair.

"Is he worthy?" he finally said.

"Worthy?" said Buddy. "Worthy of what?"

The old man looked intently at Buddy as he tried to divine the inner truth of a boy and his father. Beneath the thin shell of indifference and pride, he could see goodness and grace in the boy. But was that enough? "These clubs could change his life. And yours."

"Well, he'd take good care of them, if that's what you mean. We have a finished basement, and he has a display of all the majors he's covered. He has framed media credentials, photos, bag towels, flags, and some other stuff. If it makes any difference, I could buy him a wall rack and he could put the clubs on it."

"No, no, no," the old man said, his tone deadly serious. "These clubs aren't museum pieces. They need to be *played*. A Stradivarius wasn't meant to be confined to its carrying case. It was meant to fill a concert hall with its sublime sound. These clubs are no different. They were meant to do battle with the course, with the elements, with a nestled lie in the rough, a plugged ball in a short side bunker. They were made to have grass stains, dirt, and sand in their grooves. Otherwise, you dishonor them. You understand?"

"Sort of, I think," Buddy said.

"I'm unable to play," the old man said, patting his legs. "I had to give up the game I love. I need to know that the clubs will have a purpose."

"But my dad already has a set of clubs. Clubs from, you know, this century."

"You must listen to me," the old man said, his voice strong and insistent. "These clubs have a soul, a spirit, a heritage. They are pure originals. Most of all, they are unalterable. That's what gives them their strength. They are the sum of what can be imagined . . . and what can't be. They are waiting for their history to be written. That's why I ask if your father is worthy."

Buddy edged away, wondering what he had said or done to trigger the old man's ravings. *Waiting for their history to be written?* Since when did a bag of garage sale clubs make history? But there was something about the *way* Gordo spoke of the clubs that resonated with Buddy. There was passion. There was belief—and when was the last time Buddy had believed in anything that mattered? Here was an old man in a wheelchair, and yet his imagination allowed him to dream in ways that the younger Buddy had long deemed worthless. Maybe this was Buddy's chance to dream again, to believe as Gordo believed.

The car horn honked again. Buddy turned and held out both palms to his mom and mouthed, "Hold on." He turned back to the old man. He had made his decision.

"I've got $1,180 in my Venmo account," Buddy said hurriedly. "I've got a paid internship in the city. I don't know how much you want for the clubs, but I'll make sure they have grass stains and dirt on them. If you saw my dad play, you'd know I'm telling the truth. Nobody has laid the sod more than him."

The old man smiled, pondered the offer for several moments, but then shook his head.

"No, I can't sell them to you."

Buddy nodded, and then offered a handshake.

"It was worth a try, right?" he said. "You never know unless you ask."

Buddy tried to move away, but the old man held on tight.

"I said I wouldn't *sell* them to you. Instead, I will give them to you."

"*Give* them to me? Why?"

"Because, young man, I have more fuel than runway."

"I don't understand."

"Nor should you. But this gift comes with a condition: You must promise that you'll play again—and do so with your dad."

Buddy loosened his grip.

"I don't know," he said.

The old man squeezed harder. For someone who looked semi-frail, he had a surprisingly strong grip.

"Deal?"

"OK," Buddy said, his hand throbbing. "Deal."

"And you're a man of your word?"

"I am. I promise."

"Then we have concluded our transaction. The clubs are yours."

"I won't let you down."

"I'm not your concern. Be true to yourself. The clubs will show you the way."

Buddy retrieved the clubs from the garage, grabbed the bag by its handle, and got into the front seat of his mom's car. He wedged the bag between his legs, and as they drove off, Buddy waved to the old man. Gordo gave him a smile and a crisp salute.

"Took you long enough," Chet said.

Laurel glanced at the bag and then saw the look of contentment on Buddy's face.

"Garage sales aren't so bad, are they?" she said.

"Not this one," said Buddy.

He pulled off the plastic cover on the 7-iron. He marveled once again at the clean face of the club. Then he noticed a signature on the back of the iron.

"Holy crap!" he blurted.

"What is it, honey?" said his mom, instantly concerned. Chet strained against the seat belt and leaned forward.

"I think Dad is going to like his birthday present," he said.

Chet plopped back in his seat. "Yeah, what he always wanted: some crappy garage sale clubs."

Buddy said nothing. Instead, he pulled the plastic covers off the rest of the irons. Each one had the same engraved signature on the back.

JACK NICKLAUS.

CHAPTER THREE

Division

The cake was chocolate, the ice cream vanilla, and the singing spectacularly off-key. But Joe Riley didn't care. He was surrounded by family and friends at his forty-third birthday party.

The presents ranged from practical (ties, a pair of GFore waterproof walking shoes, an umbrella), to mocking (a fake trophy from his bank naming him the Last Paper Check Writer on Earth), to serious (a framed photo of Riley's old man—USAF Capt. Chester T. Riley—from his days flying F-4s for the 555th Tactical Fighter Squadron).

It took Riley three tries to blow out all forty-three candles.

"What'd you wish for, Dad?" asked Chet, who was named for his grandpa. "Better lung capacity?"

"To never take these moments for granted," Riley said, hugging his younger son. Chet squirmed away in embarrassment.

"Hugs are so sketch, Dad."

Riley stood up and surveyed the crowded dining room.

"I'm a lucky man," he said. "Tonight, the road rises up to meet me. To my family and to my friends, thanks for this."

Laurel blew him a kiss from across the table. Then Buddy stepped forward.

"Dad, there's one more present," he said.

Buddy disappeared for a few moments and then came back into the room holding the wrapped gift in his arms as if it were an oversized bag of mulch. There was the unmistakable sound of irons clinking against each other, and of course, there was no hiding the shape of a golf bag. Buddy placed the gift next to the table.

"I wonder what this is?" Riley said, smiling.

Buddy pawed at the floor with his foot.

"I hope you like it. It's different."

"That's one way of putting it," Chet said. Buddy glared at him.

Riley tore off the wrapping paper and saw parts of an iron.

"Buddy, you bought me an extra set of clubs? My other set is practically brand-new."

"Keep going," Buddy said.

Riley pulled off the rest of the wrapping. Ten Jack Nicklaus signatures and the three polished persimmons—driver, 3-wood, and 5-wood—gleamed under the dining room light.

"These . . . these are beautiful," Riley said as he pulled the 8-iron from the bag and examined it. "Old MacGregors. They're in mint condition. Those were the days before hybrids and exotic wedges."

Buddy beamed with pride.

Riley pulled out the driver.

"These are perfect. Did you get these refinished?"

"No, Dad. They came this way. The guy I got them from said they're originals."

"We got them at a garage sale," Chet said. "For free."

Buddy shot Chet another menacing look.

"I don't care where he got them," Riley said. "They've been restored to perfection. And there's even a replica White Fang in here. I love them."

"I thought you would, Dad. But just so you know, I think they're the originals and were made for Jack Nicklaus. Well, everything except the beat-up putter. That's what the guy said."

Laurel's brother, Aaron, inspected one of the irons.

"It does have his signature on it, Joe," he said. "Maybe you can ask Nicklaus when you cover the Memorial?"

"Jack was a longtime endorser for MacGregor," Riley said. "I already interviewed him about it a few years ago. MacGregor made his clubs and golf balls, but they also made product with his name on it—obviously mass-produced, not custom—for the general public. It would be like Rawlings selling a signature Aaron Judge glove. He endorses it, but it's not the exact same glove that he uses in games. His is custom-made."

"That makes sense," Aaron said.

"I don't know, Dad," Buddy said. "This guy knew a lot about clubs."

"Buddy, I appreciate the gesture," Riley said, his tone gentle and professorial, but also a little dismissive. "But a set of irons and woods made specifically for Jack would go for tens of thousands of dollars, probably a lot more. Nobody would just give those away, especially someone who knows clubs like you said this man did."

"Maybe I misunderstood him," Buddy said softly, embarrassed by the rebuke in front of family and friends.

"It doesn't matter," Riley said. "He was nice to give them to you. They're still vintage clubs. They're just not Jack's actual clubs."

"Yeah, I guess that would be crazy," Buddy said. "But he did tell me you should use them, that they shouldn't be displayed on a wall or something."

Riley smiled.

"Buddy, I couldn't hit a blade like this in ten thousand years. I'm lucky if I can hit my new irons."

"I can vouch for that," said Aaron, a frequent playing partner of Riley's.

"And persimmon woods?" Riley said. "The clubheads are the size of a baby's fist. I wouldn't have a chance. I need all the technology I can get. Plus, they're too pretty to scuff up on a driving range."

"I'm just telling you what the guy told me," Buddy said, his tone suddenly sharp and defensive, more so than he had intended.

"And I'm just telling you," said Riley, his own tone rising with impatience, "that even if they were what your friend says they were—which they aren't—I still couldn't hit them."

Laurel tried to rescue the moment by offering everyone an extra scoop of ice cream, but by then the damage had been done. Buddy excused himself, leaving everyone else at the table to eat their desserts in awkward silence.

In the quiet of his room, Buddy lay on the bed and took inventory of the walls. There was a poster of Soldier Field, a Spotted Cow beer sign he had found on Madison's famed State Street, a handful of cheaply framed photos from high school prom and spring break with his best friends from his frat. Above his dresser was a photo of a younger Buddy teeing off at a junior golf tournament. Next to the photo was a scorecard his dad had brought back from the Masters when Buddy was only ten. On it, Buddy had scrawled his score on every hole, signed it "Buddy Rory McIlroy Riley" with a child's flourish, and underneath his name had added, "Masters Champion." He had done so because when McIlroy, his favorite player, was a kid in Northern Ireland, he had signed his scorecards "Rory Nick Faldo McIlroy," in honor of the six-time major champion and knighted Englishman. Now the scorecard was just a reminder of what wasn't and never would be.

Buddy sat up, opened his desk drawer, and pulled out a five-inch-thick collection of scorecards from his junior golf competitions. The years-old rubber band snapped in two as he removed the cards.

He could remember every match, remember the faces of every opponent. He had that kind of memory.

There was a gentle tap on the door. His mom cracked it open.

"Can I come in?"

"I guess."

She carried a small plate with a slice of cake on it. "You never came back down."

"Yeah, sorry about that."

"Your present was a big hit."

"My present was a fake. I can't believe Gordo lied to me about those clubs."

"He didn't lie, Buddy," she said sympathetically. "He's an old man. Maybe he was just trying to impress you. Maybe he was lonely and he wanted to tell a story. I'm sure he didn't do it to deceive you."

"Well, I fell for it."

Laurel hugged her son.

"You made that old man's day. And you made your dad's night. That's never a bad thing."

"Dad made me look bad in front of everybody," Buddy said, pulling away.

"He didn't mean it that way."

"It doesn't matter. I learned my lesson."

Laurel noticed the pile of scorecards.

"I used to love to watch you play in those matches. You'd lay out your clothes the night before. Polish your golf shoes. Clean your clubs. Mark your golf balls just so. It seemed to mean a lot to you."

"I just realized something," he said, collecting the scorecards in his hand. "You were always there. Dad wasn't."

"Buddy."

"It's fine, Mom," he said, tossing the scorecards into the wastebasket under his desk. "I've moved on."

"Have you?"

"I'm kind of tired. Can we talk tomorrow?"

"Sure, honey. But I need you to come down and empty the garbage and move the clubs from the dining room."

"Why can't Dad do it?"

"Aaron convinced him to have a beer over at his house. They just left."

Buddy returned downstairs, tossed the garbage bag into the trash container in the garage, and then carried the clubs down to the basement. He placed them near the water heater and gave them one last look before climbing the stairs and closing the door.

Before going back to his room, Buddy stopped in the kitchen for a fork and a glass of milk to go with his cake.

"Buddy!" his mom said from upstairs. "Your dad and Aaron were watching TV. Can you see if they turned it off, please?"

Buddy walked to the family room, where a replay of that year's Masters was airing on AGN. The sound was on mute, but at that exact moment, his dad appeared on the screen with a news report of some sort.

Buddy began to turn up the volume, but then he stopped. He aimed the remote at the TV, and his dad disappeared into the darkness.

CHAPTER FOUR

The Hired Help

It had been a brutal day for Hard Way. He and his man had gotten the worst side of the first- and second-round draws at the Memorial. On Thursday morning, the winds had gusted, and from every direction. And now on Friday, their 1:56 tee time had come just as the humidity in the Columbus area had reached Philippine rainforest levels. There were occasional gusts, but not enough to keep the mosquitoes, Ohio's state bird, from diving like Stukas at bare arms, legs, and necks. What they siphoned could have supplied blood banks for months.

Hard Way had sprayed four coats of Off! on himself, but the skeeters all but laughed. The sleeves of his golf shirt looked like he had been attacked by a paintball team, with each red splotch a burial ground for the latest mosquito smooshed by the palm of Hard Way's hand.

He had worn pants instead of shorts, which helped protect his legs, but they didn't do much for ventilation or comfort. And then there was the course itself. If the Memorial wasn't the hardest walk on Tour, it was close, just behind Kapalua and Augusta National.

Jack Nicklaus, who had played at nearby Ohio State before turning pro in late 1961, won eighteen majors, the most ever, and went on to design hundreds of courses, including his hometown pride and joy, Muirfield Village. What made Jack's place so torturous wasn't just the hills but the rough, which was grown cornstalk high. You needed a machete to get through it.

Each blade of the Kentucky bluegrass seemed to wrap around the ankles like a tearful toddler clinging to their mama's leg as she left for work. And the way Hard Way's guy was playing, they were in the tall stuff all afternoon. By the time they made the turn, Hard Way's thighs felt as heavy as cinder blocks and his knees were making that mushy, crunchy sound that comes when what's left of your cartilage is having a fistfight with bone. His right shoulder always hurt (the result of that thing in that hot tub with that woman from the Ryder Cup welcome committee at Medinah), but now his left shoulder was filing for divorce, too. It didn't help that the bag was stuffed with an umbrella and enough rain gear to keep the crew of a shrimp trawler dry during a nor'easter. The 55-pound behemoth now had a beer belly and weighed closer to 60-something pounds. Hard Way's man didn't like to get wet.

Hard Way had swamp butt, and even his caddie bib was soaked in sweat. His socks squeaked from the moisture, and the tape job on his mangled big toes had come loose. The Hokas helped, but they could only do so much. What was that line by Indiana Jones? "It's not the years, honey, it's the mileage." How many miles of yardage book–scouting rounds, practice rounds, pro-am rounds, and tournament rounds had Hard Way walked during his two decades as a professional caddie? Figure twenty-five tournaments a year, times an average of five rounds per tournament, times at least 5 miles per round, times twenty years . . . equals 12,500 miles. That was half the circumference of the Earth. And that didn't count the couple of summers he caddied at Chicago Golf Club during his college days.

Just as they reached the 13th tee box, which happened to be the farthest point from the clubhouse, torrential rains swept through. In a matter of ten minutes, the fairways turned into the Suez Canal and the greens into infinity pools.

By the time the courtesy vehicle arrived, the downpour had washed away the mosquito corpses and blood stains from Hard Way's sleeves. His player was dry, though, thanks to the Gore-Tex rain pants, rain jacket, and rain hat and the four-foot-long umbrella that when opened was wider than some of the fairway landings.

Hard Way began to open the back door.

"Sorry, luv," said the tournament volunteer as she cracked the window of the Escalade. "Only have room for the players and bags. We'll try to send some golf carts your way."

Hard Way's guy shrugged his shoulders, settled into the front seat, and closed the door. The other two players in the group ducked into the back seat.

The volunteer popped open the rear liftgate, and the caddies loaded the bags into the cargo area. Hard Way kept an umbrella for himself before pressing the button to close the liftgate. The taillights of the SUV disappeared into the distance.

Soon the water began to puddle and wash over Hard Way's Hokas. The bill of his Titleist ball cap had given up long ago. In the distance, he could see a crackle of lightning, which was followed moments later by a roar of thunder.

"Well, gentlemen, that's my cue," Hard Way said. "I'm outta here."

"You gonna walk?" said Cornelius Ford, known by his peers as Sand Man. Nobody raked a bunker with more care than Sand Man, who believed you should leave a bunker better than you found it. When he was done smoothing out the footprints and divot (he always pushed the sand forward rather than pulling it toward him), it looked like a Zen garden. "That's all carry."

"It's either that, float back, or get electrocuted," Hard Way said. "I'm a fan of not being charred."

"Sheeet," Sand Man said. "I believe I'll wait for those carts the nice lady mentioned."

"You mean the nice lady who left us here to drown?" Hard Way said. He turned to the other caddie, "Bang Bang" Bowlen, so named for his prodigious work when he caddied on the LPGA Tour, where he banged nearly every player who wasn't gay, and several who were. "Join me for a brisk two-and-a-half-mile trek back to civilization?"

"Nah, dude," Bang Bang said. "Can't leave your wingman—or your Sand Man. That's my credo."

"'Preciate you," Sand Man said.

"Plus, Sand Man is right," Bang Bang said. "That walk in this rain is all carry."

In golf, *all carry* meant having to cover a certain distance to ensure that your shot landed safely. To miss by even a single foot could mean disaster to your scorecard. That meant carrying the murky artificial lake to reach the island green on 17 at Sawgrass, or clearing the inlet of the Pacific Ocean that separates the tee box from the peninsula green on 16 at Cypress Point, or flying a ball over Rae's Creek and a front bunker to reach the pencil-thin green on 12 at Augusta.

Hard Way, Sand Man, and Bang Bang had adopted the phrase as their own and used it to describe something that was theoretically possible but unlikely to be achieved. And if it *were* achieved, it would require a heroic and unthinkable effort.

Vanderbilt winning the College Football Playoff. All carry.

The Masters allowing cell phones. All carry.

A delicious microwave pizza. All carry.

And now, walking through a sideways downpour to the Muirfield Village clubhouse. All carry.

Hard Way pinched the bill of his cap to them, and then made his way down the 13th and 14th fairways, cut across the 15th tee box, and was starting up the 18th fairway when a maintenance crew member pulled over and gave him a ride in the back of his UTV.

By the time Hard Way got back to the clubhouse, his guy had showered, been served one of those world-famous Memorial clubhouse milkshakes, and left for the day. Hard Way was soaked to the marrow, but he squished into the storage area next to the locker room and retrieved his guy's bag. He left a water trail that earned him the stink eye from the locker-room manager, but Hard Way could live with the disapproval. Years earlier at a tournament in Singapore, when he was caddying for another player, someone had stolen his guy's clubs from a storage room. Ever since then, Hard Way always looked after the bag himself.

When the rain finally subsided, Hard Way loaded the clubs in the back of his rental car and drove the thirteen minutes from Muirfield to the Marriott Columbus Northwest in Dublin.

The hotel was pricey and always sold out during the Memorial, but the general manager was a former Ohio State golfer, and Hard Way made it a habit to bring him a shirt and hat from Augusta National. They weren't the ones with the Masters logo sold at the gigantic merchandise center—where the great unwashed spent more than $10 million per day during the tournament—but the ones with the members' club logo sold exclusively at the tiny pro shop located about 35 yards from the iconic oak tree and clubhouse. There was a difference.

Months earlier, Hard Way had spent nearly $2,000 in the shop when he was invited by a longtime Green Jacket to play the course as a guest. He used the shirts and caps as currency during the season.

Hard Way took the bag up to his room and lovingly cleaned each clubface. Next, he took the hair dryer from the bathroom and dried each club grip. He used a bath towel to wipe the moisture from the interior of the golf bag. After that, he took one of the five longest hot showers of his life, followed by a nap.

The "Tennessee Waltz" ringtone woke him. He knew who it was without looking.

"You got my bag, right?" his guy said, not bothering with pleasantries. His guy was known for that.

"Got 'em," Hard Way said. "Everything is drying out now. By the way, you left your watch in there."

"It's not a watch, it's a Rolex Daytona, the 126506," his guy said dismissively.

"Ah, the 126506," Hard Way said. "Of course."

"It's worth more than what some of those poor bastards on the Korn Ferry make in two years," his guy said. "I've been offered $140,000 for it, cash."

"It's a watch, right?" Hard Way said. "It doesn't perform aortic valve surgery. It has a big hand and a little hand."

"It's a racing chronograph," his man said. "It perpetuates the spirit of Hans Wilsdorf."

"For $140,000, it should bring Hans Wilsdorf back to life."

"I'll swing by your hotel later to pick it up. What room you in?"

"Why don't I just bring it in the morning? Saves you a trip."

"I've got to go to a fundraiser near your place. And I don't feel good about you babysitting the Daytona."

"No offense taken. OK, I'm in 924, conveniently located next to the ice machine, elevator, and housekeeping supply room. They take good care of me here. What time you coming by?"

"Late," he said. "I got roped into some sort of Make-A-Wish thing. They don't pay dick—in fact, they want *me* to donate money—and the night lasts forever. It's cheap, chewy prime rib and the usual blah-blah-blah with the four corporate EVPs sitting at the table who want to tell you about every shot they hit at Pasatiempo. Like I give a shit that they got up and down for par at 18. Go fucking tell Alister MacKenzie, for all I care."

"Well, it's a worthy cause," Hard Way said. "The kids and all."

"Whatever. I'd like to make a wish: I wish I didn't have to go to this goddamn thing. My ass is going to be a quarter inch from the ground in the morning."

And with that, his man ended the call without a goodbye.

Hard Way was constantly amazed by the tone-deaf comments made by his man, who had been spoiled by the perks of the Tour, corrupted by his own avarice, and slowly humiliated by his descent in the world rankings. It was as if he tried to hide his disappointment with anger and bluster.

He hadn't always been that way. When Hard Way had consulted with his man's first-ever caddie, Sugar Pie Wheeler, about taking the gig, the caddie had issued a warning.

"He was going to be the next big thing, remember?" Sugar Pie had said that day. "He had that swagger when he first came out here. I thought he was my meal ticket. My new-house ticket. My fishing-boat ticket. He had that kind of game. And he treated me like I was family."

Hard Way had asked why they had split up.

"He lost his confidence, man, and I couldn't help him get it back. Maybe you can. The Tour can break you that way. But he isn't the same guy, and I have the teeth marks to prove it. He's a good person gone bad. I'm not waving you off—there's a helluva player still in there—but I'm telling you, be careful. He bites."

The words came spilling back to Hard Way as he stared at his phone. He threw on a pair of TravisMathew shorts and a Pearl Jam T-shirt from the United Center gig. He slipped on a pair of Nike flip-flops and then found himself staring at the front pouch of his man's golf bag.

"Why not?"

He pulled the Rolex from the velour-lined pocket and slipped it on his left wrist. Then he headed to the hotel pub for a burger and beers. He had earned them.

The Reds game was on the TV above the bar. They were losing—what else was new?—this time to the Brewers. Hard Way grabbed a booth across from the bar, sat with his back to the wall, stretched out his legs on the bench seating, and watched in wonderment as the Reds loaded the bases with no outs and then went strikeout, strikeout, strikeout.

The waitress arrived. She was wearing a beauty-pageant-like sash that read "Birthday Girl" in silver sequins.

"You see that?" she said. "Three whiffs in a row? Not even a foul ball. That's hard to do even if you're trying."

"My condolences," Hard Way said. "Been a bit of a dry spell for the Big Red Machine."

"I was born and raised in Cincinnata before I moved here," she said. "I still root for them, but they're like those Stormtroopers in *Star Wars*. They can't hit a thing."

"Not much of a birthday present."

"It gets worse. The bartender told me the brain is fully developed at twenty-five. I just turned twenty-six."

"The crosses we bear."

"Right? Anyway, whattya drinking?"

"Something I won't regret. Let's go with Shiner Bock, if you have it, Yuengling if you don't. Burger, medium well. Fries, piping hot. When you see my beer bottle half full, that means it's getting lonely and will soon need a companion."

"Understood. Shiner on the way, food to follow."

Between innings, Hard Way took in the clientele seated at the bar. His best guesses, from right to left: two male flight attendants, sales rep, sales rep, married couple, golf fan, mom and high school daughter on Ohio State visit, three twenty-something bruhs, open seat, and then . . . *hello*. A woman of considerable stature.

Problem was, the three bruhs had noticed her, too. Fortified by a conga line of empty shot glasses, the bruhs nudged one another and then moved like a collective hoodie-attired amoeba, their pseudopods drawing them closer to her barstool. Hard Way leaned forward to hear the exchange.

"We couldn't help noticing that you're all by yourself," Bruh No. 1 said to the woman.

"Definitely by yourself," Bruh No. 2 said.

"Aw, that's sweet of you," the woman said, her back still to Hard Way. "I'm just waiting for a friend."

"Well, while you're waiting, how about if we keep you company?" Bruh No. 3 said, trying—and failing—to avoid slurring his words. He had had one too many shots of the cut-rate well Scotch. "A smokeshow like you shouldn't be sitting by yourself."

"Definitely shouldn't be doing that," the human echo chamber, Bruh No. 2, said.

The woman glanced sideways and looked them over with an air of practiced disdain. How many times had she endured the clumsy, hormones-on-parade efforts of jamokes such as these?

"I'm flattered, gentlemen. But I'm going to take a pass. You have a nice night, though."

Then she returned to her drink—a margarita, guessed Hard Way.

"'I'm flattered, gentlemen,'" Bruh No. 1 said mockingly as he repeated her response.

"I got an idea," Bruh No. 3 said, leaning against the side of the woman's barstool. "It's the waitress's birthday, so why don't you blow out a candle?" He pointed toward his zipper.

The three bruhs exploded in laughter.

"I appreciate the offer," the woman said, this time not even bothering to look at him, "but I don't do short wicks."

Two of the bruhs burst out laughing again. Bruh No. 3, laid bare by the remark, didn't join them. It didn't help that the two flight attendants and one of the sales reps at the end of the bar were laughing, too.

"Hey, bitch," Bruh No. 3 said, his tone and mood instantly menacing. "Be a shame if you slipped and fell off that chair."

"Be a real shame," Bruh No. 2 said, edging closer.

Hard Way dropped his head in resignation.

"All I wanted was a beer and a burger," he muttered.

Hard Way noticed a box of cheapie surgical masks behind the hostess stand; remnants of the Covid era. He grabbed a handful and then saw a box of disposable food service gloves near the door to the kitchen. He stuffed the gloves into his pockets.

Meanwhile, the bruhs had ordered four more shots: three for them, one for her.

"Drink up," Bruh No. 3 said, "and then you can try to make it up to me."

"I don't like cheap Scotch," she said, pushing the shot glass away. "And I don't like cheap imitations of men."

"You just don't know how to get along," Bruh No. 3 said, whispering harshly in her ear. "But you're about to find out when I—"

"Hon!" Hard Way said, wedging himself between a startled Bruh No. 3 and the woman. "The news is not good. In fact, it's frightening."

"Who the hell are you?" Bruh No. 3 said, recoiling at the sight of Hard Way.

Hard Way wore a surgical mask and began gesturing wildly with his blue-gloved hands.

"The lab results are in, darling!" he said dramatically. "They suspect the worst: either rat pox or a new strain of Pythagorean. You must put these on immediately." He handed the stunned woman the gloves and began placing the elastic mask straps over her ears. As he did, he winked at her.

"Rat pox?" Bruh No. 2 said.

"Did any of you touch my wife?" Hard Way said. "I don't blame you—she's ravishing." He paused to adjust her mask. "But I need to know NOW! You might have been exposed too."

The Bruhs, confused, backed away from the woman.

"Exposed to what?" Bruh No. 1 said, his mind trying to process this sudden explosion of information.

"Are you familiar with virulence?"

The bruhs looked at each other, confused, suddenly worried. *Virulence*?

"Never mind," Hard Way said, now almost frantic in his tone. "We're research scientists for the Department of Defense. My wife and I have been exposed to virulent strains that employ a mechanism that avoids immune cells. The bacterium colonizes the host, and then the disease overpowers the system with toxins too numerous to count. There are extracellular results, as well as antigenic cross-reactivity that is horrifying on an entirely different scale. So I ask you again: DID YOU TOUCH MY WIFE?" Hard Way was practically screaming now as the bruhs, panic in their eyes, began to back away from him and the woman. Hard Way was enjoying himself. "If you did, then put these on now. I've called for a medical scrub team, and we'll be taken directly to Wright-Patterson Air Force Base for oral and anal probes, as well as blood tests."

Bruh No. 3 ran so fast that he hydroplaned on a rain spot outside the door and cartwheeled into a parked car. The three bruhs vanished into the Dublin, Ohio, ether.

Hard Way calmly removed his mask, pulled off the gloves as if he had returned from the opera, then bowed to the woman like an actor taking a short curtain call. He spied his waitress in the corner, pointed toward his booth, and made a circular motion with his forefinger, as in *Another round, please*. Then, to a smattering of applause from the sales reps, he returned to his seat and resumed watching the hapless Reds give up a pair of runs when two outfielders collided on a routine fly ball.

The Shiners were doing their job. He had an appropriate buzz for a Friday night. Screw the early wake-up call.

The waitress appeared, not with another beer but with a note.

"You've got a fan," she said, winking.

Hard Way unfolded the cocktail napkin.

Mad Scientist,

I didn't get a chance to thank you. Will you accept a complimentary adult beverage from a rat pox survivor?

"Whattya think?" he asked the waitress.

"I think I wouldn't keep the nice lady waiting."

A few minutes later, Hard Way heard a voice.

"May I enter the Fortress of Solitude?" she said, holding two freshly made margaritas.

Hard Way glanced up and immediately lost the use of his motor skills.

On a scale of 1 to 10, she was a 16. She was beyond beautiful. There was no other way to put it. During the actual bruh confrontation, he hadn't had a chance to get a good look at her. He had been too busy attaching masks and flailing his arms.

Hard Way had seen more than a few stunners leaning over the gallery ropes in his day. But this woman—mid-to-late thirties, tops, sort of Connie Britton circa *Friday Night Lights* and Season 3 of *The West Wing*—didn't resemble any of those Phoenix Open types: the Barbies who could be seen stumbling around the TPC course in their stilettos and tiny sundresses, beer sloshing out of their cups and over their wrists like water over a bow. They were there to drink, to party, to aerate the grounds, and maybe to meet a Scottsdale bougie in one of the 16th hole corporate suites and then possibly procreate. This woman wasn't one of those women.

She wore a Levi's denim jacket and jeans, a pair of patent leather Docs, and a T-shirt featuring David Wooderson of *Dazed and Confused* and "L-I-V-I-N" on the front. And Hard Way couldn't help but notice that she also wore a wedding band and engagement ring with a diamond the size of a Pro V1.

Hard Way unfolded his six-foot-four frame from the booth, stood up, and tried not to stare.

"The waitress said you were having an intimate relationship with beer tonight, but I brought these," she said, handing him one of the margaritas. "The curse of Clooney."

"Casamigos," Hard Way said as he took the glass. "Thank you. One too many of these and I start singing show tunes from *Hamilton*."

She raised her drink. "To men with manners."

"There are so few of us," Hard Way said, clinking the glasses.

"By the way, I wasn't scared," she said.

"I was," he said.

"They were creeps," she said. "They were drunk. And the birthday boy was about to get a face full of riot-police-grade mace. But then you came out of nowhere."

"I specialize in nowhere," Hard Way said.

"Pythagorean?" she said.

"It sounded contagious," he said.

"It's a mathematical theorem," she said.

Hard Way shrugged. "I figured they skipped school the day Pythagoras was introduced."

"I figured they skipped school every day," she said. "They think

The Catcher in the Rye is a baseball book. But I have to admit, your lecture series on extracellular results—and what was it, antigenic cross-reactivity?—was excellent."

"Blame Kevin Lawrence, my best friend in college. He majored in chemical engineering. Osmosis, I guess."

"Where was that?"

"The University of Tennessee, the Harvard of East Knoxville."

"They're the ones who play that obnoxious 'Rocky Top' song."

"Excuse me? That's a song sung by a choir of angels, ma'am. And please don't tell me you're a Gator, or even worse, an insufferable Vandy grad. I respect Bama, grudgingly, but Florida or Vandy . . . that would ruin the evening."

"Nope." And then she made a V sign and started humming, "Duh . . . duh, duh, duh, duh, duh . . . duh, duh, duh . . ."

"Winston Churchill U?"

She frowned and then persisted with the humming.

"I know that one—USC. 'Troy' something," he said.

"Close. It's called 'Tribute to Troy.' "

"And you think 'Rocky Top' is obnoxious? And what's with the white horse and the Marvin the Martian–looking dude who stabs the grass with a sword?"

"Said the man whose school has a bad Davy Crockett knockoff and a dog that needs a blankie when it gets cold."

"Well done," he said, raising his glass with admiration. "I'm Max, though most everyone calls me Hard Way."

"I'm Kat," she said, "though don't tell my parents that. I'll always be Katherine Marie to them. Why Hard Way?"

"Turns out I have a medium-sized jones for the Vegas craps tables. I bet the pass line with full odds, then place bets on six or eight depending on what the point is, and I always toss a chip or two on the hard ways. Those are—"

"Two twos for the four, two threes for the six, two fours for the eight, and two fives for the ten," she said, completing his sentence.

"You know craps?"

"I know that the house edge on rolling a hard six or eight is 9.1 percent, and 11.1 percent for a hard four or ten. You have a better chance of surviving a lightning strike than rolling a hard four or ten."

"I see," Hard Way said. "So you're saying that's a strategic mistake."

"I'm saying that the stickman and the two dealers at the table would prefer you just toss them those chips as tips instead of wasting them on the hard ways."

"So noted," he said. "Just so you know, I almost got to test your odds about lightning strikes today. And I haven't used this line in years, but what was your major?"

"It's going to sound more impressive than it really is," she said.

"This will be interesting," he said.

"Undergrad was applied mathematics," she said. "Then a master's in computational and mathematical engineering at Stanford."

"If I had a nickel for every time I heard those two," he said. "And you thought I was going to be impressed."

She stuck her right leg out and pulled the jeans over her ankle to reveal a tiny tattoo: the iconic interlocking SC logo. Then she did the same with her left leg, this time to show a Stanford tree logo.

Her legs were as impressive as those degrees—maybe more so.

"My parents never forgave me," she said.

"I can see why, what with you being such an academic washout. Please tell me you weren't one of those smug, despicable sixteen-hundred-on-the-SAT kids."

She dropped her head in mock shame.

"Really? Let me guess: You split the atom *and* lettered in swimming."

"How'd you know about the swimming?"

"The shoulders are a giveaway."

"Got a half scholly out of high school but only lasted a couple of years. Just wasn't fast enough."

"So you *are* human."

"I quit the team . . ."

"Look, there's no shame in that," Hard Way said.

". . . and became a Song Girl."

"Annnnnd we're back to not being human. White turtleneck sweaters, red shoes, everyone's favorite sideline sight at a Southern Cal football game . . . *those* Song Girls?"

"They actually just changed the name to Song *Leaders,* but yes. 'Pride without arrogance; confidence without conceit.' That was our pledge. And the shoes are cardinal, not red," she said, clearly appreciating the irony in the lack of irony about the specific details.

"On behalf of all cardinal-blooded American men, nobody noticed the difference. Well, I feel like a complete slacker."

"Don't apologize. After all, you've still got that job at the Department of Defense." She smiled. It was a great smile.

"That's true. So what do you do now?"

"Consulting work. Spent a few days at Ohio State this week. The pay is obscene."

"I'm going to stop you there. It's *The* Ohio State. They insist on it. They even trademarked it."

"If ever a school needed pride without arrogance, it's this one. I refuse to say the *The*. What are they going to do next: trademark all definite and indefinite articles? Make a run at prepositions?"

"Exactly," said Hard Way, who ordered another pair of margaritas. "And if you don't mind me asking, where do you and the husband call home? I couldn't help but notice the lug nut on your finger. With a rock that big, I'm guessing Monaco?"

Kat stared at the engagement ring with a look first of indifference and then sadness. The Tiffany diamond sat like royalty atop the six-pronged throne.

"My husband—if you can call him that at this point—is in town, also for work. We've been separated for months. I was supposed to meet him tonight to discuss our divorce—happy, fun talk in Columbus, right?—but he canceled on me. Keeping promises isn't one of his strengths."

"Yikes. That got serious fast. My bad."

"No, it's OK. He's a prick. We should have called it a day ten years ago, but we were trying to gut it out for the kids. We've been frayed around the edges for so long that we didn't notice our marriage had eroded." As she spoke, she covered her ring finger with her right hand.

"I'm sorry to hear that," Hard Way said. "And I mean this in the best possible way, but you have kids? What'd you do, adopt as a teen?"

Kat shrugged, ignoring the compliment. It was a shrug of resignation.

"We were sort of the golden couple out of college. He was an All-American, I had some bona fides. But he was on the road a lot—still is—and he got sloppy. Word traveled fast. It was only a matter of time."

She took a sip of her drink and sighed. "You know, when you get married, they say, 'For better or for worse.' The better didn't last long, and the worse seemed to go on forever. But look, everyone has their version of the truth. And you don't need to hear mine."

"How about this?" Hard Way said. "I'll go find the bruhs to kick your husband's ass."

"If only it were that easy. The truth is—" she said, before catching herself. "You don't want to really know about this, do you?"

Hard Way could hear the sorrow in her voice. "Of course I do. It's either this or go count the shower curtain rings in my bathroom."

Kat looked at him with a tilt of the head.

"You're an odd one, aren't you?"

"I like to think of myself as a sympathetic ear."

Kat considered whether to continue. "You know what? I'm not proud," she said. "I could use a little sympathy."

She took a swig of her drink.

"He wasn't always a prick. When I first met him at SC, he'd barely say a word. He came from a working-class family in Long Beach. His dad was a car mechanic, and his mom made the trains run on time. Without that athletic scholarship, he'd probably be changing plugs on a Camry right now."

"Blue-collar is good," Hard Way said.

"He was sweet, humble, appreciative. But little by little, as he became a factor on the team, he began to change. It was by degrees; I didn't really notice the difference until we were seniors—and by then everything had been set in motion: the engagement, the wedding, my postgraduate degree plans, his own career plans."

Hard Way nodded. He tried to imagine what they might have looked like back then: the two bronzed USC swimmers, hair turned streaky blond by the sun and chlorine, accustomed to success, armed with diplomas, the famed Trojans network of alumni contacts at their disposal, their futures already aimed in the right direction.

"Sounds like you were both destined for greatness," Hard Way said.

"I would have settled for happiness. And for a while, we had that too. We didn't have much money, but we made the best of it. We were like Tom Cruise and—what was her name?—in *The Firm,* where they lived in a tiny apartment near Harvard Square and thought it was a big deal when they could afford moo shu pork from Wong Boys."

"Jeanne . . ."

"Tripplehorn!" Kat said. "That's her. And that was us, at least for a little while. Happy where our feet were. Happy to be together."

"And then?"

"And then life got in the way. We had a couple of kids—two daughters; they're the best. His job got stressful and he struggled. He wasn't everybody's All-American anymore. My mom got breast cancer. He was on the road too much. I felt isolated. And when he was home, he felt neglected. The male ego is a monstrous beast."

"Insecurity isn't our finest quality, I'll give you that much."

"He was a good husband, and then he wasn't. He was a good dad, and occasionally he still tries to be. He was there for me and my mom during her treatments and recovery. But more and more of his best qualities were in the past tense. There just came a point in our marriage when there *was* no point. He had mutated. I decided he wasn't worth the tears and the effort. Our marriage died of inertia."

Kat laughed at her lament. "You know, the more I think of it, maybe you and the bruhs *should* kick my husband's ass."

"Not me. I'm a pacifist."

"Well, thanks for listening. And for not judging. Gawd, I sound like the lyrics to a bad country western song. I need to keep the small talk small."

"Nah. I have my own long list of flaws. I'm on the road, geez, thirty weeks a year, maybe longer. Relationships and the road go together like ketchup and ice cream."

"Thirty weeks? Are you a pilot?"

"I'm a caddie. I'm in town for the Memorial."

Kat straightened and then smirked. Hard Way noticed the change.

"You don't like caddies?" Hard Way said.

"I used to follow golf, but I quit watching years ago."

"I don't blame you," Hard Way said. "The pace of play is so slow I can see my fingernails grow during rounds."

"How long have you been a caddie?"

"Going on almost, let's see, seventeen years. I didn't think I was going to last six months. When I got out of UT, I taught English and social studies at an elementary school in Cookeville, Tennessee. We called it 'Cookevegas.' "

"Sure, fourth graders, pro golfers. Same attention spans," Kat said.

"Anyhoo," Hard Way said, not taking the bait, "a buddy was trying to make it on the mini-tour circuit, so I tagged along during the summer. He couldn't afford a real caddie, so I carried his bag and probably cost him three shots a side. I didn't know how to read a yardage book, or even bother to check which way the wind was blowing. And I damn sure didn't have a clue about Bermuda greens.

"We were somewhere in Florida—Ocala, Palatka, Pensacola . . . all I remember is that it ended with an *a*—and my buddy was tied for the lead with two holes to play. First place paid $1,250, which wouldn't cover what a Tour pro spends to get his G 550 detailed. But it would have been all the money in the world to us, enough to splurge on dinner and the chocolate fountain at Golden Corral. And maybe we could stay at a motel where the palmetto bugs weren't as big as the ice machine."

"They're like cockroaches with wings."

"Not like—*are*."

"It sounds dreadful."

"Anyway, my guy had a chance at a win—or at least a playoff—until I mis-clubbed him on a par-3 and he hit it 20 yards over the green and into a pond. I can still see the ball splash on the fly. He fell apart and ended up hockey-sticking it for a nine. And then he birdied 18. Go figure."

"And he didn't fire you?" Kat said.

"I would have fired me!" Hard Way said. "But here's the thing: He never blamed me for talking him into hitting a 4-iron instead of the 5 he wanted to hit, or for not telling him to step away when we got a wind gust—mostly because I didn't notice the wind gust. I tried apologizing to him, but he stopped me cold. He said, 'You make the suggestions, but I make the decisions.' I've never forgotten that."

"So what happened?" Kat said, leaning forward.

"We ate a bag of pork rinds on the curb outside of a 7-Eleven. That was dinner. The hockey-stick nine dropped us, like, twenty spots. He got a check that barely paid for a tank of gas."

"No, not that—what happened to your player? Did he ever make it as a pro?"

"He knocked around on the Asian Tour for about six months, came back home, and gave up the game. Total cold turkey. He became a carpenter—makes good money in the trades—and every year, he sends me a Christmas card photo of him and the family standing in front of the tree. There's a staircase in the background, and every railing is made from one of his old clubs. And every year, he writes the same thing: 'My heart wasn't in it, but yours is.' "

"So you made it to the Tour, but he didn't."

"This is interesting to you?"

"Oddly, it is. Plus, you listened to my Tammy Wynette saga."

"After my buddy quit, I stumbled my way into a couple of bags on the mini-tour. One time, the sponsor of a tournament in Florida made the caddies wear plus fours, argyle socks, wool sweater-vests, and long-sleeved shirts in the dead of summer. You know that hot air that comes out of the dryer vent?"

"Yeah."

"That's what it was like in the canvas tent where we changed clothes after the round. No air circulation. It was a sweat box. It was like taking a swim in a Porta Potty."

"Very glamorous," Kat said.

"That same summer, I was in Chattanooga and my new guy shot 78-79 to miss the cut by a thousand. After the round, this old guy walked up to me and introduced himself. His hands were like lobster claws; you couldn't break his grip. He said his name was Cemetery and—"

" 'Cemetery'? What kind of name is that?"

"I'll get to that. Anyway, he said he used to work at Augusta National back when the pros had to use the club's caddies during the Masters. You know what the Masters is, right?"

Kat nodded, again with a slight smirk.

"I just wanted to make sure," Hard Way said. "Anyway, he was in Chattanooga visiting his grandsons and wanted to spend an afternoon on a course again. He had walked the last eight holes with us."

"But you said your player was going to miss the cut. Why would he want to follow your guy?"

"That's what I said. But he tells me, 'I wasn't watching your man. I was watching you.' So I said, kind of smart-assy, 'How'd I do?' That's when he poked that lobster claw at my chest and said, 'You either get serious about what you're doing, or you get serious about not doing it at all. Your man deserved better than what you gave him today. This is *professional* golf. A donkey can carry a bag. You wanna be a donkey or a caddie?' "

"He called you out."

"Yes, ma'am, he did. He said, 'When your man is struggling, a *professional* caddie walks beside him. You acted like he was contaminated, like you were ashamed to be near him. Your body language told me everything I needed to know. I saw you shaking your head when he three-putted from 9 feet. I saw you make fun of your man to one of the other caddies. You're the one who should be embarrassed, not your man. At least he was out there grinding."

"What'd you tell him?"

"I told him he was right. I phoned it in that day. I *was* embarrassed to be seen with a guy who could barely break 80. I wasn't professional. And I swore I'd never do that again."

"And what about Cemetery's name?"

"Oh, yeah. So five or six years later, I finally make it to the Masters. I'm on the bag of one of the amateurs who qualified. Good kid, Had a good move. Little bit of Keegan Bradley in his swing."

"You lost me."

"Caddie habit. We always find comps for swings. His was a little homemade, like KB's. But it worked."

"So you're at the Masters . . ."

"And we came in a few weeks early for some practice rounds. As usual, they assigned the kid a club caddie. Those are the rules. During one of the rounds, I asked the caddie if he'd ever heard of someone named Cemetery. He said Cemetery was a legend at Augusta National, that more than a few members had flown in for his funeral."

"Oh, no—he died?" said Kat, her voice soft with sympathy. "Well, then here's to Cemetery." She raised her glass.

Hard Way raised his and drained half the glass, all the time looking at Kat.

"What?" said Kat, suddenly self-conscious.

"Nothing. It's just that I like your style."

"Finish the story," she said.

"Roger that. Well, he got his nickname because nobody read those greens at the National better than Cemetery. They said that if Cemetery gave you the line—and you didn't screw up the speed—every putt would die in the bottom of the cup."

"Funny the things we're remembered for," Kat said. "A man and his craft."

"I went out to his gravesite and paid my respects. Caddie to caddie."

"Then I like your style, too," Kat said. "But I've got a question."

"As long as it's not about computational and mathematical engineering, sure," Hard Way said.

"Why do caddies refer to their players as 'my man . . . my guy?' The whole Lord Voldemort thing seems strange."

"Habit, I guess. It's old-school, sort of our language. I've worked for seven players in seventeen years, and each one was 'my man.'"

"It sounds almost Byzantine, in a way, like there's a wall between you and the player."

"There is. Some of my closest friends were the players who eventually fired me. It's always a business. And the caddies are usually the first casualties. We're disposable, like a broken tee."

"So you can get fired anytime?"

"Unless you're Bones. Or Greller, LaCava, Greiner, Skovron, or Scott. And even then, there's no absolute guarantee. I've been fired by text—that's the worst. Been fired by the parents of a player, by the sister of a player, and by the agent. I know caddies who got canned by a wife, even by a girlfriend."

"That's awful."

"That's nothing. I know one caddie whose man finally qualified for the Masters. It was going to be the first time for the caddie, too. The player knew the caddie's dad had always dreamed of attending a Masters, so he told the caddie he'd give him one of his complimentary tournament badges issued to the contestants."

"What a sweet gesture."

"It was. The caddie paid for his dad's plane tickets. Paid for the nonrefundable hotel room—at $750 a night. It cost a fortune, but his dad deserved it."

"He must have had a great time."

"He never got there. The player fired the caddie two weeks before the Masters and stiffed the dad on the badge."

"The player reimbursed the caddie, right?"

"Good one," Hard Way said. "You've got a lively sense of humor."

"Incredible."

"You have to understand that there's always a little bit of distance between your man and you. After a round, when you're shooting the shit with the other caddies, you might say something like, 'My man had a 9-foot downhill slider on 18 for an extra zero, but he put too much hair on it and it didn't take the break.' "

"You really know how to sweet-talk a girl," Kat said.

"You asked."

"So let me see if I can translate your language," Kat said. "A 'slider' can break right or left? 'An extra zero' means, what, the difference between a five- and six-figure check? And 'too much hair on it' means it was going too fast?"

"Very good," Hard Way said, impressed. "And the other caddie might say to me, 'At least you had a chance at the extra zero. On 16, my man checked out of the hotel and I could never get him back. He drove it into the marsh on the right. Instead of hacking it out to the short stuff and taking his Robitussin, my man said he could put the clubface on it and fly the bunker with a seven. I told him I loved his creativity, but that wedge was the play. Get the bogey. But he went Captain America on me and the ball stayed in the gunk. So we had to take an unplayable and walked off the green with a triple. My man had clam chowder for brains.' "

"OK, don't tell me," Kat said. " 'Checked out of the hotel' is he basically lost his mind?"

"Exactly," Hard Way said.

" 'Robitussin' is . . . You got me on that one."

"Take your medicine."

"Ah, good one. And 'Captain America' is . . . trying to be a hero?"

"Ding, ding, ding."

"It all makes sense," Kat said. "But you still haven't told me who your man is."

"Ha, he's a prick, too," Hard Way said. "If you don't follow golf anymore, you wouldn't know him. He has game, but he's not a closer. He was a top-50 or -60 guy for a half dozen years—and fairly well-liked and respected on Tour—but he's been in a free fall for the last couple of seasons or so. He got mean, too. I picked up his bag about two months ago, and we've been trying to deploy the parachutes ever since."

"Any luck?"

"We've slowed the free fall, but if he's not careful, he could lose his card. He needs to cash some checks soon. For both our sakes."

"Are you friends?"

"With him? Nooooo. He almost never talks about anything personal. And I don't know him well enough to push it."

"So it's all golf."

"Mostly, which is fine. I get the bare essentials. I see the wedding band, but he doesn't offer any details—and he doesn't have to. If he has kids, I've never heard him mention them. He's out here by himself. And I guess he likes it that way."

"So it's you and him. You're a team."

"Theoretically. But it's more like, you're *of* him, you're with him, but mostly you're a professional blame-ee. It's a partnership with conditions. All it takes is one too many missed cuts and missed reads, and you're looking for a new bag. The truth is, it's the greatest and worst way to make a living."

"And you're good with that?"

"A lot of these guys have never had dirt under their fingernails. They were coddled as juniors, and they're coddled as adults. Equipment guys put their clubs together for them. They've got a manager who handles all their arrangements and a swing coach who handles their golf game. Some of them have personal trainers, personal chefs, life-therapy coaches. A few have ultra-clingy parents. They've got me carrying their bag. They've got attendants in the clubhouse. There are cold plunges on-site. Dedicated workout rooms. Player-only dining rooms. They walk out of the locker room, and their courtesy car is waiting for them. I'm surprised they don't have grape peelers. It's a culture of entitlement. They begin to think they're better than you just because everyone treats them that way."

"You think they're spoiled."

"Not all of them. I didn't mean it like that. I just like rooting for the players on the fringes, the guys who came up through the ranks, the guys who don't take anything for granted."

"Ever consider a career change? Teach again?"

"I've thought about it, but I'm at the wrong end of my thirties. Plus, there's nothing like being in the thick of things on a Sunday afternoon. You don't get that teaching social studies in Cookevegas. It doesn't happen very often. If a player wins eight percent of his career starts, he'll be in the Hall of Fame. That's how hard it is to win on Tour."

"You're all about the chase, the jolt," she said. "I get that."

"You're right. Look, I'm not scrubbing latrines for a living, but I'm exhausted at the end of every day with my guy. He's high-maintenance and gets triggered easily. When he feels the pressure, he'll call me in to read a putt. If I get it wrong, I have to instantly tell him it was my fault. The trick is to not let it affect your confidence the next time he calls you in for a read. But it's hard when you're taking heat from your man all the time."

"I didn't know any of this."

"Not everyone is like him. There's one guy out there—he won a U.S. Open—who called in his caddie for a read on No. 7 at Augusta during the Masters a few years ago. It's a par-4 with a green that can fool you."

"Did the player always ask him to read putts?"

"Smart question. No, it was the first time the player had asked him that day."

"And?"

"He butchered the read, which can happen on that green. The player didn't come close to making the putt. When the caddie apologized, the player said, 'That's all right, pal. We'll get the next one together.' *That's* being a team."

"How many times have your guys won a tournament?"

Hard Way scrunched his face. Kat understood.

"OK," she said. "How many times have you come close?"

"A couple of seconds, a handful of thirds, some other top 10s where we could have, should have won," he said. "But unless you're Rocco Mediate or Tom Watson, nobody cares or remembers who finishes second."

"Rocco lost a playoff to Tiger at the U.S. Open," she said. "I remember that. And Watson—didn't he lose to someone dressed in fluorescent green?"

"Very good," Hard Way said. "It was Stewart Cink at the 2009 Open Championship. Cinky won fair and square, but Watson was fifty-nine and had a chance to become the oldest major winner ever. So I guess I was rooting for history."

"But to even get that close at that age was amazing."

"It was. But it's like getting five of the six numbers in Powerball."

"Don't you win a prize for five?"

"You win a prize, but you don't win *the* prize. He got a nice payday, but he didn't get to kiss the Claret Jug that day. And his caddie didn't get to keep the flagstick flag on No. 18."

"That's a big deal?"

"It is if you're a caddie," he said. "Back in the day, I used to carry a pocketknife in the bag at every tournament, just in case my man won."

"Because . . . ?"

"Because you'd have to cut the top of the flagstick to pull the flag off. Now you just unscrew the top."

"It's only a flag."

"That's what every caddie who has never won a tournament tells himself."

There was a silence between them as they contemplated the realities of their respective lives. It wasn't an awkward quiet, just . . . quiet. A Patti Smith cover of the Byrds' "So You Want to Be a Rock 'n' Roll Star" played in the background. Someone behind the bar appreciated the way Smith could bend a song to her will.

"But you love it," Kat said. "You love that world."

"I do," Hard Way said. "I had a respectable game as an amateur, but I knew I wasn't good enough to play professionally. Still, I wanted to be close to it. I wanted to be inside the ropes. I wanted to see golf played at the highest level. I wanted to travel the world. I wanted to walk the most famous courses in the world. And if that meant I had to carry someone's bag to do it, then sign me up."

"You're telling me why you did it, but you're not telling me why you love it."

Hard Way had never thought about it in those terms. "Do you know why you loved swimming?"

"I didn't love it, but I needed it. I had spent more time in water than on land. By the end, I was almost relieved that I was done. Every lap was a competition against the same four opponents: the water, the other swimmers, myself, and the clock. Always the clock. I could never swim fast enough to outrace that second hand. But you—you sound like you couldn't live without being a caddie."

"I could, but I don't want to," Hard Way said. "It's a joyful affliction. I love everything about it, even the stuff that I should hate. I love that every Thursday, everyone in the field starts at even-par and you have to prove yourself again. I love that it's the rare sport where the ball doesn't move unless you make it move. I love that you have to call a penalty on yourself, that cheating is golf's original sin. I love that you have to repair a divot, rake a bunker, take your hat off when you shake hands at the end of a round. I love standing on the 18th tee box at Pebble, the 17th tee box at the Old Course, the 12th tee box at Augusta, the first tee box at any Ryder Cup. I love the history and nuances of the game. I love that the game can crush your soul but also bring you an indescribable happiness—and do it all during the same 18 holes. I love that it makes you face your demons and that it reveals your better angels. I love talking about golf. Thinking about golf. I love the sounds of golf. I even love the tedium of it. But here I am, giving you my version of the truth."

"The caddie poet. Who knew?"

Hard Way was half embarrassed.

"It's just golf," he said. "What does Rory say? 'I hit a little white ball around a field sometimes.' But it's hard to hit that little white ball, especially when you're having a fistfight with your swing, and 15 feet away there's an audio guy aiming a shotgun mic at you, and the lead analyst is in the booth zesting you into a thousand pieces, and there's some drunk in the gallery yelling, 'Mashed potato!' in the middle of your takeaway. And even though my man hasn't sniffed a leaderboard since Jesus wore sandals, I have respect for his effort. Anyway, I haven't found a woman who makes me want to choose her over that . . . yet. But I'm trying."

The waitress appeared.

"Last call, folks."

Hard Way glanced at his borrowed watch. It was closing in on midnight.

"Uh, I don't know . . ."

"Two more Casamigos," Kat said, handing the waitress a credit card. "These are all on me. And add 35 percent to the bill for the birthday girl."

Hard Way began to reach into his pocket.

"Sorry, hon," the waitress said. "First card in my hand gets the bill. She beat you to it."

The waitress nodded at Kat and headed toward the bar, calculating her tip.

"Let me split it with you," he said to Kat. "I make a living wage."

"I know you do. Lousy caddies don't wear Rolexes."

Hard Way posed as if he were a wrist model.

"Thanks," he said. "It's a Daytona. It perpetuates the spirit of Hans Wilsdorf."

Kat reached out for his wrist and examined the watch with admiration and curiosity. Her hands lingered.

"It's a beautiful timepiece. Truly."

The margaritas arrived. Kat signed the bill and handed the plastic folder to the waitress. The house lights flickered on and off as Pearl Jam's "I Got ID" ended the night.

"Well, this was an unexpected evening," Kat said.

"I'll be here all weekend; that is, if my man makes the cut. So maybe I'll see you tomorrow—or actually today," he said as he glanced at the time again.

Kat's phone pinged. Text message. She glanced at it, hurriedly typed a response, and returned the phone to its home in her Tod's bucket bag.

"Sorry," she said.

"Everything OK?"

"It is now," she said, offering no details. "And another apology: I'm a one-and-done. I'm flying back home to Mission Viejo—no Monaco for me—later in the morning. My mom is watching the kids, so I won't be sticking around."

They walked to the hotel elevator, its door open and waiting. He pressed the button for the twelfth floor.

"Awkward," she said. "Same floor."

Hard Way sipped at his drink as the elevator made its way up. She stared at the floor. When the doors opened, Hard Way stepped aside to let Kat out first.

"I'm this way," he said, nodding toward the arrow pointing to his side of the hallway.

"I'm the other way," she said. "Good night."

"Safe travels," he said.

Kat took a step and then stopped.

"This is, uh, unlike me, but I'm half divorced and you're half lonely," she said. "I'm retiring the lug nut tonight." She pulled the rock off her finger, then the band and dropped both into her bag. "Two halves equal a whole. Whattya say?"

Hard Way took her ringless hand and walked her two doors down to his room. Once inside, he slipped off her jean jacket.

"Whattya say?" he said as he pulled her closer and began to untuck her T-shirt. "In the immortal words of David Wooderson, I say, 'Alright, alright, alright.' "

CHAPTER FIVE

Fight On

Hard Way reached blindly for his iPhone on the bedside table. He knocked over a lipstick-stained glass that held the remnants of a Casamigos and a jalapeño strip. When he finally located the phone, he tapped at it until it obediently displayed the time over his screensaver photo of the par-3 15th at North Berwick, his favorite hole on his favorite course in the world. The news wasn't good: 2:32 A.M.

He groaned. In less than three hours, he'd have to drag himself back to Muirfield Village Golf Club, finish what was left of the second round, sweat out making the cut, and, if he and his man survived, then slog through eighteen more holes, weather and daylight permitting.

He put the cell back on the nightstand. The glow from the screen revealed Kat's bra dangling from one edge of the lampshade, and his J. Crew boxers—the ones with the pattern of black Labradors—hanging from the other edge.

"Everything all right?" Kat said groggily as she turned around to face him. The contours of her body were backlit by the moonbeams that snuck in through a gap in the hotel room curtains.

"Bubblelicious," he said. "I can never sleep when I know I have to get up early. Was just checking the time. Sorry I woke you up."

"That's OK," she said. She ran her foot along his leg. "And if I didn't tell you earlier, you have nice calves."

"And you look like you could still swim the 400 IM," he said.

"I could, but it would take me longer than it takes Sergio to grip and regrip."

"Geez, you did pay attention back in the day."

Hard Way began doing the calculations in his head: Get up at 5:15, shave and take a quick shower, be at the course by 5:45, wait near the players' parking lot for his man to arrive by 6, be on the range by 6:15, be in place and resume play at 7:35.

"You need me to leave?" Kat said. "I can hear your brain working."

"Just doing the sleep math."

"Sleep is overrated," she said, working her way on top of him. "They've got twenty-four-hour room service here. Let's order some breakfast—I'm starving; I never got a chance to finish my dinner last night. We'll regain our strength, and, you know, tee it up one more time."

"Are you getting paid by the golf metaphor?" he said, reaching for the room phone. He ordered her the left side of the breakfast menu.

"Only one thing missing," Kat said as she navigated her way to the window. "We need to see the full moon."

She pulled apart the blackout drapes to reveal the moonlight . . . and that Class of 2008 Song Girl body. As she turned, she stepped on the clubhead of one of the irons that Hard Way had leaned against the wall. Her foot caught it just so, causing the shaft to bend and then snap near the base of the club. Kat fell against a small chair and ottoman.

Hard Way jumped out of bed and helped her up.

"You hurt?"

"I'm good," she said. "I can't say the same for whatever I stepped on."

Hard Way turned on the desk lamp. The 7-iron, his man's favorite club, had died a hero's death.

"It's my fault," he said, picking up the two pieces. "I meant to put the clubs back in the bag."

"I feel terrible," she said. "Where's the bag?"

He pointed to the closet door. "In there, drying out. But don't worry.

I'll text the TaylorMade rep right now and see if we can get a replacement shaft. The equipment trucks left on Wednesday, but one of their guys is based in Columbus. He has all the loft and lie specs, and the True Temper shaft is stock."

"I followed most of that," she said. "Why do you have clubs in your room? Don't you just leave them in the locker room?"

"I used to, but early in my career my man's clubs got stolen. Never again. Anyway, you sure you're OK?"

"How'd you put it? 'Bubblelicious.' I'm going to hop in the shower. You're welcome to join me."

"You go first—just in case room service gets here."

She kissed him. "Like I said, 'To men with manners.'"

The door closed. The toilet flushed. The shower sprang to life.

Hard Way collected the clubs and put them in the corner. Then he put on his boxers and a T-shirt. He sat at the edge of the bed, elbows on knees, head in hands. Minutes later, there was a tapping at the front door.

"Room service," the voice said.

That was fast, Hard Way thought.

He opened the door.

It was his man. And his man was four kinds of drunk.

Hard Way, who had forgotten about the watch pickup, flattened himself against the door of the closet as his man nearly ran him over with the room service cart. The metal domes over the plates of food clattered like cymbals as he barreled in. Outside in the hallway was the actual delivery kid.

"He gave me this," the kid said, holding up a $20 bill, "and said he knew you."

Hard Way held up his forefinger to the delivery kid.

"Don't leave. Hold on."

Hard Way shut the door, walked into the room, and found his man eating a piece of wheat toast.

"The charity thing lasted fuck-ing for-ev-er," his man said. "They had an auction, and I got bought by some guy whose family invented string cheese. He wanted me to give a lesson to his wife, who, by the way, was sizzling. So we went outside the ballroom and I've got my arms around this hottie, and we're using an umbrella as a club, and she starts swinging it, and she hits the string cheese guy in the crotch because he's standing too close. So he doubles over, and when he does, she turns around and whispers, "I've been wanting to do that for years." So I help the guy out to his car, go back inside, and then get cornered by three Nationwide execs who want to tell me about their member-guest at wherever the hell they play. That's forty minutes of my life I'll never get back. But I'll give 'em credit: They kept the Macallan coming, the twenty-five-year-old Sherry Oak, the good stuff. And, wait, why is your shower on?"

"I've got, uh, company."

"Look at you, Mr. Big Swinging Dick."

The shower stopped.

"Food here yet?" yelled Kat from behind the door and over the bathroom vent fan.

"Just got here!" Hard Way said.

Hard Way began to herd his man toward the room door.

"You gotta go," he said as he held it open.

His man stared at the bathroom door, and then snapped out of his momentary daze. "Not before you take my fucking watch off your fucking wrist."

"Oh, sorry," Hard Way said, opening the clasp and sliding the three-piece stainless-steel bracelet over his hand. "I put it on when I grabbed dinner tonight. Didn't want to leave it in the room when I was gone."

"Come to papa," his man said as he slipped the watch over his own left wrist and clicked the clasp in place. That's when the bathroom door popped open enough to reveal a steam-shrouded figure with one towel wrapped around her torso and another wrapped on her head like an updo.

"Max?"

"Be right there."

Hard Way nudged his man out the door. His man stopped, tilted his head, and then headed toward the elevator bay.

"Don't leave your A game in the sack," he said as he half staggered away. "Need to make this cut."

"See you in a few hours," Hard Way said. He then signed for the room service and put another $20 down for the kid, who had been patiently waiting in the hallway.

Hard Way and Kat ate breakfast in bed. She turned off the lights and ducked under the covers. Hard Way felt something soft and fuzzy just south of his belly button. He pulled up the sheets and aimed his iPhone, the ambient light from the screen revealing the unexpected.

"What are we doing down there, Woman of Troy?"

She was holding a head cover, the one with the old-school wool pom-pom on the top.

"Since you can't sleep," she said, "and now *I* can't sleep, I figured, let's see if you can hit driver again."

CHAPTER SIX

The Incident

Hard Way got up a little before four-thirty and did his best not to wake Kat. Rather than run the shower, he shaved, brushed his teeth, and dressed in the bathroom. He left a note near the sink.

Kat,

I should have left a rose or the driver cover on the pillow, but . . .

Here's some aspirin (I have a two-alarm hangover). And here's to future intersectional meetings between Tennessee and USC/ Stanford.

Safe travels westward.

Max

He carefully pulled the bag from the closet and loaded the clubs out in the hallway. He put the broken 7-iron clubhead in one of the pockets of the behemoth and dropped the snapped steel shaft next to the wedges.

The equipment rep was waiting for him in the darkness of the nearly deserted clubhouse parking lot.

"Should be easy-peasy," he said as Hard Way handed him the pieces. "I brought a couple of shafts and a spare clubhead. And I checked with the pro shop here and they have your grips. You might have to sandpaper them down a little bit for tackiness, but otherwise it's boilerplate stuff."

"I owe you," Hard Way said.

"Part of the job," he said. "You break it on a tree root or something?"

"Not exactly," said Hard Way, smiling.

"I don't want to know," the rep said as he headed for the workstation inside the pro shop. "I'll find you out at the range."

Thirty-five minutes later, the rep walked up with the repaired club.

"This is the original," he said. "This is a spare. The spare has this little piece of red tape on the top of the grip." He checked his Apple Watch. "It's 4:50. Your guy isn't going to be here until . . ."

"Right around six," answered Hard Way.

"OK, we're cutting it close on the grip glue and epoxy having enough time to dry and cure. But it should hold. I'll stick around until you guys tee off, just in case you have any problems on the range."

"Thanks, Bobby. You're a steely-eyed missile man."

"I'm going to grab a cup of coffee. I'll see you out there."

Hard Way put the two 7-irons in the bag, found a bench near the lot, and began checking box scores. He was in a fantasy baseball league with a dozen caddies and club reps. His team was dying. As always, he blamed Giancarlo Stanton.

A few other caddies began to arrive. They sat in the darkness, complaining about the usual: the travel, the oversized bibs, the heat, the length of the rough at Muirfield.

"I don't think Jack even bought blades for those mowers," said Stevie DiMaglio, nicknamed D-9 because he always ate his meals from vending machines to save money.

Bang Bang and Sand Man joined the conversation.

"Jack wants us to suffer," Sand Man said. "He ain't happy unless we're unhappy. Sheeet, I thought we'd lost Ian Woosnam in that rough one time. He was like Shoeless Joe in *Field of Dreams,* damn near disappeared into the vegetation."

"Don't be talking that way about the Golden Bear," Bang Bang said of the great Nicklaus. "Him, Mr. Palmer, and Tiger—that's the holy trinity right there."

"Amen to that," Sand Man said.

"Been meaning to ask you, dude, but what were you and your man talking about on No. 11 yesterday?"

Sand Man spit out a sunflower seed shell.

"You heard us?"

Sand Man and Bang Bang had been part of the same group.

"Heard part of it. He wanted to give it a go in two?"

The par-5 11th at Muirfield Village Golf Club was 588 yards long and reachable in two—if you bombed your drive and landed it between the creek on the left and the bunker on the right. But Sand Man's man hadn't bombed it. He never did.

"Sheeet, I wanted him to hit hybrid off the tee and we'd play it nice and smart to the green. Get on in three and see what happened on the birdie putt. But my man thought he was in a Marvel movie. Thought he was the Hulk or something."

Sand Man didn't believe in coddling his players. He told them the truth, and he didn't wrap the honesty in euphemisms. It had gotten him fired on several occasions, but Hard Way respected Sand Man for standing his ground. He secretly wished he could do the same—all the caddies did—but he didn't have the nerve.

"So what'd he say?" Bang Bang said.

"He goes, 'I'm feeling *strong*, Sand Man. Gimme the 3-wood.' I almost fell down laughing. I handed him an iron and told him to lay up. He says, 'I can do it, Sand Man. I can get there with the 3-wood.' I say, 'Beyoncé gonna leave Jay-Z and have your baby before you ever reach that green in two. Now hit the damn iron I'm holding for you and let's get on with it."

"You got the 'nads, dude."

"Sheeet, once he quit whining, what'd my man do?"

"He hit iron, wedged it close, and made birdie."

"Sand Man rests his case," he said, spitting out another sunflower seed. "Course, it coulda been worse."

"I know what you're gonna say," Bang Bang said.

"I coulda had the Boy Genius's bag," Sand Man said.

"The Boy Genius!" Bang Bang said.

The Boy Genius, as Jackson Van Stout III was called on Tour, was an insufferable and humorless nineteen-year-old whose mother owned half of Montana and happily doted on her only son. The Boy Genius had game—there was no denying his talent—but he had a belligerence and dry-ice coldness to him that made Hard Way's man look benevolent. He treated his caddies as if they were his servants, and he had already gone through a half dozen of them in his young career. Sand Man had been the first to go, partly because the Boy Genius overanalyzed everything. Every shot was a five-minute SAT exam.

"Tell him the Players story," Bang Bang said.

"How many times you need to hear that?" Sand Man said.

"There aren't enough times. C'mon, for me?"

Sand Man sighed and looked at Hard Way. "I ain't never told you this one?"

"Don't think so," Hard Way said.

"We're on 17," Sand Man said.

Bang Bang began laughing.

"I ain't even said anything and you're chuckling like a damn fool," Sand Man said.

"I know," Bang Bang said. "Can't help it."

Sand Man turned to face Hard Way. "The Boy Genius asks the distance to the pin. I tell him 149. Distance to cover the water? I tell him 132. Distance to cover the bunker? I tell him 141. Wind? Left to right, at about ten-thirty, hurting. I figure we're done. Now we just decide on a club."

"This is my favorite part," Bang Bang said.

"Then he says, 'Give me the distance in meters, not yards.' I tell him I don't have that particular information at that time. He gets all pissy about it. Then he wants me to tell him—and I ain't never going to forget this—'the magnitude of the vector.' Magnitude of what? Then he says, 'Never mind, just give me the displacement.' I'm turning the pages of my yardage book, trying to find whatever the hell he's talking about. So I say, 'Wedge feels like the right club.' And he says, 'I need the barometric pressure.' Baro-who? The Boy Genius loses it. He starts yelling at me in some damn language; it wasn't English. Then he asks if I've ever been to Helsinki. And I said, 'Hell no.' "

Bang Bang was heaving with laughter.

"How have I never heard this?" Hard Way said.

"What happened next?" Bang Bang said between horselaughs.

"I quit. I put the bag down, but before I left, I told him to hit wedge."

"And?" Bang Bang said.

"And the damn fool hits it to a foot. With the wedge. Never thanked me."

"The Boy Genius didn't deserve you," Bang Bang said.

"Truer words," Sand Man said. "Truer words."

Hard Way jumped up and slung the bag straps on his shoulders.

"My man's here," he said. "See you, fellas."

Hard Way walked over to the courtesy car. His man popped the trunk for him.

"Grab the shoes," his guy said. "I'm gonna take a piss and then we'll try to find a decent patch of dry grass on that shithole of a range. The place is going to be a swamp."

"Good morning to you, too," Hard Way said.

They walked to the clubhouse, where Hard Way waited outside before they made their way to the range. A handful of kids, their dads and moms in the background, leaned over the security rope as they strode by.

"Can you sign, please?!" said a little girl while waving a tee sheet. She wore orange shorts, an orange shirt, and an orange cap—a tribute to Rickie Fowler.

Hard Way's man gave her a thumbs-up and a wide smile. "Rickie is coming around the corner in about a minute or so," he said. "He's gonna love your outfit."

"Really?!" she said, craning her neck to see if Fowler was in sight. "Thanks, sir. Good luck today!"

Hard Way hurried his walk to catch up.

"Boss, Rickie finished his round yesterday. He isn't out here until later."

"I know," said his man. "I was just jacking her around. I'd rather have hemorrhoidal itch than stop and sign."

When they reached the range, his man started to slowly work through his bag, starting with the wedges. When he eventually reached for the 7-iron, Hard Way stepped in.

"Boss, when I was cleaning the clubs last night, I noticed that the epoxy was a little loose," he said, reciting his well-rehearsed lie. "Maybe it was the rain, but I didn't want to take a chance. I got Bobby out here this morning and he did a quick refurbish, and brought a spare, too."

His man examined the original.

"This is the gamer?" he said.

"That's it," Hard Way said.

"Grips need some work."

Hard Way pulled out a piece of sandpaper and ran it across the grips.

"Try it now."

His man hit a half dozen shots, shaping them differently on each swing.

"Give me the backup."

Hard Way handed him the other 7-iron. He went through the same shot routine.

"Lie and loft the same?"

"Exact to our specs," Hard Way said.

"Feels different. Let's stick with the gamer."

"Roger that."

After hitting balls, they went to the short-game area, and then to the practice putting green. It was almost time to catch a cart ride out to the 13th tee box. Hard Way checked every pocket in the bag: tees, extra gloves, a couple of Sharpies, three sleeves of balls, the Rolex, ball markers, energy bars, a bag of trail mix, an extra pair of socks, sunscreen, lip balm, an emergency yardage book, a dry towel, and a pack of gum. No rain gear today—it was going to be pushing ninety, zero cloud coverage. Then he counted the clubs, just as he had done a thousand times during his career. He had nightmares at least once a month about forgetting to count the clubs before a round began.

One, two, three, four, five, six, seven, eight, nine, ten, eleven, twelve, thirteen, fourteen, and, wait . . . fifteen? One too many.

Hard Way snapped his fingers. The extra 7-iron. He started to pull the spare from the bag.

"I gotta get this over to one of the range guys," Hard Way said to his man. "They'll put it in your locker."

"I'll take care of it," said his man. "You go grab us some extra waters. My sweat is already sweating."

"Affirmative," Hard Way said.

Hard Way jogged back to the oversized Yeti cooler next to the putting green, grabbed three waters, stuck two of them in his bib pouch, and then doused the end of his towel with another one. When he got back to the cart, he draped the towel across the top of the bag, transferred the bottled waters to the bag side pouches, and then climbed into the rear seat.

"Everybody in?" the volunteer cheerfully said.

"It's a golf cart, not a Formula One car," his man said. "Let's go before I die of old age."

The volunteer didn't say another word during the drive.

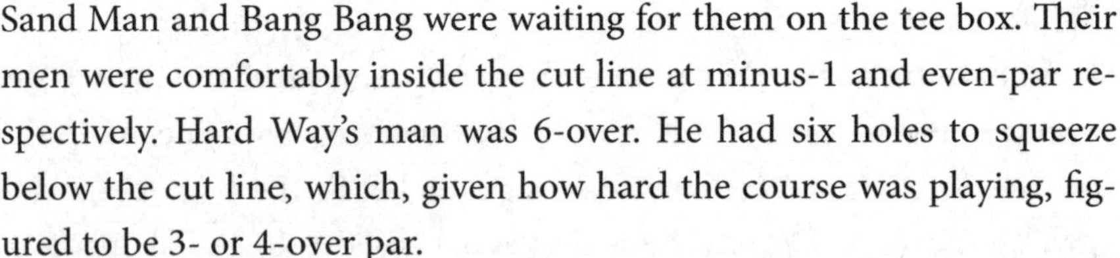

Sand Man and Bang Bang were waiting for them on the tee box. Their men were comfortably inside the cut line at minus-1 and even-par respectively. Hard Way's man was 6-over. He had six holes to squeeze below the cut line, which, given how hard the course was playing, figured to be 3- or 4-over par.

The 13th hole was a 455-yard par-4 that never seemed to fit his man's eye. He had doubled it on Thursday. From the tee box, the landing area looked about as wide as Billy Horschel's waist: tiny, only about 22 yards across. Jack had put in some trees on the left so you couldn't miss the fairway there without paying a price.

The horn sounded exactly at 7:35. Hard Way's man teed off last. He twirled the driver in his hand and set up for a baby draw. He had a functional, compact swing. What it lacked in aesthetics, it made up for in power. He could get the ball out there with the upper quarter of any field.

As soon as he hit it, Hard Way knew it was perfect. There wasn't much wind, and what little puff there was helped guide the ball toward the left side of the fairway. His man pulled the tee from the ground before bothering to see where the ball landed. Then he walked over and dropped the driver in the bag.

"Where was that yesterday?" he said to Hard Way.

"Doesn't matter," Hard Way said. "It's here now, right?"

With 109 yards to the pin, his man was between a hard lob wedge and taking something off the sand wedge. His stock yardage on the lob was 105, 110 max; the sand wedge, 119 max, 100 with a three-quarter swing.

"Whattya think?" he said.

"I love the idea of dialing down the sand wedge," Hard Way said.

"I'm feeling good, though. I can get there with the lob."

"Oh, I know you got that shot," Hard Way said (which was caddie-speak for "But don't try it"). "But the way you were pure-ing it on the range, you don't need to redline this. Just smooth it in there with the sand wedge."

"I don't know," he said.

"You will when you see it on the highlights package tonight."

His man stared at his yardage book, stared at the pin, tucked the book in his back pocket, and then pulled the sand wedge from the bag. It was tracking from the moment he hit it.

The ball landed 5 yards past the hole and spun back to a foot and a half. Kick-in birdie.

Five-over.

"Nice call there," his man said as they walked to the next tee box. "Really nice call."

Hard Way said nothing. It was rare for his man to offer compliments.

On the short par-4 14th, Hard Way read left inside edge on the birdie putt. His man agreed and made the 9-footer.

Four-over.

On the par-5 15th, his man wasn't sure whether to lay up or go for it in two. He had the length to reach it, but the risk/reward was considerable: almost a half stroke lost to the field if you missed the green in two but almost a full stroke gained on the field if you knocked it on in two.

"I think the cut's going to be 3-over," his man said. "I can lay up to my distance, take a bogey out of play, and still have a chance at a birdie."

"Makes a lot of sense," Hard Way said. "But another option is taking a calculated risk."

"Go for it?"

Hard Way went all in. "This hole is built for your game. Get on in two, make birdie for sure. Let's be aggressive."

His man stared at him.

"Screw it. Let's go."

His man had 248 yards to the pin. If he stepped on a 3-iron, he could reach it.

The ball was on line from the moment it left the club. But a breeze knocked it down just as it cleared the stream. It reached the green but was still a long way from the hole.

"Dammit," his man said. "That was tracking."

"You're on, boss. Let's have some fun with this next one."

And he did, dropping a 52-foot, left-to-right bleeder into the right edge of the cup for an eagle. Hard Way couldn't take any credit for the putt—his man had seen the line from the very beginning—but he was proud of talking him out of laying up.

Two-over, one shot inside the cut line.

"Let's keep it going," his man said. "Keep me focused. You're doing great."

He blew his 6-iron into the back right bunker on the par-3 16th—adrenaline rush—but got up and down for par. If he could par in, he was a lock to make the cut.

Instead, his man birdied the 485-yard par-4 17th to move to 1-over.

"Great read there," his man said, slapping him on the back. "I didn't see left edge, but you did."

On the par-4 18th, his man chipped in from the fringe to birdie the hardest hole on the course. Hard Way pumped his fist as if they'd just won the Claret Jug. His man had played those last six holes at 6-under, which doesn't happen every day at Jack's place. In fact, Nicklaus himself was watching from just off the 18th green. Hard Way saw Jack and his wife, Barbara, applaud with the rest of the crowd.

When everyone had finished the hole, Hard Way removed his cap and shook hands with the group.

"Whatever your man had for breakfast," Sand Man said, "make sure you give it to him for lunch."

As it stood going into the third round, they were even-par for the tournament and eight shots out of the lead. Another low number and they could be right there on Sunday—and that hadn't happened for a while.

Hard Way grabbed the wedge that his man had dropped against the side of the bag on his way off the green. He put the bag on its butt, wiped off the wedge, and then tried dropping it into the opening. For some reason, it got stuck. Hard Way walked off the green toward the scorer's area, all the while trying to shove the wedge down into the bag.

Halfway to the green, he slung the bag off his right shoulder, pulled the wedge out, and pushed aside the other clubs. One of the clubs was stuck under a separator and turned upside down, clubhead on the bottom. Hard Way pulled up on the separator, freeing the club.

"Oh, shit," Hard Way said softly.

Up ahead, his man looked like POTUS working a rope line at the Iowa State Fair. Fans patted him on the back, held out flags for autographs and knuckles for fist bumps. He looked as happy as Hard Way had ever seen him.

With a huge smile on his face, he waved at Hard Way to join him in the celebration. Hard Way walked head down toward him. His man gave him a playful hug and told the crowd, "You should get his autograph, too. Best caddie in the business!"

When they had made their way to the scorer's room, Hard Way pulled his man aside.

"Boss, we've got a problem."

"I know," his man said. "I'm still opening the face on some of those putts, and they're squirting right. Let me grab a quick bite and I'll meet you on the practice green."

"No," Hard Way said, reaching for the bag. He tapped the top of a grip.

His man leaned over to look. And there it was: the red piece of tape.

CHAPTER SEVEN

Rule 4.1B (1)

"What the hell?" said his man, removing the spare 7-iron from the bag with two fingers as if it had been dipped in sewer waste. "I thought you were going to give this to someone."

"I was, but then you said you'd take care of it."

"You're blaming *me* for this?" his man said, his voice and his anger rising. "It's not my job to do your job. I told one of the range guys that you needed to talk to him—because that's what you told me."

Hard Way's mind was doing figure eights. He remembered telling his man that he was going to get a range kid to run the club back to the locker room. His man said he'd handle it, but had Hard Way confused the two? And in Hard Way's rush to grab the bottled waters from the cooler, had he somehow stuffed the extra 7-iron in the bag backward?

"Boss, I don't know what to say."

His man walked into the scorer's room and asked a rules official to join him. Hard Way could see them talking. Then the rules official gently patted his man on the back. His man dropped his head, nodded in agreement, scribbled something on his scorecard, signed his name, and walked out of the room.

"Come with me," he said to Hard Way.

They walked outside, where a small group of reporters, including

AGN's Joe Riley, were waiting to ask about the miraculous comeback. Riley started it off.

"You went from missing the cut to working your way into the edge of contention," said Riley. "How do you explain what happened during those last six holes?"

Riley aimed his stick mic in front of the player. Hard Way could see his man sigh, place his hands on his hips, and then push the bill of his cap up so the reporters could better see the tears welling in his eyes.

"Fellas, you know it's no secret that I've been scuffling out here during the last year or so." He paused to compose himself. "This morning was special. To have Jack himself there at 18 was the honor of a lifetime." He paused again, pinching the bridge of his nose. "But we play by rules, and unfortunately my caddie didn't adhere to those rules."

He gestured toward Hard Way.

"Because there was a fifteenth club in my bag during the entire round, I've been penalized a total of four strokes for breach of Rule 4.1b (1). That's two penalty strokes for each of the first two holes, a maximum of four for the entire round."

Riley said the obvious. "Then you've missed the cut by one."

"I have. It's crushing. But fair or unfair, the rules are the rules, and I have to abide by them."

"How did it happen?" an Associated Press reporter said.

"I wish I could say it was an honest mistake, but sadly, it was laziness."

Hard Way could see the reporters glance his way. And as word spread of the four-stroke penalty, Hard Way could hear some of the fans in the background.

"That's him," said one. "He's the caddie who screwed up."

"Today was a learning experience," continued his man. "For me, I learned the painful lesson of depending on those who are unprepared for big moments. I learned that no matter how much I personally like someone, this is a business, this is my livelihood. So I've made the difficult decision to part ways with Max. I'll continue to support him in any way I can. But this was an unnecessary and preventable mistake."

His man—his *former* man—thanked the reporters and walked away, grief-stricken. The assembled fans applauded *their* man . . . the victim. The reporters moved toward Hard Way.

An SI.com reporter, Robert Harrick, spoke first. Harrick was playfully nicknamed the Vicar, in mocking honor of his volcanic temper and inventive use of four-letter words, especially if his parking space was located too far from the media center, or if there wasn't a proper supply of cookies in the buffet line. But he was a terrific reporter, respected by all.

"I don't know how to ask this delicately, but do you think you deserved to be fired?"

Hard Way was numb. He had been fired before, but never so publicly, and never for something that he was unsure was even his own doing.

"I—I—don't really know what to say," Hard Way said. "It's my job to count the clubs before we tee off. I've always done that. I did it today. There was a miscommunication."

"So it wasn't your fault?" the GolfChannel.com reporter said.

"I'm not sure it was anyone's fault. I'm really not sure what happened."

"You've been out here a long time," Riley said. "Why do you think you didn't get the benefit of the doubt?"

Hard Way stared at Riley, not unkindly. By a quirk of geographical fate, they lived in the same town. Riley, a St. Francis High School grad, on the West Side and the younger Hard Way, a Wheaton North man, on the more established North Side. They were separated by a few miles and a few years. They had each caddied at Chicago Golf, but their summers there never overlapped.

On occasion, Hard Way would see Riley and his family at the pizza place in town. He'd wave hello from the bar and Riley would wave back from their table in the dining area. One time, for no reason at all, Riley picked up Hard Way's dinner and beer tab. But they weren't friends per se. They shared the same town and the same sport, but nothing more. Riley never tried to pump Hard Way for inside Tour info (not that Hard

Way would have given it to him), and Hard Way never tried to increase his profile through Riley or the media. Among the caddies, Riley had a reputation for being fair, trustworthy, and prepared. That's all you could ever ask of a reporter.

Hard Way considered Riley's question. It wasn't an unreasonable one.

"Joe, you've been out here a long time, too," Hard Way said. "We don't sign lifetime contracts as caddies. The player is the boss; we're the employees. My man played legendary golf today. He was playing well enough to win this tournament. I'm so sorry it worked out this way."

"But you didn't answer the question," Riley said. "Do you think you should have gotten the benefit of the doubt?"

"Does it matter?" Hard Way said softly.

Hard Way excused himself, walked inside the clubhouse, and found his man sitting in the locker room. Another player was standing next to him.

"That was a class act, dude," the player said to Hard Way's man. "Nobody would have ever known the extra club was in the bag if you hadn't said anything."

"Rules are rules," his man said bravely.

"Well, it was a shitty thing," said the player, glaring at Hard Way, "but there are a lot of guys in this locker room who admire your honesty."

They shook hands and the other player left. A moment later, Hard Way approached his man.

"Boss, can you give me a second chance on this?" Hard Way said. "Nobody feels worse about what happened than me. You played beautifully."

His man looked around the locker room and then hugged him.

"I want to tell you something," he said, his voice seething as he whispered into Hard Way's ear. "I didn't fire you because we had fifteen clubs in the bag."

Hard Way tried to move away, but his man had the palm of his right hand on the back of the caddie's neck.

"I fired you because you slept with my wife last night."

Hard Way broke free.

"What? Your wife? You're out of your mind."

"Let me paint you a picture," his man said. "About five-foot-nine, legs up to here, a swimmer's body, but this one actually needs a bra."

Hard Way checked the boxes in his head but refused to believe it.

"There's no way. I mean, I did meet someone last night at the bar. But she was in town on business."

"She was in town on business . . . and to talk to me. I got stuck at the charity gig and texted her late."

Hard Way remembered Kat's phone dinging at the booth in the bar.

His man continued. "She said it was too late, that she was too tired, that she had an early flight back home . . . *our* home. I guess she got a second wind, huh?"

"I think this is all a mistake," Hard Way said. "She swam at USC and ended up marrying an All-American swimmer there."

"She told you that?"

Hard Way's mind was racing. "Yes. Wait, I think so. When she said All-American, I assumed it was another swimmer."

"You assumed wrong. Read my bio: I was a three-time All-American at USC. Swimmer? I couldn't beat her if I was wearing fins and she gave me a fifty-meter head start. Damn woman was part fish. She would have made the Olympics if she hadn't torn her rotator cuff."

"She said she quit."

"Quit? They had to drag her out of the pool. She was trying to race with one arm."

"I'm . . . confused."

"I bet you are. She show you the tattoos on her ankles? I thought I heard her voice from the bathroom, but I figured I'd had too much to drink. But then this morning, when you first walked up, I could smell her perfume on you. When you're with a woman for as many years as we've been married, you know that smell."

He leaned against a locker. "I don't know what to say, man. I had no idea."

"Well, now you have no job."

"So you're doing this to spite me?" Hard Way said.

"No," he said. "I'm doing it to spite her. I'm doing it to *ruin* you."

"Why? I didn't know she was your wife. She said she was splitting up with her husband."

"That's rich. I was getting ready to put *her* on injured reserve. And you had a lot of nerve to wear the watch she gave me."

"What?" Hard Way said.

His man unlatched the Rolex and shoved it near Hard Way's face. "See this?"

Hard Way read the engraving inside the wrist band. *'Til the End of Time—Love, Kat.*

"I think you're going to need to get that re-engraved," Hard Way said.

"Hell, thanks to you, Rolex will probably send me a brand-new one for free."

"At least be honest with me: You stuffed that 7-iron in the bag so I wouldn't see it."

"Framed you like a painting," his man said with satisfaction.

"But you had made the cut! You could have won this thing, or at least made a run at it."

There was a noise behind a nearby row of lockers. Neither man could see who it was. Perhaps another player getting ready for the third round? A security guard who'd heard the raised voices?

Hard Way waited a moment and then continued, this time with his voice slightly lowered.

"You're a fraction of a man."

"And you're unemployed. And I'm going to make sure you stay that way."

"There are plenty of reporters outside," Hard Way said, stiffening. "Maybe they'd like to hear the truth."

"Maybe you didn't pay close enough attention to my post-round performance," his man said. "I had those reporters all but dabbing the tears from my eyes. I thought Barbara and Jack were going to invite me back to the house for a family dinner and a group hug. And the fans, they love me. So do the other players."

"Not for long," Hard Way said as he turned to leave.

"You go do that. In fact, let me get the door for you. But you'll sound like a desperate caddie willing to throw your player under two buses. Whatever chance you have of getting back in the game—and it ain't much—evaporates if you go out there with that story. And just think if I happen to leak it that I caught you with my wife. You'll be lucky to get a loop at a muni in Salina, Kansas."

Hard Way knew he had no options. In the he said, he said scenario, the caddie would always lose to the player. And the truth was, his man knew it was all a bluff. One of the reasons his man had hired him was because of Hard Way's reputation for never breaking golf's version of attorney-client privilege. Hard Way considered it a breach of trust when a caddie spoke to the media about private matters.

"You really want to do this?" Hard Way said.

"It's done."

Hard Way untied his caddie bib and tossed it on the locker-room floor.

"You're a vindictive tapeworm," he said. "Had I known it was your wife, I would have never—"

"Screwed her? But you did. Now get the hell out of here. This area is for players only. You're nothing more than a human grocery cart. An app. A hired GPS. You carry and point for a living. Or you did."

Hard Way walked in a daze to the parking lot, all the time wishing there were a way to somehow reverse the last seventeen hours of his now shattered life. *Had to be a hero, didn't you? Had to show how clever you were at the bar. You were so busy being charming that you missed the clues: Her husband was in town on business . . . The look on her face when you mentioned you were a caddie . . . The way she looked at the watch. If only you'd taken a shower, there would have been no perfume smell. But no, you had to be polite. What were the chances of accidentally sleeping with the wife of your boss? A zillion to one? And how could you have missed the extra club in the bag? That was the kind of thing that happened to careless and inexperienced caddies. How do I recover from this?*

As he reached the lot, Hard Way looked up to see a delegation of caddies waiting for him at his car.

"We heard," Bang Bang said. "That could have happened to any of us, dude. Unbelievable that he cut you loose."

"Sheeet," Sand Man said, "he's the world's oldest living heart donor. There ain't no way you had fifteen clubs on purpose. Hell, you've counted the clubs in *my* man's bag, just to help me out."

Hard Way wanted to tell them what had really happened, but he didn't. And couldn't.

"Fellas," Hard Way said, "you know what Bobby Jones said: 'You have to play the ball where it lies.' So I'm gonna pack my bag, get in the car, and drive back to Wheaton. Hope to see you somewhere down the road. If not, it's been an honor."

One by one, the caddies hugged him and promised to stay in touch. Hard Way settled into the front seat and let the reality of his excommunication wash over him. In an hour's time, he had become the elder Inuit banished to an ice floe by the rest of the tribe, never to be seen again.

His cell rang. It was another caddie.

"Hey, man, how you holding up? I mean, it ain't plane-crash tragic, but you must feel like you've died, right?"

"Yeah, something like that."

The caddie paused for a beat.

"I know this isn't super cool, but any chance I could get your man's number? I'm looking to trade up from my bag."

Hard Way pressed the red disconnect icon and dropped the phone on the front seat. He pulled the parking pass from the stem of his rearview mirror and handed it to the attendant on the way out.

"Missed the cut, eh?" the attendant said sympathetically.

"Afraid so," Hard Way said. "So instead of shuttling in from the employees' lot tomorrow, why don't you use this?"

The attendant broke into a smile. "Been working this tournament for sixteen years. First time anyone gave me their pass."

"My pleasure."

"Who's your player? From now on, I'm rooting for that guy."

"Nah. Save it for someone who deserves it."

Hard Way made the short drive to the Marriott and shoved his clothes into his suitcase. In the bathroom, there was a note from Kat leaning against his toothbrush. He didn't bother reading it. Instead, he crammed the note and his kit bag into his backpack. In fifteen minutes, he was on I-70 West headed toward Indianapolis. If the traffic wasn't bad on I-65 North, he'd be back home in Wheaton in five and a half hours. Wheaton—hometown of John Belushi, Bob Woodward, and an unemployed caddie.

CHAPTER EIGHT

Eight Weeks Later

Spring and most of summer had been a blur for Riley. There was the U.S. Open in mid-June, followed by several other Tour tournaments. In July came the Scottish Open and the Open Championship. Now there was a brief vacation window before the playoffs began in August.

Riley needed the break. He was tired of living out of a battered Samsonite, tired of waking up some mornings having to think of where he was.

He and Laurel's brother, Aaron, played golf every other day. Aaron was a 4-handicap, Riley an 18 and not getting any better. Riley never asked Aaron for advice, and Aaron never offered any. He wanted Aaron to enjoy the rounds without the added weight of giving playing lessons.

Riley's short game was solid. "You've got good action there," Aaron would tell him. But his full swing would have sent Butch Harmon screaming into the night.

When covering tournaments, Riley would always spend time on the range watching the pros go through their practice routines. They made it look so effortless. He would return home with another dozen swing thoughts: head farther behind the ball, shallow out the angle of attack, take the club back faster, take the club back slower, rotate the lead shoulder under the chin, rotate the right hip, lead with the legs, uncoil from the top, keep the knees flexed, don't transition too fast, imagine a right angle between the target line and the clubface . . . on and on it went. Riley would stand over a shot and swing thoughts would bounce around his mind like lottery balls in an air blower. He was the only player Aaron had ever seen with a three-way miss.

On this sun-drenched fall day, Riley was stuck in the storage area of the basement assembling a metal shelving unit. The instructions were simple enough, but the only tool included in the kit was an Allen wrench so small that elves would have had difficulty using it.

When he was done, Riley gathered up the empty box and plastic wrapping. Just before turning off the light, he noticed the birthday clubs Buddy had gotten him in the corner of the room.

Riley hadn't thought about the clubs since the night Buddy had given them to him. He had never asked Nicklaus about the MacGregors while covering the Memorial. Jack's formal press conference wasn't the time or place to inquire about such things, and the impromptu session with a few reporters afterward had lasted only a few minutes. Anyway, Riley already knew the answer: They were restored clubs, nothing more.

Between Riley's travel schedule and Buddy's downtown internship with a risk management company, father and son hadn't seen each other very often. When they did, it had a perfunctory feel to it, as if they were going through the motions. Riley didn't know how to cut through the barrier that Buddy had created. And now Buddy was back in Madison, having moved out of the Delta house and into an apartment with several of his frat brothers before classes began in early September. There had been a handshake and a half-hearted hug from him when he left. Since then, an occasional text of no consequence.

Riley picked up the empty box and wrapping and made his way to the staircase. He turned off the light and then almost instantly turned it on again.

"OK, let's see what you got," he said out loud as he dropped the box and returned to the white golf bag. He pulled the driver and a few irons from the bag and carried them and the box to the garage. The box went in the garbage can; the garage sale clubs went into his own bag in the trunk of his 1974 BMW 3.0 coupe, which Riley had lovingly restored over the years.

Riley drove to nearby Glen Ellyn and a local muni with a grass driving range (if you count clover as grass) and found an open spot near the edge of the line. To the right of him was a beer-bellied middle-aged man wearing a Chicago Bears bucket hat, a long-sleeved shirt, shorts, calf-high white socks, and some form of ancient golf shoes. A lit cigar rested on the metal bag holder. His swing, though, was surprisingly effective.

To Riley's left was a man in his late twenties. He had alignment sticks everywhere: two laid parallel to his feet—24 inches apart—two more poking up from the ground behind, and another one held in his hands pressed against his left pocket. Riley had seen the Tour guys use alignment sticks, but never five at a time.

Riley pushed aside several of Buddy's clubs and instead pulled his brand-new 8-iron from the bag. He held the club against his chest and rotated his shoulders. He stretched his legs. He took some easy half swings. Then he dragged one of the range balls with the clubface, perched it on a clump of clover, picked his target, took a small breath, checked his grip, swung . . . and shanked it nearly into the ankles of the Chicago Bears bucket hat man.

"Almost got me on that one," the man said, more amused than annoyed.

"I've really been working on that shot," Riley said weakly.

The man gave him a courtesy laugh and returned to his own bucket.

Riley went through his routine again: target, breath, grip, swing. This time he topped the ball 20 yards.

He stepped back, looked at the clubface as if it had acted on its own. He dragged another ball out of the bucket.

"Here we go," he muttered to himself.

At least the next shot went airborne. The ball traveled 30 yards—about the same distance as the clump of dirt and grass that followed it.

Riley tried another of his newly purchased clubs, a 6-iron. He hooked his first shot. Sliced his second. Skulled his third. About four stations away, he heard a young girl say to her father, "Daddy, that man isn't very good, is he?"

Riley wiped the dirt off the 6-iron and went through his mental checklist of swing thoughts.

"Don't think, just swing," he told himself.

What better club to swing than his recently purchased carbon-faced driver, the one with the massive 460cc clubhead and all sorts of MOI benefits. He had spent nearly $700 on it. The salesman had said it was a game changer.

Riley teed up a ball, stepped behind it, and picked out his target. He walked toward the ball at a 45-degree angle, never taking his eye off the target. He set his feet, waggled the driver head, took one more glance at the target, and then swung. The ball flared to the right, barely sneaking past the 150-yard sign.

"Hey, pal."

It was the man with the alignment sticks.

"Mind if I give you some friendly advice?"

"I appreciate it," Riley said, "but I like to figure things out on my own. It's the best way to learn."

He had heard Scottie Scheffler say that once. Or maybe it was Riley's neighbor, Larry.

"Pal, I'm just trying to help."

"That's nice of you, but I'm reworking my swing [which was a lie] and my instructor [Riley didn't have one] said that you have to take two steps back to take one step forward [which was another lie]."

The bucket hat man chimed in.

"You're coming too far inside on your takeaway," he said. "And your right elbow is flaring on the downswing."

"And you're bent over like a greater-than sign, so your swing plane is all screwed up," the alignment stick man said.

"Fellas, thanks for trying to help, but I'll work out the kinks," Riley said.

"Suit yourself," bucket hat man said.

Riley teed up another ball. He smother-hooked the drive. The next ball was a hard slice.

"OK," he said to bucket hat man and alignment stick man. "I'm listening."

By the time they were done with him, there was an alignment stick parallel to his feet and another one pointing up between his legs, the tip only a few inches below his crotch. "That's an incentive to keep you from swaying to the right," alignment stick man said.

There was also a stick positioned 4 feet across from him and pointing at his chest.

"Is that for club arc, or something?" Riley said.

"No," alignment stick man said. "That's pointed at your heart. It's a reference to *The Hunger Games: Mockingjay—Part 2*."

"You're joking."

"I never joke about Katniss."

Bucket hat man put a towel under Riley's right armpit and a ball under his right heel. "I'm trying to get you to stay more connected," he explained.

Bucket hat man teed up a ball for him.

"Pronation is the key here," he said.

Riley never had a chance. He nearly impaled himself on the crotch stick when his right heel slipped off the ball. Meanwhile, the towel somehow got caught on the top of the club grip during his backswing. The ball dribbled only a few feet.

"See?" alignment stick man said, arms crossed, a look of satisfaction on his face.

"Exactly," bucket hat man said, nodding. "Much better."

"Better?" Riley said. "I almost whiffed and sang soprano at the same time."

"But you didn't sway as much, and I loved the way you front-loaded," alignment stick man said.

Bucket hat man agreed. "Takeaway line was cleaner, pronation went from an F-plus to a C-plus, and like the man said, the front-loading gave me chills."

"I hit the ball 3 feet," Riley said.

"But terrific traj," bucket hat man said.

"Every journey begins with a single step," alignment stick man said.

Riley hit a dozen more shots, each one a separate illustration of failure.

"Fellas, I give up," he said. "I just don't have it today." He stepped away from the sticks and began removing them from the ground.

"Pal," alignment stick man said, "let's give it three more tries. I'll pick the club."

He began to reach into the bag. "Whoa! How many clubs do you have in here?"

"I threw some extras in before I left today," Riley said.

Alignment stick man pulled the cover off the persimmon driver.

"Isn't this supposed to be in a museum?" he said. "I've got hybrids with bigger clubheads than this."

Bucket hat man began poking through the bag too.

"You've got some Nicklaus counterfeit irons—I've seen these things on eBay. They make them in China," he said. "The driver is actually a high-quality knockoff. Not bad."

"My kid got them at a garage sale," Riley said. "The guy gave them to him."

"Sounds about right," bucket hat man said. "They're worthless."

"I just thought they were old MacGregors," Riley said.

"Look at them," bucket hat man said. "These things just came off the assembly line in some Guangzhou sweatshop."

Alignment stick man handed Riley the wooden driver.

"Just for fun, try hitting this," he said.

"I don't know," bucket hat man said. "Who knows if they used actual wood. It's probably some cheap composite. The thing could explode in your hands."

"I'll hit one," Riley said.

He teed up a ball and set the driver behind it.

"May the odds be ever in your favor," alignment stick man said.

"Pronation," bucket hat man said.

Riley swung. It was a swing just like the two dozen swings before it. Except this time, when the clubhead collided with the ball, there was a crackling explosion of unnatural sound. It was so thunderous that bucket hat man ducked and alignment stick man gasped. The range ball shot forward for nearly 200 yards and then rose as if it were propelled by a second-stage rocket. The three men lost sight of it for a moment and then it finally reentered Earth's atmosphere far beyond the edge of the range.

An astonished bucket hat man could say nothing. Alignment stick man mumbled something about "negative sway." Riley, almost delirious in his happiness, turned to both and bowed down with arms outstretched, just as Katniss had done to the game makers.

"Thank you for your consideration," he said.

Bucket hat man shook his hand.

"I can't believe what I just saw," he said. "How did you do that?"

"It had to be three bills easy, maybe 350, maybe more," alignment stick man said.

"I didn't even feel it," Riley said. "I've never caught a ball that flush."

"Try another one," bucket hat man said.

Riley pulled a ball from the pile, placed it atop the tee in the palm of his right hand, and plunged the peg into the ground. He barely looked at his line. For the first time in his adult golf life, he was too excited to think, to hear, to tie his mind into knots with his usual checklist of swing tips. He just wanted to hit. And hit it far.

When struck, the ball disobeyed every law of physics. It ignored gravity. It mocked common sense. It simply refused to land—that is, until it had traveled 415 yards.

He was no longer Joe Riley, but Kal-El from the planet Krypton. This artifact, this garage sale afterthought, this lightbulb-sized piece of lacquered wood, had turned him into some sort of golf superman. How? Why?

He hit another one. It sounded *far*. The father and his daughter drove a golf cart to the third ball, aimed a range finder at Riley, and then reported back: 421 yards.

"Pal," alignment stick man said, "Alan Shepard didn't hit a ball that far—and he was on the moon."

Fifteen minutes earlier, Riley had almost broken bucket hat man's ankle with a shank. Now his shots were flying like the Blue Angels. The only thing missing was a contrail.

Someone summoned the club pro from the shop.

"Have I seen you on TV or something?" asked the club pro, who had been at the muni for years. "You play professionally?"

Riley was wearing sunglasses and a hat. There was no way the club pro could have recognized him from AGN.

"Nope. Don't play professionally."

"I didn't think so—not with that swing," the club pro said. "But you hit it far."

"I've got some good help," Riley said, nodding toward bucket hat man and alignment stick man.

"Those who can't, teach, I guess," the club pro said. "Is that persimmon?"

"It is."

"Mind if I take a look?"

Riley handed him the driver. The club pro carefully examined it as if he were a forensics expert. He ran his fingers along the grooves. He checked the wrapping of the leather grip. He looked hard at the metal plate.

"A Tommy Armour 945W," he said, reading from the plate.

"We're pretty sure it's a knockoff, or something MacGregor flooded the market with way back when," Riley said.

"Hmmm," the club pro said, still looking at the club. "That's what you think, huh?"

"My son got the whole set free at a garage sale," Riley said.

"You usually hit the ball that far?" the club pro said.

"Not usually."

The club pro glanced up.

"OK," Riley said, "not ever."

"Mind if I look at the irons?"

"Sure. We think they're counterfeits from China."

The club pro pulled one of the garage sale blades from the bag, an 8-iron. He turned it over in his hand.

"Mind hitting one of these for me?"

Riley took the club and teed up a ball in the grass.

"I was having some problems with my new 8-iron earlier," he said nervously.

"That's fine," the club pro said. "You swing, I'll watch."

"I haven't hit a blade in years," Riley said.

"Then this will be a thrill for all of us."

"Don't expect much."

Riley could feel everyone watching him as he stood over the shot. He blew out of a puff of air and then loosened his grip in an effort to relax. As he stared down, the 8-iron looked as thin as a wafer cracker, the sweet spot seemingly the size of a bottle cap. He was already preparing himself for failure.

When he hit the ball, Riley initially thought he had caught too much grass behind it—an unhappy tendency of his. But the ball burst from the clubface and arched high in the sky . . . and stayed airborne for 190 yards. It bounded forward another 8 yards upon landing. Riley turned to the club pro for some sort of explanation.

"I—I—I don't know what's happening," Riley said.

"Well, whatever it is, don't stop doing it," the club pro said. "I wouldn't have believed it if I hadn't seen it myself."

"So how do you explain this?" Riley said.

"I have no earthly idea," the club pro said. "But you just hit an 8-iron 20 yards longer than Rory McIlroy—and he's hitting real golf balls."

"So what should I do?"

"Well, the next time you go to a garage sale," the club pro said, "bring me with you. By the way, those clubs are the real deal."

The club pro walked back to his shop. Alignment stick man and bucket hat man beamed with pride.

"Well, we got you fixed," bucket hat man said.

“Sure did,” alignment stick man said.

“Couldn’t have done it without you, fellas,” Riley said.

“Can I ask you a favor?” bucket hat man said. “Mind if hit your persimmon?”

“Uh, I don’t know about that,” Riley said.

“Just one,” he said.

“Yeah, I guess.”

Bucket hat man took a couple of easy practice swings and then placed a ball on the tee.

“If you can blast it that far with your swing, I think I can do a little better,” bucket hat man said, not unkindly.

“This’ll be fun,” alignment stick man said.

Bucket hat man didn’t catch the ball in the center of the clubface, but it was close. Had they taken a video of the swing, it would have shown a near-perfect club path and an impressive follow-through. The ball rocketed directly over the 175-yard marker and came to a rest slightly to the right and just past the 200-yard sign.

“I thought I thumped that thing,” bucket hat man said, perplexed. “Two hundred? That’s it?”

He handed the club back to Riley.

“Do me a favor. Hit one more, but this time swing as hard as you can.”

Riley did as he was told. He swung so hard that he came out of his left shoe and nearly fell down during the follow-through.

“Where’d it go?” he said once he regained his balance.

“If I had to guess,” alignment stick man said, “I’d say somewhere in Joliet.”

That night, Riley called his son. Buddy just had returned to Madison for his own version of vacation time before classes began in three weeks.

“Buddy, you need to come home this weekend.”

“I can’t, Dad. I’m taking a Chi O to a party.”

"I'm not asking you, I'm telling you," Riley said. "Get up early Saturday, drive down, and we'll be done in time for you to make the party."

"Dad, c'mon," Buddy said. "Is everything OK? What's so important that I gotta schlep back and forth?"

"We need to see someone."

"Who?"

"The man from the garage sale."

CHAPTER NINE

To Absent Friends

The first thing Riley and Buddy saw as they rounded Menomini Drive was a SOLD placard on top of the real estate sign in the front yard of the Dutch Colonial. The garage door was closed, and there were no cars in the driveway. Riley pulled in front of the mailbox on the curb.

As Riley and Buddy approached, they could see through the glass in the front door and into a bare living room. The walls were faded where the sun had slowly bleached out the paint over the years. But there were also blocks of the original dark mustard color where framed artwork or photos had once hung. On the door handle were brochures attached by rubber bands. One touted the miracle of gutter coverings; the other was from a local Realtor who said he could sell properties for top dollar. Too late.

Riley rang the doorbell. There was no movement inside. He rang it again. Nothing.

"Dad, I don't think anybody's here," Buddy said. "Gordo told me he was downsizing."

"Gordo?"

"That's his name."

They stood on the stoop for another minute or so. Across the street, a neighbor cracked open her front door and yelled, "Are you Mormons?!"

"We're members of The Church of Jesus Christ of Latter-day Saints!" Buddy yelled back. "I'm Elder Buddy and this is Elder Joe. Could we share our testimony with you?"

The woman slammed her door.

Riley didn't know whether to laugh or scold. Instead, he smiled on the inside.

Buddy rang the doorbell a final time. Again, silence. As they turned to leave, they heard a voice and then saw someone fast-walking to the door.

"Hold on! Sorry! I was in the basement!" she said.

It was Gordo's granddaughter. Buddy recognized her from the garage sale. She was in her early twenties, and prettier than he had recalled.

"Hi, remember me?" Buddy said.

"No," she said, slightly out of breath. "Are you here to pick up the FOR SALE sign? We need it out of the yard before the closing on Monday."

"We're not here for that," Buddy said. "I met you and your granddad at the garage sale this summer."

"You did? I'm sorry, there were a lot of people here that day and it's been a difficult few months."

Riley took over.

"My name is Joe Riley, and this is my son," he said. "We apologize for bothering you, but we were hoping to talk to your grandfather."

"About what, please?" she said.

"Actually, we wanted to ask him a few questions about a set of golf clubs," Riley said. "I have them out in the car."

"I wish I could help you," she said. "But my granddad's not here."

"We can come back at another time if that helps?" Riley said.

The woman paused before answering.

"My granddad died about two weeks ago," she said. "Everything's been a blur ever since."

"Gordo died?" Buddy blurted.

"I think what my son meant to say," Riley said, giving Buddy a sideways look, “is that we’re very sorry to hear that. We’ll leave you alone. It isn’t that important.”

The woman turned to Buddy. “He let you call him Gordo?” she said.

“Yeah, he told me to call him that,” Buddy said.

“That was my granddad’s middle name,” she said. “Well, it was Gordon, but only his Navy buddies called him Gordo.”

“What was his first name?” Riley said.

“Standish,” she said. “He usually went by SG—he was a bit formal that way—so you must have made quite an impression on him . . . I’m sorry, I forgot your name?”

“Buddy. My name’s Buddy.”

“I’m Sadie. I’m just cleaning up the place before the final walk-through. My parents were supposed to help, but it’s been hard on them.”

Her voice cracked as she mentioned her parents. “And I guess on me, too.”

“Our apologies,” Riley said as he stepped off the stoop. “We’ll let you finish up.”

Sadie had closed the door and was locking the dead bolt when the names suddenly registered with her. She flung open the door.

“Wait—you’re Buddy!” she said. “And you’re the golf reporter guy!”

Both men nodded.

“Come in!” she said. “My granddad left something for you.”

They walked down a short hallway and into the kitchen. On the counter was a cardboard box with a Coffey Law & Associates logo on the side. Coffey Law & Associates was a well-regarded Chicago law firm known for its work with the powerful and influential Daley family in years past. Leaning against the box was a Tumi leather backpack.

As Sadie unzipped the largest of the backpack compartments, she nodded at the box.

“I interned there this summer.”

“I interned downtown, too,” Buddy said. “At Aon.”

Sadie didn’t look up but said, not unsarcastically, “Risk mitigation—thrilling.”

She pulled out an iPad, powered it up, typed in her password, and propped the screen on one of the case slots.

"SG recorded this three days before he died. He had me set it up and hit Record, and then he ordered me out of the room. When he was done, he had me email the video to myself but made me promise I wouldn't watch it until you did. He knew your names, but he didn't know how to reach you. Honestly, I'd forgotten all about it, what with his death a few days later, then the funeral, then this house sale. I still can't believe he's gone."

"What is it?" Buddy said.

"I have no idea," she said. "By then, he was just hanging on. So whatever it is, it mattered to him."

She called up the email and clicked on the link to the video. Gordo appeared. He looked much thinner than Buddy remembered him from the garage sale. His USS *Higbee* hat seemed to sit lower on his head. There was a frailty to him, but also a look of determination.

"Ready?" she said.

Riley and Buddy leaned in. Sadie hit Play and turned up the volume.

Gordo cleared his throat and began, haltingly at first.

> *"Buddy, if you're watching this, then there is such a thing as destiny.*
>
> *It also means that your father is probably with you, and that he has used the clubs I gave you from the garage sale."*

Buddy turned to his dad.

"You hit them?" Buddy said. "Why didn't you tell me?"

"Shhhh," Riley said. "Listen."

> *"When we spoke that day, my medical condition was deteriorating rapidly," Gordo continued. "I said that I was 'downsizing.' It*

wasn't a complete falsehood—that is, if you consider hospice downsizing."

Gordo coughed, and it took him some time to gather his strength again.

"I've lived a long and full life. I wish it could have been longer, but mortality has its own stopwatch. Someone once asked the great sportswriter Dan Jenkins what he would put on his tombstone. He said it would read 'I knew this would happen.'

"In my case, I know my remaining time is short—which is why I enjoyed our conversation so much. I sensed that you have deeper feelings for the game of golf than you'll admit. And deeper feelings for the bridges that golf can build between a father and son."

"I think I'll watch the rest of this later," Buddy said as he reached for the iPad.

"No," Riley said. "He's saying this to me as much as he's saying it to you. We both need to hear it."

Gordo said:

"What I didn't tell you that day—what I have never told anyone—is the story of those clubs. As you know, I am, or was, for the purposes of this video, a keen admirer of the classically made golf club. Some people are aficionados of vintage sports cars or artwork. I have always been fascinated by how things are made, how they work, and why some things are made better than others, especially golf clubs. Once a machinist's mate, always a machinist's mate.

"When I was much younger, I made a pilgrimage to Jupiter, Florida, to see the master clubmaker Jack Wullkotte. I mentioned him to you when we spoke, Buddy.

"I made the trip in the early 1970s, after I had returned home from Vietnam. I was looking for simplicity in my life, and the idea

of making golf clubs, of being an artisan, of doing something solitary and peaceful, had great appeal to me.

"I drove the thirteen hundred miles straight through, stopping only long enough to fill the tank and take short naps at rest areas along the way. Wullkotte must have thought I was a vagrant when I showed up at his shop door. I hadn't shaved or showered, and my clothes were wrinkled and matted.

"He was tall, at least six-foot-one, and as thin as a tine on a bunker rake. He wore glasses and had an intense, scholarly look to him. He was in his forties, but his hands seemed older to me. They were a sculptor's hands commanded by the mind of a master clubmaker.

"He was understandably suspicious at first. Who would drive such a distance and arrive unannounced? But as soon as I mentioned that I had served in Vietnam, he welcomed me in. He, too, was a veteran and had fought in the Korean War.

"The shop was filled with rows and rows of clubs in varying stages of completion. They were laid horizontally, the clubheads sticking out over the edges of the wooden shelves like feet over the end of a bunk bed.

"I had a thousand questions, it seemed, and he patiently tried to answer each one. His tone was even and measured. He had made clubs for many of the greatest players in the game—Jack Nicklaus, Ben Hogan, Byron Nelson, Jimmy Demaret, Tom Weiskopf, Curtis Strange, Greg Norman, Ben Crenshaw, Nick Price, JoAnne Carner, and Dottie Pepper—"

Gordo had another brief coughing episode.

"I'm sorry for the interruptions. Where was I? Oh, yes, . . . the equipment and tools were old, almost primitive, but reliable. He told me of the time that Pepper brought her clubs to him for an assessment. She nearly fainted when Wullkotte took out a massive

lead sledgehammer and began pounding away at her irons as he made loft and lie adjustments. Several weeks later, after the equipment session, Pepper set a record for most shots under par in a LPGA major championship. You could hear the pride in his voice as he told the story of her victory.

"But at my urging, he talked most about his long affiliation with Nicklaus. Wullkotte had been a caddie when he was younger and had even competed against Nicklaus in the Ohio Open in the late 1950s. But their working relationship was the capstone of his career.

"Buddy, there's a story about how the two Jacks met."

"I think I know this one," Riley said.
Buddy and Sadie instantly shushed him.

"Nicklaus broke the shaft of his 6-iron while playing in a tournament and had his personal pilot fly the club to the MacGregor plant in Cincinnati for repairs," Gordo continued. "But the plant was closed for two weeks to allow for the vacations of all employees, including Wullkotte, who worked in the Custom Club and Repair Department. A supervisor pleaded with Wullkotte to delay his vacation so he could attend to Nicklaus's 6-iron. Wullkotte drove a hard bargain: He would fix the club—a thirty-minute job, at most—but MacGregor had to pay him a full day's wages. The supervisor quickly agreed.

"Wullkotte repaired the club, and his next paycheck bulged with the extra day's wages: $32."

"He only made $4 an hour?" Buddy said.

"You're a business major, Buddy, so I assume you're probably thinking, Only $4 an hour?"

"How'd he know that?" Buddy said.

"But that $32 paled in comparison to what happened next. Nicklaus was so pleased with the quality of the repair that he insisted only Wullkotte work on his clubs. Not long after that, Nicklaus hired him as his personal clubmaker—a position he held for almost fifty years."

"The clubs, SG," Sadie said impatiently. "What about the garage sale clubs?"

Gordo paused to take a sip of water.

"I spent the entire day at the shop. It was like watching Michelangelo create something from a block of marble. Wullkotte was meticulous and pursued perfection in every detail.

"As I shadowed him, I noticed a large gray plastic garbage can in the far corner of the shop. Poking out from the top of the can, among the wood shavings, empty soda bottles, and scrap paper, was a full set of woods and irons. I pulled the driver out. It was a driver made for Nicklaus. The entire set had been made for him. They were beautiful.

"When I told Wullkotte that someone had accidentally placed the clubs in the garbage, he shook his head and without looking up said, 'That was the finest set of clubs I ever made for Jack. The persimmon was flawless. Every groove of every iron was without peer. But now they're worthless orphans without a future. They'll be destroyed by the end of the day.'

"I was astounded. Destroyed? 'Why?' I asked him.

"Wullkotte stopped his work, cleaned his glasses with a fresh handkerchief retrieved from his back pocket, and sighed wearily.

"He told me, 'I dropped them. It was an accident, of course. I stubbornly tried to carry all of them to a finishing rack, and one of the irons slipped through my arms. As I tried to stop its fall, I leaned too far forward and all the clubs bounced against the ground.'

"Wullkotte pointed to the shop floor. It was polished, unforgiving concrete.

"He said he had gathered up the clubs and put each one under an industrial-grade lighted magnifying glass. It was there that the perfectionist saw the imperfections: the tiniest of scratches and nicks in every iron and wood. To sand or grind them out would have meant to change, however miniscule, the exact specifications demanded by Nicklaus—to say nothing of compromising the standards set by Wullkotte himself. His reputation was built on such standards.

"I pulled a few of the clubs from the garbage can and examined them. To the naked eye, there wasn't the faintest hint of a defect. I told him, 'Nobody would ever know.'

"He stuffed the handkerchief back in his pocket and said, 'I would.'

"The day seemed to be over in minutes. I asked him if I could buy him dinner for his time, but he said he already had a date with his wife, Jeannine. He was going to leave after he completed one final task: destroying those disgraced irons and woods.

"He walked to the garbage can, and with each hand grabbed seven club shafts like wheat stalks and spread them out on a nearby work table. He picked up the massive hammer and raised it high above his head as if he were Abraham about to do harm to Isaac. I couldn't bear to witness it, so I leaped forward and held his arm.

"I said, 'Let me keep them!'

"He turned, and there was a flash of astonishment in his eyes.

"I kept talking—and kept tight hold of his arm. I reminded him that he had said they were the finest clubs he had ever made for Nicklaus. I told him I wanted to study the clubs, learn from his work, and one day in my own basement shop, try to replicate them. I said that if he would spare them from the hammer, I would treat them with the reverence they deserved, that I would never sell them, and that if he didn't want me to ever use them in play, I would honor his request.

"He pulled his arm away with surprising strength and then gently laid the hammer on the table. He stared at me for a few moments, smiled and said, 'I thought you'd never ask.'

"Wait, that's what he said to me at the garage sale!" Buddy said.

"I was speechless as he handed me the clubs," Gordo said. "I'll never forget his next words.

"He said, 'These clubs deserved better than my own clumsiness. They were made not for mere mortals but for the greatest golfer in the history of the game. They are unfulfilled. It's up to you to use them in a way that merits their powers.'

"I asked him, 'What powers?'

"He said, 'You'll have to discover that for yourself.'

"I drove back to Illinois with the clubs swaddled in a pair of blankets. A few days later, on a rainy, late Monday afternoon in June, I parked my car on a gravel cutout on the side of Hawthorne Lane, which runs—"

"Just behind the No. 1 green and No. 2 tee box at Chicago Golf Club," Riley said, in sync with the old man.

"Buddy," Gordo said, "I told you that many years ago, I played one round of golf there. This was that one time. And I was uninvited.

"I squeezed through an opening in the trees, dropped my bag over the five-foot-high chain-link fencing, and then climbed over the top. The course was closed on Mondays, and the soft, steady rain had kept even the caddies from wanting to play that afternoon. By then, all maintenance work on the course had been completed for the day. By teeing off on the second hole, I reduced my chances of being seen by anyone who might be in the clubhouse or pro shop. By my calculations, I had three hours and twenty-eight minutes before sunset.

"I didn't have an official scorecard, but I had a piece of paper and a pencil in a plastic bag. The markers on each tee box would give me the hole's distance, and I had studied the routing map countless times. Actually being on the course, and the danger of possibly being caught, was somehow thrilling.

"My plan was to play from the member tees—6,571 yards, par 35 on the front and back—but skip the par-4 first and 18th holes because of their proximity to the clubhouse area. Whatever scores I had on the par-4 second and 17th holes would be entered for the two holes I couldn't play. Under the circumstances, it seemed like an honorable solution.

"I pulled the white athletic sock off the MacGregor driver, took a few hurried practice swings, and then hit my first-ever shot with Wullkotte's masterpiece. The ball pierced through the rain and I lost sight of it. I began walking down the left edge of the fairway and finally found it just 55 yards from the pin. I had driven the ball 385 yards, nearly 165 yards longer than I had ever hit a driver.

"Every shot with every club on every hole was near perfection. I birdied my first two holes, eagled the third, and then went birdie, par, birdie, par, birdie on the final five holes on the front nine. I'm not sure I had ever been happier in my life. It was as if Wullkotte's clubs were swinging themselves and all I had to do was hang on.

"The rain had blown through by the time I reached the par-3 10th hole, and the early-evening sun was glorious as it stretched across the work of Macdonald and Raynor. In the distance, I could hear the rope snap hook clang against the metal flagpole behind the first tee box. I was walking the same grounds that Harry Vardon, Francis Ouimet, Chick Evans, and Bobby Jones had walked. U.S. Opens had been played there. So had the Walker Cup and the U.S. Amateur. As melodramatic as it might sound, I felt the presence of those players.

"I parred the par-3, birdied the 11th and 12th, parred the 13th, and then birdied the 14th. A poor decision on the 15th resulted in

a bogey, but I finished with a birdie on the 16th hole, and as dusk began to give way to darkness, I made another birdie on the 17th.

"There was no time to celebrate, though, because I could see someone driving a golf cart toward me as I retrieved the ball from the cup. He was waving his hand and yelling something as he sped forward.

"I grabbed my bag, ran across the No. 2 tee box, clambered over the fence, and made it to my car as he arrived at the fence line. I could hear him shout through the foliage, 'You should be ashamed of yourself!'

"But I wasn't ashamed; I was exhilarated. I had never hit a ball so true or so far. I had never scored like that. No one had! Wullkotte was right: The clubs had an unexplained, unimaginable power. They had been made for Nicklaus, and Nicklaus ran through the veins of those clubs . . . and through me.

"I sat in my car and lovingly cleaned each iron and wood before placing each club in the golf bag and putting the bag in the trunk. Then I took out the plastic bag and recorded my round on the piece of paper. On the sixteen holes I had played myself, I had shot 11-under. If I applied the birdies from No. 2 and No. 17 to the two holes I couldn't play—the first and 18th—I was 13-under for the round. A 57! My hands shook as I checked and rechecked the totals.

"As I drove to downtown Wheaton for dinner, the euphoria of the round overwhelmed me. I kept glancing down at my makeshift scorecard and marveling at the numbers. A gust blew through the open windows, and my paper floated into the air just as the light turned green and I began to cross the intersection at Roosevelt Road. I reached for the paper and then heard a skidding sound to my left. I turned at the exact moment a pickup truck, its tires hydroplaning on the rain-slickened street, slammed into my driver's-side door.

"I remember the flash of pain. I remember hearing voices and the sound of an ambulance in the distance. I remember the taste of

blood in my mouth and the plaintive cries of the truck driver as I was pulled from my car: 'Oh, God, did I kill him? Please tell me I didn't kill him.'

"When I awoke, whenever that was, the surgeon informed me that I was fortunate to be alive. He added, almost as an aside, that my legs and hips had been crushed by the collision and that I would never walk again. In that moment, my first thought wasn't about the miracle of my survival but about the cruelty of not being able to swing those clubs again. I was alive, but part of me was now dead.

"The police later ruled the collision an accident in the truest sense, a tragic combination of a rain-slickened road and fateful timing. Had I spent another five seconds checking my score in the parked car, or a few more moments cleaning those clubs . . . how different my life might have been. The only consolation is that no one else was injured.

The clubs had also survived the crash, but they were returned to my basement, where they stayed undisturbed for decades. That is, until my wonderful granddaughter Sadie mistakenly brought them upstairs for the garage sale.

"When you showed up that day, Buddy, I recognized it as an opportunity to give the clubs meaning again. Wullkotte believed that each club he made had a soul of sorts, a sense of being. I think he was trying to tell me they possessed a mystical connection with the player. During my one round with them at Chicago Golf, I felt something. I felt that connection.

"Despite your best efforts to feign disinterest in the game, I gave you those clubs as a way to connect not only with golf again, but with your father. Wullkotte said the clubs were unfulfilled. But I believe you and your father can change that.

"I've often asked myself: Would I give up that one day at Chicago Golf for a lifetime of walking? And until this moment, I couldn't answer the question. But now I know. I know that day was worth it. Just as Wullkotte passed the clubs along to me, I was

able to pass them along to you. And you have passed them along to your dad.

"Given your father's golf background, I know he will use the clubs in the spirit in which I gave them. They have powers. But there are limits to those powers. It will be up to him to learn each.

"Remember the words of P. G. Wodehouse: 'Golf . . . is the infallible test.'

"With or without those clubs, the game will test you. And you will be the better for it."

Gordo smiled, pinched the bill of his cap, and then leaned forward to press the red Stop button on the screen. His image disappeared.

Buddy folded the cover over the iPad and handed it to Sadie, who was wiping tears from her eyes. Riley also had to collect himself.

"Buddy," said Riley, his voice filled with emotion, "I owe you an apology. And if Gordo were here, I'd owe him one, too. Those clubs aren't ordinary clubs."

"I tried to tell you, Dad."

"You did, and I didn't listen. I'm listening now."

"Hold on," Sadie interrupted. "I loved my granddad. He was a romantic, especially when it came to golf. But clubs with secret powers? Father-son counseling sessions? As much as I adored him, I'm going to assume this video is the result of a haze produced by the opioids given to him during his final days of hospice. I spent hours at his bedside and he *never* mentioned any of this."

Riley began to speak, but Buddy cut him off.

"Dad, when did you use the clubs?"

"The day I called you at Madison," Riley said.

"You're at Madison?" Sadie said. "I'm going to be a 2L there."

"I'm a junior there," Buddy said. "You're on Bascom Mall."

"Let me get through this, if you don't mind," Riley said. "I went to the range and brought a couple of Gordo's clubs: the driver and the 8-iron. I wasn't even going to hit them, but a couple of guys there talked me into it."

"These are the garage sale clubs?" Sadie said.

"Yes, the clubs you wouldn't sell me," Buddy said. "They were in the white bag."

"Right, the white bag," she said. "Those clubs were his babies."

"He's the one who told me to look at them," Buddy said. "He said that my dad might like them. And when I tried to buy them, he said he'd give them to me—if I made a deal with him."

"What kind of deal?" Sadie said.

Buddy had divulged more than he had wanted to. He decided to tell the truth—or at least most of it.

"He made me promise that the clubs would be used by my dad. He said they could change our lives. We shook on it. Then on the way home, I saw Jack Nicklaus's name on the irons and I thought they really could be one-of-a-kind clubs. But my dad said they weren't."

"Your dad was wrong," Riley said.

"Whattya mean, wrong?" Sadie said. "You're not telling me they really *do* have powers."

"I can't believe I'm saying this, but they do—at least the two I hit," Riley said. "Do you play?"

"SG insisted on it," she said. "But law school and leisure time don't go well together. I haven't played in a few years."

"Then you know the game," Riley said. "And if you saw my swing, you'd know I can't hit a driver 350 yards."

"You hit that driver 350?!" Buddy said.

"Actually longer, I think," Riley said. "And I hit the 8-iron about 190."

"This is through the looking glass," Sadie said. "It's fantasia."

"It is," Riley said. "It's also true. I thought they were medium-quality replica clubs. I was even told they were knockoff clubs made in China. That's a real thing these days."

"But we just saw the video. They're not from China; they're from Florida," Buddy said.

"I'm not sure they're from this planet," Riley said.

"Maybe you got lucky on a few shots," Sadie said. "It happens."

"Maybe it does, but it doesn't happen to me," Riley said. "It looked like the ball was shot out of an air cannon. I'm a forty-three-year-old golf reporter who weighs 181 pounds and has never broken 80 in my life. What happened yesterday at the range wasn't a fluke; it was a miracle."

"So you're saying this is *a priori,*" she said.

"I don't speak legal," Riley said.

"An assumption that is true without further proof," she said. "Water is wet. Or, your swing is terrible, therefore you can't hit a drive 350 yards."

"Yes, *a priori,*" Riley said. "If I'm lucky, I usually hit an 8-iron 135 yards, a driver 215, and that's with the wind."

"This can't be real," she said. "Show me."

"Yeah, Dad, we gotta see this."

They drove a half dozen miles to the SmashGolf facility in Naperville. The battered white, single-strap golf bag that Riley carried by the handle earned a few snickers from the staff. Riley picked a hitting bay at the end of the elevated row.

The netting that surrounded the range was 150 feet high, and the farthest distance from the hitting bay to the end of the range was 250 yards.

Riley pulled off the driver head cover and tossed it to Buddy. His warm-up lasted no more than sixty seconds.

"Does he always swing like that?" whispered Sadie to Buddy.

"Sadly, yes."

"It looks like . . ."

"A convulsion?" Buddy said.

"Something like that," she said, giggling.

Riley adjusted the glove on his left hand. "You know I can hear you, right?"

"Dad, I looked it up online," Buddy said, staring at his phone screen. "Someone did an analysis of what it would take to clear the fence here. According to this guy's data, an 18-handicap like you has absolutely no chance. You don't generate enough ball speed, you create too much spin, and you probably don't have a high enough launch angle."

"Clear it?" Riley said. "That fence is 50 yards high. I'd have to fly the ball 300 yards."

"More like 330, 335. This guy says the average Tour pro couldn't clear it, and that McIlroy would be inches short—even if he used his regular golf ball, not these limited-distance range balls."

"Any other good news?"

"Well, there's a link to McIlroy hitting a persimmon driver at the Scottish Open."

"How'd he do?"

"Spin rate was double, had about 50 yards less carry than his regular driver—255 yards vs. 307—and his total distance was 65 yards shorter. Big differences."

"You guys are making my head hurt," Sadie said. "What about the French guy? My grandpa said he hit a ball over a lake one time."

"French?" Riley said. "No, you're thinking of Bryson DeChambeau, and he's American. He was pushing 220 miles per hour on ball speed. He'd clear the fence."

"So would some of those long driving champions," Buddy said. "Martin Borgmeier reaches 230 on his ball speed."

"This is fascinating," Sadie said. "Can you hit the damn ball, please?"

Riley placed a ball on the white rubber tee, which poked up through the hole in the mat like a single whisker on an otherwise clean-shaven face.

"Swing easy, Dad. Don't want you to rupture an oblique."

Voices swirled through Riley's head: *Pronation . . . No swaying . . . Daddy, that man isn't very good, is he?*

Riley took the club back, paused ever so slightly at the top of his backswing, and then tried to remember to keep his right elbow in his right pocket during the downswing.

When the club hit the ball, there was a whooshing sound, not unlike the noise made by a freight train as it sweeps by. The ball sped toward the back of the range and rose majestically and easily over the netting.

Riley held the driver in both hands, as if it were Excalibur. Buddy and Sadie, overcome by the sight of it all, began yelling, hugging, and jumping up and down.

"Dad, I can't believe it! I watched it, and I still can't believe it!"

"I hit it, and I can't believe it," Riley said.

"You must have cleared that fence by another 50 yards," Sadie said.

They turned to the monitor for information. It had frozen.

"Dad, there's something wrong with this machine," Buddy said.

"Maybe because he hit it so far?" Sadie said.

"Maybe," Buddy said. "You can't hit a ball—especially *these* balls and that wooden driver—that far with that slow of a swing. Try another one, Dad."

Riley waved the clubhead at the sensor light, and a ball rolled from the dispenser. He teed it up and swung once more. This one carried like a Barry Bonds dinger during his juiced-up days. The netting never had a chance.

Riley put his hands on his knees and dropped his head.

"Gordo was right!" he said. He turned to Sadie. "Your grandpa was right!"

"That ball had to go at least 400 yards to clear the fence like that," Buddy said, confused and awestruck at the same time. "And with these balls, you probably lose 5 to 10 percent of distance. I don't understand how this is happening."

A SmashGolf employee appeared. He had a size-20 neck, and his polo shirt clung to his biceps and chest for dear life.

"Sir, we're going to have to ask you and your party to leave, please," he said.

"We just got here," Sadie said. "He's only hit two balls."

The employee pointed to a sign on the pillar next to the hitting bay.

DON'T MAKE US DQ YOU! NO BALLS OVER THE FENCE, PLEASE!

"Not my rule," the employee said. "We gave you a pass on the first one. Can't do it on the second."

"I understand," Riley said.

"But Dad . . ." Buddy said.

“It’s OK,” Riley said. “Let’s go.”

The employee leaned in conspiratorially.

“Our supervisor said he’s never seen anyone fly the netting by that much,” he said. He slipped a half dozen cards into Riley’s hands. “Here are some drink and food coupons. Bring the family the next time, but leave the woodshop driver at home.”

He slapped Riley on the back, nearly sending him off the platform and into the safety net.

Riley, Buddy, and Sadie drove in silence back to Gordo’s house. Everyone was deep in their own thoughts. Riley pulled into the driveway and shut off the ignition. He stared straight ahead.

“Dad?” Buddy said.

“I know what you’re going to ask,” Riley said.

“Well, do they?”

“I’ve only hit two of the clubs, but I think you know the answer.”

“Do they what?” Sadie said.

“Do they all go that far,” Riley said.

“Dad, do you understand what you could do with these clubs?” Buddy said. “You could win the Masters. You could be World No. 1. You could be unbeatable. It’s like—”

“Don’t say it,” Riley said.

“—you’re Jack Nicklaus,” Buddy said, completing the thought.

“This,” Sadie said, opening the back passenger door, “has been unlike any morning I’ve ever had. I have to finish up here today, and then I’m driving to Madison Sunday night.”

“Buddy is driving up today,” Riley said. “He has a party date with—what’d you say?—a Chi O.”

“Dad.”

“Chi-O, Chi-O,” Sadie began singing, “it’s off to bed we go . . .”

Buddy blushed. “It’s just a party.”

Sadie got out of the car.

“What’s your number?” she said impatiently to Buddy.

He gave it to her. A few moments later, his cell phone dinged with her contact info.

"If you get tired of sorority girls, give me a call," she said.

She started to walk toward the front door but then peeled back to the driver's side of the car.

"Mr. Riley, I don't cover golf for a living," she said. "But I know my grandpa would be glad you and Buddy have those clubs. I know you'll do the right thing. I know you'll do, as he would say, the honorable thing."

"I wish I could have asked him how he would have used the clubs."

"He'd tell you what he told Buddy: They were meant to be played. So play them."

"So you're saying water is wet?"

"I'm saying if you can hit Jack Nicklaus's clubs like Jack Nicklaus . . ."

Riley nodded and smiled. "*A priori.*"

CHAPTER TEN

Needle Movers

"Joe, this is Audio in the truck. Can I get a sound check, please?"

"One, two, three, four, fi—"

"We're good," the voice said in Riley's ear, abruptly cutting him off. "Thanks."

It was late August, and the first round of the Tour Championship had just ended. For now, the possibilities of the Nicklaus clubs would have to wait. Riley had told no one about the clubs—not Laurel, not Chet, not his brother-in-law, Aaron—and he had instructed Buddy and Sadie to do the same. Riley was careful by nature. He needed to think this through. Plus, Riley had a day job.

The weather was mercifully moderate in Atlanta. Humid, but not its usual torturous, stifling self. Riley used his thumb to gently push the rest of the fitted IFB earpiece into his left ear and then double-checked to make sure the coil tubing was hidden and clipped securely to the back of his shirt collar. He was in position at the auxiliary set near the driving range at East Lake Golf Club.

Even though he had transitioned to TV from digital nearly six years earlier (and before that, from newspapers to digital), the earpiece still didn't feel comfortable. Nothing about doing TV felt natural to him. Not holding a mic. Not wearing a coat and tie (a Windsor knot still confounded him). Not the cornea-melting lights. Not staring into a camera lens and being unable to shake the thought that he was looking into the eye of a chicken. Not the performance sweat that would leave his dress shirts soaked under the armpits. Not the voices of others on the set chatting casually as he completed a report from another location. Not wearing makeup. Not anything, actually. It was as foreign to him as Portuguese.

The truth is, he had never fully recovered from his first-ever AGN appearance, a debacle so spectacularly awful that there should have been yellow police tape stretched around the Old Course practice green, which was where he did his standup that day at St. Andrews.

The assignment had seemed simple enough: a two-minute report that would involve the anchor teeing him up on three different news and notes items. Item No. 1: a brief anecdote about Arjun Atwal, a little-known player from India who had established an unlikely friendship with Tiger Woods. Item No. 2: a small scoop about the R&A's plans for its next Open Championship site announcement. Item No. 3: a feel-good nugget on a St. Andrews local who was celebrating his fiftieth Open as a volunteer worker in the iconic yellow scoreboard just off the 18th green. Riley would do his report about ten minutes after Tim Rinello "wrapped" his latest heartwarming feature. In TV-speak, wrapping a story meant appearing on camera to introduce the piece to the viewer (the "lead"), and when the story was done, appearing once again on camera to add an anecdote or additional information (the "tag") before tossing it back to Neil Lassiter, who was anchoring AGN's coverage.

Rinello, whose bookshelves were lined with Emmys and Murrow Awards, had a gift for finding the heart of every story and then framing it in a way that resonated with all viewers.

As Rinello took his place in front of the camera, Riley stopped looking at his own notes and instead watched as a master prepared for his moment. Rinello pinched the dimple just under the knot of his paisley tie and tugged it tight. He made sure the fold of his purple pocket square was just so. He patted the top of his hair. He turned to the side and softly recited what he planned to say to the camera during his lead.

Riley couldn't see the program feed on the monitor facing Rinello, so he live streamed it on his phone.

As always, Rinello was flawless as he took the toss from the anchor.

"Thanks, Neil," he began. "Just a lob wedge away from the first tee here at the Old Course is the R&A World Golf Museum, where the history of the game—and the towering figures who helped define that history—is lovingly detailed for visitors.

"You know all about St. Andrews legends Old Tom Morris and Young Tom Morris. They're buried not far from where I stand. But about a month ago, the Auld Grey Toon paid homage to an unlikely hero: a little dog . . . with a big heart."

Riley shot a thumbs-up sign to Rinello and began watching the story on his phone. Rinello turned his attention to the monitor. In moments, Riley was hooked.

About ten years earlier, a crippled street dog had tried to find refuge in a dark corner of an outdoor maintenance structure adjacent to the Old Course during an unseasonably cold December. Workers had shooed the mutt away, only to see the shaking, malnourished, three-legged dog attempt to sneak back in.

Late one night, the Old Course greenkeeper drove to the maintenance office—through an unexpected dusting of snow—to retrieve some papers from his office for an upcoming trip. As he settled into his desk chair, he heard the sound of barking outside. He looked through the window and there was the ragged mutt. Hoping to scare away the dog and end the noise, the greenkeeper rapped his knuckles hard against the cold glass. The dog limped toward the light of the office and, if possible, barked even louder.

The greenkeeper tried to return to his work, but it was impossible with the barking. He put on his coat and stormed to the door. The dog was waiting for him, and it began to hop away from the main office and toward an adjacent building. The greenkeeper began to chase after the dog and soon caught up to the lame animal—just in time to see the growing flames coming from a generator located outside the building.

He ran back to the main office, pulled a fire extinguisher from the wall, and sprayed down the generator. Fire officials were called, and they later told him an electrical malfunction had been at fault. Had the greenkeeper not been there that night, they said, the building, his own nearby office, and perhaps much more would have been destroyed.

After the firefighters had left, the greenkeeper searched for the dog. He eventually found it in a grimy corner of an outdoor storage area. He scooped it up, brought it inside, and laid it on the worn couch in his office. He gently placed his down coat on the dog, which watched suspiciously as the greenkeeper brought a bowl of fresh water and an unopened ham sandwich left across the hall in the fridge of the employees' lounge. The dog lapped slowly at the water, and then ate the strips of torn ham from the palm of the greenkeeper. It fell asleep thirty minutes later, curled up next to the greenkeeper, who kept tender watch over the mutt.

In the weeks and months that followed, the greenkeeper—and the local vet—nursed the dog back to health. He was named Prince, in honor of the Principal's Nose bunkers on the 16th hole of the Old Course. And when the greenkeeper made his daily rounds, Prince was always by his side. It was that way for years.

Prince had died of a kidney disease a month before this Open Championship was to begin. And Rinello had been there, along with an AGN camera crew, to chronicle the tribute paid to a beloved dog by the citizens of the Home of Golf. The dog had been buried near the practice range, and a small plaque had been placed on the exterior of the building he had saved years earlier.

As the story ended, Rinello raised his stick mic and returned on camera.

"It is no coincidence that there has been a surge of donations to the local animal shelter here in the past month," he said. "Some of those donations come from players in this Open Championship field. Several of them have even placed dog bone stickers on the backs of their hats. In their own way, Neil, they are treating a Prince like a king."

The final line was too much for the audio tech, who cried openly. As soon as Rinello was cleared by the production truck, the tech gave the feature reporter a long hug. Then suddenly he released Rinello and waved frantically at Riley.

"They want you in position right now!"

Riley shook his head.

"I've got ten minutes before they need me," he said casually.

"Not anymore, you don't," said the tech, who plugged Riley into an audio device and attached it to his belt. "There's some lighting screwup on the main set. You're buying them some time to fix the problem."

So quick was the turnaround that Rinello had no choice but to drop to a knee in front of Riley, just out of the sight line of the camera.

"Pretend I'm not here," Rinello whispered.

Unlike Rinello, Riley didn't have time to check the dimple of his tie or review his notes. There was no jaunty thumbs-up sign to the truck. Instead, he stared at the black lens as the anchor spoke glowingly of Rinello's story and then mentioned that they were dealing with technical issues on the set. Just as Riley heard Lassiter begin to segue to him, the producer got in his ear.

"Our lighting is funky here, so no tee-ups," he said matter-of-factly. "We'll just run B-roll over each item."

Riley tried to understand the information, but he was disoriented by the last-second change. *B-roll. What was this B-roll they spoke of?*

"And we welcome in our colleague Joe Riley, who is stationed in the shadows of the historic R&A building," Lassiter said. "Joe, what do you have for us?"

Riley stared at the eye of the chicken, the red light now shining brightly just above the lens.

"Go," the producer cued him.

"Go, what?" Riley said.

"Go!" the producer said again. "Talk! Now! You're live!"

The meltdown was epic.

Riley referred to Arjun Atwal as Atwal Arjun. There was no mention of his friendship with the great Woods. Instead, Riley panicked to the point where he began reciting Arjun/Atwal's play at Nassau Community College back in the day.

From there, Riley all but lost consciousness. He froze while trying to remember which courses on the Open rota were going to be selected next by the R&A. Worse yet, he forgot what the A stood for and called the ruling body "the Royal and Old."

The producer did what he could.

"Wrap it up!" he frantically ordered. "Get it back to Neil!"

But Riley persisted, partly because his earpiece had dislodged and he couldn't fully hear the producer yelling in his ear, and partly because his brain had malfunctioned. For a moment—but only for a moment—he put a noun and verb together while describing the Open Championship's yellow scoreboard.

He could hear himself say the words: "For decades, the majestic hand-operated scoreboard has stood over the 18th green of this historic championship . . ."

OK, here we go, thought Riley. *We'll salvage something out of this. Take a breath. It's not as bad as you think.*

Except it was. Because as Riley congratulated himself for making it through a single sentence without incident, he had quit talking out loud. The AGN viewing audience saw a man staring straight ahead, apparently deep in thought, followed by a spasm of incoherency as he realized there was more to say.

Panicked, Riley referenced the volunteer, but he failed to mention the gentleman's name or that he worked in the belly of the scoreboard. Instead, Riley made it sound as if the man was homeless and lived inside the scoreboard during tournament week.

By report's end, Riley was a prisoner of his own confusion, a bewildered mouse searching for a way out of a horrifying maze. There was no graceful exit. His mind could only channel his inner Forrest Gump.

As the director cut to a two-box of Riley and the anchor, an exhausted and defeated Riley said in full Gump mode, "And Neil, that's all I've got to say about that."

As he finished, Rinello, still kneeling below him, dropped his head in sympathetic resignation. Meanwhile, Lassiter, a pro's pro, deftly maneuvered away from the on-air disaster as if it had never happened. He ran through a few of the marquee pairings, referenced the weather forecast, and then took the program to break.

As they were in commercial, Riley nudged the earpiece back in and could now hear the producer and anchor discuss the next segment.

"Here's our traffic coming up," the producer said. "We'll preview the Road Hole, and then you'll get to Maria's feature. After that—"

"Hold on," Lassiter said. "What was that clown show with Riley? Seriously, what the eff was that?"

"We'll get it cleaned up for the next time," the producer said.

"*Next* time?" Lassiter said. "There shouldn't have been a *this* time. I don't mean to be callous, but this is big boys TV. If Riley can't ride the bike without training wheels, get him out of here."

Riley pulled his IFB plug from the audio unit. As he did, Lassiter saw Riley on one of the monitors at the main set.

"Was my mic open during that?" Lassiter said to the truck.

"Affirmative, Neil."

"That's unfortunate," Lassiter said as he took a final look at his notes before they were back on the air. "But someone needed to say it."

Rinello put his hand on Riley's shoulder. "Don't beat yourself up," he said. "It happens to everybody."

The audio tech, eyes averted, took the stick mic from Riley as if it were a murder weapon. The cameraman, who had done live sports for decades, clicked off his headset and stepped in front of the lens so no one in the truck could see or hear the exchange.

"Look, there's no way around it: You just shit your pants on live TV," he said. "That's the bad news. The good news is that you can only get better."

Riley shook his hand and said, "I don't think you'll have to worry about it. I'm never doing television again."

As he walked down the steps of the scaffolding that supported the set, Portia Pendersmith appeared. While her name seemed like something from a Harry Potter book, she was, in fact, an award-winning golf writer who had transitioned from the London-based *Times* to the UK network Star Sports, where she quickly earned praise and more awards for her on-air work. It was Pendersmith who had encouraged Riley to take the career leap of faith.

"Hiya," she said cheerfully.

"Portia," Riley pleaded, "don't say a word. I know you mean well, but I need to be alone."

"Understandable, of course," Pendersmith said. "After all, it *was* utter rubbish in every conceivable way. Why bother to sprinkle it with anything other than the truth?"

"Portia, seriously."

"I am serious. We all watched in the media center. It was like witnessing a loved one cutting off his arm with a dull popsicle stick. I fear many of our colleagues have been rendered speechless for the foreseeable future."

Riley began to walk away.

"Don't do that," Pendersmith said. "Don't feel sorry for yourself. It was admittedly a massive fail, but it happens to us all. I once got tongue-tied on the air and called the Firth of Forth 'a fifth of whiskey.' The wisdom is in the scar tissue."

"That doesn't make me feel better," Riley said.

"Right. Yes, I suppose you'd like to drown yourself in both at this moment."

Riley tried to suppress a smile but couldn't.

"Joe, it is only television. And golf television at that. There is an illusion of importance, but that's only because it is beamed indiscriminately to all."

"My implosion was not an illusion."

"Oh, don't be daft. Here's what you're going to do. Tonight, eight-thirty at the Dunvegan. You're going to meet me and a small contingent of sympathetic Brits who don't hold a grudge for Yorktown. We will drink to bloody forget. And to offer humble and proper suggestions for your improvement whilst holding a microphone."

She hugged him, and for a moment, Riley felt better. But that didn't stop him from making the long walk to the dusty and massive TV compound, where AGN's trucks and trailers were located on beds of gravel. He waited outside the office of AGN's vice president, production, Mike McMullins.

McMullins was known as "the Prince of Darkness," a nickname born from his preference for working in rooms almost entirely devoid of light. He was Dickensian in nature: consumed by work, oblivious to niceties, uninterested in human interaction. He was admired more than beloved, which was fine with him. What he lacked in social skills, he tripled in work ethic and intuition. He rewarded those who shared his ethos with a loyalty unmatched at the network. He despised the petty politics of AGN, and that had hurt his career advancement. He was a general stuck with a major's gold oak leaf.

Riley tapped lightly on the door.

"Come in."

Riley entered the darkened room. McMullins was seated at his desk, his face illuminated by the meager glow of his laptop and a green banker's lamp. On the opposite wall were two monitors set to AGN programming.

"Whattya need?" McMullins said, finally looking up from the screen. His expression was impassive, almost expressionless.

"I just wanted to apologize in person for disintegrating on live TV," Riley said. "I embarrassed myself and AGN."

"You did," McMullins said flatly. "Anything else?"

"I think maybe it's best for everyone if I don't do any more TV," Riley said.

McMullins returned to his keyboard and began typing.

"That decision has already been made," McMullins said. "It was made in the middle of your report."

"Well, I appreciate you giving me a shot," Riley said as he turned to leave. "I'll let you get back to work."

"Noon," McMullins said.

"Noon, what?" Riley said.

"Be at the fairway set at noon. You're doing the preview show."

"But I was awful."

"You were."

"So why would you give me another chance?"

"Because we didn't put you in a position to succeed. That's on me. The next one is on you. Close the door on your way out."

That night, as Portia and the Brits bought round after round, Riley stood up in a wobbly stupor on the outdoor patio at the corner of North Street and Golf Place and raised a pint in honor of a certain vice president/producer.

"Here's to Mike McMullins!" Riley announced to the entire pub.

"Or as you like to say on live telly, McMullins Mike!" Portia said, laughing.

At that exact moment, a man rounded the corner and walked past their table. They instantly recognized the veteran player, and without breaking stride or turning around, the man shouted into the evening air, "It's Arjun, not Atwal! Get my name right!"

The seven reporters stared at each other in disbelief and then fell in a clump against the table. Their laughter could be heard for blocks.

Riley did get better, starting with that noon appearance. Not Rinello better. Not Emmy better. But passable. Proficient. And with each day and each rep, there were occasional moments of noteworthy work. Lassiter had pulled him aside late Sunday night after AGN's final wrap-up show of the Open and apologized for his outburst.

"I deserved everything you said that day," Riley said.

"You didn't deserve *that,*" Lassiter said. "Someone I respect reminded me of the first time I anchored the desk at a major."

"Which was?" said Riley.

"It would have been 2011 at Congressional."

"Rory's win at the U.S. Open."

"Exactly."

"You scuffled, did you?"

"Like Aaron Altman. I was so nervous that I sweated through my socks. The makeup person went through a roll of Bounty trying to sop up the sweat on my forehead."

"I find that hard to believe. You look so comfortable, so natural when you do TV."

"I'm telling you, the producer saved my ass that day. The USGA blue coats were so unnerved after they saw me open the broadcast that they 'strongly suggested' I be replaced immediately. The producer told them to go pound bunker sand."

"The producer could do that?"

"Not really, but he did. He also did everything he could to keep from showing me on camera until my sweat glands calmed down: player arrivals, driving range, putting green, weather reports, hole layouts, tee times. I'm surprised he didn't send an ENG crew to shoot the locker-room attendants folding towels."

"You recovered."

"I did. But it was a valuable lesson—one that I forgot until today."

"Whatever happened to that producer?"

"He's standing right over there," Lassiter said. "He paid for this party out of his own pocket."

Riley looked across the room. There was McMullins, nursing a beer by himself.

"I should have known," Riley said.

"Now you do," Lassiter said.

"Joe."

It was the cameraman. Riley was jolted back to the present tense.

"Can you take a half step back and to your right? I want to get more of the range in the shot."

"You got it," Riley said.

The Tour Championship was Riley's favorite tournament of the season, mostly because it was, for all intents and purposes, the last tournament of the season. There were fall events, but those didn't have much muscle mass. Riley was looking forward to weeks of no sprints through airport terminals, lumpy hotel beds, smoke-scented rental cars, TSA random searches, 5 A.M. call times, late-night drive-throughs, expense reports, player entourages, self-important agents, dust bowl TV compounds, elbow wrestling with the fat guy in the middle seat, chowderheads who thought everyone needed to hear their phone conversation on speakerphone, or delayed and canceled flights. (The motto of his Chicago-based airline should have been "We landed. What else do you want?") Whoever thought being a sports reporter was glamorous work had never traveled for a living. Riley just wanted to go home.

Atlanta was not his favorite city. ("America's Parking Lot" is how one player described it and its legendary traffic.) East Lake was not his favorite course. But the tournament had its moments, and East Lake had its history. It was the oldest course in the city, and there was a perpetual bond with one of its own: Bobby Jones. Adding to its stature was the redesign done by Donald Ross.

"Joe, you got me?" It was the AGN morning show lead producer.

"Yes, sir," Riley said.

"Still good on the McIlroy note, the field updates [there had been a couple of player withdrawals], and course conditions?"

"All set."

"OK, Cynthia will be in the chair this morning. You'll be talking to Maury for this. Toss back to him when you're done. When he has a second, we'll have him say hello."

If AGN had had a Mount Rushmore, Maury Walsh would have been one of the four faces. So impactful was his career on the network's success that he probably deserved to be on the mountain face twice.

He was one of the network's original anchors. Riley had been watching him since his college days at Madison. AGN had hired Walsh away from a Los Angeles station, where his nightly local sports segment had the highest ratings in that market, and brought him to the studio headquarters outside Charlotte. Walsh didn't know much about golf then—he still didn't—but he used his oversized personality to pull the casual fan into broadcasts. He was one of them: a 22-handicap who didn't take himself or the sport too seriously. In a game of hushed tones and reverence, Walsh treated golf with respect but not adoration. He thought most of the players were pampered adults in arrested development, more concerned about their courtesy cars than showing courtesy to the fans who paid hard-earned money for a tournament ticket. He converted lawyer jokes to agent jokes. ("What do you call twenty-five player agents buried up to their chins in cement? Not enough cement.") With the exception of Butch Harmon, Randy Smith, Leeds Sargent Jr., and a handful of others, he thought swing coaches were witch doctors. He had no patience for self-important course architects who framed themselves as mystical interpreters of all things mineral and water. And he thought there should be a congressional hearing into Pebble Beach charging $675 for a round of golf at a "public" course, and another $20 for a pull cart.

He was an everyman. He was popular. He made a weekly tournament feel bigger than it had a right to feel, and a major feel bigger than it already was. One year, he decided to come over to the UK early and attend the men's singles final at Wimbledon before making his way to Sandwich and Royal St. George's for the Open Championship ten days later. He created a medium-sized uproar when he refused to stand when the royals entered the Centre Court stadium. He was hissed at and even booed for his lack of decorum. When confronted at his seat by reporters from the London tabloids, Walsh asked, "What day is it?"

"You twit," said a reporter from *The Sun*. "It's Sunday. The Gentlemen's Singles Championship is always played on Sunday."

"And today is Sunday the what?" Walsh said.

"Sunday, July—" the reporter said before stopping himself.

"You were saying . . ." Walsh said.

"Sunday, July fourth," the reporter said.

"No taxation without representation, baby!" Walsh bellowed. "Any other day, I would have stood. But not today."

Walsh was pilloried in the London tabs, but across the pond he was hailed as a hero by flag-waving Americans everywhere. AGN issued a tepid apology for Walsh's actions, but the corporate wrist slap only solidified the anchor's standing with his viewership.

Walsh was getting older, and more forgetful, and he didn't spend as much time on the range with the players and caddies as he had in past years. Rarely did he walk a course these days, and if he did, it was only down the first fairway and back. The lack of preparation sometimes showed on the air.

Riley glanced at his note card and then heard Walsh's booming voice.

"Joel, it's so good to see you on the monitor," Walsh said. "Ready to make some television? I smell Emmy!"

"It's Joe," Riley said. "And yes, it's always a thrill to work with you."

"You're very kind, Joel. This will be fun."

In the back of the production truck, pressed uncomfortably against a sound-deadened carpeted wall, stood a small man writing in a small notebook. His name was Stanley Pierre, and he was a programming and efficiency consultant hired by AGN to identify, in his words, "the needle movers" at the network. His mission was known, but his presence was unwelcome. When he appeared on-site, it usually meant that someone on the staff was going to disappear in the weeks to come.

The production truck, with only two rows of seating and limited standing space in the rear, was cramped to begin with. There were two associate directors, a graphics operator, a technical director, a producer, a second producer, the primary director, and a spotter. But now here was this outsider whose job it was to evaluate talent, to pretend to use objectivity in a medium that was built on subjectivity.

The people in this truck had seen it before: Pierre's recommendations could fast-track or end careers. His words carried weight at AGN headquarters, though nobody quite knew why. He had no on-air or production experience. He saw the world through a TV screen and then wrote what he saw in that little spiral notebook, the cheap kind that TV detectives pulled from their inside breast pockets at the crime scene.

Pierre watched as Walsh was handed a rundown of the segment. Walsh flicked the page away.

"Highlights . . . a little Maury analysis . . . tee up Joel . . . a little more of the Maurinator . . . and then get us to break," Walsh said, his mic live. "We're not covering appellate court here. It's just golf. Give me a ten-second count coming in and getting out. Capisce?"

There was a general uneasiness in the truck. Walsh was about to go rogue.

The producer, Cynthia Maxson, who had come to AGN only several weeks earlier and had yet to work with Walsh, pressed the talkback button to the anchor mic.

"Maury, love the freestyle thinking here," she said nervously, "but let's try to color inside the lines on this one."

There were forty-seven seconds on the countdown clock.

"Maury?" she said, pressing the button again.

Thirty-one seconds.

Walsh took a sip of water. He amused himself by rolling his *r*'s. He noticed that one of his shirt buttons was undone and fumbled with it until Mike the stage manager rushed over to fix it.

Sixteen seconds.

"Can Maury hear me?" Maxson said. She stabbed at the button again. "Maury!"

Nothing.

"Mike, we've lost audio with Maury," the producer said. "Cue him up at ten."

Mike held his fingers under the camera and began the countdown. At five, Maury pressed his talkback button to the producer.

"Got you!" he said. "Welcome to AGN!"

One second later, Walsh was live on the air.

The producer threw her hands up in exasperation. She was speechless. The same couldn't be said for Walsh, who welcomed the audience with his signature phrase—"Hello, good people of planet Earth"—and began a stream-of-consciousness journey that featured an anecdote about Bobby Jones and his love of macaroni and cheese, a verse of Ray Charles's rendition of "Georgia on My Mind," a personal remembrance of Tiger's win at East Lake in 2018, a demand to know why there were so many streets in the city named Peachtree, and a story about a chance meeting with Hank Aaron years earlier at the Varsity while ordering a chili dog.

The producer looked at the director. "What is he *doing*?"

"He's being Maury," the director said.

The producer pressed the talkback button. "Maury," she said calmly, "is there actual golf in our future?"

Walsh continued on. It was as close to a psychedelic experience as you could have on network television without taking mushrooms. He meandered through the highlights, rarely syncing the B-roll with his own analysis. Maxson tried to steer him back to the rundown, but he ignored her.

There was a moment during the highlights, when Jordan Spieth could be heard pleading openly for his iffy tee shot on the par-3 ninth hole to clear the left greenside bunker—"Fly, baby, fly!"—that Maury was vintage Maury. As the ball did indeed carry the bunker, land at green's edge, and come to a stop a mere 6 inches from the back pin placement, Walsh said simply: "The Dude abides."

The production crew applauded in the truck. Maxson turned in confusion.

"*The Big Lebowski,*" the director said to her.

"Who?" she said, looking frantically at the rundown.

Walsh then began to tell a story.

"I was in Belfast years ago to visit the Harland & Wolff shipyard, which, as we all know, is where it took two years for the supposedly unsinkable *Titanic* to be built."

Maxson pressed the talkback button.

"Maury . . . the *Titanic*?"

She turned back to the director, who shrugged and said, "Patience. He'll get there. He always does."

"The *Titanic*!" she said. "I feel like *I'm* sinking!"

In the back, Pierre jotted down something in his spiral notebook. And Walsh continued his soliloquy.

"After my visit, I took a taxi from the shipyard to the Crown bar—I guess the full name is the Crown Liquor Saloon—in the middle of Belfast," he said. "I sat alone in one of those ancient carved mahogany booths and pondered the meaning of life."

"Oh, dear God—he's pondering life," Maxson said.

"And as I sipped from a freshly poured pint," Walsh said, "I thought of a young man who had likely visited that same shipyard as perhaps part of a school field trip. He lived less than five miles away but was a curious young lad. He didn't think of building great ships but of building a great career of his own."

"Wait for it," the director said, nudging Maxson with his elbow. "We're almost there."

Maxson got in Riley's ear.

"Be ready," she said. "Apparently there's a point to all of this."

Riley gave a thumbs-up to the lens.

Walsh continued.

"This young man, born and raised in a modest nearby town, has built not only a career but a legacy," Walsh said. "We once knew him for his disarming smile, for the curly hair that fought to escape from under his cap, and, of course, for a golf swing touched by the gods themselves. Let's bring in Joe Riley, our intrepid reporter, who looks splendid in bespoke attire. Joe, tell us, please, about the one, the only Rory McIlroy of Holywood, Northern Ireland."

Maxson dropped her head on the desk in exhaustion.

"Told you," the director said.

Riley provided his post-round update of McIlroy's day. He then segued to three injury-related withdrawals from the field, and then detailed the winds that were supposed to sweep through the Atlanta area the following day—and how they would affect playing conditions for Round Two.

"Maury, I spoke with a handful of players who said those winds could make East Lake play at least five shots tougher tomorrow, maybe more," Riley said. "Today was about birdies. Friday could be about carnage."

"Well put, my friend," Walsh said. "But it was the great Bobby Jones who said that a gale wind puts hair on a golfer's chest. Or I might have made that up."

Maxson pressed the button again.

"Maury, for the love of all things holy, can we land this plane now? Coming up on ten . . . nine . . . eight . . ."

"Ladies and gentlemen," Walsh said, "I vote for carnage. We'll see you back tomorrow at East Lake. A pleasant evening to all."

"Two . . . one. We're out," Maxson said, slumped in her chair, unnerved by the experience.

As the crew gathered its things and began to file out the back door and down the grated metal stairs, there was a piercing scream. It was Maxson.

"I quit! I quit! I quit!" she said as she rushed out the door, squeezing herself past the others on the stairs.

Right behind her, scribbling frantically in his notebook, was the efficiency and programming consultant Stanley Pierre.

CHAPTER ELEVEN

A Barroom Tale

Towne Tap was proudly an old man's bar. The Shiners cost $3.25, cash only. Shots were optional, and the pours were heavy. Sloppy Joes and patty melts on the lunch menu. Fish fry on Friday nights. Pizza available next door at Al's after 4 P.M. every day except Sunday. College football and, on this night, the MLB playoffs on the TVs. Neon beer signs. Basement-style knotty pine on the walls. A row of video slots. A CD jukebox stuffed with country. A couple of working-class moms taking the orders and keeping the peace. A line of chairs at the bar and a half dozen tables against the wall.

The clientele was decidedly local and blue-collar: pipe fitters, plumbers, a handful of construction workers, teachers, a couple of firemen, some retirees, a half dozen couples, and the remnants of a slow-pitch softball team.

Hard Way had been a Towne Tap regular for years. It was a neighborhood bar stuck happily in a time warp. It survived because it had high self-esteem and an uncomplicated nature.

It was a little after eight-thirty on a chilly Tuesday night. Hard Way, wearing shorts and a Bandon Dunes sweatshirt from years earlier, sat at the Tap bar by himself, working on his second pint of Shiner. He had polished off a ten-inch pepperoni and sausage pizza for dinner. The unopened envelope from Kat sat under the Styrofoam plate.

Bang Bang was on his way. His older sister was a chef at a Chicago restaurant that had just earned two Michelin stars. The entire family had flown in to celebrate her success. Now he was making the drive from the city to Warrenville—from molecular gastronomy to pepperoni and sausage, all in one night.

Hard Way had last seen Bang Bang at the BMW Championship at Olympia Fields, where his man was on a late-season heater. Bang Bang had gotten Hard Way a pass and then sneaked him into the caddie room. He was met with a combination of hugs and handshakes, but also a few sideway looks, as if he were an outsider, *persona non* caddie.

It was all so strange. Hard Way had walked a few holes, but this time as a spectator, not a caddie. The distance between being inside those ropes and being outside them was less than a half inch, but in reality, it was the difference between being an insider and being an outsider. He was jealous as he watched the players and caddies walk down the fan-lined fairways like royalty.

Hard Way's former man had been true to his word: He had devoted considerable time and energy to blackballing Hard Way from getting another bag. The irony of Hard Way's dismissal was that his former man had put together a strong second half of the year. There were a couple of top 10s, even a nice Friday-Saturday run at the Open Championship at Hoylake. He had squeezed into the top 70 to play in the first playoff event, advanced to the BMW, improved his world ranking, but then failed to reach the Tour Championship. Still, it was an impressive recovery.

There was a moment near the range at the BMW where Hard Way saw his former man, and his man saw him. Hard Way said nothing, but his former man scratched his nose with his middle finger.

Hard Way had mixed feelings about being there. But he wanted to support Sand Man and Bang Bang. And if a player agent saw him and wanted to talk about a possible gig, well, what was the harm in that?

But there were no job offers. No players acknowledged him. Just as his former man had vowed to, he had rendered Hard Way radioactive.

Hard Way had tried getting another bag, but no one would return his calls. He made a run at a couple of fringe Tour players whose caddies had bolted for higher-ranked guys. They ghosted him. He asked about some open bags on the Korn Ferry Tour. Nothing. The Champions Tour. Nothing. The DP World Tour. Nothing. The LPGA Tour. Nothing. The Challenge Tour, the Asian Tour, the Japan and Korean tours . . . nothing.

There were occasional vague, polite pledges to reach out to him if something became available, but follow-up calls and emails by Hard Way went unanswered. A player agent whom Hard Way had known for years and considered a friend pulled him aside that day at the BMW.

"You committed the worst kind of mistake," he said. "You don't come back from that. Your former guy has everyone on Tour believing that you stole his Rolex and stole money out of his pocket because of your ineptitude. You're the caddie who can't count clubs. You're untrustworthy. You're a pariah out here. There's even a crazy rumor in the locker rooms that you tried to steal his wife."

"So then that's a hard no about getting Scheffler's bag?" Hard Way deadpanned.

"I'm not making this up, Hard Way. I like you, but you somehow made your man a hero. People feel sorry for him. I didn't think that was possible."

"So what do I do?"

"You had better hope a lot of people in DuPage County want to hit range balls."

Months later, the conversation still stung. Hard Way had read an item on Geoff Shackelford's golf website that noted that his former man and Kat had "reconciled" after "the incident." Hard Way didn't have her number, and she didn't have his—an oversight during that night and morning in Columbus. What had begun as a rescue of a woman being harassed at a hotel bar had become a career-ender for Hard Way. No good deed goes unpunished.

"Done with the pizza, dear?" the bartender said, waiting to clear away the paper plate and cardboard circle.

Hard Way awoke from his daze.

"Yeah, Deb, sorry," he said. "Daydreaming, I guess."

The envelope fell to the floor behind the bar. Deb picked it up and started to hand it back to Hard Way.

"No," Hard Way said. "I'm done with that too."

Deb shrugged and tossed it into the trash can under the counter.

Bang Bang arrived a little before ten. Every woman in the bar, including Deb, tracked him the entire way to his seat. He made handsome an art form.

"Dear?" said Deb before Bang Bang could settle into his seat.

Bang Bang threw down a foursome of hundos on the bar.

"Whatever Hard Way is having, but let's add a chaser," he said. He looked around the bar, counting eleven other patrons. "Buy them a round, too. And what's your name?"

"Deb," she said, leaning closer.

"You are a sight for sore eyes," Bang Bang said. "Tell you what." He pushed one of the $100 bills toward her. "You keep this for yourself. Just make sure I'm in an Uber at the end of the night. I gotta get back to the city."

"Dear, I'll drive you myself if I have to," she said.

Hard Way stared at the $100 bills with envy.

"Do you know how many cans of Dinty Moore I could buy with those?" he said.

"Dude, I'd give you $100 for a can right now," said Bang Bang. "I love my sister—and I know she's like the Tiger Woods of cooking—but I'm not a foodie. My taste buds aren't that smart. First of all, the portions were the size of ball markers. And do you know what cured Arctic char is?"

"I think it's a fish," Hard Way said.

"Is that so? Well, I guess I ate that tonight. Plus, I thought Michelins were tires. Swear to God, when she said they got two Michelins, I almost offered to buy two more so they'd have a full set for the car."

"Pizza's next door at Al's," Hard Way said. "Still a mushrooms-and-green-peppers guy? You might want to take off that blazer. Don't want to get any red sauce on that puppy. Armani?"

"Are-who?" Bang Bang said.

"The blazer," Hard Way said, reaching inside the single-breasted jacket to look at the stitched label. "Yeah, it's Armani. What'd that run you, two grand?"

"Three, I think," he said. "Good coat?"

"Bang Bang, you could wear a brown tarp and look good."

"I'll say," interrupted Deb. "And don't worry, dear, about the pizza. I'll get it for you."

"Look at you," Hard Way said. "You're already making friends."

As Deb walked through the connecting doors to Al's, Bang Bang lowered his voice so no one sitting nearby could hear him.

"You need a loan, dude? I'm flush. My man played his ass off down the stretch. Hit some bonuses on his equipment deal and threw some my way. And you'll love this: Some New York modeling agency wants me to do a test photo session. Said they love my cheekbones and my 'rugged authenticity.' I wear a bib and carry a bag! Only in New York do they think that's rugged. But the cabbage they're talking about paying me is outrageous."

"I appreciate the offer, but keep your money," said Hard Way, who was too embarrassed to tell his friend about the "courtesy reminder" sent by the bank about his late mortgage payment.

"Seriously, I don't know how many times you helped me when I was living week to week, sofa to sofa, meal to meal. Just say when."

"I'm OK. There's still the plasma bank."

"Seriously?"

"Actually, I think I might be out there again soon. I got a couple of things working."

"Dude, that ain't what I'm hearing. Sand Man, me, and a few other guys have dropped your name to some players who are looking to make a change. You'd be perfect for them."

"Let me guess what they said."

"It's not what they say, it's what they don't say. These guys know you'd help them, but they act like you don't exist anymore."

Hard Way drained his pint glass. "Yeah, I'm not going to be out there anytime soon. I just didn't want to admit it."

"How 'bout this: Come back to the city with me. They upgraded me at the Four Seasons, so I've got a suite. Some of the servers at my sister's restaurant are coming over after they get done with work tonight. They're lookers. There will be tits and asses all over the place. Might do you some good."

"Is there a state where you haven't screwed a woman?"

"Three: Alaska, Vermont, and New Hampshire."

"I'm from the Granite State," said Deb, back with the pizza in one hand, paper plates in the other.

Bang Bang winked at Hard Way.

"You'd break my heart, Deb," Bang Bang said.

"I'd die trying, dear."

Someone at the end of the bar yelled for some barbecue chips. Deb pulled a bag from the rack on the wall and walked them over to the customer.

"Bang Bang, you'll have more women tonight than I've had in the last five years," Hard Way said.

"Yeah, but none of mine are player wives."

Hard Way winced at the memory of Kat, and the repercussions of their night together.

"Oops," Bang Bang said. "Too soon?"

Hard Way shook his head. "I guess not," he said. "Been more than four months since it happened. Thing is, I liked her. She was all carry, like hitting a 3-wood 290 over water to a front pin, but she had style."

"Call her. Email her. Send a drone. Do something, dude."

"Don't have her number."

"I can get it."

"Probably best to let it go," Hard Way said, glad that he hadn't read Kat's note.

"Well, if you change your mind about her number or the Four Seasons, you've got a standing offer, dude."

"I've learned my lesson, but I appreciate the offers, sir."

They downed a shot of Jameson, clinked their pint glasses, tapped them twice on the counter Ted Lasso–style, and then drained their beers. Two more were waiting before they were done.

"Deb, you're gonna have to order me an Uber, too," Hard Way said.

"Already on my to-do list, dear," she said.

Hard Way listened as Bang Bang talked about his upcoming trip to the Zozo in Japan and the Hero World in the Bahamas. The more he talked, the more jealous Hard Way became. For all the bitching that caddies did on a weekly basis—the 180 days on the road, the loneliness, the weather, the aches and pains, the airplane food prepared in microwaves three feet from the crapper, the egos and whims of the players, the almost-constant worries about money—they loved their jobs. There were only about 135 players in the world who earned Tour cards (and only 100 of them had full-exempt status), which meant there were only about 135 caddies in the world carrying their bags. There were another 10,000 caddies . . . 20,000—who knew for sure?—hoping to be part of that 135. Hard Way had been one of them. Now he was an outcast.

"I'm happy for you, Bang Bang."

"Come a long way, haven't we?" Bang Bang said. "Remember when we were sleeping four caddies to a hotel room?"

"With only two twin beds," Hard Way said.

"And the caddies with the two highest scorecards each day slept on the floor."

"And there were mousetraps under the beds."

"And mice in them, dude. But better than sleeping in a car."

"Not much better—and I slept in my car a lot," Hard Way said. "Couldn't find a $39-a-night truck-stop room and couldn't afford an $80 room. Used a garden hose next to a gas station to take a shirtless shower. Then did a quick wipe under the armpits with the pine tree air freshener from my car."

"Eighty?" Bang Bang said. "I couldn't afford the $39 room."

"You didn't miss much. But they did throw the bedbugs in for free."

"Where was it that someone broke into our room in the middle of the night and wanted to rob us?"

"Flint, Michigan."

"But they left because we didn't have any money."

"We *never* had any money back then," Hard Way said. "You didn't do it for the money. You did it for the adventure.

"What was the name of the caddie whose man shot 82 on Thursday at Carnoustie, got piss drunk because he was sure they were going to miss the cut the next day, passed out in the bar, and we drew a chalk outline around him?"

"That was Charlie the Clavicle," Bang Bang said without hesitation.

"That's him!"

Deb walked over. "Charlie the Clavicle?"

"He got the name after he sustained—how should we put it—some shoulder trauma during a visit to De Wallen before a tournament began in Amsterdam," Hard Way said.

"De Who?" Deb said.

"It's part of the Red Light District in Amsterdam."

"You lost me."

"Amsterdam. Capital of the Netherlands. Home of the Van Gogh Museum, Amstel beer, and a vibrant, legal prostitution district."

"Never been east of Pittsburgh or west of Denver, so wouldn't know the place. How did Charlie hurt himself?"

"Let's just say she went one way and his clavicle went the other," Hard Way said. "It was twist and shout. He can only carry a bag on his left shoulder now. But the name stuck."

"And the Clavicle got drunk in Carnoustie?"

"Different year, but, yeah, the dude was *out,*" Bang Bang said. "He had an early tee time on Friday and we didn't want him to lose his gig. We stuffed a note and his caddie badge in his shirt pocket, poured him into a cab, paid the driver, and told him to drop the Clav off at the clubhouse."

"What'd the note say?"

"'I've lost my player. Can you help me?'" Hard Way said, laughing.

"They found him the next morning slumped against the locker-room door," Bang Bang said. "They coffee'd him up, got him to the range, and he spent the whole round with his hands over his ears."

"Why?"

"Because his man shot 63 and made the cut!" Hard Way said. "The crowd noise almost killed the Clav. They finished third that week, and the Clav has been going to AA meetings ever since. He even paid us back for the cab."

"Tell her about the Open Championship," Bang Bang said.

"You interested in any of this, Deb?" Hard Way said.

"Dear, until you and Jack Reacher Jr. walked in, the highlight of my night was restocking cocktail napkins."

"When you caddie at the Open in the UK, it costs a fortune," Hard Way said. "You get killed by the exchange rate and the price gouging. One caddie was so desperate that he convinced a farmer to rent him a tiny trailer next to the crops. It was like sleeping in an aluminum coffin on wheels. He woke up to roosters every morning."

"And he still had it better than you," Bang Bang said.

"I was getting to that. The Open was at Muirfield that year, and there were eight of us trying to find a place to share in North Berwick. That's a little town about five miles from the course. We were going from pub to pub asking the locals if any of them would rent us a place for the week. They laughed at us. We were on our last pub when a guy playing pool said he had a 'Bohemian' apartment, but he might be willing to relocate if the price was right. We gave him a number, he gave us the address and one of his keys, and said he'd be out in an hour."

"American ingenuity," Deb said.

"We were so proud of ourselves," Hard Way said. "But when we got there, the place was smaller than a high school book locker. Two of us slept in the same munchkin bed with an ironing board between us. Two other caddies slept on the living room floor. Another caddie on a ratty love seat. Two caddies on the kitchen floor. And the eighth caddie actually slept in a dog bed. He's still picking German shepherd fur out of his clothes."

"Glamorous," Deb said.

"That's what you did back then," Hard Way said. "You piled into a car and drove from state to state. You chipped in for gas money. You bummed a few bucks from other caddies. We were all just trying to get by. We had guys with two or three aliases. Guys who were heavy drinkers and druggies. Guys running from the law. Guys running from their ex-wives and the alimony payments."

"Why are you smiling?" Deb said.

"Because we didn't care," Hard Way said. "We just wanted to be out there."

"You make your money on tips—like me?"

"Don't ask me, ask him," Hard Way said. "He's solvent, I'm not."

"Hard Way's been at it longer than me," Bang Bang said. "Nowadays, if you're caddying for a decent player, you get a guaranteed $2,000 to $3,000 for the week you work. But you don't work every week."

"You're rich!"

"Not if you're flying from Phoenix to Orlando for Bay Hill, then renting a car, then paying full boat during spring break for a hotel room, then paying for your meals," Bang Bang said. "You're lucky if you break even."

"But what if your player wins?"

"Then I buy an engagement ring for you and me," Bang Bang said.

"I wish," Deb said.

"It usually works like this: A caddie gets 10 percent of the winner's share, 8 percent if his man finishes in the top 10, and something like 7 percent for a fortieth-place finish," Hard Way said.

"What's a winner share these days?"

"The Masters is what, $4.2 mil and climbing?" Hard Way said.

"And the U.S. Open is north of $4 million," Bang Bang said.

"So if your player wins the U.S. Open—" Deb said.

"I get $430,000," Bang Bang said.

"That's almost as much as Tiger made for *winning* the 1997 Masters," Hard Way said.

Deb crossed her arms, not completely convinced. "You mean a caddie gets that for only four days' work?"

"But if he misses the cut, Bang Bang gets 10 percent of zero," Hard Way said.

"I should have been a caddie," Deb said.

"No, you should have been Ted Scott in 2024," Bang Bang said.

"You lost me again," Deb said.

"Ted Scott is now the patron saint of caddies," Hard Way said. "In 2024, he earned about $5 million for carrying Scottie Scheffler's bag."

"Get out!" Deb said. "Five million?"

"Five-point-two, if you believe the reports," Bang Bang said. "If he'd been a player, he would have finished in the top 25 on the Tour money list."

"You can get legitimately rich out there," said Hard Way. "I bet some of the caddies have stock portfolios."

"I'll drink to that," Bang Bang said.

"Really?"

"Dude, strictly blue chips and some fixed-income positions."

Hard Way gave him a sideways look.

"When I started, the best caddies got $500 a week in salary, and if they had a big year, maybe made somewhere between $150,000 and $180,000," Hard Way said. "But there weren't many of those guys. Most of us got half that."

"And most of the tournament directors treated us like we were going to steal their daughters," Bang Bang said.

"Which you did," Hard Way said.

"It was the daughters' idea, not mine, dude."

Deb was puzzled. "I thought the players were pampered."

"The players were—and still are—but not the caddies," Hard Way said. "We were never allowed in the clubhouse. If we were lucky, there might be a caddie shack where we could hang out. And if we were really lucky, they'd give us a little meal ticket that we could use at the concession stand for a hot dog and a small drink. Thank God for Gypsy Joe."

"Who's that?" Deb said.

"Gypsy Joe Grillo," Bang Bang said. "Was a great Tour caddie, but also a great chef. He'd cook these huge meals for all the caddies and charge us just $4 per plate. It was usually the only decent food we'd eat the whole week."

"And he did it every week on Tour," Hard Way said. "He was the best."

Deb excused herself to retrieve an order from the kitchen. Hard Way leaned toward Bang Bang.

"I want to ask you something, and you're going to think it's the Jameson talking," Hard Way said once Deb was out of earshot.

"Dude, anything."

"You can't tell anyone; it's that ridiculous."

"I'd eat Arctic char before I said anything."

"A couple of days ago, I was at my range and a guy came in and bought a bucket of balls."

"Whoo, I can see why mum's the word. A bucket of balls at a practice range. That *is* unusual."

Hard Way ignored the sarcasm. "I was dicking around with a crossword puzzle and never got a look at him. He paid the extra couple of bucks for the grass area. I didn't think twice about it."

"So far it's a mystery wrapped in an enema."

"Enigma, but whatever. When I was closing up that night, I fired up the Pickermobile and did a quick circuit of the range. And this is where it gets weird: I think this mystery guy sent a large bucket out there."

"How far did he send it?"

"Four bills and change."

"No way."

"I told you it was ridiculous."

"How many?"

"All of them. I lasered it myself."

Bang Bang took a long chug. "There are, what, sixty balls in a bucket?"

"About seventy-five."

"And you want me to believe that Mr. Mystery bombed seventy-five drives with shitty *range balls* 400-plus yards?"

"He didn't just bomb them. You could have thrown a bag towel over them. There was barely any dispersion."

"Someone's playing with you."

"That's what I thought, but now I'm not so sure. At first, I figured it was the high school kids. But they usually just spell out swear words with the balls. Then I thought maybe Streelman was back in town—he went to Wheaton South—and was checking up on me. But he can't send it 400."

"Maybe it was one of those long-drive kids who had a good day?"

"Thought that too. Those guys are good, but not like this. No, this was the work of a professional golfer, not a professional long driver. These shots were shaped. There was a purpose. It wasn't somebody just swinging out of their FootJoys."

"Dude, there's nobody on the planet that can do what you say this guy did. Seventy-five drives in a perfect pattern? You don't have to worry about me repeating this, because I don't believe it."

"I don't blame you. Plus, why would he come to my range? Medinah isn't far away. Butler and Butterfield are in Oak Brook. Chicago Golf is just down the road. Rich Harvest and Black Sheep are in the vicinity. Those are proper places. I've got a patch of bent grass and a vending machine."

"But?"

"But he knew the answer to one of the crossword questions."

"If I guess it, will you think I play on Tour, too?"

"What's a ten-letter golf saying that dates back to 1681?"

Bang Bang scratched his head. "Figjam?"

"That's only six."

"I'm concise."

"It's 'Far and Sure.'"

"Dude, there are two places where that's the club motto, and we've been to both: Royal Liverpool and—"

"Chicago Golf," Hard Way said. "F me. The guy's a local."

"Give up the ghost, Hard Way. This guy bought a bucket of balls, but he didn't send them 400 yards. We do this for a living, dude. It didn't happen."

"I'm gonna find this guy."

"And if you do, then what?"

Hard Way downed another shot, tapped his pint glass twice against the counter, took a gulp, and said, "I'm gonna carry his bag and win a major."

"That," Bang Bang said, "would definitely be all carry."

CHAPTER TWELVE

The Plan

Only a few days remained before November 1, the date when Hard Way always closed To the Linksland for the winter. The highs were still in the sixties, but the lows were beginning to creep into the thirties. He couldn't afford heated hitting bays for the mats, and he didn't want to risk any damage to the bent grass once it got cold. A buddy who was a retired groundskeeper would spread a turf cover over Hard Way's prized grass before the December freeze arrived.

It had been a good week, relatively speaking. Business had been brisk—a rarity for To the Linksland—as golfers tried to squeeze in their last range sessions of the fall season. Today was no different; almost every space was occupied. But the temporary bump in cash flow wouldn't be nearly enough to get Hard Way through the winter.

Bang Bang had called with a proposal: come to Scottsdale, stay rent-free at his place near Kierland (he was going to be on the road most of the winter, anyway), and make some money as a caddie at Whisper Rock. Bang Bang had joined a few months earlier after having been on the waiting list for years.

The Rock, as it was called by the members, was known for its aura of cool, for making hanging out an art form. Its two tracks, the Upper and Lower courses, were included in the annual national rankings done by the golf magazines. Its membership featured more than a few Tour members, Tour caddies, and reportedly the lowest average handicap number of any club in the country. The practice facilities had no equal. The clubhouse was understated and comfortable. The surroundings were gorgeous. The service was world-class. The food was prepared perfectly. It was a place for serious players who didn't take themselves seriously.

Hard Way had been invited there in the past when in town for the Tour stop. He loved the vibe, how relaxed it was. There was nothing wrong with the formality and history of such places as Muirfield in Scotland or Augusta National, where coats and ties were required for dinner, and traditionalism and gentility ruled the day. Hard Way never had a problem if a club proudly committed itself to the more time-honored ways. What he couldn't stand was a club where the membership thought it was somehow better than, somehow superior to, everyone else, to say nothing of its waitstaff, locker-room attendants, club pros, and caddies. At Whisper Rock, everyone was equal. Didn't matter if you drove a million-dollar Singer Porsche or a used Subaru up to the valet circle. Once you walked through the thick wooden clubhouse doors, money, stature, titles, championships, portfolios, and celebrity didn't matter. It was the most egalitarian big-time club that Hard Way had ever seen.

But he didn't want to be a caddie there. At least not at first. He knew the Tour pros there. He knew the Tour caddies there. He knew other members. Now he was going to loop for them at their club?

Pride, though, was one of the seven deadly sins. Hard Way couldn't afford the luxury of ignoring his financial plight. While nobody got rich looping at a golf club, the Rock's members had a reputation for treating and tipping their caddies well. With his range closed for the winter, Hard Way needed an income source. Plus, Bang Bang reminded him, it was fifty degrees warmer in Scottsdale than in Wheaton, and maybe, just maybe, one of the Tour boys would realize that Hard Way was worth giving a second chance. The logic was undeniable.

"OK, you convinced me," Hard Way told him.

"Only one condition," Bang Bang said. "You gotta take care of my dog when I'm gone. His name is Oscar. He's a cocker, and he's a pig in a dog suit. Last week he ate a jar of Vaseline. Crapped petroleum jelly for a week. But you'll love him."

"Sounds adorable," Hard Way said, indifferent to all pets. "Just as long as he doesn't sleep in the bed."

"Oh, he'll sleep in the bed. He'll sleep under the covers and with his head on the pillow. And he'll snore. But it beats you paying rent, right?"

"Dog people crack me up," Hard Way said.

"Could be worse," Bang Bang said. "I could be a cat person."

Hard Way had three days before he made the twenty-five-and-a-half-hour drive to Scottsdale. He sat at the counter in the range shack with his earbuds in, Pearl Jam playing on his phone, and examined the route: Wheaton to St. Louis, St. Louis to Tulsa, Tulsa to Oklahoma City, Oklahoma City to Amarillo, Amarillo to Albuquerque, Albuquerque to Scottsdale. The only question was whether the Big Ass—that's what everyone called his ten-year-old cherry-red F-150 SuperCrew—could cover the seventeen hundred miles without breaking down.

He hadn't heard the shack door open. It wasn't until someone tapped him gently on the shoulder that he looked up. It was Joe Riley, the AGN reporter.

"You here as a golfer or as media?" Hard Way said as he removed the earbuds. His antennae were up, and his voice harder than he'd intended. "If you're media, then I've got nothing to say."

"I come in peace," Riley said. "I'm just a guy standing in front of a caddie, asking him to sell him a bucket of balls."

"*Notting Hill*. Nice pivot."

"I heard that you worked here," Riley said.

"It's worse than that: I own the place. Well, me and the mortgage company."

"Decent crowd today."

Hard Way looked out the window at the eclectic collection of swings.

"Like being at the range before a pro-am," Hard Way said. "Got some people making some real interesting passes at the ball."

"You doing all right?" Riley said. "And I'm just asking as a regular person."

"Doing OK, thanks. You were there that day. Takes a while for that bruise mark to heal."

"Hope to see you out there again."

"Me too. Anyway, what size bucket?"

"I'm feeling Vijay-ish. Give me the large."

Hard Way scooped out a bucket from his container.

"On me," he said.

"Can't take it," Riley said. "AGN policy." He dropped a $20 bill on the counter and grabbed the plastic bucket handle.

"It's only eight bucks."

"I'm going to hit off the grass, away from the others. The rest is for services rendered."

"What services?"

"I don't know," Riley said as he headed out the door. "I'm just trying to support our local small businesses."

Hard Way stuffed the $20 in the register and watched as Riley walked to the far end of the bent-grass area, where he placed the bucket on its side and then set his stand bag on the ground. Its flamingo-thin legs splayed wide as it struggled to deal with the weight of Riley's clubs. *What's he got in there, copper piping?* thought Hard Way.

He could see Riley put on his glove, pull out what looked like a wedge, and then take some practice swings. *Woof*, thought Hard Way. *Is that a swing or a seizure?* He put the earbuds back in, returned to the counter and to his plans for the Arizona trip.

After lunch, Hard Way fired up the Pickermobile and worked through the shorter and medium distances: 100 yards to 200 yards. That's where the heaviest volume was. It didn't take him long to fill up the three picker containers, though his ears were ringing as a couple of meatheads made it their mission to hit the metal cage with knockdown 4-irons. He emptied the containers and then made one more sweep, this time toward the 225-yard sign.

As he got closer, Hard Way noticed a cluster of ten or so balls at the marker. He looked beyond it and saw another cluster at the 250 mark, the 275 mark, as well as the 300 mark.

"This can't be happening."

Hard Way kept driving. There was another cluster between the 300-yard and 400-yard markers, and then one final cluster just beyond the 400-yard sign.

He was here, and I missed him! thought Hard Way. He did a hard U-turn and made a beeline for the grass area. Range rats scattered as he pulled up in front of them and emerged from the cage.

He inspected each of the five stations. The first four were what you'd expect of high handicappers: a mishmash of divots and broken tees. But the fifth station looked as if Tiger himself had gone through his bag club by club. There were six long divot strips, each one straighter than the next. They looked like stripes on the American flag.

Hard Way turned to several golfers who were standing nearby. "Did anyone see who was hitting balls here?"

He was met by befuddled looks and head shakes.

"We just got here," said one of the golfers. "You were picking up balls, so we left money on the counter. Nobody was hitting on the grass, so . . ."

Hard Way tried to remember who had come through the shack that morning and paid the upcharge for the grass area. There had been a couple of women prepping for their weekly league matches—but none of them resembled a bionic Nelly Korda. There had been a few twenty-somethings who looked like they could swing hard. There was a thirty-something—Hard Way had seen him in the past—with the kind of a swing that could win a club championship. Then again, if he belonged to a club, what would he be doing at To the Linksland? There had been a forty-something who clearly had done some powerlifting in his life. The muscled-up guys like him could crank one out there every so often. But that kind of distance with that kind of consistency? No way.

And there had been Joe Riley. Hard Way immediately remembered those practice swings. *That's a hard pass,* he thought.

During his 25½-hour drive to Scottsdale, Hard Way pondered questions that lacked obvious answers.

Who was the player?

Why had he chosen Hard Way's range twice for his hitting sessions?

How could that kind of talent remain a secret?

Why wasn't he on Tour? Or was he already?

Hard Way had spent hours online researching the existence of a player that fit the profile of Mr. Mystery. There were stories about golf prodigies, but none of them were from the Chicago area or even the Midwest. There had been a recent qualifier for a regional long driving contest in nearby St. Charles, but the winning yardage was only 363. A young pro from New Zealand had made headlines for his hitting length in a tournament in Auckland—averaging nearly 351 yards with his driver. But Auckland was 8,100 miles away.

This much Hard Way knew: There was a person in the greater Wheaton area who could hit a golf ball farther and more accurately than he had ever seen—or in this case, hadn't seen. But the person was hiding in plain sight.

CHAPTER THIRTEEN

Westbound

Hard Way had left Wheaton on a Monday and arrived at Bang Bang's townhouse at midafternoon on Wednesday. As he entered the code on the door's touch pad, he heard a combination of whining and barking from inside. When he walked in, Hard Way almost tripped over the wire crate that held the infamous Oscar, the buff-colored cocker spaniel who was wagging his tail and pawing to get out.

"No, you can't play through yet," Hard Way said to the dog, who tilted his head sideways as the stranger spoke. "Let me get my stuff in first."

Hard Way emptied the Big Ass and brought his bags and clubs into the newish two-story, two-bedroom townhome located only a couple of blocks from the restaurants, bars, and stores of Scottsdale Quarter. No wonder Bang Bang had chosen this location. It had a target-rich environment for dating, was only about fifteen minutes from Whisper Rock, and was a bit more refined and restrained than Old Town Scottsdale.

A day earlier, as Hard Way had made his way past Amarillo and into New Mexico, Bang Bang had called just after boarding a flight to Seattle for a pair of five-digit corporate speaking gigs. After the speech in Seattle, he said he was meeting his sometime girlfriend in Vancouver for a couple of weeks, then flying to the Bahamas. He gave detailed instructions on how to walk, feed, bathe (like that was going to happen), and amuse Oscar. Hard Way had half listened. Now, as he knelt to open the crate to let Oscar out, he could feel his cell phone buzzing with texts. *I'll check those in a minute*, he thought. *First, let's release the hound.*

Oscar barreled out of the crate and knocked Hard Way over. The dog did a frenzied loop around the living room, skidding across the kitchen floor, slamming into a wall, regaining his balance, then sprinting toward and leaping at Hard Way, who was on his back laughing at the sight of this crazed animal. Hard Way caught the dog in midair, but Oscar wrestled free and began bathing his new friend with licks. That done, he jumped off, walked calmly to the front door, and pooped.

"No, no, no, no," Hard Way said. But it was too late. Hard Way grabbed some paper towels and a plastic grocery bag from the kitchen and cleaned up the mess. His phone buzzed again. Hard Way glanced at the screen. There were six text messages, all from Bang Bang.

Dude, you should be there by now. Greta, my next-door neighbor (that little Chiquita does the nightly weather for Channel 15 and is hotter than Death Valley but unfortunately is duded up with the starting strong safety for the Cardinals), fed and walked Oscar early this morning. You need to feed him a late lunch.

Mail key is on the counter. Fridge is stocked.

Fitzy at the Rock knows you're coming over tomorrow. He looks like Colt Knost, but better-looking. He'll set you up.

You're in for a surprise. 🤔

See you in a month. Mi casa es su casa.

And remember, you've got to walk Oscar as soon as you let him out of the crate. Otherwise, he'll do a deuce near the front door. Collar and leash on hook next to door.

"Now he tells me," Hard Way said.

Hard Way fed Oscar and then walked him down to the pool house and small park near the front entrance of the development. The pool area was hidden by green mesh fence coverings and bougainvillea vines. A woman's voice rang out.

"Oskie!"

Oscar broke free of Hard Way and ran, leash trailing behind him, to the fence door. It opened, revealing a woman no taller than five-foot-two, perfectly proportioned, and wearing a pink floral bikini and an Arizona State ball cap. She crouched down to hug Oscar, who melted in her arms.

"Come here, my little baby," she said before looking up. "You must be Hard Way."

"Right now, I wish I were Oscar, but, yes, I am Hard Way. Or Max. Or really whatever you prefer."

She rolled her eyes.

"I'm going to stop talking now," Hard Way said.

"I'm Greta. Gerald said you'd be here today."

"Who's Gerald?"

"He's Oskie's daddy," she said, rubbing the dog's ears. "Isn't he, baby?"

"You mean Bang Bang?"

"Who's Bang Bang?"

"Apparently that's Gerald—a fact that I didn't know until this exact minute. He's 'Bang Bang' in our world."

"Are you a caddie, too?"

"I was. Am? I'm in a period of transition."

Hard Way grabbed the leash and tugged at Oscar, who reluctantly returned to walk mode. "I better get back to my bonding time," he said, nodding toward the dog.

"See you around campus," she said, closing the fence door.

The next day, Hard Way found a spot in the employee lot at Whisper Rock; stopped by the office to sign his papers; was issued a white caddie onesie, a pin sheet, and a yardage book; and then received an orientation tour of both courses. He had played the Upper and Lower tracks in the past and knew some of their nuances, but it was helpful to get a refresher from one of the regular caddies.

"We'll get you a bag tomorrow," said Fitzy when they met at the end of the day in the caddie room near the chipping and bunker practice area behind the front range.

The reception from the other caddies that day had been somewhere between friendly and frosty. Hard Way had tried to introduce himself to as many of them as possible. He didn't want any of the regulars to think he was big-timing them because he had caddied on Tour. The club had reopened in August after the annual month off in July, but the out-of-town members didn't start trickling in until October, when the face-of-the-sun temperatures finally relented in the Valley. Hard Way knew he was starting at the bottom of the seniority list, which is the way it should work. He just wanted to keep his head down, do his job, and try to earn as much money as possible during the fall and winter. Bang Bang had done him a solid; he didn't want to make his friend look bad after the recommendation.

The Rock caddies, like a lot of caddies at elite clubs such as Cypress, Seminole, Pine Valley, and Shinnecock, certainly were good enough from a golf perspective to work on Tour. But to be a successful Tour caddie, it took more than reading a putt or a yardage book. You had to be able to read the room, as well as your player. You had to develop a calm, even demeanor that remained unshakable in all circumstances: in contention late on Sunday, grinding to make the cut on Friday, playing a pro-am with Steph Curry on Wednesday, meeting a former U.S. president at a Ryder Cup function, handling the pressure when paired with Rory or Tiger. In addition, you had to know your place in all of those situations. The best caddies, like the best refs, blended in like cream in coffee.

Hard Way had never caddied for the likes of Rory, Rahm, or Scheffler, but he had worked for players who had reached the top 50, including one who had been a Ryder Cup captain's pick. He had caddied in majors, caddied when the difference between a made and missed putt could mean hundreds of thousands of dollars. He had caddied for guys who were so nervous on the first tee that they couldn't speak.

There was no substitution for hard work. He had seen the effort put in by the best caddies in the business: Mackay, Greller, LaCava, Greiner, Williams, Skovron, Scott, Tesori, Waldman, Foster, and Jackovac, to name a few. Their prep work was impeccable. Their instincts during a round equally so. At the Masters, you could see those guys on the 10th hole and know they were already thinking ahead to Amen Corner and the 11th, 12th, and 13th holes.

Hard Way watched, listened, learned, and adopted many of their routines. At majors especially, he rolled lots of putts on each green and made detailed notes. If his player called him in for a read, he wanted to be ready. Everything was about preparation.

When he walked a course on his own, he'd walk it at least twice. He played the round in his head as he envisioned his man would play it. *What tee shots are going to make my man uncomfortable? If he misses the fairway—and almost nobody hits every fairway—how will he get to that pin from that rough? Where are the places he's instantly dead if he hits it there? Where are the places he can miss and survive? What language and tone do I use to get him back to neutral and focused if he makes a mess out of a hole?*

Compared to caddying on Tour, looping at a club was like going from commanding a submarine in the Bering Sea to puttering around Lake Havasu on a pontoon. That didn't mean that Hard Way wasn't working hard at the Rock—he wanted to give the member or guest their money's worth—but it didn't come with the same pressures. On Tour, a caddie and player were together at least five days a week, seven if they made the cut. At the Rock, Hard Way would have ten to fifteen minutes to watch his member or guest on the range and get a quick idea of ball flight, distance, and skill set. Within a hole or two, he'd be able to determine if a player wanted him to read every putt, suggest clubs and strategy, tell stories, or simply be quiet.

As the weeks passed, Hard Way began to feel more comfortable. A few of the other Rock caddies invited him out for beers or a round of golf on a day off. Others were polite but distant, as if they had been told to avoid Hard Way. Turns out, they had.

Bang Bang's texts about the pooch had been true. Oscar did indeed sleep in Hard Way's bed, starting at the bottom, then working his way under the covers, and finishing with his head on the pillow. Hard Way had tried to keep the dog in the crate, but Oscar would have no part of it. Instead, Hard Way awoke to the gentle snoring of a three-year-old cocker whose tongue stuck out between his top and bottom teeth.

On a Wednesday morning in late October, Hard Way had been assigned as a forecaddie for a foursome: two members and their guests from Mobile, Alabama. The members were good players. It was going to be an easy, fun loop.

As he stood behind the group on the range, Hard Way heard someone call his name in a voice that was immediately recognizable.

It was his former man.

Hard Way could feel his stomach muscles tighten, much like when a highway patrol car, lights flashing, siren wailing, suddenly appears in the rearview mirror.

His former man walked directly to Hard Way and extended his hand. There was a smile on his face.

"The rumors are true," he said. "You're back in the business. Isn't this a great place?"

Hard Way was disoriented, unsure how to respond. He shook his former man's hand, but did so in a daze. His man then turned his attention to the foursome, who were well aware of the history between the two. They, too, didn't know how to respond.

His man killed them with kindness. Hard Way had seen him do it countless times at pro-ams. When in the mood, his former man could pretend to be interested in their every life detail: job, family, hobbies, favorite teams. He soon had the foursome laughing, as if he had known them for years.

"Gentlemen, can I ask a favor?" he said. "Can I steal my old buddy here for this round? I'm only here for a couple of days and wanted to spend some time with Hard Way. You mind swapping caddies?"

Nobody had any objections, except Hard Way. "I'm sorry, but this is my group for the day, so I'm going to have to beg off."

"I cleared it with Fitzy," his former man said jovially. "He said if it's OK with the fellas here, it's OK with him."

They all nodded in agreement.

"Good," his former man said. "Let me buy you beers when we're done today. Have a great round, boys. Hard Way, I'm set up over here." He pointed to his bag, which was about 20 yards down the range.

Hard Way was introduced to the rest of the group. One was his former man's accountant, the other two were marketing executives with a New York financial house. It was clear the execs were being romanced in hopes they'd make an endorsement offer.

"Hard Way and I go back a little bit," he told them. "He's a great caddie, as long as you don't ask him to count your clubs."

They laughed, and one of them slapped Hard Way on the back.

"Good one," said the guest.

Hard Way could feel his temples throb as he tried to control his anger.

Handicaps were exchanged and bets were made on the first tee of the Upper. Hard Way left the foursome at their carts and ran out to the left edge of the fairway to track their tee shots on the par-4 first hole. His former man outdrove the other three by 50 yards.

Hard Way gave the amateurs their distances and then made his way to his former man's drive. He was determined to keep the conversation to a minimum when the two carts pulled up.

"You've got 120 to the front, 131 to the pin," he said, looking at his pin sheet. "Wind coming in from two o'clock. Everything will roll right to left once you're on."

His former man pulled a gap wedge from the bag. "Fellas, I'm just getting used to this place, but the ball flies a little farther in this dry air." He took a practice swing and then smoothed his shot to about 8 feet. As he handed the club to Hard Way, he said, "Guess you're the last to know that Bang Bang isn't the only new member here. I just bought a place in Troon North off Dynamite. Couldn't handle those California taxes anymore."

Hard Way wiped the club, returned it to the bag, and then reached for the sand container on the side of the cart. As he did, his former man hit the accelerator, nearly taking Hard Way's arm with him. Hard Way did the best he could, patting down the divot with his foot, and then ran to the green, the whole time wondering if Kat and the kids were in Scottsdale, too.

Hard Way gave the players their reads and then stepped away. His former man drained the putt for birdie. "That's the first good read Hard Way has given me in years, isn't it, buddy?"

Hard Way said nothing as he returned the flag to the hole.

For the next three and a half hours, his former man walked the delicate line between insults and supposed friendly trash talk. But when the others weren't looking, he would drop his club at Hard Way's feet, toss the ball to him for cleaning just out of his reach, or make an unnecessary sharp left or right turn when the caddie was standing on the back of the cart as they drove.

His former man played well, but Hard Way couldn't help but notice that he didn't play *that* well when the execs had a chance to win a hole. He would purposely hit to the fat part of the green, leave a putt a half foot short, or lay up on the par-5s when he could easily have reached them in two. It was the kind of golf you played when you wanted your guests to feel good about themselves and their games. And the better they felt, the better chance his former man would leave the course with a new deal.

"Oh, did I tell you, Hard Way?" his former man said as they walked off the 17th green. "I'll be out here tomorrow afternoon doing something with AGN out on the range. Maybe you can shag balls."

Once again, Hard Way said nothing. He didn't want to give his former man any reason to complain to management.

When the round ended, Hard Way began cleaning each player's clubs. The accountant started to reach in his pocket to pay Hard Way. The execs began to do the same.

"I've got this, fellas," their host said. "I'll meet you in the grill in a few minutes and start paying off my debts. You guys fleeced me!"

The guests laughed and then thanked Hard Way as they began the walk to the clubhouse. Hard Way knew his former man was keeping his clubs there for the night, so he grabbed the guests' bags and slung them over his shoulders for the walk to the front valet circle.

"Hold on. You forgot something, didn't you?" his former man said as he stuffed a wad of cash into the front pocket of Hard Way's onesie. "You earned every penny of it. See you again—but not for long."

Hard Way took the bags to the drop-off area and then stopped by the caddie room to pick up his car keys. Fitzy, the caddie master, was waiting for him.

"How'd it go out there?"

"Good group. Had fun," he lied.

"Your man said that you had requested his foursome on the tee sheet. Sorry about the confusion before the round."

"He said *I* had requested them?"

"You didn't?"

"If that's what he said, sure. Anyway, see you tomorrow."

"Got you down for the afternoon wave."

"Sounds good. Gives me time to sleep in, walk that damn dog, and get over here."

When Hard Way reached his car, he pulled out his earnings from the front pocket. It was a wad of one-dollar bills—forty-seven in all. Hard Way had been stiffed. He began to return to the clubhouse and confront his former man. But that was the whole point of the $47, to get Hard

Way to create a scene. His former man would swear that he had been more than generous to Hard Way. In fact, he would say that he had added a $100 bonus for a job well done. Once again, it would be his word against Hard Way's.

During the drive home, Bang Bang called.

"Heard the prick busted your balls today."

"He's still America's sweetheart."

"He's trying to get you booted from the place. He's telling everyone that you can't be trusted. But the owner, the GM, and a couple of the other caddies stood up for you. Said you deserved a second chance. So did I."

"I know, man, and I won't forget it. But of all the gin joints in all the towns in all the world, he walks into mine."

"You're doing that movie thing again, aren't you?"

"I am. When you back in town?"

"TBD. But soon. How's my boy doing?"

"You mean your *dog*? You realize he's a canine. He doesn't recite Proust. Can't fix a carburetor. Won't run for public office."

"Don't make fun of our bond. He's family."

"He's doing fine. I'm teaching him French, and he's teaching me how to scratch my ears."

"Hang in there, dude. You had a bad day, but you survived. Tomorrow's going to be better."

"Not that much better. He's out there again tomorrow. Doing something with AGN."

"Bummer. But I've got some news that might perk you up."

"Let me guess: I don't have to take Oscar to get his glands drained?"

"Kat is in Scottsdale. And here's the kicker: She's single and she's trying to track you down."

Hard Way didn't know how to react. Kat, him, and his (and her) former man all in the same town at the same time?

The car behind Hard Way laid on its horn. The light had been green for five seconds. Hard Way, flustered, gunned the Big Ass.

"Why would she be here?" he asked once he collected himself.

"It's a long story."

"Give me the short story."

"After you got shitcanned at the Memorial, Kat told your former guy she was leaving him. He blubbered like a baby. He begged her to reconsider, promised he'd go to couples counseling, even offered do a trial separation if that's what she wanted."

"I hate to admit it," Hard Way said, "but it sounds like he was at least trying."

"Kat thought so. She gave him another chance."

"Great," Hard Way said sarcastically. "Do I need to send a card?"

"Dude, you didn't let me finish. She gave him another chance right up until the moment she caught him cheating with the membership director at their country club."

"What?"

"You'll love this. Your man put an AirTag in his golf bag and paid one of the caddies to drive a cart—slowly—on all eighteen holes. That gave him a four-hour window for his straycations at a buddy's safe house in the neighborhood. If Kat checked his location, it looked like he was playing a round of golf when really he was just playing around."

"I didn't know he was that clever."

"It worked for a while. Then one day a friend of Kat's was driving by the club and saw your man duck into the car of the woman who wasn't his wife."

"The membership director."

"Bingo. They were headed to the safe house. The friend called Kat. Kat checked the AirTag location, which showed your former man on the first fairway. Kat drove over to the club and discovered that the bag, but not her husband, was on the cart at the No. 3 tee box by then. Kat called your former man, who said he was already 2-under but couldn't talk because it was his turn to hit. When he got home, the garage code and door locks had been changed. She put his clubs in the middle of the driveway and taped a ziplock bag to it. The AirTag and the name and number of her divorce attorney were in the bag. He moved to Scottsdale a week later."

"That was an expensive non-round of golf. But what's she doing here?"

"He gets the kids one weekend a month. She flies out with them, gets a room at the Westin, and flies them home on Sundays."

"The Westin that's two blocks away from your place?"

"Bingo."

Hard Way turned left into the townhome complex. The conversation had made the drive seem shorter than usual. "I don't know, Bang Bang. I'm going to have to think about it."

"You better think quick."

"Why?"

"Because she's waiting for you at my place."

Hard Way came around the block and turned into the driveway, and there on the front stoop were Greta, Oscar . . . and Kat.

Oscar, his collar and leash in place, wagged his tail at the sight of Hard Way but was content to stay wedged between Greta and Kat. Both women looked spectacular, Greta in a pair of ASU gym shorts and a blue popcorn bikini top, and Kat in a pair of torn jeans and a black Homage T-shirt that read "IF YOU HEAR ANY NOISE IT'S JUST ME AND THE BOYS BOPPIN." You had to respect a woman who understood her inner Dave Parker.

"I see you've met my foster family," Hard Way said to Kat, who stood and began to give him a hug. Unsure how to respond, Hard Way offered a tepid embrace. Kat pulled away, embarrassed by the awkward exchange.

"Way to go, Max," Greta said, amused at his level of discomfort. "It looked like you were hugging a nun."

"Yeah, that wasn't my best effort," he said weakly. He tried again, this time patting Kat on the back.

"That was even worse," Greta said. "I'm going to walk the pooch and let you guys figure it out. Kat, it was nice meeting you. One of these days, you'll have to explain to me what you see in this lug."

She blew a kiss at Hard Way and mouthed, "She's a keeper." Hard Way nodded.

As Oscar and Greta disappeared down the street, Kat and Hard Way began speaking at the same time, with Kat saying she shouldn't have shown up unannounced, and Hard Way, still in his Whisper Rock onesie, saying he looked like a member of the Apollo 8 flight crew.

"I was going to say hazmat engineer, but the flight crew thing works too," Kat said. "Heard my ex was his usual delightful self."

"Who knew: two reunions on the same day."

"Greta is nice."

"I guess, if you're into brilliant and beautiful TV meteorologists."

"Bang Bang must have needed a rabies shot. And maybe you need one, too."

"Not me. Never tempted."

"I don't believe that."

"Did she tell you about her football-player boyfriend? His five o'clock shadow could kick my ass. No, I'm a look-but-don't-touch guy."

"That's not entirely true," Kat said with a knowing grin.

They went inside, where Hard Way told Kat to grab whatever she wanted out of the fridge. He took a quick shower and traded the white onesie for shorts and a Dollywood T-shirt. When he returned, Kat was on the couch, with plenty of room for a companion. Hard Way chose the recliner, a decision that didn't go unnoticed by Kat.

Kat sipped at a can of Diet Coke. Hard Way brushed away some dog fur on the armrest.

"This was probably a bad idea," Kat said, breaking the silence. "I sort of guilted Bang Bang into arranging this meeting."

"Oh, Gerald and I will be having a chat when he gets back off the road," Hard Way said.

"Who's Gerald?"

"That's what I said. Turns out the world's sexiest man has the world's un-sexiest real name."

"Sounds like a British ambassador."

"Sounds like all the other names were taken the day he was born. Anyway, I'm not going to lie: Between spending four hours with our ex, and then you and the boys boppin in, I'm going to need a mental health day."

"I'm so sorry about what happened to you," she said. "You didn't deserve any of this. I should have told you my name at the bar. You should have told me who your player was. We would have saved ourselves a lot of trouble."

"Yeah, you sort of put me on the towel rack," he said.

"I don't understand."

"You hung me out to dry."

"You were cute and chivalrous," she said. "I was flirty and just so damn tired of being unhappy. It was the perfect storm of emotions for me. But there was a moment when I should have walked away."

"When was that?"

"When I saw the Rolex."

"Perfect. Ratted out by Hans Wilsdorf. But why didn't you just say something?"

"It looked like the one I gave him, but without seeing the engraving I wasn't completely sure. Maybe there was part of me that didn't want to believe it was the same watch. I was having too much fun. I liked you, and I thought you liked me. But all I did was get you fired."

"I got myself fired, but you helped. Mine was no venial sin."

"You didn't know I was his wife. Hell, he rarely mentioned me to anyone, especially his caddies. And I said I didn't follow golf anymore, so there wasn't much incentive for you to volunteer his name."

"Did you know he was in the hotel room that morning?"

"I heard somebody, but I assumed it was room service. He told me later about the perfume. He hasn't remembered our anniversary in years, but he remembers my perfume?"

"Lucky us."

"Can I ask you a question?" she said.

"You're on the tee box."

"Why didn't you call me?"

"I didn't have your number, and it wasn't like I could ask your ex for it. And when he vaporized me at the Memorial, I drove home and went to a dark place. I was a cave dweller for months."

"You did have my number. It was in the note I left in the hotel bathroom."

Hard Way stared at his feet.

"You never read it, did you?" she said.

"I kept it for the longest time. Just couldn't bring myself to open it."

"You should have. Do you know how hard it is to write a note in lipstick?"

More silence.

Kat glanced at her watch and began to reach for her handbag. "That was a joke, by the way. But I guess I don't blame you. If it weren't for me, you'd still have a job. Well, I better go check in on the kids."

She got up and put the purse strap over her shoulder. Hard Way popped up too.

"Before you go, my turn to ask a few things," he said.

Kat sat back down, and so did Hard Way.

"I owe you a few good answers," she said.

"Question one: Are you officially and legally the former Mrs. Former Man? Because I'm done with married women."

Kat held up her left hand. Her ring finger had a vacancy.

"Question two: What makes you think I regretted a single nanosecond of that night and morning with you?"

"To begin with, you never opened my note."

"Question three: What did the note say?"

"It said I was married to a Tour player. It said the name of the player. It said I had a good feeling about you—and us. It said to call me and included my number. It said I was reconsidering my disdain for Vols orange. It said I asked my mom to DVR the Memorial that day so I could watch it after I flew home—just in case you were on TV."

"You said all that in lipstick? And, yeah, I was on TV. I was the top story."

"All I can do is apologize, Max. That's why I came here today." She pulled her sunglasses and rental car keys from her bag. "Tell Greta I'm sorry I couldn't stick around to say goodbye." She stood up and started for the door.

"Not so fast, my friend." Hard Way was standing now too. "An additional bonus question: Is it too late to get your number? I'm a believer in mulligans on the first tee."

Kat, stunned for a moment, dropped her purse and wrapped her arms around him.

"You know you're an idiot," she said.

"I get that a lot," he said.

They were in mid-kiss when the door opened and Oscar, tail wagging at the sight of his new best friend, sprinted toward Kat. Greta took one step in, assessed the scene, and said, "Now, *that's* a hug."

CHAPTER FOURTEEN

Far and Sure

Riley wasn't AGN's first choice for the early-December assignment. In fact, he wasn't AGN's first, second, or hundredth choice to fly to Phoenix for what eventually would be a half-hour special to air months later during the network's coverage of the Drive, Chip and Putt competition. Originally considered an afterthought by the network's executives, the DC&P had become an unexpected viewer favorite to begin the Masters-week programming. Who knew that people would want to watch seven-to-fifteen-year-old boys and girls chip into a circle, try to sink a 15-foot putt, or do a kids' version of a long driving contest on a Sunday at Augusta National? But they did. As viewership numbers increased, so did AGN's interest in treating it like an actual event. The now-polished production—and the shoulder programming that went with it—made the Green Jackets happy. At AGN, it was always about putting a smile on the Green Jackets' faces. If you didn't, you risked finding yourself without a chair when the music stopped in the annual television negotiations. Augusta National kept a tight leash on its TV "partners," thanks to those yearly renewal contracts.

This latest assignment would be part of that shoulder programming. The idea was to have three Tour pros, each known for their driving, chipping, or putting skills, be the centerpieces of the special. AGN had sent crews to assorted Drive, Chip and Putt qualifying sites around the country and had instructed kids to look into the camera and ask the pros for tips. The results were a combo platter of serious questions mixed with the kind of stream-of-consciousness you'd expect from kids: *How do I chip off a tight lie? How do you line up a putt? What's the best club to use for the chipping competition? How do you handle pressure? How do I tell my dad that I don't want his golf advice? Is there a way to psych out my opponents? My dad says it's OK to put olive oil on the face of my driver—is that true? Is* MOI *French? Do you have Tiger's email address?*

The coordinating producer overseeing this specific shoulder program had wanted one of the network's anchors or one of the more polished reporters, such as Rinello, for the gig—someone to add some gravitas to the show. But because AGN's top talent usually took vacations at this time of year, the roster of available hosts was scorecard thin. Riley became the best of the least-desirable options. As always, he had volunteered for the assignment. It was his default position.

"I thought you were off for a while," Laurel had said when informed of the trip.

"It's a lucky break for me," he had said. "It will raise my profile at the network and with the Green Jackets."

"What about raising your profile with your family? Buddy's coming home this weekend before final exams begin. We were all going out for dinner. Remember?"

"He'll understand."

"You're losing him, Joe."

"I'll make it up to him when I get back."

Laurel had sighed. "You always say that, but there's always another assignment."

"Do we have to have this conversation now?"

"That's the problem, Joe. We *never* have the conversation."

It had ended there: with silence and no resolution. Riley wasn't someone who often shared his feelings, even with Laurel. Laurel liked to collect people. She had dozens of friends, and they often entrusted her with their innermost thoughts. Riley had few close friends and held his secrets tight. It was part of his emotional DNA, the result of growing up under the command of a USAF captain who had retired as a full bull colonel. His old man wasn't as dictatorial as the Great Santini, but there was no questioning his orders. You did as you were told, when you were told.

Riley had the same rigid traits as his dad. He was a workaholic in desperate need of a 12-step program. He was disciplined. Loyal. Honor bound. An overachiever. None of that made him an especially good father. If anything, his two sons, especially Buddy, felt weighed down by the very virtues that Riley had tried to instill in them.

The possibility of a higher network profile hadn't been the only reason Riley had raised his hand for the new assignment. What he hadn't told his wife was that his agent had yet to receive any details about an expected new contract. This wasn't an unusual AGN tactic. The company's talent office often waited until the final days of an existing contract before submitting an offer. It was their way of using time and doubt as a negotiating tool. In fact, Riley's previous contract had expired before AGN finally sent a new one.

"We'll get it done," his agent had assured him after this latest delay. "We'll ask for four years and some escalating salary bumps, and they'll counter with three and pretend to fight us on the money. You know, the usual."

Meanwhile, AGN had secured the help of three Tour pros who lived in the Scottsdale area, belonged to Whisper Rock, and would be in town on the shoot date. Whisper Rock had agreed to make parts of its impressive practice facility available for the daylong shoot.

"We'll coach you up," the coordinating producer had told Riley, doing little to hide his disappointment that more prominent talent wasn't involved. "And we can probably do some things in edit that will minimize your, uh, weaknesses."

"Don't sugarcoat it," Riley had said. "Tell me how you really feel."

But the CP was allergic to sarcasm and didn't realize or care how tone-deaf his comments sounded. "Jan Chaffin will field produce. She'll take it from here."

That was good. Chaffin was a seasoned producer who would have everything buttoned up. Riley had worked with her in the past.

Riley flew into PHX late that morning, bringing with him an oversized extendable plastic tube, the kind used for architectural plans. In it was the persimmon driver.

He had debated whether to bring it on the trip, but Buddy had convinced him.

"It's freezing here, it's warm there, and you're gonna be at Whisper Rock," he had argued. "You've got to take it with you."

Riley eventually agreed but decided he would use it only if he was guaranteed total privacy. If not, the driver would never come out of the case. The flight attendant had stored it in the coat closet near the front galley.

That night, Riley did his prep work and tried to fight off the time change. He was asleep by eight. The next morning, he was up so early that he decided to meet Chaffin and the crew at the course for the six-thirty call time.

"Hello, sunshine," said Chaffin, who always wore the same ensemble on shoots: jeans, a polo shirt, a long-sleeved golf pullover, and sneakers. Her blond-streaked hair was always pulled back into a ponytail. "You and Rinello might be the only reporters who show up for the setup."

"Had nothing else to do," Riley said.

She introduced Riley to the four-person local crew: a director of photography, secondary camera, audio, and grip. They began unloading their vans and setting up the equipment at the range, chipping area, and practice green.

The amount of gear required for a shoot never ceased to amaze Riley. Because of the multiple sites around the range area, the crew had brought extra metal stands, tripods, cameras, monitors, lenses, dollies, deflectors, diffusers, scrims, sliders, sand bags, lights, boom mics, MōVIs, mixers, electrical cords, hi-hats, and spare battery packs. All Riley had brought was a legal pad with several pages of notes and questions.

By 8:45, the crew was finished with the primary setup at the chipping area. The putting and driving range sites also had equipment in place for later in the day. There would be tweaks to the lighting and a series of sound checks once each player arrived for his segment, but for now, the setups worked for the perfectionist that was Chaffin.

As they waited for Tour pro Gary Lippon to finish his breakfast in the grill, the audio guy brought several shopping bags full of snacks to the staging table. Chaffin had put him in charge of making a food and drinks run the night before.

"What *is* this?" she said as the audio guy finished unpacking the bags.

"Healthy snacks," he said proudly.

Riley walked over to the table.

"Spam?" he said. "You bought Spam?"

"It's sneaky tasty," the audio guy said.

"Audio guys," Chaffin said with a sigh. "It's always the audio guy."

Lippon, among the best short-game players on Tour, emerged from the clubhouse. His bag was waiting on a cart, and he drove it to the chipping area just left of the caddie room near the front range. The audio guy dropped a lav wire under his golf shirt and clipped the mic under his collar.

Riley shook hands and thanked him for making the time.

"This shouldn't take longer than six, seven hours, tops," Riley said.

Lippon started to nod in blind agreement and then caught himself. "What? Seven hours?"

"I'm just messing with you," Riley said.

"You got me on that one," Lippon said. "OK, what do you need me to do?"

During the next fifty minutes, Lippon conducted a short-game clinic, stopping at times to answer the pre-taped questions from the Drive, Chip and Putt kids that Chaffin showed him on her iPad. Riley would step in at times with a follow-up question or introduce the next kid on the iPad. Lippon's array of chips—and the reason for using each one of them—was fascinating. Riley had seen players hit these chips for years, but Lippon broke down the swings like an English teacher diagramming a sentence.

"This stuff is so easy that even this guy can do it," Lippon said, pulling Riley into the frame and handing him a wedge.

"I didn't know there would be a pop quiz today," Riley said, trying to hand the club back to Lippon. "My game is better suited for the Shank, Top and Four-Jack competition."

Within ten minutes, though, Lippon had Riley chipping the ball to kick-in range on a regular basis. For Riley, who had always thought of himself as a decent short-game player, the lesson was a revelation. If Riley could do it, Lippon said directly to the camera, anybody could. Lippon had a future in television.

Drew Fetting, who almost always led the Tour in Strokes Gained: Putting, 3-Putt Avoidance, and Putting from 5–15 Feet, stopped by after lunch for his on-camera session. The Clemson grad dropped a ball at the 6-foot mark, the 15-foot mark, and the 30-foot mark—the distances used in the putting competition—and sank the first two and saw the 30-footer spin in and out of the cup. Riley dared him to do it again. This time, he made all three.

"You wanna know how I did that?" Fetting said, his Greensville twang as thick as SAE 30. "I don't think, I just do. I get so damn tired [it came out as "tarred"] of watching amateurs—and even a lot of the guys on Tour ["Turr"]—spend an hour over a putt. Pick a line ["lawn"], use your upper body for the stroke, square the putter face to the ball, watch the thing roll into the hole. That's it. I could even teach a Gamecock how to do it."

"A lot of the kids want to know how you handle the pressure of an important putt," Riley said.

"Son, we human beings always try to make things more complicated than they are. I'd tell these kids to trust themselves and not listen to their parents. How many damn tournaments they won? None!"

Fetting stayed on the putting green answering questions and rolling putts until 1:45 that afternoon. When he was done, he shook hands with every crew member and thanked them for their hard work.

The audio guy was so moved by the gesture that he handed Fetting a slice of Spam.

Chaffin gave the crew a ninety-minute lunch break. Next up at four o'clock: Hard Way's former man.

"We've got some good stuff so far," Chaffin said to Riley. "Keep having fun with these guys. The interaction gives it some personality."

"The next guy is going to be a challenge."

"He's the one who fired the caddie?"

"Fired him and made sure nobody else hired him. And here's a twist: The caddie now works at Whisper Rock."

"Here? You're kidding?"

"It's a job."

"But it isn't the Tour. Is he here today?"

"Don't know."

"Crazy to think they're both at the same club."

If all went as planned, the last segment would take place during parts of the so-called golden hour: just after sunrise, or not long before sunset. Producers and camerapeople treated the golden hour as if it were the Ascension. The light was softer and filled with dramatic oranges and reds. Chaffin and the DP were already talking about the possibilities of watching Hard Way's former man hit drives against the backdrop of the Sonoran Desert during the late-afternoon window.

At 4:20, they were still waiting for him. Chaffin had called his agent asking for an ETA. Riley had checked the clubhouse and locker room. Nothing. The DP was looking at his watch as he calculated the amount of available shooting time before sunset. At 4:33, the player walked onto the range.

"All right, let's get this shit show going," he said without offering an apology for his late arrival. "Who's in charge?" Then he saw Riley off to the side. "Whoa. I thought Lassiter was doing this thing."

"No, it's me," Riley said. "This is our producer, Jan Chaffin." Chaffin stepped forward, hand extended, but the player ignored her.

"Seriously, I'm wasting a half day for Punt, Pass and Kick, and I get the junior varsity squad? I think we're going to pull the plug on this right now."

He called his agent, but it didn't go well. By the player's reaction, the agent had told him there was no backing out. He stuffed the phone back in his pants pocket.

"What's the comp?" he asked Chaffin, not hiding his annoyance.

Riley began to step forward, but Chaffin said soothingly, "I'll handle this."

Chaffin was only five-foot-three, doted on her elderly dad, and volunteered at an animal shelter in her spare time. But when properly motivated, she had the defensive instincts of a mongoose. She turned her full attention on the player.

"I'm sorry, I don't understand," she said, even though she did. "Comp?"

"The comp . . . the honorarium . . . the full scholarship?" the player said. "Think of it as billable hours."

"You want money for this?"

"No, sweetheart, I want a coupon for a free Grand Slam breakfast. Of course I want money! I'm an independent contractor. Don't they pay you for *your* time?"

"They do, but we don't pay for interviews, and your agent knows that. If you don't want to do this, that's fine. I'll just walk over to the golf shop and ask the club pro if he'd like to be part of our Masters coverage package. When Augusta National asks why you were a no-show, I'll tell them you were too busy sticking your hand out."

The player took a step back in mock fear.

"Oh, please, anything but that!" he said, before his tone turned dismissive. "I'm so terrified, I'll give you the main number to the club."

"Nope. I've got it right here. Let me call right now and ask for the Chairman," she said, pulling her phone from her back pocket. "And by the way, I'm not your sweetheart."

The player stared hard at Chaffin. Chaffin didn't blink.

"Aw, shit," the player said, realizing his power play had failed. "I'm here to help the kiddies. I'll give you twenty minutes and not a second longer."

Once the cameras started rolling, Hard Way's former guy turned on the charm. There was a lot of "That's a great question, Joe," and "There's nothing better than supporting these great girls and boys as they compete at the finest golf club in the world. It's the highlight of my week." Wink.

Hard Way's former man was a world-class phony, but he was also a world-class driver. Even during the seasons he had struggled on Tour, his driver was rarely the reason. His technique was textbook: a full, wide arc with a perfect transition from the top of the backswing to the downswing and impact. It wasn't unusual for other Tour players on the range to sneak a peek at his driving skills.

A pyramid of Pro V1s was assembled for him. He used his driver to push half the balls toward Riley, who made like a caddie and tossed a new Titleist to him after every drive. The player would catch it with the palm of his right hand and tee it up almost in one motion. He wasn't the longest driver on Tour, but he could pump it out there at 300-yards-plus with regularity. And his Driving Accuracy Percentage was among the Tour's best. When the rest of his game cooperated—and it had during the latter part of the season—he was a formidable player.

During the session, the DP said they had to stop for a moment to change a malfunctioning battery. The player whistled at Chaffin and tapped his finger on his wrist, as in, *How much time is left?*

"Seven more minutes," she said.

"Clock's running, even if the camera isn't," he said. "Ticktock. Ticktock."

Once the new battery was clicked into place on the back of the primary, Chaffin gave the good-to-go signal. Riley showed the player the last remaining video question from one of the kids.

"My name is Jodie and my swing isn't very pretty, but sometimes I can hit it far for a kid," she said with an adorable smile that was missing a front tooth. "What advice would you give someone like me?"

The player pretended to ponder the question as if he had been asked to interpret the works of Kant.

"Jodie, the best way is to show you," he said, looking into the camera. He waved for Riley to join him. Chaffin nudged Riley into the shot. "A swing doesn't have to be 'pretty' to be effective. I have a mechanically sound swing, but if you want to see the prettiest swing of all time, go google an old-timer named Sam Snead. Jim Furyk looks like he's having a medical emergency in the middle of his swing, but he won $71 million on Tour, won a major, played on Ryder Cup teams, and is going to be in the Hall of Fame one of these days." He handed his driver to Riley. "Joe, you're, what, a 10- or 12-handicap?"

"Uh, closer to 18."

"Ouch! OK, so let's see what I have to work with here."

Riley, who didn't have a glove with him and was wearing a shirt and tie, took a few practice swings. "What do you think?" he said.

"I think you're the first 40-handicap I've ever met. But just for the fun of it, let's try to stretch that chest on your backswing and try to visualize tucking your right elbow into your back pocket on the downswing." He teed up a ball for Riley.

Riley added the two new swing thoughts to his already massive list of dos and don'ts. He stretched. He tucked. He hit the ball about 60 yards, its flight no higher than several feet off the ground.

"That's OK, Joe. I'll tee it a little higher for you. And Jodie, no matter how ugly you think your swing looks, it can't be worse than this."

"Thanks for the vote of confidence," Riley said, hoping his smile hid his embarrassment over the cheap dig.

Riley's next shot sprayed to the far right about 100 yards, again clearing the ground by only a few feet. Without thinking, he kicked at the grass in frustration.

"Jodie, did you see what Joe did there? He threw a little tantrum. He's an adult, so he should know better. Obviously, Joe needs to work on his temper and his game." He took the driver back from Riley and began demonstrating a fix. "In Joe's case, he's bringing the club way inside on the takeaway, his swing is too long, and he doesn't generate any power with his legs or with his shoulder turn. Instead, let's try this."

He did a slow-motion swing, and as he did, he pointed out the proper takeaway, shoulder turn, loading up of the legs, elbow tuck, downswing, and follow-through. Then he teed up a ball and swung at what seemed like half speed. The ball traveled close to 300 yards.

"That was the anti-Joe swing," he said, laughing as he put an arm around Riley. "I hope that helps, Jodie. Thank you, kids. Good luck in the finals!"

"And we're clear," Chaffin said.

The player immediately removed his arm from Riley's shoulder. "What a colossal waste of time," he said as he motioned for a Rock range worker to retrieve his bag and store it.

"Well, the kids will appreciate it," Riley said.

"Fantastic. My life has meaning now."

"And thanks for the mini-lesson. I could barely get the ball airborne."

"You were never going to hit my driver worth a shit."

"I thought I'd do better than that."

"That shaft I play is one of the stiffest on Tour. You don't have the swing speed to even flex it. You might as well have been swinging a steel I beam." He started to walk toward the clubhouse.

"Nice meeting you!" Chaffin yelled sarcastically.

Riley jogged after the player. He had dealt with difficult athletes in the past. An All-Star outfielder, angry about a newspaper story Riley had written, had screamed at him so loud and long during pregame batting practice that the opposing team's players poured from their clubhouse to watch. An NFL running back, displeased with a line of questioning, once spat flecks of a tuna fish sandwich at Riley's face. An NBA power forward had threatened to dump him in a recycling bin. But Riley had never seen behavior like this from a Tour player. He wanted an explanation.

"I'm just curious," Riley said when he caught up. "Why would you do that? Make me look bad just for fun? Disrespect my producer and our crew?"

"Because this was on my dime, not yours," he said, not slowing down. "So if I want to have a laugh at your expense, that's how it goes. You get what you pay for."

Riley stopped. The player walked across one of the practice greens, past the golf shop, and disappeared through the thick wooden double doors of the clubhouse. Riley stood with his hands on his hips.

"How'd it go out there today?" It was the club's general manager. "I was just coming to see you guys."

"We just finished. Thanks for everything."

"Our pleasure. I talked to Lippon and Fetting before they left. They said they had a blast."

"Well, two out of three isn't bad."

"Yeah, the other guy is, well . . . different." The GM specialized in diplomacy. "Your producer told me your crew wouldn't take long to pack up?"

"Yeah, they have it down to a science."

"Where you staying?"

"I'm over at the Boulders. Close by."

"Nice place. By the way, we're closing the range soon, so feel free to hit what's left out there."

"Tempting, but I probably shouldn't."

"If you change your mind, we've got a demo bag next to the pro shop if you need some clubs to hit. Anyway, good meeting you."

"Quick question: Do you know if Max Mitchell is working today?"

"I've been stuck inside most of the day, so I'm not sure," the GM said. "If he is, I'm guessing our caddie master gave him an early group or a late one. We're trying to avoid any drama."

"Drama?"

"We knew his man—you know the story—was doing the shoot with you guys today. So Hard Way either was done by noon or he went out late and is on the back nine somewhere."

"I was there the day it happened."

"Yeah, we were watching in the clubhouse. What a mess. But the members love Max—except one."

When Riley returned to the range, the crew had already broken down all of the equipment and was beginning to load the bags and cases onto the specially designed storage racks and metal slideouts of their Mercedes cargo vans. With the DP's approval (DPs were protective of their gear), Riley helped carry the last of the bags to the customized Sprinters.

"You guys are fast," he said.

"Always easier to pack up than to set up," said the DP.

"Hey, sunshine," Chaffin said. "We're going to head back to the hotel and do all the media management there. It's going to take some time to transfer and organize the files. Want to meet us for a late dinner?"

"Probably will grab something at the hotel, but let me know where you're going and maybe I'll drive over and buy the first round."

After the crew drove off, Riley walked to his rental car, which was one of only a few remaining vehicles in the members' lot. He peered down a cart path located near the far end of the range and saw a half pyramid of balls stacked on the grass. He looked at his watch. There were still ten minutes before closing time.

No harm in going out there and taking a look, Riley said to himself.

Riley unlocked the trunk, pulled off the container's plastic lid, and slid the driver out of the case. A golf glove was secured to the grip with a thick rubber band. He fast-walked to the range and found the most isolated spot.

The slowly setting sun was directly in his sight line. He tried to shield his eyes as he made a sweep of the surroundings. As best as he could determine, there was no one on the opposite side of the back range. He had the place to himself.

Riley stuffed the fat end of his tie between the buttons of his dress shirt, slipped on his golf glove, and took a handful of practice swings. He decided to concentrate on the three earlier tips from the pros: stretch the chest, make a smooth transition from backswing to downswing, tuck the elbow into the back pocket.

He teed up a Pro V1, checked his target line, and swung. He lost the ball in the sun, but he knew he had struck it well. He hit another ball. He saw it leave the club, tracked it for the initial part of its flight, but again failed to see it land. *I should have brought a hat,* he thought. In the distance, he heard the faint sound of someone yelling.

Riley wasn't the only person to hear the yelling. Hard Way was standing on the tee box of the ninth hole on the Lower Course, which was located about 60 yards from the back range. He was a forecaddie for a group that had started on the back nine and was finishing on the front. Through an opening in the trees, Hard Way could see two members huddled behind a cart.

"Hey, you fellas mind if I run over and check on those guys?" Hard Way said.

"Be careful," said a member of the foursome. "There were javelinas over there yesterday. If their babies are with them, those nasty monsters will make a run at you. One of 'em rammed the side of my cart."

"Tell those guys to get the hell out of there," another member said.

"Be right back," Hard Way said.

As he jogged past the second of two practice chipping areas behind the range, Hard Way heard something whoosh over his head and settle into the brush and cactuses behind him. The two members frantically waved him over.

"Get down, for God's sake!" one of the members said, pulling Hard Way's onesie sleeve. "Someone's trying to kill us!"

"It's not javelinas?" Hard Way said.

"I wish!" the other member said. "At least you can hear them bastards coming at you. Someone is shooting at us with some sort of rocket launcher!"

"A rocket launcher?"

"Or mortar. Four or five of the things have sailed over our heads," the first member said. "I thought it was coming from one of the houses a couple of blocks over. Then I saw somebody on the front range, but that's gotta be 350 yards."

"More like 380, 390 where we are," the second member said.

Moments later, another projectile flew overhead. It hit the base of a tree behind them and bounced back toward their cart. Hard Way could see the object. It was a Whisper Rock range ball.

"Fellas, I think I know what's happening," he said. "Some of the shag bag kids are hitting errant balls back into the range from the desert and can't see where they're aiming."

"With what, a bazooka?!" the first member said.

"I saw them out there when our group got to the tee box on 9. They find the range balls in the waste areas."

"Well, those kids are like artillery gunners," the second member said.

"I'll let 'em know," Hard Way said. "Give me a minute and you should be OK. Look at it this way, fellas: You've got a story to tell."

"Some story," the first member said. "I think I wet myself."

Hard Way patted them on the backs and began to run along the cart path between the range and the ninth fairway. He waved to his group, who gave him the thumbs-up as they drove toward the green.

It wasn't long before Hard Way tracked down one of the range workers.

"You guys trying to reduce the membership numbers?" Hard Way said.

"Huh?" said the kid. At about the same time, another of the workers emerged from the desert carrying two full shag bags of balls.

"You guys almost clipped a few of the members on the back range," Hard Way said.

"Wasn't us," the second kid said. "We punched a few out to the middle of the range for the pickers, but that's about it."

"You didn't accidentally hit any toward the back?"

"We've got sand wedges," the second kid said. "Even if we tried, we couldn't reach that."

Hard Way had heard enough. He began sprinting toward the front range and could see a lone figure teeing up a ball. As he ran, one of the members of his foursome yelled for him to come to the green. Hard Way stared at the unknown man—*He's wearing a tie?*—and then glanced back at his foursome. *Damn.* Duty called. He stopped and ran back toward the foursome.

Riley's room service dinner had arrived blazingly fast, only twenty-five minutes after he walked into his junior suite. He turned on the TV—the Thursday-night game between TCU and Texas Tech was deep in the second quarter—and pulled the room service cart close to where he was sitting at the edge of the king-sized bed. He took the metal cover off his salad and was in mid-bite when there was a knock on the door. Riley noticed that they had forgotten to put a glass of iced tea on the tray. The server must have noticed too.

Riley took a $5 bill from his wallet, opened the door, and before he looked up, said, "Thanks for circling back with the tea. Here you go."

"Thank you," Hard Way said, tugging the fiver from Riley's hand and stuffing it into his pocket.

Riley stepped back in surprise. Against the outline of the hotel room doorframe, the six-foot-four Hard Way was a semi-imposing figure, especially in a Whisper Rock onesie.

"I thought you were room service."

"No, still a caddie."

Riley stepped to the side and waved Hard Way in. "I'm eating dinner."

"That looks better than what I'm having. Impressive room."

"I can order you something."

"No, I have a dinner date with a cocker spaniel named Oscar. Our GM said you were asking about me. Said you were staying here."

"How'd you get my room number? They're not supposed to give that out."

"I have friends in the house. And how'd you know I was working at the Rock?"

"I have friends, too."

"You can't report that. Check that," he said, his voice more conciliatory. "I'd appreciate it if you wouldn't report that."

"Your man—"

"My former man," Hard Way corrected him.

"Your *former* man did a thing with us today for a Masters show that'll air during the Drive, Chip and Putt."

"I'll say this much about him: He's great with a driver in his hands. Some of the other clubs, not so much. And he can be convincing in front of a camera."

"He faked it."

"It's a specialty of his. Anyway, what does any of this have to do with me?"

Riley wasn't sure how to answer the question.

"Nothing. I just wanted to say hello."

But that was only half the truth. There was a part of Riley—the AGN reporter part—that had ulterior motives. He did want to say hello. But he also hoped that Hard Way might consider doing a story with him about his life post-firing.

"That's it? Just hello? You sure there's nothing else you wanted to discuss?"

Riley felt exposed. The caddie could read putts *and* people.

"No, that was it," Riley said unconvincingly.

"Well, hello and goodbye." Hard Way headed for the door.

"Wait. I'm playing TPC tomorrow, if you want to join me. Got a 10 A.M. tee time."

"You lugged your clubs out here?"

Riley hesitated. "Not really. Going to rent some. Brought my shoes and a few sleeves of balls."

"Thanks for the offer. I'm off tomorrow, so I'm going to take it easy."

"If you decide otherwise . . ."

"I won't, but thanks."

The door shut, and Riley returned to his meal. Five minutes later, there was another knock. Riley looked through the peephole. It was Hard Way again.

"Forgot to ask you something," Hard Way said. "Didn't you once tell me that you caddied at Chicago Golf?"

"When I was in high school and college. You've got a good memory.

I told you that a couple of years ago in the players' parking lot at . . . the John Deere, wasn't it?"

"That sounds right. And I told you I was there for a couple of summers after you."

"I remember now."

"So you know golf history?"

"I suppose so," Riley said, an uneasiness beginning to form.

"Then you probably know the club motto at Chicago Golf." Hard Way stepped toward him. "I'll even give you a hint: It's a ten-letter golf saying that dates back to 1681."

Riley froze. But his silence said everything.

"You got sloppy today. You couldn't see us, but I could see you. Or the outline of you. That was you today on the range at the Rock, right? And that was you on my range back home, too."

More silence.

"You know what," Hard Way said as he began to leave, "I think I *will* join you tomorrow. You're going to show me how that homemade swing of yours hits a ball that damn far and sure. By the way, nice tie."

Hard Way disappeared down the hallway. Riley closed the door and stared at the stuffed chile. He had lost his appetite.

CHAPTER FIFTEEN

Moving Day

There were ninety-four names in all. Spread across the nearly eleven hundred employees of AGN, the list amounted to about 8.5 percent of the network's workforce. The layoffs during Phases Two and Three would be fewer, but that would mean little to those whose jobs would disappear with a phone call from HR. What was the term they used? *Separation.* The company wasn't firing you; you were simply drifting away.

AGN was owned by Seneca Media, which was owned by shareholders, which was owned by the bottom line. AGN made money, lots of it, but not enough for the liking of Wall Street and Seneca's CEO and corporate board. There had been cord-cutting, but AGN's direct-to-consumer option had eased that financial pain. But the decree had been issued, Caesar-like, and all citizens of corporate Seneca had to obey. In this case, those citizens resided at AGN.

Stanley Pierre, the programming and efficiency expert, lived for such layoffs. The more carnage, the better. He liked to tell his subordinates that it was his job to "create churn, execute action items, and amplify those who provide a bleeding edge." Nobody knew what he meant. But in his spiral notepad were his observations. Those observations coagulated into some form of fact—Pierre's version of fact.

Of the ninety-four names on the layoff list, Pierre had been responsible for twenty-seven of them. He had argued during a "thought shower" with department heads that some of the positions were redundant and, thus, expendable. After all, how many graphics producers, mobile unit engineers, news editors, remote operators, researchers, directors, stage managers, production managers, assignment desk staff members, and makeup artists did you really need?

As for on-air talent, Pierre targeted those whose presence lacked what he called "pop." He couldn't quantify it, he said, as much as he could feel it. The needle—there was that word again—simply didn't move when they appeared on camera. Only a "blue-sky thinker" (another favorite Pierre corporate-speak phrase) like him could see it. It was his gift.

Pierre had reviewed a handful of recent tournament broadcasts and identified several on-air candidates for firing and/or nonrenewal. Their work was solid, informative, occasionally entertaining. But when in doubt, Pierre resorted to his standard two questions: Did anyone turn on their TV or streaming device to specifically watch that person? And all things being equal, could AGN survive without their services? According to Pierre, the answers were a resounding, cost-saving no and yes.

McMullins disagreed with the assessments and said so loudly, forcefully, and repeatedly in the meetings. A live sports broadcast was a Jenga game of pieces, he argued. Remove too many blocks—even small-to-medium-sized pieces—and the broadcast soon loses its stability and watchability. Worker bees added to the structure and success of the golf coverage, McMullins said. It needed them, even if AGN, Pierre, and the viewers didn't realize it.

Pierre listened with feigned interest, even pretending to jot some of McMullins's arguments in his notebook. He let McMullins bark himself out, but the decisions had been made. The company would wait until a soon-to-be-determined Friday—"Take Out the Garbage Day"—to inform the unfortunate ninety-four. In fact, the obligatory somber press release had already been crafted. There would be a brief mourning period for the deceased, and everyone else would report to work on Monday.

Joseph James Riley would not be one of the returnees. He was No. 92 on the list.

CHAPTER SIXTEEN

Proof

Hard Way found the TPC club pro sipping a cup of coffee in his small office down the hall from the golf shop. On the wall behind his desk were framed photos of him and his Florida Southern teammates with the NCAA Division II championship trophy.

"That was a helluva team you played on," Hard Way said as he walked in. "Mind if I photoshop myself into that group?"

"Ancient history," said the club pro, who shook hands and waved for Hard Way to take a seat.

Hard Way had known him for a half dozen years. He was a good guy—and a good player—who had made a run at the Tour when he was younger. Had a half dozen putts dropped here or there during Q School, the club pro might have been a Tour pro. But there were a thousand of those stories. It had always been a game of almosts.

"You on the tee sheet today?" the club pro said.

"Late addition. Playing with Joe Riley from AGN."

"Slumming with the media? Couldn't find a game at the Rock?"

"Mercy mission. He was there yesterday filming something. He asked me to take a look at his swing. We're from the same hometown."

"Someplace in Illinois?"

"Wheaton."

"What time you playing?"

"He said he booked something for ten."

The club pro picked up the phone and called the golf shop desk. "Jimmy, make sure to comp Riley and Hard Way at ten," he said of the $550-apiece green fees. He covered the phone's microphone with his palm. "Need anything else?"

"Was hoping we could go out as a twosome. And I know he needs rentals."

"Jimmy, throw a set of those new Ping sticks on the back of Riley's cart. Comp those, too. And squeeze them in as a twosome. We can juggle some of the times a bit."

The club pro walked from behind the desk and put his hand on Hard Way's shoulder. "You've got a lot of friends in the business. Hang in there. You'll be back."

"Thanks for taking care of us. Dinner and beers on me at Lamp."

"I can't turn down free pizza. I'll text you later this week. Have fun out there today."

TPC looked completely different without its tournament makeup on. No country bands playing across the street. No blimp overhead. No TV towers. No coliseum spectator stands on the par-3 16th. No Bourbon Street booze garden near the practice range. No overserved guys passed out on a hill overlooking the 18th green. No women spilling out of whatever tiny swatch of clothing they were wearing. This was the church-picnic side of TPC: wholesome, civilized, the antithesis of debauchery. Hard Way had never seen it like this.

Riley showed up fifteen minutes later and was driven out to the range, where a cart, clubs, and Hard Way were waiting for him. He had brought with him the plastic case holding his persimmon driver.

"What's that, the Mayall Telescope?" Hard Way said.

"It's my driver."

"In that goofy case?"

"It's all I could find to bring it on the plane."

"Is that what you were hitting yesterday?"

Riley nodded.

"And at Wheaton, too?"

Riley nodded again.

"So when you hit whatever's in there . . ." Hard Way said, pointing at the tube.

"It goes really far," Riley said. "You want to see it?"

Hard Way looked up and down the TPC range. There were a half dozen other players warming up. "No. Keep it in there until we're out on the course. We're not looking to attract any attention today. We don't need spectators."

Riley stuffed the case in between the two bags on the back of the cart and then grabbed a handful of rental clubs for a quick warm-up session. Hard Way stood behind him as Riley took several practice swings. He had an amateur's swing—mechanical, deeply flawed, inconsistent. On occasion, Riley would find the center of the face, but the rest were hit near the toe.

"You're not saying anything," Riley said. "Is it that bad?"

"It's not good."

"That helps my self-esteem."

"Tough. Your swing is longer than a city block. You take it way inside. And your grip is too weak. But I'm not a teaching pro."

"Can you help me?"

"I can help you find someone who can help you. But right now I'm trying to figure out how that swing flew a ball over the range yesterday."

"It's not the swing, Max. It's the club."

"You keep saying that. We'll see."

The Stadium Course, designed by Tom Weiskopf and Jay Morrish, was no easy track, especially when the winds kicked up. It was breezy, but Hard Way had seen worse. For the first seven holes, they played from the friendlier Resort tee boxes, which were more than six shots easier than from the tips. Riley, using only the rental clubs, was 6-over and that's only because he chipped in for bogey at the par-5 third and dropped a blind-squirrel-finds-an-acorn 40-footer for par on the par-3 seventh. Meanwhile, Hard Way was at even-par.

Hard Way stopped the cart at the back end of the par-4 eighth-hole tee boxes. He looked to see if any other groups were within viewing distance. It was clear.

"Bring two balls, the Ping driver, and the telescope," he said to Riley.

Riley grabbed a couple of ProV1s, the G430 from the bag, and the long container from the back of the cart and followed Hard Way as he walked past the Championship tees.

"Where we going, Mesa?" Riley said.

"This is where we teed off during the second round this past February," Hard Way said. "Seems like a thousand years ago."

"And from back here, the hole seems like a thousand yards long," Riley said.

"It's 491. Plus, I didn't want you to hit it until we put some space between us and any other groups out here."

Riley removed the driver from the container and took off the sock that protected the wooden head. Hard Way laughed.

"*That's* the club?" he said.

"That's one of them," Riley said defensively. "The rest are back in my basement."

"What does it want to be when it grows up?"

Riley made a face.

"I'm sorry, did I hurt its feelings?" Hard Way said. "There is no way that piece of . . . *kindling* is responsible for what I saw yesterday."

"It is," Riley said.

Hard Way raised his voice and did his best to imitate the late, great Ivor Robson, who was the official starter at the Open Championship for forty-one years. "This is Game No. 1," he said. "On the tee from the USA, Joe Riley." He extended his arm and swept it dramatically and mockingly toward the tee box.

Riley hit the rental Ping first. It was his best drive of the front nine, a slight draw that covered 210 yards and rolled out to about 230. Riley looked back at Hard Way for approval. Hard Way bobbed his head.

Riley teed up the second ball, took a practice swing—the MacGregor clubhead looked ridiculously small compared to the Ping's—and then found the same target line as before. The breeze freshened, blowing gently toward him.

When club connected with ball, Hard Way flinched involuntarily. There was a crackling, thunderous sound to it. Moments earlier, the ball had laid inert in the palm of a tee. And then in a matter of seconds, it was transported 400 yards away.

Riley began to say something, but Hard Way put his forefinger to his lips. He took the MacGregor from Riley and tossed his own driver off to the side. The clubhead was half the size of the carbon Callaway driver that he used, but the persimmon felt heavier. The shaft was at least an inch or two shorter than the Callaway's.

He swung the club several times before teeing up a ball.

"Max, I don't think it's going to work for—" But before Riley could finish the sentence, Hard Way brought his finger to his lips again.

Had there been a slow-motion camera to record the moment of impact, it would have shown that Hard Way literally hit the ball between the screws of the wooden clubface. It was the absolute sweet spot of the club. His follow-through was as good as that of any Tour pro.

The drive traveled 254 yards.

Hard Way handed the club back to Riley, collected his Callaway, walked to the cart, and sat silently behind the steering wheel. He was trying to comprehend the impossible. Even after Riley sat down next to him, he stared straight ahead, almost in a trance.

"Max? You all right?"

"No, I don't think I am," he said, finally breaking the silence. "I don't know how you did that. I don't know how anybody could do that. I saw it, and I still don't believe it. I didn't believe it when I was in the picker at my range. I didn't want to believe it when I saw it at the Rock range. And I can't believe it now."

"It takes some getting used to," Riley said.

Hard Way took the persimmon driver from Riley and examined the clubhead.

"You flew the practice range with—what is that, a driver you stole from Gene Sarazen's attic?"

"It's a MacGregor, and I'm pretty sure it was made for Jack Nicklaus."

"I don't care if it was made for Thor. He couldn't hit a persimmon driver that far."

"You have to quit thinking logically. This isn't an ordinary driver. I'm not an ordinary player with it in my hand. Something happens. It's . . ."

"Magical?"

"Something like that. I tried to tell you on the tee box. The clubs don't seem to work for others."

Hard Way punched at the accelerator and drove down the cart path on the left side of the fairway.

"What about my first ball?" Riley said. "It's right out of the sleeve."

"Leave it."

Hard Way pulled up to the right of the second drive. He aimed his range finder at the pin, saw the number, and aimed it again, not sure if the device was functioning correctly. To be sure, he found a nearby yardage plate and walked it off to the ball. "You've got 80 to the front, 89 to the pin," he said. "You just hit a 402-yard drive. You outdrove me by almost 150 yards. I need a drink."

"I actually liked the other drive," Riley said. "Better angle into the green, don't you think?"

"Are you out of your—" Hard Way said before noticing Riley's smile.

Riley landed a sand wedge at the front edge and two-putted for par. Using the MacGregor on seven of the remaining ten holes, Riley parred seven of them, bogeyed two, and birdied one. Hard Way found himself forgetting his own game and instead falling naturally into caddie mode.

When they were done, Hard Way took off his ball cap, shook Riley's hand, and said, "I never thought I'd see anything better on a golf course than Tiger in his prime. But this gave him a run for the money."

"Nothing beats Tiger in his prime. I had a lucky day."

"I'm not so sure about that. I'm not so sure about anything."

They drove back to the clubhouse, and Hard Way walked Riley to his rental car.

"You'll be in Wheaton for a while?" Hard Way said.

"Until I get my next assignment. But it should be quiet for a couple of weeks."

"Don't tell anyone about today."

"I finally break 80 and I can't say anything? Why?"

"Because I have an idea. I'll be in touch."

Before getting in the car, Riley pulled his scorecard from his back pocket.

"Will you sign it?" he said. "Or else nobody is going to believe what I shot."

Hard Way used the stubby scoring pencil to scribble his name on the bottom right corner of the scorecard. Then he paused, took a scorecard from his own back pocket, wrote in Riley's hole-by-hole numbers, and handed both to the sports reporter.

"Two?" said a confused Riley.

"One for you, but now sign one for me. Because I don't believe what you shot either."

CHAPTER SEVENTEEN

So Long, Farewell

Riley was sitting at his desk in his attic office when his cell phone rang late Friday afternoon. He instantly recognized the area code—704, AGN headquarters in Charlotte—but not the extension.

"Hello?"

"I'm calling for Joseph Riley," the AGN HR rep said, her voice sterile and hurried.

"I'm Joe Riley."

The woman identified herself and then delivered machine-gun bursts of HR-approved language: "We've made the difficult decision . . . Your separation is effective immediately . . . You'll receive instructions on how to return your laptop . . ."

A stunned Riley asked through the haze why his contract wasn't being renewed. The HR rep would only say that the decision hadn't been made "lightly." What about all the assignments he had volunteered for during his time at AGN? Perhaps there was still time to prove his value? "That won't be necessary," he was told. What if AGN spoke to his agent about signing a new deal at a reduced salary? "I'm afraid that isn't an option. We wish you the best and thank you for your years of service. Should you need transition assistance, please don't hesitate to call. Thank you."

There was a harsh click, and she was gone, no doubt moving on to the next name on her list. In three minutes' time, his career had ended. It was like being pushed out of a plane with an anvil strapped to your back.

Chet, who had just gotten home from school with Laurel, walked into Riley's office. Riley surprised his son with a long hug. Chet squirmed away.

"Dad, you're messing up my hair product."

As Chet dashed out of the room, Laurel walked in and plopped herself on the wingback chair next to Riley's desk.

"The school year is three months old, and I already want an IV hookup to a box of wine."

"Sweetie, I need to talk to you about something."

"My turn first. Did I tell you the fifth graders are trying to organize a boycott of the cafeteria? They're demanding Uber Eats. You can't make this stuff up."

"It's kind of important."

"Is it as important as your younger son raising his hand in Mr. Pecora's class today and announcing that he needed the bathroom key to 'take a big, squishy dump?' "

"I just got a call from AGN."

"Oh, c'mon. You just got home from Arizona. They're not sending you out again. It's the holidays. This is your offseason."

"No, they're definitely not sending me out again."

"I likey this kind of AGN call," she said playfully. "Does this mean you can finally clean the crawl space?"

"I got fired."

Laurel shot up in the chair. "What?!"

"Not fired, I guess. But not renewed. Well, yeah, fired. I'm done."

"Fired? How can they do this? *Why* did they do this? Can't your agent do something?" The sentences ran together as her voice and emotions rose.

"There was no warning. My agent was blindsided."

She got out of the chair and hugged Riley. There were tears in her eyes. "I'm so sorry. Are you OK?"

"I feel anesthetized."

"Who called you?"

"Some AGN droid."

"Not McMullins?"

"He called later. Said he wanted to be on the call, but HR wouldn't allow it. He said the cuts were across the board: studio production, live event, technical support, administrative, managers, on-air . . . it was a bloodbath. Almost a hundred people got the call."

"Severance pay?"

"Not a dime. I'm off the books in less than a week."

"Joe, then we're in serious trouble."

Riley had been one of the lowest-paid on-air talents at AGN. Still, his salary covered the mortgage, the second mortgage (for a long-ago addition on the small house), credit card charges, assorted other monthly bills, the beginnings of a college fund for Chet, health care, a small 401(k) commitment, and a summer vacation every other year. Laurel's teaching salary was devoted entirely to Buddy's out-of-state tuition and expenses at Wisconsin, which were creeping toward $70,000 per year. A third loan filled the gap between Laurel's salary and Buddy's college costs. There was a small emergency savings account, but it totaled barely $4,000.

"We might have to pull Buddy from Madison," said Laurel, who oversaw the family's finances. "I don't know how we're going to pay for his spring semester, much less his senior year."

"Can't we dip into our 401(k)? Or maybe he takes out student loans."

"We'd get penalized on the withdrawals and wipe out our retirement fund. And do you want Buddy to owe $100,000 in loans, plus interest?"

"If we take him out of school, he'll never forgive me," Riley said. "He'll blame me forever. He loves that place."

"It would be temporary, until we can figure something out. But, Joe, if we don't take him out, we might have to sell the house."

They sat in silence, each trying to invent solutions that didn't yet exist.

"Do people know?" Laurel said.

"The media beat reporters will get most of the details," Riley said. "They always do. It'll be online soon enough."

"Another network will hire you," Laurel said. "You're too good to go unemployed."

Riley appreciated her optimism, but he knew better. As devastated as he was by the call, he had seen good reporters at other networks, newspapers, and digital sites all deemed expendable by their corporate ownership. There were no guarantees about the future, especially in the field of journalism, which was under siege by forces inside and outside the profession.

"What about your agent?" Laurel said.

"He didn't sound optimistic. But I still have some friends in the business."

"And if they can't help?"

"I don't know."

"We need to tell the boys."

"I'll call Buddy right now."

"What about the little dude?"

"We'll tell him after I talk to Buddy. But we're not saying anything about Wisconsin until we absolutely have to."

"Then what?"

"Then I'm taking you and Chet out for pizza at Barone's. And we'll worry about tomorrow tomorrow."

CHAPTER EIGHTEEN

Green Eggs and Ham

The texts, voicemails, and emails came in a steady stream over the weekend. Almost all of them had a funereal quality, as if they should have been accompanied by an arrangement of lilies and chrysanthemums. The sentiments were well-meaning and sincere, but they were also a reminder of a certain type of failure. There was talk of some sort of farewell party for the dearly departed, but the logistics became too complicated, and the idea was quickly abandoned.

Maury Walsh had left a message. It didn't waste time with hushed tones and profound sadness.

"Heard you got whacked," the voicemail began. "If Steve Jobs, Bill Belichick, and Oprah can get fired during their careers, then so can you. Nobody died, so you'll be fine. Call me—I'll help you any way I can."

Riley saved that one.

Hard Way waited until Monday to reach out.

"Welcome to the Unemployment Club," Hard Way said. "Saw it in Marchand's column. I wanted to give you some space. How are you enjoying your life of quiet desperation?"

"I never saw it coming."

"You never do, pal."

"Nobody hires anybody in December, so I'm scrambling. I've got one more paycheck coming and then Laurel and I have some tough decisions to make."

"That's why I'm calling. I can offer you a job right now."

"Whisper Rock caddie? I don't look good in jumpsuits."

"I told you I had an idea. How about if I'm the caddie and you're the player?"

"You lost me."

"I want to caddie for you on Tour. I think you can win. I think you can win big."

"The Tour? The *PGA* Tour?" Riley began to laugh. "The one with Rory, Scottie, Collin, Xander, Ludvig? That Tour?"

"Hear me out."

"Wait. You're serious about this? I thought you were just trying to make me feel better after AGN fired me."

"I'm doing both. You getting canned actually makes my plan easier."

"Max, there's only one plan: I have to get a job. A real job."

"It doesn't get more real than the Tour. If I didn't think you could do it, I never would have called. I've seen you play."

"You've seen me play one round with just one of the Nicklaus clubs."

"That's my point. Just think what you could do with the rest of them."

"C'mon, Max. I'm nothing without those clubs. I know how to cover the game but not how to *play* it. It's the difference between singing in the shower and singing at Carnegie Hall."

"Whattya have to lose by trying?" Hard Way said. "You're walking away before you belt out a note."

"I'm walking away before this goes too far. I just lost my job. I need a new one fast. I have a family to support."

Hard Way couldn't argue with the logic, but that didn't stop him from trying.

"Talked to Sarge this morning," he said. "He's totally in. He'll make time for us next week."

"You mean Leeds Sargent Jr.? You talked to him about me?"

"I did. He can't wait to meet you."

"For what?"

"For dialing in your distances. For chipping. Pitching. Putting. For waxing and buffing that swing of yours."

"He charges, what, a couple grand per lesson? That's a mortgage payment for us."

"He said he'll give you a pass until we cash our first tournament check."

"Cash a check? Don't we have to get in a tournament first?"

"I've seen how far you send it. This could work, Joe."

"No, it can't. Name me all the World Long Drive champions who have won on the PGA Tour. The answer is one: Lon Hinkle in 1981. That's it. Some of those guys are plus-2, plus-3, plus-4 players—and they still can't get their card. A few years ago, someone crunched the numbers for Tour players: The *average* handicap index was plus-5.4, and for the top players it was 6.0 and higher. Tiger's best index was 8.3!"

"Respectfully, those Long Drive champs don't have me on their bag, and they don't have Sarge on the range."

"They're actual players. I'm not. I'm an out-of-work sports reporter who has clubs that were made for the greatest champion of all time. Hitting the ball far isn't enough."

"What if I told you that by the end of January, you'll be good enough to play in a Tour event."

"I'd tell you to get a CT scan."

"I'm being serious."

"Me too."

"Give Sarge and me two months. If we can't turn you into a real player, we'll be the first to tell you."

"What do I tell Laurel?"

"Tell her the truth. Tell her that your clubs are the golf equivalent of Wonderboy. Tell her that the only string that runs through this entire fantastical story is the power of fate and family. You told me the story yourself: Your wife wanted to go to garage sales that day . . . your son found the clubs . . . the old man wanted you to have them. Don't you see? None of this is a coincidence."

"Even if she buys any of that—and she won't—I can't be gone for two months. I'm not single like you. I can't leave my family so I can learn how to hit a knockdown wedge."

"Sarge has an endorsement deal with one of the private jet companies. He says he has flight hours up the wazoo. We'll get you from O'Hare or DuPage to Scottsdale and Vegas for the sessions. You can stay with me and Bang Bang for free. And I have a buddy in Wheaton who just bought a $50,000 simulator. It has 250 courses in its library, and 50 of them are Tour venues. We can use that when you're back home."

"I don't know, man . . ." Riley's voice trailed off.

"You've got nothing to lose, Joe. All I'm asking is that you come to Sarge's place in Vegas for a meeting. I'll even pay for the plane ticket. If it doesn't feel right, walk away. But try to remember what it felt like that day when you added up your score at TPC."

"That was before I lost my job."

"You'll talk to Laurel? You'll do that much for me?"

Riley sighed. "I'll talk to her." But he had already made up his mind.

Hard Way ended the call with a tap of the forefinger. In his lap was Oskie, curled up in blissful sleep. Bang Bang sat nearby.

"Well?" Bang Bang said.

"I figure 10 to 90 odds he says yes, maybe 20 to 80 if he's been drinking."

"But he didn't say no."

"He's going to talk to his wife. That'll be interesting."

"Hey, you did what you could. By the way, free private jet? How'd you swing that with Sarge? He'd rather lose a testicle than give up flight time."

"I lied. There are no jet hours. There is no simulator. I'm not even sure there's a Sarge."

"Whoa."

"I took a calculated risk. If he doesn't say yes, then the lies don't matter."

"Magic golf clubs?" Laurel said incredulously, unsure if her husband was completely well.

"Pretty much," Riley said.

"The ones Buddy got in a garage sale? You're telling me they do magic things?"

"Yes."

"And only *you* can hit them far?"

"Really far. Like farther than anyone on the PGA Tour, by a lot."

"You've been under a lot of stress, hon. Maybe you should talk to someone?"

"Sweetie, I'm not crazy. The clubs were made for Jack Nicklaus. And I hit them like Jack Nicklaus, even better."

"You've had these clubs for months. Why didn't you tell me about them back then? Why didn't Buddy?"

"At first, we didn't know what they could do. And when I did know, I didn't believe it."

"Maybe *I* need to talk to someone," Laurel said. "And now you want to play on the Tour? Good God, Joe, you can't beat Chet."

"She's right, Dad!" Chet yelled from the living room. He had been listening to the entire conversation.

"Go upstairs, Chet!" Riley and Laurel shouted in unison.

There was a pause, until Riley said, "I already told Hard Way I was having serious doubts."

"I can't imagine why. And who are Hard Way, Sarge, and Bang Bang? What kind of names are those?"

"You know about Hard Way. He's a former Tour caddie working in Scottsdale at a private club. He would be on my bag. Sarge is one of the best golf instructors in the world. Hard Way has arranged a meeting with him in Vegas. And Bang Bang is a Tour caddie for a pretty successful player. Hard Way is living with him."

"Why do they call him Bang Bang?"

"Let's just say he's popular with the women."

"What?"

"He has a reputation for, well . . ."

"Bang banging women?" Laurel said. "That's disgusting. It's prehistoric."

"He's actually a good guy."

"He is? Great. Then why don't we invite him to the house and he and the boys can go pick up women in the produce section of the Jewels. He can teach them about the benefits of casual sex, toxic masculinity, and the minimization of women."

"Can I go with them?"

Laurel punched her husband on the arm.

"Seriously, I'm hurt that you and Buddy didn't tell me about any of this."

"And if we had, what would you have said?"

"That I think this idea of magic clubs is straight out of J. K. Rowling. And the only thing crazier than magic clubs is you trying to play professional golf."

Her arguments made sense. It *was* ridiculous. Riley reached for his cell phone on the counter. "I'm going to call Hard Way now and tell him I'm out. You're right: We can't afford this."

"You didn't let me finish," Laurel said. "When I was teaching first graders, there was a passage in a Dr. Seuss book that I always read to them:

How did it get so late so soon?
It's night before it's afternoon.
December is here before it's June.
My goodness how the time has flewn.
How did it get so late so soon?"

She took Riley's hand. "I love you. You've worked so hard your entire adult life. You've helped raise two extraordinary boys. I don't fully understand any of this, but it doesn't matter what I think."

"What about Buddy and Wisconsin? The bills? Our house?"

"Classes don't start until mid-January, so that buys us a little time.

We can scrape by until then. But the question isn't 'Should you do this?' The question is 'What if you don't?' What if you wake up one day and wonder how it got so late so soon?"

Hard Way answered the phone on the second ring.

It was Riley. "I'll come out for the meeting. That's all I can promise."

"That's all I can ask," Hard Way said as he pumped his fist in the air. Oskie, roused from sleep, barked out of habit. "I thought we'd lost you."

"You still might."

"I'll drive to Vegas and pick you up at the airport tomorrow night. I have the next few days off."

"Funny, so do I."

"An unemployment joke," Hard Way said. "I like it."

CHAPTER NINETEEN

Bright Light City

By eight-thirty the next night, Hard Way and Riley were sitting in a booth—Frank Sinatra's booth—at the Golden Steer steakhouse. The iconic Vegas restaurant was located in a nondescript cluster of stores off Sahara Avenue just north of the Strip. The two men had come directly from the airport, their luggage and Riley's golf bag locked in the cab of the Big Ass, its security alarm at full alert.

"You look nervous," Riley said to Hard Way, who kept glancing at the entrance from their seats in the main dining room.

"No, not really," Hard Way said unconvincingly, "but it might be a good idea to let me do the talking at the start."

"You know him better than I do. I'm a little nervous, too."

"We're not signing papers or anything," Hard Way said. "We're just going to talk."

"What'd you tell him about me, about our round together?"

"I didn't get into a lot of details over the phone. Better to do that in person."

The Golden Steer was the oldest steakhouse in a town that had seen them come and go since the restaurant had opened in 1958. The Rat Pack had dined here. Elvis, too. So had Nat King Cole, Joe DiMaggio, Natalie Wood, and assorted wiseguys. Some of the waiters had been there for four decades. It wasn't known for its cutting-edge decor or avant-garde interpretation of red meat. It was a place for Caesar salads prepared tableside, bowls of whipped potatoes and side dishes of bubbling mac and cheese, and, of course, USDA Prime steaks. For dessert, you got the angioplasty. The Golden Steer's charm was its indifference to culinary trends and cholesterol levels. It didn't mind having a history. It was so out, it was in.

Riley and Hard Way each ordered beers from the tuxedo-clad server. As the drinks arrived, so did the legendary golf instructor Leeds Sargent Jr., who was old enough to have shaken Sinatra's hand and good enough to have been courted by the best players in the world. "Sarge," as he was known by his friends, could be gruff, searingly honest, and demanding. He was in his mid-seventies and had the build of a former Marines DI. He was thick, but not fat. He looked like the kind of man you'd want on your side during a bar fight. He didn't suffer fools, nor did he believe in stroking the egos of players. He coached hard and expected his clients to work hard. Otherwise, what was the point?

For those amateurs with disposable incomes, second wives, and fourth homes, an hour-long lesson cost $2,000—and that's if there was space available. Sarge was picky, and the prospective client list was long. Riley had introduced himself to Sargent at Royal Birkdale a half dozen years earlier. There was a brief grunt, a handshake that made Riley wince, and no attempt at small talk. Sargent did everything with a purpose.

"Am I late?" he said as he approached the table with a warm smile for Hard Way, followed by a look of confusion when he saw Riley. "*This* is the guy?"

"This is him, Sarge," Hard Way said.

Riley and Hard Way moved over in unison to make room for Sargent in the tufted, red-cushioned booth. Almost instantaneously, the waiter appeared with a bottle of wine.

"Mr. Sargent, so nice to see you again. Please accept this 2018 Darius II Cabernet with our compliments," he said as he expertly removed the cork, placed it on the table, and poured a healthy splash of the Cab Sav for Sargent's consideration.

"Thank you, Marcus. You're very kind."

He gave it a quick, practiced swirl in the wide-bowled glass, took a deep sniff to make sure the wine wasn't corked, and then declared it more than suitable for the table. The waiter tried not to show it, but a small wave of relief washed across his face. Sargent, who was an expert on California Cabernets (his extensive wine cellar at home also included a collection of his cherished French favorites, Château Margaux and Petrus), could have gotten a second job as a sommelier in one of Vegas's finest restaurants, such was the extent of his knowledge.

Marcus poured wine into the three glasses and then disappeared as quickly as he had arrived. Sargent was famous for his generous tips, his constant business, and his insistence that his corporate clients, with their deep expense accounts, dine at the Golden Steer while in town.

Sargent raised his glass. "To old friends . . . and new ones," he said, looking half suspiciously at Riley. There was a pause as they sipped at the wine. "Now then," Sargent said, "what's this shit about hitting it 400 yards?"

"You're on," Hard Way said, turning to Riley.

Riley was caught off guard. "I thought you wanted to start us off?" he said to Hard Way.

An impatient Sargent pointed at Riley. "You. Speak. Now."

"We met at—" Riley began. Sargent cut him off.

"I know where we met," he said curtly. "I know who you are. You mostly get it right on TV. What I don't know is why I'm here, and how, according to Hard Way, you can send it longer than the best players on the planet."

"I thought Max had already explained," Riley said, confused.

"Just tell the story, Joe," Hard Way said quickly.

Riley nervously explained how his older son had found clubs at a garage sale, how the owner of the clubs had said they had special qualities, how they'd been made specifically for Nicklaus decades earlier and had never been used, and how the old man had said he wanted Riley to have them. He told Sargent of his own skepticism, and how those doubts had disappeared after he'd hit the clubs for the first time.

He told him of the visit to the old man's house, of the old man's final video referencing the "powers" of the clubs.

"I brought them with me," Riley said. "They're in Max's truck. Do you want to see the driver?"

"No," said Sargent sharply, already regretting his decision to take the dinner meeting. "This is a restaurant, not a golf shop."

Riley shrank back in his seat after the scolding.

Sargent sighed. "My closest friends say I can be unmannerly at times," he said, his tone slightly less brusque. "It isn't my finest quality. Why don't you tell me about the specs of the clubs."

Hard Way had predicted the question on the ride to the restaurant. Riley was prepared.

"Tommy Armour 945W driver," Riley said as he read from his notes. "Lamkin leather grips, paper underlisting, $^{1}/_{64}$th of an inch over standard size, $^{3}/_{8}$-ounce wooden dowel with lead in it and positioned at end of grip."

"Length?"

"It's 43$^{1}/_{2}$ inches long, 9$^{1}/_{2}$ degrees loft."

"The irons?"

"MacGregor Limited Editions, Pro-81 template, Dynamic Gold X100 shafts with 5-inch tapered wooden dowels, flat sole, standard toe on grinds, straight leading edge with only a slight heel-to-toe radius."

Sargent took a deep breath and then exhaled. He swirled the remaining wine in his glass and finished it off. "Was there a putter in the bag?"

"A White Fang replica. Basically worthless."

Sargent motioned for Marcus. "I'm going to need something stronger than the Cab. Bring me a Pappy 15," he said, referring to the fifteen-year-old Pappy Van Winkle. "And let's go ahead and order while you're here."

"Yes, sir—the usual for you: rib eye, medium rare?" Marcus said.

Sargent nodded. "Bring three appetizers, too, your choice, for the table."

Hard Way chose the porterhouse, medium. Meanwhile, Riley ran his finger slowly down the menu. Sargent tapped his fingers on the table.

"Found it!" Riley said with an air of satisfaction. "I'll have the eggplant parmigiana." He looked up to see Sargent glaring at him in disgust.

"What'd I do?" Riley said.

"For chrissakes, this isn't Olive Garden," Sargent said. "You don't order eggplant at a steakhouse. That's like ordering cock at a whorehouse."

"But I like eggplant."

Sargent ignored him and turned to the waiter. "Eighty-six the vegetable garden. He'll have the New York cut, medium." There was no more discussion about meal choices.

The glass of famed Kentucky straight bourbon whiskey was on the table in less than two minutes. Sargent took a full sip. "I've known Jack Nicklaus for nearly fifty years," Sargent said, his voice at first affected by the whiskey's burn. "I never had the honor of working with Jack—Mr. Grout was his only swing instructor—but we've talked about his equipment choices over the years. What were you told about the designer and grinder?"

Riley, still stinging from the meal rebuke, remembered the names without looking. "Wullkotte and White."

"Then you, sir, own a set of Jack's personal clubs. The 945s were used by him from the mid-1970s to about 1990. He also used the Limited Editions for years and years. I'll take your word about the replica White Fang. So the question isn't how you got the clubs. The question is how are you able to hit them like that?"

"I was hoping you could tell us," Riley said.

"Shit if I know. A 400-yard drive with persimmon? I'd need two swings with one of those drivers to reach that."

"Sarge, his swing needs help," Hard Way said.

"Help? You said he hits it almost a fucking quarter of a mile!"

"That's his driver, Sarge. I'm worried about how his bag is configured. Joe, tell him about the rest of the clubs."

"I've got 2 through 9 on the irons, a pitching wedge, sand wedge, driver, 3-wood, and 5-wood. And, oh, the White Fangy thing. But I've never used it."

"So what's the problem? I assume you hit the shit out of the irons, too."

"I do," Riley confirmed before Hard Way could answer.

"The problem is there's no 60-degree, no gap wedge, no hybrids," Hard Way said. "We need some clubs for 110 yards in, and for some bad lies from longer numbers. So we might need to swap out two or three of those clubs for new stuff. And he ain't Nicklaus when he's not swinging the Nicklaus clubs. He's just Joe, the guy with the crappy swing who orders eggplant at the Golden Steer. We need your help with *that* guy."

"Help to do what? You got an AGN employee outing you want to win?"

Riley dropped his head, slightly embarrassed.

"He just got fired by AGN," Hard Way said.

"Shit," Sargent said. "I didn't know. But I hope you're not thinking about trying to make a buck on those state mini-tours, are you? That's a young man's game—I don't care how far you hit it."

"Mini-tours?" Riley said. "I thought we were going to talk about the PGA Tour. That's what Max said."

Sargent turned to stare at Hard Way. "He did, did he? What else did Max say?"

"He said you wanted to help me get on Tour, that you'd give me free lessons, that you'd let me use some of your charter jet hours. He said you wanted to meet me in Vegas. Out of respect to both of you—and your generous offer—I agreed to hear what you had to say."

"Hard Way," said Sargent, his voice rising in anger, "before I use this steak knife to cut your hamstrings, is there anything you want to add?"

"In retrospect," Hard Way said, covering Sargent's knife with a dinner napkin, "I might have taken some liberties when describing your level of interest."

"You told me you had a friend who could fly it 400, and asked if I would offer a little advice. I don't recall anything about lessons and jets."

"Yes, well, that might have gotten lost in translation."

"I'm not following," Riley said to Hard Way. "You mean you never told him what you told me?"

Hard Way could feel the walls closing in. There was only one option left: honesty. He took a deep breath and then spoke.

"You're right—I lied to both of you," Hard Way said. "But I needed you in the same place. Sarge, this is going to sound batshit crazy, but I think Joe can win a major."

"A major?!" Sargent said, nearly doing a spit take with the precious Pappy 15. "He couldn't win a minor!"

Sargent's raised voice attracted the attention of several tables nearby. He apologized to them before turning his attention back to Hard Way and Riley.

"A guy in street clothes doesn't beat these Tour guys," he said. "He doesn't beat them in the most watered-down field you can think of. And he sure as hell doesn't beat them in a major. You've been out there, Hard Way. You know that. At least I thought you did."

"Sarge, this guy in street clothes shot 79 with rental clubs and that persimmon driver at TPC—and he played the last ten holes from the Tour tips. I helped him with some of his lines, read a few putts, but not much else. He shot 79 without knowing what he was doing. With that length, those clubs, and your help, he could shave a dozen shots off that, maybe more. Do that and he would have finished T-3 at Phoenix last year."

"And you'd be his caddie—is that how this works?"

"Yeah, I would."

Sargent looked at Riley. "Did he talk you into this? Because this is lunacy."

"I didn't know that you didn't know," Riley said. "I thought you and Hard Way were working together on this."

"Joe, I can explain," Hard Way said, knowing he really couldn't.

"You've done enough damage," Sargent said.

A defeated Hard Way said softly, "Sarge, he could win."

"The less you say, the better," Sarge said. "The next thing out of your mouth should be an apology."

"No, it shouldn't," Riley said, with sudden conviction.

"Joe," Hard Way said, "he's right."

"No, he's not—not completely," Riley said, before looking at Sargent. "It *is* lunacy, I'll give you that. Do I really think I can win a major? No. I don't even know how I'd qualify for a major. But a dying old man gave my son a set of special clubs and wanted me to have them—and do something special with them. And for reasons that defy explanation, only I can hit them far, *really* far. I don't blame you for thinking this is ten kinds of dumb. It is. If word got out, you'd be ridiculed for helping us. But Martin Luther King Jr. said, 'Faith is taking the first step when you don't see the whole staircase.'"

Sargent rolled his eyes. "Really? MLK and golf? And see the whole staircase? I don't see *any* staircase."

"Sarge," Hard Way said, "sometimes things don't have to make sense to make sense."

"Stop at a metaphysics seminar on the way over here?"

"I'm serious, Sarge."

"You should hear yourselves. Magic clubs with special powers? You two are a confederacy of dunces."

"You wouldn't say that if you'd seen what I saw at TPC."

"Tell me this—and I have trouble saying this out loud—why are they magical?"

"I don't know," Riley said.

"Whattya mean, you don't know?"

"They didn't come with an instruction manual," Riley said. "Maybe I wasn't meant to know. Does everything have to have a reason?"

"Yes."

"You're a cause-and-effect guy."

"I am."

"A believer in only empirical evidence. A worshiper of fully formed equations."

"Makes life easier."

"What about faith?"

"I'll take logic over faith."

"These clubs defy logic."

"Look, I'm just a humble swing instructor."

"Used to be," Hard Way said under his breath.

Sargent ignored him. "I've been doing this long enough to know there are absolutes in golf. You want me to believe the impossible rather than the plausible. I can't do it. It's impossible for you to hit a persimmon driver 400-plus yards."

"Mozart was five when he wrote his first composition," Riley said.

"I think it was six," Hard Way said.

"I'm almost positive it was five."

"Save it for your *Jeopardy!* auditions, fellas," Sargent said, not hiding his irritation.

"The point is, it wasn't plausible until he wrote it," Riley said. "Einstein was only twenty-six when he published his theory of relativity. Was that plausible? How do you explain a foursome of teenagers from Liverpool changing the world of music? How was Ali plausible? Or Tiger?"

"Mozart, Einstein, the Beatles, Ali, Tiger," Sargent said. "Do you hear yourselves?"

"I didn't realize it until a moment ago, but this guy," Riley said, nodding toward Hard Way, "actually believes in me. My wife believes in me. My sons believe in me. The old man believed in me. AGN didn't. I didn't—until now."

Sargent held up his hand like a crossing guard.

"Hard Way," Sargent said, his voice softening, "I agreed to come here tonight as a courtesy because I think you're one of the good guys. You got a rough deal with your man, and I want to help you get back on your feet. But you can't honestly think a—" Here he paused and looked at Riley. "How old are you, Joe?"

"I'm forty-three."

Sargent immediately looked back and resumed talking solely to Hard Way, ignoring Riley. "A forty-three-year-old amateur with an—"

"Eighteen."

"—eighteen handicap is going to win a major."

Riley chimed in. "Mickelson was almost fifty-one when he won the PGA at Kiawah. Julius Boros was forty-eight, Jerry Barber forty-five, Lee Trevino forty-four. Jack won the Masters when he was forty-six; Tiger did it when he was forty-three. Hale Irwin won the U.S. Open when he was forty-five, Raymond Floyd when he was forty-three. Tom Watson almost won the Open Championship when he was fifty-nine."

"Stop it," Sargent said. "Every one of those guys is in the Hall of Fame except Barber. You can't compare yourself to Tiger, Jack, Phil, Raymond, Hale, and Tom."

"I'm just saying that age doesn't matter."

"Like hell it doesn't." Sargent looked directly at Riley. "You ever play competitive golf?"

"Does fifth man on my high school team count?"

Sargent threw up his hands. "The last amateur to win on Tour was Phil . . . in 1991. An amateur hasn't won a major since 1933. The days of Ouimet and Jones are done, fellas. The subject is closed."

They finished their meals in silence. When Marcus later removed their empty plates from the table, he didn't bother offering dessert options. Thirty years in the service industry had taught him how to read body language. Instead, he wordlessly placed the bill behind the candle ball holder.

Riley began to reach for the tab.

"You touch that and I'll have a mob guy break all your fingers in a car door," Sargent said. He picked up the folder, took a quick glance, peeled off six hundred-dollar bills, and returned the folder to the table's edge. Marcus whisked it away.

"You don't drop coin in my town," Sargent said as he began to slide out of the booth. Hard Way and Riley started to get up.

"Thanks for dinner," Hard Way said.

"No, stay put. Have another drink on me—Marcus knows the drill. And if you don't have rooms yet, go to the Wynn and ask for Genevieve. She's a VP there and always works nights. Tell her I sent you."

Hard Way began to protest. Sargent stopped him with a cold glare. "Fellas, I'm sorry I couldn't help you. Safe travels home."

On his way out the door, Sargent was stopped by several diners asking for his autograph. One requested a quick photo with him in front of the small Christmas tree near the entrance. And then he was gone.

In Sargent's honor, Riley ordered a Pappy 15. And then two more bourbons after that, but this time he downshifted to Knob Creek 12 and put it on their own tab. Hard Way splurged on a bottle of Pellegrino.

"That was some soaring oratory," Hard Way said.

"That was the liquor talking," Riley said.

"Are we making a mistake?" Hard Way said.

"Yes," Riley said. "I've never had this much bourbon in my life. I can't feel my thumbs."

"I mean you. These clubs. Trying for a major."

"The mistake would be not to try," Riley said.

"Who's seen you hit the clubs?"

"You. A few people at the ranges. My son Buddy. And Gordo's granddaughter. Gordo is the one who gave Buddy the clubs."

"What does your son think?"

"I don't know for sure. We don't exactly have the closest relationship."

"You don't have to answer this—it's none of my business—but what's the problem?"

Riley swirled the liquid in his glass before knocking back the rest of it.

"I suck as a dad. That's the problem."

"Like you said, that's the bourbon talking. I'm sure you're a good dad."

"Wolves could raise our youngest, Chet—he's eight—and he'd be fine. But Buddy has always been more sensitive."

"He's in college? Gets good grades?"

"A junior at Madison. Yeah, smart kid."

"He's good to people? Respects others?"

"He didn't want Laurel and me to know, but he volunteers a couple of nights a week at the homeless shelter near campus."

"Then you raised him right."

"Not me. Laurel. She's a hundred times the parent that I am."

"Then what's the disconnect?"

Riley started to squirm in his seat. "If you can believe it, it's golf. He loves the game . . . or did. He had some serious talent as a junior player."

"What happened?"

"First time out as a caddie at Chicago Golf, he got caught cheating for a guest. I came down on him pretty hard. It didn't end well."

"He quit."

"Quit playing. Quit caddying. Quit watching. Since then, there's always been scar tissue between us."

"Geezus, Joe, do you know how many times a club caddie gets put in that situation? Didn't it ever happen when you were looping?"

"Not once."

"Well, we all can't caddie for the Twelve Apostles. The rest of us get stuck with the guy who wants us to fluff up a lie in the fescue, or, hell, just foot-wedge it out of there when nobody's looking. They want illegal drops and expect you to say nothing. Happened to me last week with a guest at the Rock."

"And you let them?"

"I'm not their mommy. They know they're breaking the rules. I know they're breaking the rules. I get paid either way."

"That's not how I raised my sons."

"When a player cheats, they reveal their character—or lack of it. Buddy didn't cheat; the player did."

"He was an accomplice."

"He was a kid working his first-ever loop. The guest was what, some slickster auditioning for a membership interview? A 12-handicap posing as a 7? Wanted to put a low number on the card in front of the members? Buddy never had a chance with a guy like that."

"I would have walked away. You always have a choice."

"Bullshit. You would have been scared shitless, just like Buddy was. You think your kid *wanted* to cheat for that douche?"

"So you think he did the right thing?"

"I think he did the only thing he could do."

Riley looked at his empty glass. Marcus appeared, just long enough for Hard Way to swirl his finger in the air. The waiter disappeared, returning a minute later with a fresh drink.

"You trying to get me drunk?" Riley said. "Because it's working."

"I'm trying to understand you. That's what caddies do."

"And this is your truth serum," Riley said, holding up the Glencairn glass. "But what about you?"

"What about me?"

"You called bullshit on me. I call it on you."

"Really?"

Riley leaned forward. "You'll give me a straight answer?"

"Try me."

"What really happened at the Memorial? You didn't get fired because there were fifteen clubs in the bag."

Hard Way took a deep breath. "No comment."

"I knew it!" Riley slammed his hand down on the table.

"Whatever you think you know, you don't. And as long as you're a member of the Fourth Estate, all you'll ever get from me is 'No comment.'"

"I'm not a member of any estate. I got fired. Remember?"

"Doesn't matter."

"So there *is* more to it?"

"I got canned. End of story."

"Bullshlit," said Riley, who was beginning to slur his words.

"Time to get you home, Sparky." Hard Way waved for the check. It was on the table an instant later.

Hard Way had to boost Riley into the front seat of the pickup. Riley tried to stage a comeback during the ride to the Wynn.

"You were pretty tough on me about Buddy."

"That's only because you keep forgetting something."

"What's that?"

"That Gordo wasn't the only one who thought you were worthy of those clubs. Your son did, too."

There was a long silence in the car. Both of the men looked out their respective windows.

Finally Riley spoke.

"I hate that you're right. So what do we do next?"

Hard Way continued looking out his window, then turned and looked right at Riley and said, "We keep trying."

CHAPTER TWENTY

Hard Sell

Early the next morning, Hard Way and Riley climbed back into the truck for the short drive from the Strip to the airport. As they reached the Terminal 1 entrance, Hard Way sat motionless behind the steering wheel, deep in thought.

"We're here," Riley said, his head pounding. "Thanks for the ride. I gotta go or I'm going to be late for my flight."

Hard Way didn't respond.

"Hard Way?"

"No, you're not going," Hard Way said.

A car honked its horn behind them. Riley winced at the sound. "What are we doing?" Riley said, confused. "I actually have to get back, you know, to my real life."

"I didn't come here for a steak dinner."

It took about twenty minutes to reach the Esperanza Canyon clubhouse in Henderson. A sign pointed them to an adjoining facility, the Leeds Sargent Jr. School of Golf. They found Sargent standing alone on the range, the morning dew still covering the grass. He had a cup of coffee in one hand and a driver in the other. At each hitting station was a metal rack to hold a golf bag and a small green crate filled with Sargent-logo'd Titleists.

Sargent turned and saw Hard Way walking with purpose, while Riley moved noticeably slower as he struggled to balance the golf bag on his shoulder.

"You fellas don't give up," Sargent said. "What, dinner wasn't enough? Now you want me to buy you breakfast, too?"

He turned his full attention to Riley.

"For chrissakes, Riley, you look like you've been embalmed."

"I wish I *were* dead," Riley said. "My head hurts so much I can hear my temples screaming."

"Did you sleep in those clothes?" said Sargent, who was known for his classic golf wardrobe of expensive tailored pants, custom-made leather belts, and golf shirts with perfect creases in the sleeves. "I told you—"

Hard Way interrupted him. "I don't care what you told us," he said, his tone rude and harsh. "I don't care that you've given lessons to presidents, royals, actors, captains of industry, and half of the top 100 in the world rankings. I knew you when you were a nobody who got fifteen bucks for an hour lesson at the muni. I knew you when you bought your clothes off the rack at secondhand stores. You were begging anybody on any tour to give you a chance. And when we first met, I was the guy who introduced you to a player who was *this close* to losing his card. He didn't know you. Nobody did. But he trusted me, and you helped save his career. Then word spread—as it always does—and you became *the* Leeds Sargent."

"You done?"

"Actually, no. I liked the original version of you. That guy would have jumped at the chance to help another nobody."

Hard Way reached into his pocket and waved a doubled-over wad of cash as thick as his porterhouse the night before.

"If you won't watch Riley hit a few for old times' sake, then I'll pay the two grand for a lesson!"

"*Now* are you done?" Sargent said.

"Damn straight I am," Hard Way said.

"First of all, those are $1 bills. How many are in there? I'm going to guess fifty, tops."

"Fifty-three," Hard Way said indignantly.

"Second, I wanted to test your commitment. The old Hard Way wouldn't have let me walk out that door last night."

"That's true."

"Third, what took you so long to get here? I've been waiting almost forty-five minutes."

"You're in?"

"I'll look at his swing, that's all I'm promising you. But you owe me $15 for the lesson. For old times' sake."

Riley's head was throbbing, and nothing was making sense. "But why, Sarge? Why do you really want to do this?"

"Why, son? Because if what you say about your clubs is true, I want to see the whole damn staircase."

CHAPTER TWENTY-ONE

The Lesson

During his long career as a swing instructor, Sargent had witnessed hundreds of thousands of shots, perhaps millions. Who knew for sure? But it was an indisputable fact that the majority of those shots were more bad than good, and because of the bad, there was always a demand for his services.

The swing itself—and what happened when clubhead met ball—was a matter of high school physics. Mass. Energy. Impact. Torque. Velocity. Aerodynamics. Those were the constants. Sir Isaac Newton never played a round of golf, but he would have understood the relationship between player, club, and ball flight.

On this day, though, the natural science of physics called in sick.

The session began at the outside lesson tee. The temperature would warm to the low eighties as the day went on, but for now the early morning air was chilly enough for a light flannel.

Riley wore a borrowed Esperanza Canyon golf shirt and pullover shell as Sargent peppered him with a constant stream of personal questions: Where did he live? How many kids? Favorite teams? Favorite Tour pro to interview? Preferred pizza topping? On and on it went. Meanwhile, an assistant appeared for a few minutes and used his iPhone to discreetly shoot video of Riley.

The questions served a purpose: to distract, to relax. Pablo Picasso said, "Bad artists copy, great artists steal." Sargent had stolen the idea of distraction from the great Butch Harmon. Harmon had explained in a *Golf Digest* interview how he would start a lesson by asking a new client to hit a few wedges. To reduce nervousness, Harmon would make conversation about non-golf topics. Rather than think about their swing, the player would think about the answers to Harmon's questions. It was a simple mind game, but effective. It gave Harmon—and now Sargent—time to assess the swing without the player feeling self-conscious. Harmon's goal, which became Sargent's goal, was to identify the most glaring flaw of the swing and then fix that one thing.

Riley's swing had so many flaws that it was difficult for Sargent to choose just one. He settled on widening the arc. Riley's backswing was too upright, and his downswing was too narrow. The fix wasn't complicated: a better turn of his left shoulder. If he could get that shoulder to turn behind the ball, it would create more extension, a shallower downswing, and improved contact and distance.

"You sure?" Riley said.

Sargent, his eyes hidden by sunglasses, leaned against his driver. How many times had he heard that question from amateurs and pros alike? They all wanted to cling to what felt comfortable to them, even if it was wrong.

"Am I sure?" he said evenly. "Come with me."

Sargent motioned for Riley to follow him back to the main facility. Hard Way came too. This was going to be fun.

Sargent entered a six-digit code on the building's outdoor security pad and then pressed a red button next to it. Retractable floor-to-ceiling doors began to open, revealing a half dozen state-of-the-art hitting bays. The back walls were covered completely with framed tournament flags.

"I love what you've done with the place," Riley said. The joke fell flat.

Riley noticed that there was writing on each flag. He moved closer to inspect the messages.

On an Open Championship flag: IT'S MY NAME ON THE CLARET JUG, BUT YOUR NAME SHOULD BE RIGHT NEXT TO IT.

On a Players Championship flag: YOU CHANGED MY LIFE. I OWE YOU EVERYTHING.

On a Masters flag: I CAN'T GIVE YOU MY GREEN JACKET, BUT WILL THIS DO FOR NOW?

On a U.S. Open flag: YOU TAUGHT ME TO BELIEVE IN MYSELF.

On a PGA Championship flag: I DIDN'T KNOW SO MANY BOTTLES OF WINE FIT INTO THE WANAMAKER! NOTHING BETTER THAN TO DRINK IT WITH YOU—THE MAN WHO MADE IT ALL POSSIBLE.

The testimonials were endless. It was a museum wall of the best players in the world offering their heartfelt thanks. Riley walked the width of the building as he read row after row of the Sharpie-written messages.

"These are incredible," he said. Riley looked up to find only himself and Hard Way in the building. Sargent had returned to the range. "Why'd he leave?"

"You dipshit," Hard Way said. "You don't ask Leeds Sargent if he's 'sure.' All these autographed flags? Each one of them come from wins at majors or near-majors."

"I get it. I'll apologize."

"Don't apologize. Just follow his lead. If he says you need to widen your arc—and by the way, you do—then let him show you how to widen your arc. This isn't the floor of the Senate. There's no debate."

"You're right. Message received."

They returned to the range, where Sargent stood with his crossed forearms perched on top of the butt of the grip. Riley took his place at the lesson tee.

"Sarge, you were making the excellent point that my swing is too narrow," Riley said. "I was hoping you could teach me how to do it the right way."

"You sure?"

Both men smiled.

"I'm ready to work," Riley said.

Sargent handed him an 8-iron from the teaching facility equipment rack.

"Let's start with this."

"Don't you want me to hit my Nicklaus 8-iron?" Riley said.

Sargent simply stared at him. Riley instantly realized his mistake.

"Your 8-iron is the perfect choice," Riley said obediently. "You want to establish a baseline with a regular iron. I get it."

Now with a borrowed 8-iron in his hand, Riley began to learn the mechanics of the fix. Sargent had him execute those mechanics in slow motion for a dozen reps and then increased the speed little by little. They returned to the inside hitting bay to videotape the new and improved swing. When that was done, Sargent pressed a button on the monitor and a split screen appeared of Riley's old swing vs. his new. The difference was dramatic. Riley could see that the new swing was wider and shallower.

"Can we take the swing for a test drive?"

"That's what I like to hear," Sargent said.

Riley's "feel," Sargent said, was to make sure his left shoulder turned behind the ball. "A skinny guy like you is flexible enough to do it."

The first half dozen shots were a variety of mishits. But on the seventh try, Riley caught it flush, and according to the monitor, the ball flew 152 yards with a slight draw. Riley was giddy.

"I've never hit an 8-iron like that."

"Not bad," Hard Way said.

"Don't obsess over distance," Sargent said. "I just want you to concentrate on shoulder turn. Do that and everything else falls into place." He glanced at his Breitling. "I've got a playing lesson at ten and then I'm catching a flight out this afternoon. Let's go back outside and see what you can do with that driver of yours."

Riley took the club out of the bag.

"You mind?" Sargent said, hand outstretched. Riley gave him the persimmon.

Sargent inspected the head. Then he wrapped his meaty hands around the grip. "Original leather? It must have been stored in a humidor. It's perfect."

"That's the way it came."

Sargent took a few practice swings. "I haven't hit one of these in decades."

"Give it a whack," Hard Way said, adjusting the portable Trackman.

Even though Sargent was in his mid-seventies, his swing was still impressive. As he stood over the tee shot, you could sense that he was going back in time. He aimed the face of the club at a striped range marker some 200 yards in front of him and then set up with a slightly open stance. Sargent always loved to hit the fade.

This was no different. The ball bent slightly left to right in flight, cleared the marker by 10 yards, and rolled another 5.

"That's 30 to 40 yards less than with my regular driver," he said, handing the club back to Riley.

"Sounds about right," Hard Way said, "but remember, you're also getting penalized for the cool air. More drag, more resistance on the ball when it's cold outside. But wait 'til you see this."

Riley did as Sargent had taught him: a few slow-motion swings to promote muscle memory, then a couple of swings at 60 to 70 percent. Then it was time.

The ball rose above the tree line and then the Black Mountains in the background. It stayed in the air seemingly forever.

"Jesus H. Christ," Sargent blurted out.

He had never seen a ball struck like that. Not by Tiger. Not by anyone. This was breathtaking.

It was one thing to be told by Hard Way that Riley, with his double-digit handicap and a swing that screamed, "Help me!," could hit a ball that far with a wooden clubhead. But to witness it in person was like watching Greg Norman in his prime—but times fifty. Nobody, including Nicklaus and Arnold Palmer, had ever hit a persimmon driver better than Norman, who could routinely squeeze 300 yards out of those ferocious swings. But these drives by Riley were 100 yards longer, and it wasn't the Great White Shark behind the wheel. It was the Thin Weak Minnow.

It took a moment for the monitor to display the radar tracking data.

It was as if the processor couldn't believe its own calculations. Hard Way read the numbers. "That, my friends, was 414 yards. In this air."

"Something's wrong," Sargent said, looking at the screen readout. "His swing speed is only 93.4 miles per hour! To hit it that far with a persimmon, you'd have to be at 160! This is impossible."

"Look at the ball speed, though," Hard Way said. "It's 201. That makes sense: For every mile per hour of ball speed, you get 2 yards of distance. Add in the rollout . . ."

Sargent took off his sunglasses and peered hard at the numbers again. "This just can't be," he said. He handed Riley his own personal driver.

"This should be fine for you. Put the same swing on it that you just did."

Riley went through his new routine. He hit it well—the swing was shallow and had an improved arc—and it carried 212 yards and rolled another 15.

"That swing was better than the first," Sargent said, the reality of it all sinking in, "and it's 187 yards short of the persimmon."

Riley hit ten more persimmon drives for Sargent. They were all within the 400-to-415-yard range. Sargent looked at Hard Way for an explanation.

"I told you," Hard Way said. "Freak show."

"What about the other clubs in the bag?"

"Haven't had a chance to dial in the distances for the irons and fairway woods, but we will. If they're anything like the driver, the numbers will be crazy long."

Sargent looked at his watch again. "I have to go. But we'll be seeing each other again, that's for damn sure."

As Sargent walked away, Riley turned to Hard Way.

"What does that mean?"

"It means you just got a swing coach."

Halfway to his teaching facility, Sargent yelled over his shoulder. "Finish third at Phoenix? That skinny little shit would have won it!"

CHAPTER TWENTY-TWO

The Lump of Clay

There was no official announcement. No Tiger-like "Hello, world" press conference. No social media post. Riley decided to go from amateur to pro while packing his bag for a weeklong golf boot camp trip to Scottsdale and Vegas.

Chet had suggested that his dad write a book about his upcoming experience and then sell the movie rights. Laurel asked Riley if AGN might be interested in a trade: his exclusive story for his old job back. Buddy, though, had said surprisingly little about his dad's firing and his decision to work with Sargent. He had such mixed feelings. Was it selfish to be secretly glad that his dad had lost a job that had kept him on the road for so many days for so many years? Was it wrong to want to see what his dad could do with the Nicklaus clubs—the clubs Buddy had discovered? So he had chosen semi-silence and offered his dad a generic "Good luck," which Riley took as indifference.

As for a book or a movie, there was no story—not yet, and probably not in the future, either. There was only an audacious idea. In fact, Riley laughed out loud at the preposterous nature of what he was attempting to do.

Hard Way, Riley, and Sargent had discussed all the possibilities. Remain an amateur and try to win the Latin America Amateur Championship in January, with a victory guaranteeing entry into the Masters,

U.S. Open, and Open Championship? Or if that failed, travel to the UK in June and compete in the Amateur Championship, which gave the winner an exemption to the Open Championship in July?

Worried that Riley wouldn't be competition-ready by January, they decided there were more opportunities to reach a major by turning pro. Of course, first he had to qualify for a Tour event, and there were only two feasible (and it was a loose interpretation of the word) options for Riley: finishing in the top four of a Monday qualifier, or receiving a sponsor exemption. The competition for either would be fierce.

Monday qualifiers were Darwinian, the natural selection process played out on a golf course. To even compete in the Monday event, many of the players first had to come through a pre-qualifier tournament held a week earlier. Based on demand, some tournaments had as many as eight or nine pre-qualifiers, with the survivors funneled into the Monday qualifier.

Riley had covered a few "pre-Qs," as they were called, during his time at AGN. The fields were a mix of professional players, club pros, and talented amateurs, but also more than a few imposters who would have had a tough time winning a $2 Nassau with their buddies at the local muni. To get in the field, the imposters either registered as amateurs and lied about their handicap indexes (a 2.0 or better was required), or registered as pros, which allowed them to bypass the index disclosure. Then they'd shoot 110 but have a story to tell their friends. In 2022, an amateur posing as a pro shot a 65-over-par 135 in a Texas Open pre-Q.

The Monday qualifier itself was the equivalent of a hundred-yard sprint featuring seventy-five or so players, including those who came through the pre-Q's as well as actual Tour, Korn Ferry, and Champions Tour members, former Tour members, nonmembers with significant bona fides, and several teaching pros from the local area. They were all competing for those four precious tournament openings. If you didn't shoot in the low-to-mid-60s, you had no chance.

Adding to the degree of difficulty was the likelihood of a playoff to determine who advanced to the tournament. It wasn't uncommon for there to be five remaining players for only two spots, or four players for three spots, or in the case of the Honda Classic in 2022, sixteen players for one spot. For the pre-Qs, it was more difficult to come through a Monday qualifier than it was to win the Tour event they were trying to qualify for. One multiple-major winner once said that if he had had to depend on qualifiers, he wouldn't have made it into more than three tournaments a year, if that.

As for Riley's other option, an unrestricted sponsor exemption had become much harder to secure. In the past, Tour tournament directors or chairpersons had used those exemptions to invite whomever they wanted: a sixteen-year-old Tiger at Riviera in 1992, a sixteen-year-old Jordan Spieth at the Byron Nelson in 2010, former NFL quarterback Tony Romo at the Byron Nelson in 2019, et cetera. But Tour policy changes had reduced the number of unrestricted exemptions to a precious few.

Riley wasn't Tiger, Spieth, or Romo. He did know many of the tournament directors and had played in some of their media day functions. But to expect any of those directors or chairpersons to give him one of their coveted exemptions (especially after having seen him shoot a sporty 94 in the media outings) was fantasy.

In the end, Riley, Hard Way, and Sargent settled on a pre-qualifier. It was the lesser of two long shots. He could register as a pro and not submit an index. There almost certainly wouldn't be any media coverage, so he and Hard Way could stay under the radar. If he failed, nobody would likely know or care, and there was usually another qualifier the following week.

Laurel drove him to O'Hare. Chet sat behind her, chattering away during the thirty-five-minute drive as only Chet could. Next to him on the fold-down seat was the top end of a hard plastic travel case Riley had bought to hold his Nicklaus clubs and several of his non-Nicklaus wedges and hybrids. The case was massive, large enough to hold a staff bag or an Egyptian mummy, and sturdy enough to survive the indifferent care of airline baggage handlers.

"I forgot to tell you guys that you might be getting a call from school," Chet said.

"What?" Laurel said, her eyes now peeled on Chet via the rearview mirror. "None of your teachers said anything to me about it—and I work there."

"It was a non-classroom incident, Mom."

"What does that mean?" Riley said.

Chet was the smartest student at James Keogh Elementary School. He completed his assignments with ease and often took time to explain the work to his classmates. His teachers knew this was no ordinary eight-year-old. But Chet's lively mind wasn't appreciated by all.

"I was in the cafeteria line and the girl in front of me asked the hairnet lady if she could have a salad instead of the shepherd's pie because she doesn't eat meat," Chet explained. "And the lady told her, 'Quit being a Karen.' I informed the woman that 'Karen' was a pejorative term and especially inappropriate given that the girl had politely asked if she could have a salad. Then I asked the server if I could have a salad, too, and said, 'Maybe *I'm* the Karen.' The server refused to give us any food at all and told us to move along. So there's that . . ."

Riley tried to suppress his reaction. Laurel didn't bother, bursting into the throaty laughter that never ceased to make Riley smile.

"You are definitely not a Karen," Laurel said. "You're one of a kind."

"Does that mean I can quit using this booster seat soon?"

"Twelve more pounds, honey. That's the law."

"It sucks being a little dude."

O'Hare was its usual congested self in the morning. Buses, Ubers, Lyfts, taxis, limos, and civilian drivers darted in and out of openings like jockeys at the once-fabled Arlington Park. Laurel squeezed the minivan into a space near the kiosk of the United curbside check-in. Riley gave her a quick kiss.

"I feel guilty about this," he said.

"Don't. We'll be fine. We love you."

Riley turned around to say goodbye to Chet, who rarely gave him more than a fist bump when he left for a trip. This time, though, Chet unlatched his seat belt, leaned through the opening of the front seats, and buried his head in his dad's chest.

"Little dude," Riley said softly as he hugged Chet, "I'll be home soon."

Chet pulled back to reveal tears in his eyes. "True," he said, instantly composing himself. "What was I thinking?"

Laurel laughed out loud again.

One of the airport traffic patrol officers approached the car.

"It ain't a movie set, folks. Kiss, get your bags out of the car, and move."

Riley slung his backpack over his shoulder and then opened the liftgate, where he first removed his roller board and then wrestled the wheeled travel hard case containing his clubs to the curb. As Laurel pulled away, Chet turned around, thumped his fist against his chest and pointed at Riley. This time it was Riley's turn for tears.

It was winter-coat weather when Riley's plane climbed over O'Hare, the temperatures in the low thirties, a dusting of snow covering the rooftops and lawns of Chicagoland. When he landed in Phoenix that afternoon, it was eighty-three degrees and the cactuses were waving hello.

Riley got his rental car, drove to Scottsdale, and dropped off his luggage at Bang Bang's townhome, where an excited Oskie introduced himself by peeing on Riley's shoes. He unpacked his golf bag from the monster case and drove immediately to Troon North, where Hard Way was waiting for him at a table on the balcony of the clubhouse bar. Nearby Pinnacle Peak was to the south, and the mountain ranges were in the distance to the north.

"And so the journey begins," Hard Way said, rising to give Riley a handshake and a hug. The lower part of Hard Way's face was tan, but his forehead was Elmer's Glue–white, the result of him smartly wearing his Whisper Rock floppy hat during his loops, including the one he had just completed an hour earlier. "Ready to begin Phase One?"

"Phase One?" Riley said.

"Think of it as a reeducation process. Right now, you approach the game like an amateur. Even when you were working for AGN—and again, a pox on their house for laying you off—you viewed the game through the eyes of an educated amateur. I want to teach you how to think through a shot and a round like a pro. Make sense?"

"Whattya mean, exactly?"

"I'm glad you asked. Where are your clubs?"

"Out back on the rack."

"No, no, no," Hard Way said. "We *never* let the clubs out of our sight in a public place. Especially *those* clubs."

Hard Way had called in a favor from the club pro. The Monument Course, another well-respected Tom Weiskopf design, was supposed to be open after a three-week shutdown for overseeding, but there was an issue with the No. 17 green. Play was limited to the front nine until the next day, but the club pro gave Riley and Hard Way free rein on the back nine.

Riley found his bag on the rack, and one of the clubhouse guys lugged it to the back of a cart.

"How many clubs you got in this thing?" the clubbie said as he strained to lift it.

"Nineteen. Brought some extras to try out."

"Nineteen? That's worse than that caddie at the Memorial."

Hard Way sat grim-faced in the cart, his knuckles white as he power-gripped the steering wheel. As Riley sat down on the white bench seat, Hard Way stabbed at the gas pedal with his right foot and then made a hard left turn toward the No. 10 tee box. Riley almost tumbled out of the cart.

"Hey, that kid was just making a joke," Riley said, desperately gripping the yee-haw handle on the roof frame. "He didn't know any better."

Hard Way said nothing, but he knew Riley was right. If anything, he was embarrassed by his reaction. When they arrived at the tee box, Hard Way apologized.

"I guess the nerve endings are still sensitive."

"Let's get to work. Talk to me, Yoda."

"To quote the great green-skinned Jedi master, 'You must unlearn what you have learned.'" They stepped to the back tees. "As a reporter, you're out there walking with groups, doing your interviews, writing your essays and stories. You might be working with a producer, but for the most part, you're on your own, right?"

"Mostly, yes."

"That's not how it works when you're playing. Some of the old-school players will tell you different, that a caddie has three jobs: show up, keep up, shut up. They didn't want or need a lot of input. And it's still that way for some guys on Tour. But you and me, we need to be a team."

"Like Greller and Spieth."

"Uh, that's a little ambitious. Those boys are next-level. I don't know how Greller does it. Jordan is brilliant but exhausting. He's like a border collie; he'd wear me out."

"He's a border collie with a green jacket, a Claret Jug, and a U.S. Open trophy."

"And he'll win more. You'll get no argument from me. But I once saw a player move to another spot on the range because Jordan was talking through every warm-up shot. His brain works in mysterious ways. Greller's gift is being able to do the mind meld with him."

"So what's your point?"

"That I'm not just going to carry your bag. We need to be connected on every shot."

"A little dramatic, don't you think?"

"If we're going to have any chance of not embarrassing ourselves, I'll have to understand every nuance of your game. Not just your yardages, but the way you decide on a shot. The mental game is as important as how far you hit it—maybe more important. When I walk the course on my own, I need to be able to think through it as if I'm you."

"Good luck with that. *I* don't even know how my mind works during a round."

"Look, 95 percent of what we do as caddies can be done by almost anyone. But the other 5 percent is what a professional caddie does. And by the way, I get veto power on ten of your shots."

"Ten? Bones only got one or two a season from Phil. Greller gets a half dozen or so."

"You ain't Phil or Spieth. If you're about to do something dumb, I get to use one of my ten. In fact, I might need more than that."

The 10th hole at the Monument course was 396 yards from the tips. Hard Way had to remind himself that the green was driveable for Riley and his MacGregor persimmon.

"Whattya thinking here?" Hard Way said.

Riley walked to the cart and returned with his driver. "I'm thinking it's time to make an early statement."

"I'm thinking it's time to use a practice-round veto."

"I can reach this thing."

"You can. But the wind is helping toward two o'clock on the dial and the temp is already eighty-something degrees. So the ball is going to carry a little more because the air is lighter and less dense. It's also dry, and the rough is cut to resort-course height, so if you're off line even just a bit, it could run through and into the gunk. You've got some room behind the green, but it's no bargain. There's not much slope on the hole, so nothing to really calculate there. But the pin is back right, which brings that greenside bunker into play. You haven't hit any balls, so who knows what you'll do with that first swing. The way the fairway is contoured, most of the shots are going to funnel back to the short grass. But if you roll over those humps, then everything feeds into the gunk. So I'll ask you again: Whattya thinking here?"

"You do all that for one shot?"

"A good caddie does that for *every* shot. Slope—uphill, downhill, or flat? Wind. Temperature. Adrenaline. Is the grass dewy or dry? Are we at sea level or an elevation? Identify the places where you absolutely don't want to be and then figure out where to miss. And if you do get into trouble, have a plan B ready to go."

"So much for 'Show up, keep up, shut up.'"

Despite Hard Way's speech, Riley remained mesmerized by the white flag fluttering in the far distance. "I'm still thinking driver."

"Hit driver, then try the 5-wood," Hard Way said. "We'll see how it plays out."

Even without a proper warm-up, Riley hit a tee shot that caught the eight-mile-per-hour afternoon breeze and seemed destined for the green. As always, the ball flight and distance still caused Hard Way to shake his head in amazement.

"That's one small step for man," Riley said proudly as the ball disappeared into the horizon, "and one giant step for Joe Riley."

"Not so fast, my friend," said Hard Way, who was watching through his range finder.

The breeze pushed the ball over the bunker and toward the brush-filled hill overlooking the green. It appeared to plop into the middle of a bush.

"Hello, trouble," he said.

"What?"

"I'm pretty sure you're cooked—deep fried, as we say," Hard Way said. "Now hit the 5-wood. But aim toward the left side of the fairway. That gives us a better angle at the pin on the second shot."

Riley took a couple of practice swings and then launched the tee shot. It towered toward the middle of the fairway—nothing wrong with that—and came to a quick stop after landing.

"You just hit a 5-wood farther than Rory can hit a stock driver. I'm never going to get used to this."

"Me neither."

"You are going to freak those boys out, my friend."

They drove to the ball. Hard Way chuckled as he calculated the distance.

"You hit it 351. You've got 45 to the pin, and you've mostly taken that bunker out of play." He aimed the range finder at the waste area where Riley's first drive had landed. "You were right: You could reach the green, but the risk/reward wasn't worth it."

"A 45-yard shot off a tight lie isn't my strength."

"Yeah, we're going to make those shots a priority. With your distance off the tee, you're going to have a lot of those kind of yardages."

"What do I do?"

"Well, you've got the Nicklaus nuclear option with your sand wedge. We'll dial in those numbers, but I'm guessing you can probably hit that in the 135-to-140-yard range, which is nuts. Or we can try your non-Nicklaus 60-degree wedge, or the non-Jack gap wedge. For someone like you, that probably is in the 70-yard range. So let's try all three: a little more than a quarter swing on the Nicklaus, a three-quarter swing on the 60, a half swing on the gap wedge."

Riley tried to keep his swing short on the sand wedge, but he didn't have the muscle memory for it yet. The ball still flew 50 yards over the green. With the 60-degree wedge, he took a divot the size of a dish towel and the ball traveled only 20 yards.

"I'm better than that," Riley said.

"Don't worry about it. That's why God invented Sarge. He'll get you fixed. Try the gap wedge."

Riley's half swing had the length but not the direction. It missed the green.

With each hole, Hard Way began to get a feel for Riley's game. His swing wasn't anywhere near Tour, Korn Ferry, mini-tour, or college quality, but it wasn't entirely grotesque. In short, what you'd expect from a double-digit handicap. Sarge had sanded down some of the edges with the first lesson, but there remained a lot of work to be done. Still, with a persimmon or one of those Nicklaus irons in his hands, Riley's distance created options that Hard Way had never imagined. Only 127 yards for a second shot into the par-5 11th? A bump and run off the fringe after a 400-yard drive on the par-4, 426-yard 12th? An 8-iron into the 222-yard par-3 13th? Driver and pitching wedge into the 570-yard par-5 14th? Drive the par-4, 299-yard 15th with a 4-iron? Easy 7-iron into the 244-yard par-3 16th? Three-wood to the middle of the green on the 370-yard par-4 18th? It was madness. Better yet, Riley had a decent—for an amateur—short game. And his putting stroke with the rental putter was consistent and relatively sound.

They skipped the par-4 17th because of the green repair. Riley gave himself an imaginary five on the hole, but even with the fake bogey and the real bogey on No. 10, he shot a 1-under-par 35 with his first ball.

"I can't believe I just shot 35 on a nine," Riley said.

"Big difference between this and tournament golf, but it was a nice start. We still have a lot of work to do, especially 100 yards and in." Hard Way handed him the scorecard. "Turn it over."

Riley tried to decipher the scribbled numbers. "Did John Nash write these?"

"No. These are your yardages today with the Jacks—the Nicklaus clubs. They'll change as we refine your swing and play in some other climates."

Riley squinted at the numbers.

Dr—407
3W—368
5W—351
2i—332
3i—320
4i—299
5i—280
6i—265
7i—250
8i—228
9i—210
PW—177
SW—136
Gap W—93
60-degree W—68

"Seriously?"

"Seriously. A couple of them were wind-aided, and you didn't hit some of these clubs more than a few times, so don't hold me to all the numbers. But it gives you an idea. I'm going to text them to Sarge. He'll do a *Bridesmaids* and shit himself in the middle of the street when he sees the Jack-club yardages. The non-Jacks—60-degree, gap—were what I would have expected from you."

"The Jack-club numbers are one and a half times what I usually hit my clubs."

"They're more than Tiger, Jack, Rors . . . *anybody* hits their clubs, pal. I had to double-check my numbers because I thought I'd screwed up the math. They don't seem real, but they are."

"None of this seems real."

"The strange thing—what am I saying, it's *all* strange—is that your ball doesn't tail much with the persimmons. Rahm hit persimmons for fun at a tournament in the UK, and his ball leaked hard to the right. He flushed it on the screws, but he couldn't control the flight because of his swing speed."

"Which means?"

"Which means your swing speed isn't anywhere near Rahmbo's, so maybe that explains why your shots don't wander so much. You hit a couple toe-y shots today, but for the most part you kept it around the middle of the club and kept it in the fairway. And being in the fairway is always a good thing."

"What's next?"

"Phase Two. Back to Vegas."

CHAPTER TWENTY-THREE

The Smart Guy

They were halfway through the hour-long lesson at Sargent's Vegas facility when a man in his late fifties made his way from the teaching center building to the range. Hard Way was the first to see him.

"Is that who I think it is?"

"It is," Sargent said. "We need him."

Riley turned around just as the man took his place an appropriate distance behind them. The man nodded at Sargent, who said nothing but nodded back. The man wore gray slacks, a white belt, a yellow golf shirt, and custom Gucci golf shoes. His eyes were hidden by a pair of reflective Maui Jims.

"Who is that guy?" Riley said under his breath to Hard Way.

"You'll find out soon enough," Hard Way whispered.

"I didn't know Gucci made golf shoes."

"They don't. But they made a pair just for him. A lot of people owe him favors."

"Why is he here?"

The man stepped forward.

"I'm here because Sarge thought it might be to our mutual advantage if I met you. I'm always looking for possible investments in their embryonic stages."

He shook Riley's hand, then moved to Hard Way and finally, to Sargent.

"This is Jimmy Gallagher," Sargent said. "Jimmy is an old friend."

"Why do I know that name?" Riley said.

Jimmy Gallagher smiled, revealing neon-white veneers the size of Chiclets. He waited until the name registered in Riley's memory. And it did.

"Wait, 'Gimme G'?" Riley said. "The guy who supposedly won money off half the top 20 in the world rankings?"

"More like sixteen of the top 20, but you're on the right track," Sargent said.

"I heard you only got a stroke a side?" Riley asked Gallagher.

"It's best to keep that kind of information to myself," he said.

"And you beat them?"

"It isn't the strokes that matter; it's the effect they have on your opponent. Pressure is the great equalizer."

"Rumor has it that you almost beat Tiger straight up—and this was in his prime. After the round, he supposedly asked you for a putting lesson."

"You have good sources."

"So it's true?"

Gallagher shrugged. "Let's just say that Tiger had to work for his money that day. But I had to reach into my pocket and he didn't. I don't celebrate losses."

Sargent interrupted. "Joe, I asked Gimme to come by and take a look at your game."

"Why?"

"Because he's an investor, and you need working capital."

"If I like what I see today, I'll bankroll you," Gallagher said.

"I need a bankroll?"

"For the basics," Sargent said. "Decent hotels. Airfare. Rental cars. Gas. Food. Cash for the clubhouse guys. Entry fees. You don't have any endorsement deals, so you'll need presentable clothes, shoes. You'll have to pay for your own balls, gloves, hats, equipment. And Hard Way can't live off the land, so you've got pay him, too."

"Estimate?"

"At least $6,000 a week, and that's being conservative," Hard Way said. "Some of these guys fly private, hire chefs, personal trainers, physical therapists. Some of them bring family. It adds up."

Riley whistled. "Six K a week? What's the payment plan?"

"There isn't one," Gallagher said. "If you're as good as Sarge says you could be, I'm going to make plenty of money on the side."

"And if I don't win?"

"That's why they call it gambling," Gallagher said. "I'll shake your hand and we'll go our separate ways. No hard feelings."

"How do you figure out if I'm worth the investment?"

"That's where my one condition comes in."

"And what's that?"

"We're going to tee it up. You know what they say: 'To find a man's true character, play golf with him.' "

"That's it?"

"For five hundred a hole."

"Dollars?!"

"Yes, the green kind," Gallagher said, amused by Riley's naïveté. "Oh, I forgot to mention: automatic presses if you're two down."

Riley did the math in his head. There would be the original bet and the possibility of eight other presses. "That's $45,000 if I lose every hole and every press!"

"That's correct. I don't usually play for such small stakes, but let's keep it friendly."

Riley looked at Sarge and Hard Way in confusion. He could feel his heart thumping against his rib cage.

"I can't do it," Riley said, panicked. "My wife would stab me in my sleep if I lost $45,000."

"Then you've revealed your character, and I have my answer," Gallagher said with a polite finality. "Some people are built for such moments; others aren't."

As Gallagher began to leave, he glanced at Sargent and shook his head in disappointment. Gallagher was a man unaccustomed to being told no. He lived for the action. Riley, he decided, lived to play it safe.

"Hold on," Sargent said as Gallagher walked away. "I'll cover him."

"Like hell you will," Riley said. "I'm not playing."

"Like hell you aren't," Sargent said. "Either you're in this, or you're not. This doesn't work if Hard Way and I believe in you more than you believe in yourself."

"This guy is a world-class gambler. I play for $2 Nassaus. Look at me," Riley said as he extended his hands. "They're shaking."

"Sarge, your friend isn't up to the challenge," Gallagher said. "He's ice cream in the sun. He's already melting and he hasn't hit a shot."

The words cut through Riley, but he knew there was truth in them.

"My offer stands," Sargent said. "I'll cover his losses."

Gallagher shook his head again. "No. I'm not taking your money unless he has skin in the game, too. I need to see if he can handle pressure. If not, I'm walking."

"What kind of skin?" Sargent said.

Gallagher thought about it for a moment. "The first $10,000 of the bet is out of his pocket. Take it or leave it."

"Joe?" Sargent said.

Riley knew this was the intersection of logic and financial madness. He thought of Lee Trevino, the six-time major winner who used to work as a clubhouse attendant and hustler in El Paso before eventually joining the Tour. It was Trevino who said, "You don't know what pressure is until you've played for $5 a hole when you only have $2 in your pocket."

Riley was playing for $10,000 but had only $4,000—the entirety of his family's savings account—in his pocket, so to speak. If he lost, he'd somehow have to come up with another $6,000, to say nothing of Sargent having to fork over tens of thousands to the smug Vegas gambler. Gallagher was right about this being a test of will and worth. Riley knew that, too.

"How many strokes you giving me?" Riley said to Gallagher, hoping to get at least three or four a side.

The gambler tilted his head, as if he were actually pondering the question, which he wasn't. "I will give you exactly zero a side."

"That's not fair."

"No, I suppose it isn't. And yet, it bothers me not in the least."

Riley looked first at Hard Way and then at Sargent for guidance. Their faces remained impassive. This would be Riley's decision alone.

"Well?" said Gallagher as he casually brushed a blade of grass off his Guccis.

"I don't need strokes. I'll see you tomorrow on the first tee."

"Excellent," Gallagher said. "I was hoping you'd say that."

Off to the side, Hard Way nudged Sargent. "I think our boy has some balls after all."

"We'll see," Sargent said. "We'll see."

CHAPTER TWENTY-FOUR

The Match

Riley was down $4,500 after seven holes. It would have been worse, but Gallagher had been in momentary shock after watching Riley's first drive. It had been Hard Way's idea for Riley to warm up early with his Nicklaus clubs before Gallagher arrived on the range. By the time the gambler got there, Riley was hitting his non-Jack wedges to mere mortal distances.

Gallagher and his caddie had tried to hide their smiles when Hard Way handed his man the persimmon driver on the opening hole. The key fob to Gallagher's cherry-red Ferrari was thicker than the MacGregor driver. Sargent hadn't told Gallagher about the powers of the clubs themselves, only that he had found an unlikely player with an extraordinary advantage.

Gallagher had stepped forward. "I'm fine with whatever clubs you choose to play," he said, examining Riley's driver with a bemused look. "But persimmon is a curious choice for a money game. And these irons are well-preserved fossils."

"Since when did you give two shits about the age of a club?" Sargent said. "And just so things stay friendly, keep the gooey stuff in your bag."

Gallagher pretended to be offended. "Sarge, is that any way to treat a friend?"

"Gimme, I've seen you spread Vaseline on a driver face like it was cream cheese on a bagel."

Though it was forbidden by the rules of golf, Gallagher often played in money games where the players agreed to allow foreign substances on the clubface. Gallagher preferred petroleum jelly or lip balm, both of which reduced the backspin on the ball. Less spin meant a straighter ball and more rollout when it landed.

"Based on what I've seen so far," Gallagher said smugly as he handed the wooden driver back to Riley, "I don't think I'll have to resort to such measures. My game should be more than sufficient."

Gallagher's antics had triggered Sargent. He had wagged his finger at the gambler and said, "Gimme, you can save that gamesmanship shit for somebody else. I'll bet you twenty large that he outdrives you—and I'll even let you buy a mulligan right now for five large. Is *that* more than sufficient?"

"Sarge, what are you doing?" Riley had said. "Twenty thousand? Are you crazy?"

Sargent had ignored him. This was between him and Gallagher.

"Well, Gimme?"

Gallagher hadn't become a rich man by making foolish bets. He craved action, but the five-figure bet was out of character for Sargent. Something seemed suspiciously odd, beginning with a former golf reporter hitting a wooden driver.

"Maybe on the next hole," Gallagher had said.

"Once you see this on the first hole, you're not going to want any part of it on the second," Sargent had said.

Riley and Gallagher had shaken hands.

"Good luck," Gallagher had said to Riley. "You'll need it."

Hard Way had tried to lighten the mood as he picked out the line for Riley.

"Want to chuck this whole thing and go see a concert at Sphere instead?"

"Max, I think I'm going to throw up."

"If you do, can you aim for Gimme's Guccis?"

Riley had smiled weakly. His hands were trembling.

The opening hole was friendly enough: only 371 yards and straightaway, but into a breeze that topped off at ten to twelve miles per hour. Riley had the honors.

As he had stood over the ball, his thoughts collided like electrons and protons. Each thought had competed for his attention, but one reigned supreme: How was he going to pay Gallagher?

Riley, a jumbled mess, had stepped away. Hard Way had immediately grabbed the bag and placed it near his man. He had wanted to give Gallagher the appearance that they were discussing a new aiming point because of the breeze. Hard Way had even gestured at some distant cactus for effect. But under his breath, he said, "How we doing, Sparky?"

"Not good, Max," Riley said. "I can't seem to pull the club back."

Hard Way had glanced over at Gallagher. He wasn't buying any of the fake strategy talk. Instead, he had had the look of someone already counting his winnings.

"You think you're the first person to go freeze-frame on the tee box?" Hard Way said. "Know where they found Tiger before the first round of the 1997 Masters?"

"No," Riley said.

"Curled up in a ball in a corner of the locker room."

"What?"

"The attendants snuck Earl in there and he coaxed Tiger out of the fetal position and to the range. T was such a mess that he shot 40 on the front nine."

"And 30 on the back nine," Riley had said. "Everyone knows that."

"And he ended up winning the thing—his first major victory—by twelve shots," Hard Way had said. "He went from whimpering kid to Masters champion."

"I've never heard that story. That's incredible."

"It'd really be incredible if any part of it were true."

Riley looked at him and just shook his head.

"Joe, you're supposed to be nervous. Now nut up and let's make Earl and Tiger proud. You got this."

The ball had vanished as soon as Riley hit it. It departed with such suddenness that Gallagher had immediately turned to his caddie and whispered, "I saw it come off the club, but then I lost it."

The caddie had tracked the ball as it arched high over the fairway. "That thing's gonna need heat tiles for reentry," he had said to Gallagher.

Gallagher had finally located the ball just as it dropped from the heavens and rolled to a stop just short of the green.

"Nicely done," Gallagher had said to Riley, his voice calm and flat. But behind the façade of composure, Gallagher had been caught unprepared—a rarity for him. His confusion had likely contributed to a drive that squirted to the right of the fairway and settled under a Teddy-bear cholla.

"Mulligans available," Sargent had said. "I'll even give you the friends-and-family discount. Only $5,000."

Gallagher had smiled thinly. As the group walked off the tee box, Gallagher waved Sargent to his side.

"You almost got me for twenty dimes on the tee shot. And that was a nice play on the mulligan. But your boy is going to need more than driver today."

"It's early, Gimme. It's early."

Gallagher had had to punch out from the cholla, and his third shot rolled off the left fringe. He two-putted for bogey and conceded Riley's 6-inch par putt.

"This guy isn't so tough," Riley had said to Hard Way as they walked ahead to the No. 2 tee box.

"Love the confidence," Hard Way had said. "But let's concentrate on the hole, not the other guy."

"I'm already up $500."

"Focus," Hard Way had said.

By the third hole, Gallagher had flipped the match. His nickname wasn't an accident. He holed a 35-foot birdie putt on No. 2 to even the match and made an 18-footer for birdie on No. 3 to go up $500. Riley had driven the 325-yard par-4 fourth and seemingly had the hole clinched when Gallagher chipped in for birdie. A shaken Riley missed a

2-footer to tie the hole, at which point the press kicked in and Riley's anxiety level multiplied exponentially.

Hard Way had used every method he knew to try to calm his man down, but nothing worked. He had seen this happen on Tour, when a player's game disintegrated because of the possibility of money made or lost. How many times had he watched a player fighting to make a cut—and the guaranteed check that would come with it—be asphyxiated by the pressure and reality of the moment? How many times had he watched players on the cusp of top-5 finishes begin fixating on their potential payoff rather than on their next shot? More times than not, they'd make a careless mistake: a loose swing, an indifferent bunker shot, a missed short putt. In a matter of minutes, they'd tumble down and off the leaderboard, and as they did, the zeroes and commas on their payoff checks disappeared with them.

Riley's drive on the par-4 fifth had settled into a divot, and his next shot was skulled across the green and into a bunker. Gallagher's par easily won the hole. On the 184-yard par-3 sixth, they were in between clubs: 9-iron or pitching wedge. Hard Way had told Riley to hit a three-quarter 9-iron—the distance numbers still boggled Hard Way's mind—but by then Riley had quit listening. Or more accurately, was unable to listen. By then, he could think only of losing another hole, and losing more money. He had taken a full swing and flown the green by 15 yards and into the desert dirt and rocks. He had been lucky to get up and down in three shots, while Gallagher had nearly holed his 25-foot birdie putt and, true to his name, had nothing more than a 4-inch gimme to go up $2,000 on the original bet, $1,000 on the first press, and force a second press. And Riley had conceded the par-4 seventh hole after pumping each of his three 400-yard drives into the rock cliffs and vegetation that overlooked the left side of the fairway and green. The concession meant he was down $2,500, $1,500, and $500 on three bets, with eleven holes remaining.

"Your boy is crumbling," Gallagher had said as he strode past Sargent on the way to the No. 8 tee box.

Sargent had said nothing. What was there to say anyway? Riley was dead golfer walking. Remarkably enough, Riley's swing was still functional, but a swing couldn't survive on its own. It needed direction, purpose. Sargent thought back to the long-forgotten Percy Boomer and his obscure but seminal instruction book published in 1942: "Every good golf shot is the outcome of a satisfactory psychological-physical relationship." In Riley's case, the psychological and the physical weren't on speaking terms.

Under the rules of the match, Sargent wasn't allowed to offer Riley advice, but Hard Way could. Sargent caught Hard Way's attention as Gallagher and his caddie picked out a line on the tee box of the par-5 eighth hole and brushed his nose with his knuckle, an homage to one of Sargent's favorite movies, *The Sting*. Hard Way grinned and brushed his nose in response.

Desperate times required desperate measures.

Hard Way softly elbowed Riley in the side.

"All right, you can relax now," Hard Way whispered.

"Relax?" Riley said. "I can barely breathe. Can't I just concede the match, pay him his $4,500, and go back home?"

"Yeah, you can, but that means you'll concede these next two holes on the front and the whole back nine. You'll owe him all the presses, too."

"That can't be right."

"You'll be on the hook for the ten dimes, and Sarge will owe the other $35,000."

"Maybe I can make a deal with Gallagher after nine." He was on the outer edges of an anxiety attack. "Oh, my God, why did I let you talk me into this?"

"Gentlemen, are we bothering you?" It was Gallagher. "A little decorum, please."

Hard Way pulled Riley aside, out of earshot of Gallagher and his caddie.

"One, you might want to consider some yoga breaths. Two, I'm going to tell you something, but you can't show any reaction when you hear it."

"Oh, this will be good," Riley said, the sarcasm thicker than the five cash stacks that Gallagher had purposely flashed on the driving range.

"Remember, granite-faced."

"Sure. Granite-faced. Got it."

"Double the bet."

"What?"

"Double the bet. Now. Before he tees off."

"Are you out of your eff-in'—" Riley said, his voice rising just loud enough to cause Gallagher to turn and look his way again. Riley caught himself, nodded blankly at the gambler, and in a near whisper, said, "Why would I do that?"

"Because we have two par-5s in a row and because every smart guy in this town knows that Gimme fades on the back nine. He's *praying* that you'll ask out after nine. He *wants* you to negotiate a payment."

"He's kicking my ass. If I double it, I could lose $20,000 and Sarge could lose—I don't want to think about. No. Absolutely not."

"Hurry. He's teeing it up. He won't know what hit him."

Gallagher pushed the tee into the ground, adjusted the height slightly, and then stepped back to take one last look at his line. He took a relaxed practice swing, set his feet, and gave one last glance at his target. Hard Way stared at Riley—nothing.

Just as Gallagher began his takeaway, a fly settled on the top of his Callaway ball. He stepped back and swatted at it with the driver head. The insect flew off, and Gallagher began his routine again. As he settled into his stance, he heard Riley's voice.

"I wanna talk about the bet," Riley said.

About time, thought Gallagher. He had expected the discombobulated Riley to fold a few holes earlier. *I'll settle for $6,000 from the rube, $20,000 from Sarge. I want them to feel pain, but not true suffering. No reason to be greedy. I'll even buy lunch.*

"I understand," Gallagher said amiably. "If I were you, I'd do the same thing. I'm prepared to be reasonable. But obviously we have to extrapolate the bet to its full conclusion. With that in mind, I'm prepared to offer you a settlement of—"

"I want to double it," Riley said, his voice cracking.

"Pardon me?"

"Double," Riley said, firmly this time. "I'm down $4,500. We make it a $1,000 hole starting now. That means—"

"That means," Gallagher said, before Riley could finish his sentence, "that if you continue at your present pace, you and Sarge will owe me $66,500. I'll require you, of course, to double your own stake to $20,000."

Riley looked at Hard Way. Hard Way slowly mouthed, "Like a lawn chair."

He'll fold.

Riley looked at Sargent.

"Hell, let's triple it," Sargent said.

Riley detected a slight flinch from Gallagher at the words.

"Do we have a deal?" Riley said. "Double the bet?"

"Happily," Gallagher said.

Riley walked back to Hard Way. Gallagher returned to his tee shot.

"If he regrips twice and waggles the club three times," Hard Way said softly, "you've got him. He changes his routine when he's nervous."

"How do you know that?"

"I don't, but Sarge does. He knows people who pay attention to tells. Gimme's tell is the regrip and waggle. When he's nervous, he becomes Sergio Garcia Jr."

Riley hadn't noticed anything unusual about Gallagher's pre-shot routine during the first seven holes. Then again, Riley had been in a daze during the front nine. This time he counted as Gallagher regripped once, paused, regripped again, waggled his club once, twice, paused, and at the last moment, waggled it once more before slicing his drive. The ball bounced off the fairway and settled behind the trunk of a tree.

"Told you," Hard Way said. "OK, take a deep breath. Second-easiest hole on the course. You can carry the split fairway, no problem. This thing is made for you."

For reasons not even Riley could explain, a calm came over him. Maybe it was Gallagher's flinch, or the regrips and waggles, or perhaps the sliced drive. Or maybe he was tired of being scared.

When Riley took his practice swing, he felt whole again. There was no way of articulating the feeling, but every golfer has experienced it—that inner peace that comes with knowing you're about to hit a shot exactly and precisely as your mind has imagined it. There is no tension, no real feeling of any kind. You think of nothing, and the reward soon presents itself.

The ball reached warp speed in moments. Hard Way just laughed. Gallagher instantly lost sight of the ball in the desert sky and asked his caddie, "Where is it?" His caddie replied, "Boldly going where no ball has gone before." Sargent punched his fist into the palm of his hand and said to himself, *What do you think of that, Percy?*

Nobody in the group saw it land, but Hard Way knew the line was straight and true. As they walked off the tee box toward the fairway, Hard Way couldn't quit laughing.

"What's so funny?" said Riley, who couldn't contain his own smile.

"You compressed that ball so much that I think the back of it touched the front of it," Hard Way said. "We're going to have to take it out of play after the hole."

"I didn't feel the club hitting the ball."

"I guaran-damn-tee you the ball felt it. That might be the purest shot I've ever seen."

Gallagher punched out from behind the tree but thinned his third shot into the waste area that ran across the width of the fairway. His fourth shot skidded into the greenside bunker on the right.

As he walked up the side of the fairway toward his ball, he paused to watch Riley prepare to hit what he assumed was his third shot. Gallagher had been preoccupied with his own situation and thought Riley had already hit his second shot.

"We're still in this," Gallagher told his caddie. "They're hitting three and I can get up and down for bogey. That's a big green, especially with that pin front right. The TV guy can still make a mess of this."

"Their third? Gimme, that's their *drive*. They've got 77 to the pin."

"That's impossible. You're telling me he hit it 429 . . . with something made in woodshop class?"

The caddie checked his yardage book again.

"Yep, 67 to the front, 77 to the pin."

"I'll be a son of a bitch."

"I'll be one with you."

Hard Way pulled the sand wedge for Riley.

"Half swing, nothing more. Let's favor left of the pin, take the bunker out of play."

"Yes, Obi-Wan," Riley said.

But the shot wasn't left of the pin; it was at the heart of the pin. It landed a few feet in front of the hole, bounced once, and dove into the darkness of the cup for double eagle.

Riley, eyes wide and mouth open, looked at Hard Way when the ball disappeared. He turned and found Sargent, who was trailing 20 yards behind and off to the side. Sargent saluted him. Riley shrugged his shoulders and saluted back.

"I've never made a double eagle," he said to Hard Way.

"I have a feeling there's going to be a lot of things you've never done before," Hard Way said. "Let's go say hello to that cup."

With the hole won by Riley, Gallagher's caddie retrieved his man's ball from the bunker with a rake. He wiped the sand and grime off with a damp towel, and then handed it to a silent and sullen Gallagher as they walked toward the No. 9 tee box, which had a postcard view of the famed Vegas Strip located about fourteen miles away. The ninth hole was a second consecutive par-5 but measured 632 yards, 126 yards longer than the hole they had just lost.

Riley had the honors, and with his newfound confidence, he sent his drive into the stratosphere.

"Hell, that might hit one of the hotels on the Strip," Hard Way said for Gallagher's benefit. "Very saucy."

Gallagher ignored the comment, but as he took the driver from his caddie, he did what would have been unthinkable only thirty minutes earlier: He wondered if he had brought enough cash to cover his bet.

Riley didn't think it was possible for one man to carry so much money. Gallagher reached into a side pouch of his golf bag and pulled out those five, brick-sized stacks of cash. Thick rubber bands strained to keep the money in place.

With the exception of pushes on the two back-nine par-3s and the par-4 18th, Riley had won eight of the last eleven holes, and all the presses that came with them. He had played those eleven holes in 8-under.

Gallagher hadn't wilted as much as he had been steamrolled. Only his legendary putting stroke had kept him from losing all eleven.

"As agreed, here are your winnings," Gallagher said, handing Riley four of the $10,000 cash bricks, and peeling off five $100 bills from the remaining brick. "That's $40,500, and that completes our arrangement. That was a clever tactical move to double the bet."

Gallagher counted out another $2,500 and handed it to his caddie. "Here's a thousand for having to witness my demise," he said. "And here's another fifteen hundred for your memory loss of today's event. Needless to say, your silence will be rewarded by my future use of your services."

The caddie took the money, tipped his cap to the others, and departed without a word. As he walked away, he thought, *Nobody would believe me anyway.*

Meanwhile, Riley could barely grasp the crisp bills with both hands. He looked lovingly at the pile of money and then made a decision.

"Gimme, I can't take this," he said, trying to hand three of the stacks back to Gallagher.

"You can, and you will," Gallagher said, raising his hands as he stepped out of Riley's reach. "The money was won fairly."

Hard Way and Sargent said nothing.

"I did win, but I owe you for teaching me *how* to win," Riley said. "I was terrified, but your tell—when you did the extra regrips and waggles—taught me that every player has a weak spot."

Gallagher glanced at Hard Way and Sargent in confusion. *Tells*?

Sargent stepped in. "So do we have a deal? Did you see enough to bankroll him?"

"Not only am I going to bankroll him, I'm going to make a fortune doing it," Gallagher said.

"Then that's payment enough for me," Riley said, successfully placing $30,000 in Gallagher's hands. Gallagher again looked at Hard Way and Sargent, as if to say, *Who gives back money?* "But if you don't mind, I'd like to use this stack to make a dent in a couple of debts."

Riley counted out $5,000 each for Hard Way and Sargent and handed them the cash.

"This doesn't begin to pay for your time or your belief in me," he said as they tried to protest, "but thank you."

"You only have $500 left," Gallagher said. "What can you do with that?"

Riley looked at Hard Way.

"I'm going to have my caddie teach me how to roll the bones."

That night at Caesar's, aided by the advice of Hard Way and a hot roller at the other end of the craps table, Riley doubled his $500. Before heading to the cashier's cage, Riley tossed a trio of $25 chips to the table crew, and another $25 to the shooter—all on the instructions of Hard Way.

"Why did I just give away $100?" Riley said.

"Because the universe rewards graciousness," Hard Way said. "And because if you ever come back here, that crew will look out for you."

Afterward, as they waited at the restaurant bar for Sargent to arrive for dinner, Riley and Hard Way dissected the day's match.

"I was wondering," Riley said. "If everybody in this town knows about Gimme's tells, why isn't there a line of players waiting to take his money?"

"Yeah, the tells," Hard Way said uneasily. "That's a good question."

"No, seriously. As soon as I saw him do it, just like you said, he wasn't so intimidating anymore."

"Yeah, that was something, wasn't it?"

"What's wrong?"

"Well, I wasn't going to mention it to you."

"Mention what?"

"There were no tells. Gimme *always* regrips twice and waggles three times. I figured you were so worried about the money that you hadn't paid attention to his routine."

"You're kidding me?"

"I am not, sir. I needed something to build up your confidence."

"You lied!"

"I call it 'creative caddying.' "

"I could have lost $20,000!"

"Instead, you won more than $40,000. So in the words of Jim Malone, 'Here endeth the lesson.' "

A restaurant host appeared.

"Your party is seated and waiting for you," said the host as he tried to extract the still-squabbling Riley and Hard Way from the bar. Gallagher and Sargent watched with amusement from their table.

"I think Hard Way just told him that he made up your tells," Sargent said.

"Ah, yes—my imaginary weakness."

"Why'd you bail him out, Gimme? I've never seen you throw a match like that. It was a professional flop, but I never took you for someone with a heart."

"Sarge," Gallagher said as he sipped on an expertly made Sazerac, "I have many fine qualities, but losing money for the purpose of a kind deed is not one of them."

"You mean . . ."

"I mean I never take a dive. I gave him my best game, which is considerable on most days. His best, which was remarkable during those last eleven holes, was far better."

"So you really don't have a heart."

"I have one for beautiful women, for exquisite cars, and for drinks such as this one. But if I'm going to invest in someone, then I need to see how that person operates under duress. Riley was at the brink of mental destruction. Yes, Hard Way's clever use of imaginary tells had a temporary effect, but your player still needed to execute the shots."

"Gimme, you're the most honest guy I know in this dishonest town. Look me in the eye and tell me why you're doing this."

"Whatever you and Hard Way have taught him, whatever is in those inexplicable clubs, and however Riley's pedestrian swing controls their powers, he won the match and my support."

"Gimme. That's *a* reason. Now give me *the* reason."

Gallagher took a final swig of his drink, stood up, and shook Sargent's hand. "Because, my friend, I was too young to bet on Namath against the Colts in '69, too poor to bet on the USA hockey team against the Soviets in '80, and too scared to bet on Douglas against Tyson in '90. I've been waiting my whole life for a long shot like this."

The host finally herded Hard Way and Riley to the table.

"You're out of here?" Hard Way said to Gallagher.

"With much regret," Gallagher said, "I must leave the company of your motley crew. I have to attend to the needs and wants of a certain in-residence woman whose name you might have seen on a Strip marquee."

"That's why you're a legend and I'm just a caddie."

"Your humility bubbles to the surface," Gallagher said. "In my absence, take good care of our mutual investment. I assume you've thought through your next move."

"We're going to earn a buck the hardest way there is," Sargent said.

"Roulette?" the gambler said.

"Worse. A pre-qualifier."

CHAPTER TWENTY-FIVE

Bait and Switch

An AGN researcher was the first to take notice of the name.

Can't be the same guy, can it?

She prided herself on her thoroughness and decided to call the Southern Texas PGA office just to make sure. The STPGA operator forwarded her to the communications coordinator, who couldn't quite believe AGN was interested in a pre-qualifier.

"Which one did you say it was?"

The researcher checked her notes. "The entry list for the March 18 pre-Q at Woodforest. It's the second of the four pre-Qs for the Houston Open."

"OK, found the list. What's the name?"

"Riley," she said. "Joe Riley."

There was a pause.

"Sorry, don't see it—Wait, there it is. Yeah, there's a Riley."

"Does it list a city next to his name?"

"Sure does. J. Riley, Las Vegas, Nevada."

"Las Vegas? Not Wheaton, Illinois?"

"No ma'am. Just Vegas."

"No first name?"

"Just the initial J."

"All right. Appreciate you looking that up for me."

The first-year researcher hung up the phone at her desk.

“What was that about?” said a longtime researcher in the adjoining cubicle. He was a career 80-percenter, content to do the minimum while pretending to do the maximum.

“You’ll laugh, but there’s a guy named J. Riley playing in the pre-Q at Houston. I thought it might be our Joe Riley.”

The 80-percenter wheeled his office chair next to hers and in a conspiratorial voice said, “Some free advice?”

“Sure,” she said.

“I was you a long time ago. Trying to impress the higher-ups, showing initiative, doing the Employee of the Month thing. Turns out, nobody cared.”

“Thought it was worth a shot,” she said.

“I played in a scramble with Joe last summer at the company tournament. We used his ball just once during the entire round—and that’s only because we had to. Does that sound like someone who would enter a pre-Q?”

“I guess not,” she said, embarrassed now.

The older researcher leaned back in his office chair and pushed himself toward his cubicle.

“One last piece of advice,” he said before disappearing around the wall of his workstation. “If you want to last here, don’t ever tell McMullins what you told me.”

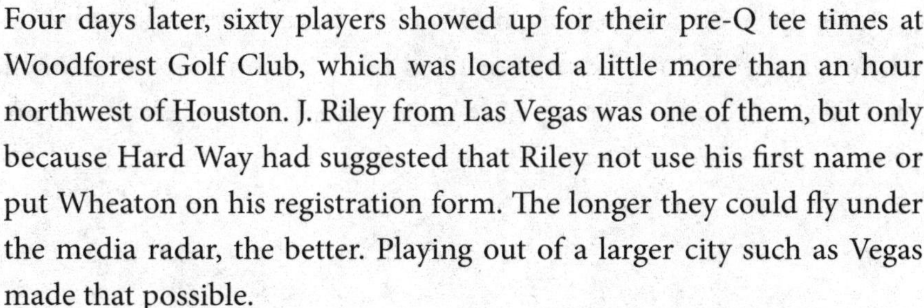

Four days later, sixty players showed up for their pre-Q tee times at Woodforest Golf Club, which was located a little more than an hour northwest of Houston. J. Riley from Las Vegas was one of them, but only because Hard Way had suggested that Riley not use his first name or put Wheaton on his registration form. The longer they could fly under the media radar, the better. Playing out of a larger city such as Vegas made that possible.

Riley had promised Hard Way and Sargent—and Laurel—a two-month commitment before looking for a real job. But after the match-play victory against Gallagher, December and January had bled into February and now early March. Everyone had agreed that the pre-Qs were Riley's best chance to reach a Tour event.

Everyone except Laurel.

"Joe, I'm playing dodgeball with the credit card companies each month," she had said in their last phone conversation. "The little dude spends part of his homework time cutting out grocery coupons for us. We're getting by, but just barely."

"I'll be home soon," Riley had said.

"I meant now."

"Dr. Seuss would want me to play in the Houston pre-Q."

"Joe, it's not funny. I don't know how much longer I can do this."

"Give me Houston. That's all I ask."

"OK," she had said wearily. "Houston. You deserve that much."

Riley didn't dare tell her that he had given Gallagher back $30,000 in match winnings, or that he had paid Hard Way and Sargent $5,000 each, or that his agent had recently informed him that his TV job prospects weren't what they had hoped.

Laurel had her secrets, too. She didn't dare tell Riley that she had lied about negotiating a payment extension with the University of Wisconsin so Buddy could attend spring semester. It was true that Buddy was a student in good standing with the bursar's office. It also was true that Laurel had sold Riley's treasured BMW to a local dealership to ensure that.

Her husband and her sons would know the truth soon enough. But for now, she had explained to Chet and Buddy that the car was stuck at a local garage as the mechanic ordered hard-to-find parts. She asked that they not mention the repairs to their dad. It was, she said, "a surprise."

Riley was paired with an amateur from Beaumont, Texas, and a pro from Bixby, Oklahoma. When they reported to the first tee, neither one recognized Riley from his AGN appearances, but they instantly knew who Hard Way was.

"How the mighty have fallen," the pro said to Hard Way, without introducing himself. "This poor sumbitch down here in the low minor leagues with us nobodies."

The amateur, no older than twenty, rolled his eyes at the pro as he shook hands with Hard Way, and then Riley.

"There's always one, ain't there? Good luck to both of you."

"Where's your caddie?" Riley said.

"Don't have one. Can't afford it. If I make it through, then I'll see if my mom will carry the bag."

Because it was a larger field, the low eight scores and ties would advance out of this pre-Q. The other three pre-Qs ranged from top six, seven, and eight and ties. In all, about thirty players would move on to the Monday Q and its field of seventy-five. Out of that field, only four would move through to the actual Houston Open.

The pro hit first. His drive on the par-4, 396-yard hole split the fairway. He had a homemade swing, but it was powerful. It traveled at least 290 yards, maybe a little more.

"Put a hurtin' on that thing," he crowed, spitting a stream of tobacco juice. "I might have to call my insurance agent and see if they cover collisions like that!"

The amateur pushed his drive to the right, and it settled in the first cut of rough, about 20 yards behind the pro's shot.

Hard Way pulled the head cover off the Nicklaus driver and handed the club to Riley. As they discussed what line to take, the pro chimed in.

"Who are you, Byron Nelson with that thing?" he said. "What kind of ball you hitting, a gutta-percha?"

The pro sidled up to the amateur.

"We won't have to worry about this guy moving through," he said, nudging the kid with an elbow.

Hard Way checked the wind one last time. It was at their back.

"Joe, take a little bit off the swing," he said. "Wind is helping just enough."

The pro nudged the kid again.

"Sure, take a little bit off the swing, Byron. Hell, the sumbitch hole is 400 yards long."

As Hard Way pulled the bag to the side of the tee box, he caught the eye of the pro and mouthed, "Buh-bye." An instant later, Riley's drive screamed through the air, landed 10 yards short of the green, bounced to the back pin position, and came to a stop a foot away from the hole.

The pro swallowed his wad of chaw and then threw up on the leg of an elderly volunteer. He knew at that moment, just as Salieri must have known the first time he heard Mozart play, that he was irrelevant. The pro was so shaken by what he had witnessed from Riley that he sprayed his second shot and needed three more to salvage a bogey. The amateur recorded a scrambling par. Riley tapped in for eagle.

As they walked off the green, the pro squeezed between Hard Way and Riley.

"What planet you from?" he said. "'Cause nobody is beating you sumbitches today."

Late that afternoon, the first-year AGN researcher checked the pre-Q scores in Houston. She couldn't help herself.

J. Riley from Las Vegas had shot a 63, two shots ahead of the next player, an amateur from Beaumont. It would be the lowest score of the four pre-Q tournaments.

Word soon spread of the unknown hotshot from Vegas with his persimmon woods, his ancient irons, and his impossibly long distances. Of course, there were always the one-round wonders who disappeared when they advanced from the pre-Q to the pressures of the Monday qualifier. The veterans of the Monday circuit had seen it happen time after time.

But Riley shot a 65 to finish second overall and secure a place with the Tour pros in the Houston field. His photo made it into the online edition of the Houston *Chronicle* sports section, which made it to the

AGN researcher, who forwarded it to McMullins with an email subject heading of *You're not going to believe this . . .*

For fun, she cc'd the longtime researcher.

It didn't take long for the national golf media to learn of the story. In AGN's case, McMullins sent Rinello to Houston. He joined a dozen other reporters who had been dispatched by their networks, papers, websites, and magazines to separate fact from fiction regarding Riley. More than a few of those same reporters, convinced that Riley would never make the cut, booked their return flights for Friday night. Who could blame them?

Despite the pleas of Tour officials on-site, Riley declined all interview requests. Rinello reached out separately.

"Tim," Riley said, "if I could, I would. But I promised Hard Way and Sarge that I wouldn't do any interviews unless I got to the weekend. And I think we both know that's not going to happen. If you still want to talk to me after Friday's round, I'll do it."

Rinello could hear the stress and anxiety in Riley's voice. He wished him well, but wondered if his friend would even survive Thursday's round.

Laurel could hear the same stress, which is why she floated the possibility of a last-minute spring break trip to Houston with Chet and Buddy.

"We'll be your cheering section," she said.

"L, you said it yourself: We're semi-broke," Riley said. "Three round-trip airfares aren't going to be cheap. Let's save the money. Anyway, I'm going to be nervous enough."

"You've done so well, and I shouldn't have guilted you about the money thing."

"You weren't wrong. Anyway, you'd have to drag Buddy here."

"Hon, it was his idea."

"Buddy?"

"You underestimate him. You always have."

As he stepped onto the first tee for the opening round at Memorial Park Golf Course, Riley couldn't help but notice that at least a dozen media members, including Rinello, were crouched down just inside the ropes. The early-morning dew had already left watermarks on the knees of their pants. A competing network was broadcasting the tournament, but Rinello would do several hits for AGN shows after the round was completed.

A handful of photographers with their Nikons and Cannons hanging from their necks and slung over their shoulders also were there. A TV crew had been assigned to follow the 7:13 A.M. threesome, too.

Riley had become a subplot for Thursday morning. He would serve as part of the news cycle until the big names and leaders established themselves later in the day. He was the opening act.

Six months earlier, Riley had been one of those reporters wearing a credential with Inside the Ropes status. It gave him treasured access and proximity. Where else could you cover a sporting event and be only ten feet away from the players?

Now he wished those armbands didn't exist. Everyone seemed too close, too *there*.

"Feeling ready?" Hard Way said.

"No," Riley said.

"You'll be fine once we get going."

"I don't know if I can do this."

Hard Way wondered the same thing. The warm-up session had been awful. Worse than awful. Unlike the pre-Q and the qualifier, when he had been locked into his swing, Riley had a two-way miss working on the range—one shot went right, the next one left. And now he had to deal with a media contingent and a bigger-than-expected fan presence on the first tee. It was something Sarge and Hard Way hadn't been able to replicate in their prep work. Riley would have to experience it for himself. All players did.

"We've got a 522-yard par-4," Hard Way said. "I'll give you $10 if you land it in the fairway."

"Just what I need, more pressure."

"And I'll give you $100 if you push the boat out and it lands wherever the hell it lands."

"Sure, just as soon as you tell me what 'Push the boat out' means."

"I heard Dame Mary Berry say it on a BBC cooking show—and yes, I watch cooking shows. It's British slang for 'be extravagant.' In other words, feel free to hit the crap out of this drive."

"All right, this one is for Dame Mary," Riley said with a slight grin.

The ever-observant Rinello had heard the entire exchange. In his notebook, he wrote, "Professional caddie work . . . Joe in knots on first tee . . . Caddie untied him."

Riley didn't completely relax, but he did concentrate on his tee shot rather than the media entourage. His drive cleared the corner of the dogleg-left hole and landed on the right edge of the fairway. It carried almost 400 yards.

The crowd had a delayed reaction. First disbelief, followed by murmuring, and then cheers. Rinello turned to watch their faces and wrote, "They saw something they had never seen before: the supernatural."

"That's the Riley I know!" Hard Way said, taking the driver from his man. "And no, I'm not paying you $100. That was a psychological ploy."

Riley still had his struggles. The two-way miss returned several times during the round, as did a half dozen unforced errors caused by nerves. But Hard Way steered him around the Tom Doak redesign for a 1-over-par 71.

The next day, a calmer Riley shot an even-par 70 and made the cut on the number after sinking a downhill 3-footer on the final hole for par. As it turned out, he was the last one to sneak into the weekend.

As promised, Riley did the interview with Rinello. It was a surreal experience to be on the other side of the questions, especially when posed by such a skillful reporter.

"What would success have been for you Thursday morning when you teed off?" Rinello said, leaning forward and lightly touching Riley's left arm.

"That's easy," Riley said. "Not hitting a spectator."

"Joe, the advantage I have in this interview is that I know you and your inclination to deflect and hide behind humor. In honor of our friendship, give me an honest answer."

Riley stared down for a moment. Rinello had caught him in the act.

"Success? I have so much respect for those players who are out there grinding in the pre-Qs and in the Monday qualifiers. Every week, they try to chase down their dreams. They try to eke out a living in the hardest game ever invented. There are no courtesy cars and player lounges for them. They just want a chance. So success for me was not letting them down."

"In what way?"

"WD because I shot a 94. I didn't want them to think I'd wasted a spot. I'm playing for me, of course, but also for them."

"And as we sit here with you now, what would success look like for you after Sunday's round?"

"To finish last with dignity."

"You think you're going to finish last?"

"I think everyone thinks I'm going to finish last."

"Why?"

"Because I'm a nobody trying to be a somebody."

"In light of your surprising performance this week, a handful of Tour players, including your caddie's former employer, have suggested that your game is too good to be true. Your response?"

The question caught Riley by surprise. Hard Way's former man wasn't in the Houston field, but it was now obvious that he was working behind the scenes to undermine Riley and Hard Way and create suspicion among other Tour pros.

"The clubs don't hit themselves," Riley said.

"So you're saying those players are wrong."

"I'm saying I'd have more respect for them if they said it to my face."

"You're angry."

"No, Tim, I'm motivated."

The interview aired on AGN later that night. When it was done, Hard Way's former man muted the TV, picked up his phone, and made a half dozen calls.

Riley shot consecutive rounds of 2-under-par 68 over the weekend to finish in a tie for thirty-seventh out of the remaining field of eighty-three and earn $43,165. At Riley's request, tournament officials wired $3,021—Hard Way's 7 percent cut of the winnings—to the caddie's bank account and the remainder to the empty Riley family savings account.

Thanks to Riley, the tournament had seen a bump in viewership. He never challenged for the lead, but his top-40 finish hadn't gone unnoticed by others in the industry—or by his older son.

"Dad, that was unreal," said Buddy, who called shortly after Riley finished the round.

"I can barely hear you," Riley said.

"Sorry!" Buddy shouted. "Everybody I know is crammed into my apartment. We watched the whole thing. I can't believe Mom wouldn't let us fly down there."

"That's what your mom said?"

"Yeah," said Buddy above the din. "She said you were all for it, but that she thought we should save the money. Sometimes I don't get her."

Laurel had covered for Riley.

"Sometimes I don't, either. But we don't deserve her."

"I lost you on that one, Dad. Too loud on my end. I'll try you back when it calms down."

Fifteen minutes later, as Hard Way and Riley were loading their bags into the rental car, Riley's cell began to ring.

"Buddy again?" Hard Way said.

"He said he'd call back," said Riley, pulling his phone from his back pocket. Except this time he didn't recognize the number. "Where's a 210 area code?"

"No clue," Hard Way said. "Wait! Answer it now!"

"Why?"

"Answer it! Two-ten is San Antonio."

It was the tournament director of the Davis Oil Open. The Davis was played just northeast of San Antonio and, more important, it was played the week before the Masters. Riley put him on speaker.

"Son, what you did at Houston was nothing short of dazzling," the tournament director gushed. "We'd like to offer you one of our unrestricted sponsor exemptions. We'll treat you like family. That's what we're famous for."

"Can I call you back?"

Hard Way slapped his forehead. He looked at Riley in disbelief. The tournament director, momentarily stunned, said, "Don't take too long. We got a press release with your name on it."

A few minutes later, with Laurel's blessing, Riley accepted the invitation.

Hard Way and Riley made the three-hour drive to San Antonio early that evening. They had a celebratory steak dinner and Monday morning drove to the TPC San Antonio Oaks course.

Their arrival at the clubhouse was met with awkward looks and averted eyes. The clubhouse manager said the tournament director was on his way.

"Maybe they ran out of courtesy cars?" Hard Way said.

"This is all new to me," Riley said.

A few minutes later, the tournament director arrived, seeming flustered.

"I've been trying to reach you all morning," he said.

"That's my bad," Riley said. "I turned off my cell late last night and forgot to bring it with me today."

The director motioned for them to step outside.

"I'm afraid we're going to have to withdraw our sponsor exemption. I'm terribly sorry."

"What?" Riley said.

"There has been"—he paused and seemed at a loss for the right words—"how should I put it?" Again, a pause. "Um, pushback from certain influential parties."

"What does that mean?" Riley asked.

"It means we're not going to be able to accommodate you. The exemption has been offered to and accepted by another player."

Everyone was silent.

"Did you see the following my man had this past week?" Hard Way asked. "The media coverage? The way he played? What happened to being 'family'? That's what you're famous for."

"It's out of my hands at this point. We'll obviously pay for any travel costs related to this misunderstanding."

"'Misunderstanding'?" Hard Way said.

"We had to make a difficult choice based on an untenable situation."

"Which was?" Riley said.

But before the tournament director could respond, Hard Way interrupted. "I'll tell you what it was. Some of the players were going to boycott the tournament."

The director said nothing.

"What'd we do wrong?"

"You finished thirty-seventh," Hard Way stated simply. "They think the Jacks are illegal. They think you and I don't belong at a Tour event. They think whatever my former man is telling them to think. Is that about the gist of it?" Hard Way looked at the tournament director.

The tournament director rubbed the back of his neck with the palm of his hand.

"Yeah, that's about right."

The drive back to the hotel was made in silence. Once he'd parked, Hard Way began to open the car door. Riley stayed put.

"You coming?" Hard Way said.

"Do you think I'm a cheater?" Riley said, staring straight ahead.

"What?"

"Do you think I'm a cheater?"

"Joe, don't do this."

"What's the difference between what I'm doing and what I accused Buddy of doing? Gawd, what a hypocrite I am."

Hard Way closed the door and waved off the hotel car valet through the window.

"You're not a cheater," he said. "Otherwise, we would have finished higher than T-37."

"You're missing my point," Riley said.

"Do you fudge the coin?"

"Fudge the what?"

"The coin. When you mark your ball on the green, do you move your coin a little to the left or right to avoid an indentation on your putting line?"

"No."

"When it's time to putt, do you place your ball just in front of your mark, or do you try to gain an inch or so closer to the hole?"

"Right in front of it."

"If your ball is buried in the rough around the green, do you use your shoe heels to 'accidentally' compress the grass behind it so you have an easier chip?"

"Of course not."

"If you're in the rough off a fairway, do you clear a path behind the ball by taking a few sideway practice swings?"

"No."

"Do you doctor your clubfaces?"

"You know I don't."

"Just like I said, you're not a cheater. Name me one rule you've broken."

"I'm talking about the spirit of the rules."

"So am I. What's the difference between what you do with the Jacks and what Nicklaus did with a club in his hand? Or Tiger. Hogan. Rory. Seve. Scottie. They hit shots that were so good that it didn't make sense."

"I'm not them."

"But your shots are! Don't you understand? You bring those clubs to life, not the other way around. Your clubs are *harder* to hit well than Rory's clubs. It's not even close. I don't know how you do it, but you do. And however you do it, it ain't cheating."

"You really think it's me?"

"I hit your driver. It went nowhere. Sarge hit your driver. It went nowhere. The guy at the range in Glen Ellyn—what's his name?"

"Bucket hat man."

"Yeah, him. It went nowhere. Trust me, it's you."

There was a tap on the car window. It was the car valet again. He held up two bottled waters.

"I don't know whether to tip this kid or run over him," Hard Way said, waving him off again.

Riley hadn't noticed the valet. His mind was still at the course.

"I can't believe they'd boycott a tournament because of me."

"Could have been a bluff, but the tournament director wasn't going to take the chance," Hard Way said.

"What should I do now?"

"Go home. Reintroduce yourself to your family. But before you do, I need to tell you a story."

"About what?"

"About why I got fired at the Memorial."

"Max, I was drunk that night in Vegas. I was out of line to ask."

"You were a reporter then. Now you're an ex-reporter. And you're a friend. You bared your soul about Buddy. And now I owe you the same honesty."

CHAPTER TWENTY-SIX

One-Man Rule

That same Monday . . .

The Chairman was a creature of habit. When in town, he was at his Augusta National office by 7:15 A.M., but only after completing his ninety-minute workout in his home gym.

His administrative assistant of ten years had been at the office since 6 A.M. She had already placed his daily schedule and the print editions of Monday's *The Wall Street Journal* and *The Augusta Chronicle* on his George III antique desk, which had been a gift from the members upon his appointment as chairman. A silver tray with the Augusta National logo held a glass of freshly squeezed orange juice and a small bowl of yogurt. The Chairman, now in his early seventies, ate judiciously.

He was a pragmatic man, a lawyer by trade, just as Augusta National co-founder Bobby Jones had been in his professional life. The Chairman had been a scratch player in his twenties, and was a member of a USA team that had beaten Great Britain and Ireland, 13–11, in the Walker Cup. But the demands of law school, his climb to near the top of one of New York's most prestigious firms, and later, the establishment of his own boutique power firm in Charlotte had contributed to his handicap reaching high single digits. He was now a respectable 10.5, but you played him at your own risk. Only a few days ago, he had shot his age.

The Chairman was traditional in ways that mattered at clubs such as Augusta National. His bespoke gray slacks and white dress shirts, his Cambridge Shell cordovan wingtips, his muted blue Augusta National ties, his freshly dry-cleaned green jacket, his Mercedes S-Class in Obsidian Black metallic . . . they all spoke a language of understated affluence. At a recent club function, a new member had arrived in the dining room with a flamboyant pocket square sprouting from his green jacket as if it were a dozen plum-purple roses. The Chairman had noticed the indiscretion and motioned with nothing more than a nod and frown for a nearby club official to handle the matter. Moments later, the member received a gentle hand on the shoulder and was invited to join the official in an anteroom, where a clubhouse attendant stood ready with a postcard-sized white box. When the member returned to his seat, his left breast pocket was bare. At night's end, the member found his offending floral fabric in its white cardboard coffin sitting comfortably on the passenger seat of his car.

It gave the Chairman no pleasure to enforce the club's dress code. If anything, he admired the new member for testing, however accidentally, the limits of the rules. What had made the Chairman especially formidable as a lawyer was his own ability to test the tensile strength of the law. He had a nimble mind and a predisposition to unconventional thinking. His reputation for honesty was unassailable, as was his allegiance to fairness.

Power as an ideal didn't appeal to him. He valued differing, informed opinions but made it clear that his voice would be the final one to be heard. Those who had foolishly challenged his rule for their personal gain suddenly found themselves assigned to the tournament's Refuse and Recycling Committee.

Mistakes had been made during his tenure, but he always found a way to correct them or ease their impact. At times, he had had to pull the membership into the future as it kicked and screamed like an infant about his diversity, community outreach, and technology initiatives. He loved his duties and his club, but he had decided this would be his last Masters as chairman. He had shared the decision with no one.

Only a very few people outside his immediate family had the

number to his private office. The list included several U.S. presidents, the CEO of the Royal & Ancient, and a handful of trusted friends. Everyone else had to go through his assistant.

One of those trusted friends called late that morning. The friend didn't make a request as much as make the Chairman aware of a golf injustice. The call lasted just four minutes, but when it was finished, the Chairman asked his assistant to send him the link to Rinello's AGN interview with Joe Riley.

The Chairman had met Riley several years earlier during his annual Masters-week visit to the main work area at the media center. Accompanied by the Green Jacket in charge of the Media Committee, the Chairman would be introduced to or reacquainted with various reporters and editors. He would linger for a few moments with each media member as he worked his way up the carpeted stairs.

Riley had struck him as pleasant and professional. The Chairman found his reports and stories competent and often compelling. He had been surprised to learn that Riley had been included in AGN's layoffs and would no longer be part of future Masters telecasts. He had sent a personal note to the reporter thanking him for his past contributions to the coverage.

When news of Riley's foray into professional golf first reached his desk the previous week, there was something about its daring nature that intrigued the Chairman. Much like he had with the pocket square, he respected the outlandishness of it. Of course, he gave Riley no chance of qualifying for or competing in the Houston tournament. In fact, he had forgotten about it until his assistant had placed a note on his desk.

Re: Joe Riley . . . He made it.

Now having just learned of Riley's sudden exclusion from the Davis Oil Open, the Chairman watched the Rinello interview, the highlights of Riley's play at the Houston Open, and his demeanor and conduct during and after his rounds. Riley's game was unlike anything the Chairman had ever seen. It was unpolished and incomprehensible. *This* was the reporter who, according to the club's communications director, had barely broken 100 at Augusta National several years earlier during the Monday lottery round? It was obvious at Houston that he had depended heavily on his caddie, but you were drawn to the possibilities. There also was a humility to his style, as well as a certain courage of conviction. Above all else, the Chairman loved an underdog. He had been one himself: a rural kid from Madison, Georgia, whose dad toiled thirty-five years as a roofer, a self-taught player who learned the game of golf at a local course with bald spots of red clay on every fairway and green, a straight-A student rejected by the Ivies who worked two jobs to help pay for his in-state UGA tuition, a little-regarded first-year associate who eventually made equity partner at the blue-blooded New York firm, and a risk-taker who eventually left to start his own shop from scratch. He was always the outsider, as was this Riley fellow.

According to existing criteria, there were twenty-six ways a player could automatically qualify for a Masters invitation. They included past champion status, winning a recent major, winning one of the established amateur championships or a gold medal in Olympic golf competition, finishing in the top 12 of the previous year's Masters or the top 4 of the previous year's other majors, winning an approved Tour event, and having finished in the top 50 of the world rankings. Joe Riley didn't meet any of those qualifications.

The next morning, Tuesday, at exactly 7:15, the Chairman walked into his office, had a small glass of freshly squeezed orange juice and a half cup of plain yogurt, and then typed a two-sentence email to his communications department instructing it to post his announcement on the Masters website at precisely noon that day. Like the Chairman himself, the announcement was direct and concise.

The Masters Tournament has extended a special invitation to Joe Riley, a player of unusual circumstance not otherwise qualified. We look forward to hosting Mr. Riley and the rest of the Masters invitees.

Roy T. Jewell
Chairman

There were now twenty-seven ways to join the Masters field.

CHAPTER TWENTY-SEVEN

Cordially Invited

That same Tuesday . . .

Hard Way was running hot. Still angry about getting booted from the Davis Oil tournament a day earlier, he now was stuck at San Antonio International Airport after yet another delay to his morning flight to Phoenix. At first it had been something about a maintenance issue with a rear lavatory door, then a staffing problem involving the flight attendants, then a malfunction of an unspecified cockpit light. Hard Way had arrived at the airport at 7 A.M., and almost four hours later, he was still at Gate 24 with no definitive departure time in sight.

He texted Riley, whose flight to Chicago was scheduled to depart in an hour from Gate 10 in the same terminal.

I'm in airline hell. You?

Flight plans changed.

Those bastards. I could have gotten home faster on the back of a sloth. What'd they do to you?

Rerouted me.

Sorry, man. Through DFW, Detroit, or Minny?

None of the above.

Houston?

You're getting colder.

I quit caring two texts ago.

That's too bad. I was hoping you'd join me.

Where?

Georgia.

No thank you. Going to regroup,
visit Kat, chill.

I've got a better idea.

What's that?

You'll find out in less than thirty seconds.

Hard Way glanced at the video screen above the ticket counter. It was 10:59 Central time, 11:59 Eastern.

Moments later, Hard Way's phone began to ring and ding as if it were playing "Carol of the Bells." He answered Bang Bang's call first.

"Dude! I just saw the news!" Bang Bang said.

"It's public?"

"They just released a statement."

"That's great. First they screw us, and then they tell everyone about it."

"Screwed you? You just got the golden ticket!"

"We got boned big-time, Bang Bang. Tournament director here pulled the bait and switch. We're out."

"Dude, we talking about the same thing?"

"Yeah, Davis Oil. We're out."

"No, man. You're in!"

"In what?"

"The Masters!"

When Riley had covered the Masters for AGN and, before that, for the Chicago *Tribune,* he would fly into Atlanta and make the mind-numbing two-and-a-half-hour drive east to Augusta, or fly into Columbia, South Carolina, and drive seventy-five minutes west on I-20. He had never imagined flying in a private jet from an FBO in San Antonio to Augusta Regional.

The truth is, he had never imagined any of this. When he had called Laurel with the news, she had burst out laughing, chided her husband about the practical joke, and said she had to cut the call short. Only when Buddy texted her a link from the AGN website did she begin to believe. Even when the green Masters invitation arrived at the house by courier, she double-checked the name and address to make sure it wasn't all a mistake.

Gallagher had arranged the private plane to Augusta for Riley and Hard Way, as well as a rental house for two weeks. Since the Masters invitation had come only nine days before the tournament began, Sargent had suggested that Hard Way and Riley get there as soon as possible and begin their prep work before the course opened its doors to the media, patrons, the Augusta National Women's Amateur, and the Drive, Chip and Putt competition. Sargent would fly in that Sunday.

By getting there so early, Riley and Hard Way would have three and a half days of relative solitude at Augusta National. The ANWA would have a practice round there on Friday, and their final round there on Saturday. The DCP kids would take the stage on Sunday. But the true madness would begin the following day, when all attention turned to the Masters itself.

This wouldn't be the first time Riley had played Augusta National. Four years earlier—and after five previous attempts—his name had finally been chosen from the list of entries in the annual media lottery. Pressroom veterans were convinced that the "lottery" was nothing more than a mirage, that the club handpicked the media field each year. The conspiracy theorists, though, were always the ones who didn't get picked.

Riley and twenty-seven other members of the media had received printed invitations on official Masters stationery, followed by a mandatory Sunday briefing on the schedule and protocol for the Monday lottery round, followed by a restless night of sleep.

Riley had borrowed a set of clubs from the manager of the Washington Avenue hotel where the lesser AGN talent was housed. He drove down Magnolia Lane at exactly an hour before his appointed tee time (any earlier and you'd have to wait in your car), was issued a locker in the Champions Locker Room, was served breakfast, was assigned a caddie (no tipping, said the instructions, though only the very cheap or the very naïve adhered to that particular Augusta National rule), hit a few practice shots on the range, posed for a photo on the first tee box, and then, palms sweaty, snap-hooked his opening drive. It took him the entire front nine before his heartbeat had settled down.

He had shot 98 that day, but it included a par on the famous par-3 12th. Despite the no-tipping edict, Riley had slipped his caddie a couple of hundos on the 18th tee box, where no member or club official could see the transaction. He finished the hole with a double bogey and a smile as wide as a fairway. It had been a memorable, carefree day.

There would be nothing carefree about this visit. As the wheels of the Embraer Phenom 305/E touched down softly on the grooved concrete runway of Augusta Regional, Riley was overcome by a sense of awe, but also by dread. He turned to Hard Way, who was unbuckling his seat belt as they taxied to the FBO.

"Skitch, how did we get here?"

Hard Way instantly recognized the movie dialogue from Tom Hanks's *That Thing You Do!*

"I led you here, sir," Hard Way said dramatically. "For I am Spartacus."

There was a long pause. "You know what happened to him, right?" Riley said.

"Good point."

CHAPTER TWENTY-EIGHT

Master Class

Nobody does rules like the Masters.

No running. No phones. No sitting on the grass. No backward hats, including for the players. No tipping. No folding chairs with arms or pointed ends. No pointed heels. No shoes without socks in the clubhouse. No playing in shorts. No cash accepted. No selfie sticks. No strollers. No flags, banners, or signs. No cameras once the tournament begins. No autograph-seeking on the course. No public comments from anybody at the club except the Chairman. No sponsor signage on the caddies. No wearing the green jacket with jeans.

The cumulative weight of the rules (and there are more of them) once prompted a longtime golf writer to say, "Can't wait to get here, can't wait to leave." Riley had repeated those words in the past, but not now. Now, incredibly, he was in the field, not the media center. Rules were the least of his worries. Hard Way and Riley dropped their luggage off at their rental house, a spacious Southern Colonial set on an acre of land with a wide circular drive, a vast front porch, and a two-story-high flagpole with the American flag and a Masters flag below it flapping gently in the early afternoon breeze. On the antique table in the foyer was a huge welcome basket that spilled over with candy, cheeses, crackers, wines, and a bottle of Macallan Scotch. Green and yellow balloons were tied to the wicker handle. A note sat on top of the feast:

Welcome to our home. It was lucky for Jordan in 2015!
All the best!

Riley had never stayed in such luxurious lodgings for a tournament. During his newspaper and digital days, the travel departments routinely placed him in low-budget hotels. There was one draconian period when they booked him into a bed-and-breakfast in Carnoustie where there was no breakfast and the bed was as narrow as an ironing board. Dinner at the house consisted of a single cucumber finger sandwich and a small glass of tap water. The same corporate travel agent also refused to approve his request for a U.S. Open media hotel room and instead booked him into a campground near Oakmont. The agent's crowning cost-saving achievement came when Riley was dispatched to cover the Presidents Cup in Melbourne, Australia. His room was located above a car wash on the outskirts of the city.

"Pretty sweet," Riley said. "At AGN, I was usually assigned the converted garage at a rental house off Aumond Road."

"It'll do," Hard Way said, ignoring the gift basket. "You take the big bedroom, I'll grab one of the other rooms. Let's go over to the course and play a quick nine before it gets dark."

It took only about ten minutes to reach the main entry gate. They took a right at Eisenhower Drive and then a quick left at Magnolia Lane, where the canopy of trees framed the back side of the stately clubhouse in the distance. How many goose bumps had the short drive produced over the decades?

Riley, like all those who had made multiple trips to Augusta National and read the work of golf historian David Owen, was well-versed in its humble beginnings.

In 1931, as the infant club struggled to attract members, the initiation fee was just $350. Almost nobody wanted to join. Three years later, in an effort to draw attention to the east Georgia course, club cofounders Bobby Jones and Clifford Roberts debuted the Augusta National Invitation Tournament, which was later renamed the Masters. Jones, the only player ever to have won all four majors in the same calendar year, provided the new tournament with its legitimacy and credibility, while the dour Roberts, an investment banker who would serve as the tournament chairman for forty-three years, assumed the role of micromanaging autocrat. He and Jones would become an adroit pair, partly for what they created, and partly for their intractable nature and unwavering commitment to perfection.

Everything at Augusta National is done in extremes. It is what makes the place singular, but also so exasperating at times. A frequent guest to the club once told Riley, “Nobody does the last 10 percent of anything better than Augusta National.”

This was true, especially at the Masters. The grounds were pristine. The high-quality merchandise was reasonably priced (compared to, say, at the U.S. Open, where you needed a home equity loan to afford a golf shirt), the employees were exceedingly helpful, and the concession stand menu was so obscenely affordable that it was hard to spend $20 on a meal for two. The players were treated like heads of state. The television broadcasts were refreshingly light on commercials. The press facilities were state-of-the-art velvet coffins: full of creature comforts, but meanwhile, meaningful access to players had been virtually eliminated.

Riley had always struggled with the contradiction that was Augusta National. So many decent and well-meaning members. So many iconic golf moments. So many new initiatives locally, nationally, and internationally to use golf as a tool of inclusion. So much emphasis on a telecast devoted to golf and not commercials.

Still, it was hard to ignore the club’s own complicated and distressing past: a history of racism, sexism, and exclusion that stretched to 1975 until the first Black player was allowed to compete in the Masters, 1990 until the first Black member was admitted, and 2012 until the first women were admitted into the membership. This was the same club whose previous chairman had publicly humiliated Tiger Woods in a 2010 address to the media by lecturing “our hero” about the player’s personal conduct and human failings. It was hypocrisy and arrogance personified, as if the chairman at the time and all his fellow Green Jackets had led flawless lives, or that the club was immune to scrutiny about its own inconvenient past, including the tragic end of co-founder Roberts in late September 1977. Overpowered by his own personal demons, the eighty-four year-old Roberts had placed the working end of a gun to his head and pulled the trigger. His body was found at the edge of Ike's Pond at the club's Par 3 Course.

For Riley, the Masters was a magnificent tournament played on a magnificent course, and he was honored to have covered as many Masters as he had. But for all its grandeur and history, it was also a fenced-in azalea fortress located across the street from a beauty salon, a gas station, and an auto repair shop.

As Hard Way pulled the Mercedes courtesy car into the circular drive of the clubhouse, an attendant appeared and arranged for Riley's clubs to be taken to the range.

"I'll park and meet you there," Hard Way said to Riley.

The attendant led Riley to the locker room and then waited at a discreet distance as Riley changed into his golf shoes. It was such a disorienting experience to be where he had been forbidden to visit as a reporter. When he finished, a pair of Green Jackets approached. Out of habit, Riley thought he had done something wrong.

"Mr. Riley?" the older of the two members said.

"Yes?" Riley said, rising to his feet, half convinced that they were going to escort him from the premises.

"I'm Richard Nielsen, and this is Ivan Johnson. And we are thrilled that you are back here, albeit under different circumstances."

Nielsen and Johnson offered handshakes and warm smiles. Riley sighed with relief.

"I thought I'd already violated some sort of protocol," Riley said.

"We were admirers of your work, and now we're admirers of your play," Johnson said. "Please let us know if there's anything we can do for you." He nodded toward the attendant. "Terrence will provide you with our contact info. Don't hesitate to call."

The two men departed. Riley reached for his hat, closed the door to his temporary locker, and followed Terrence out of the clubhouse. As they made the five-minute walk to the practice area, Riley said, "That was surprising."

Terrence didn't acknowledge the comment. Instead, he took Riley directly to the Golf Services Building adjacent to the range. To call it a caddie shack would have been like calling dinner at the internationally famous French Laundry "a bite to eat."

"Here you go, sir. I'll make sure Mr. Nielsen and Mr. Johnson's information is provided to you before you leave today."

He started to walk away, but then stopped and turned.

"Mr. Riley, as a staff, we treat all the entrants with equal respect." He winked. "But we root for the little guys. Good luck."

Hard Way emerged from the small building with an Augusta National caddie at his side.

"What was that about?" he asked as the attendant left.

"I think we're likeable underdogs," Riley said.

"Underdogs? We're subterranean. Anyway, this tournament is littered with likable underdogs who didn't make the cut. That's why I arranged for some special assistance. Joe, meet Milwaukee Fats Joyner."

Milwaukee was at least 300 pounds, and in his linen-white Masters caddie uni, the sixty-something-year-old man looked like the Pillsbury Doughboy, but without the chef's hat.

"We don't believe in irony when it comes to nicknames here," Milwaukee said as his beefy hand folded over Riley's.

According to Augusta National rules, Riley had to use a club caddie for practice rounds until Saturday. Hard Way could accompany them Monday through Friday, but he wasn't allowed to carry the clubs until Riley officially registered on the weekend. That was OK with Hard Way, who was no fan of the white onesies, or lugging around that bag for an extra five days.

"Milwaukee is one of the top three caddies at this place, and that's saying something," Hard Way said.

"Well, it's nice to be wanted," Milwaukee said. "Congrats on getting in."

"You mean it?" Riley said.

Milwaukee looked at Hard Way.

"Permission to speak," Hard Way said. "You won't hurt our feelings."

"Well, I am happy for you, and for this guy, too," Milwaukee said, patting Hard Way on the back. "But a lot of professional players would have loved that special invitation. Still, what you did at Houston caught our attention in the caddie room. A few of the fellas were cheering for you."

"But not you," Riley said, still smarting from Milwaukee's reference to *professional* players.

"I wasn't cheering *against* you. I'm just . . ."

"Dubious?"

"Yeah, that's a good word for it, I suppose. But I'd love for you to prove me wrong. I'll give you an honest day's work, and I'll tell you everything I know about the place."

"Sounds fair to me," Riley said.

Milwaukee picked up the bag. The bag strap groaned.

"Whatcha got in this thing, a bank safe?"

"Sorry," Hard Way said. "We've got some decisions to make on clubs, so there's a half dozen extras in there: a couple of 60-degree wedges, a couple of gap wedges, a couple of hybrids."

"And I see two putters."

"And two putters."

"Never mind about the painted white one. I just use the Scotty Cameron," Riley said.

"My bad," Hard Way said. "Meant to leave the fake Fang back at the rental house."

"Well, let's get to it," Milwaukee said.

"Before we start," Riley said, "I just want to say one thing: This is sooooo cool."

"Settle down, Sparky," Hard Way said. "Gotta pace yourself."

Riley walked ahead. Under his breath, Hard Way told Milwaukee, "This is *unbelievably* cool."

Riley warmed up with his non-Nicklaus wedges. The uninspiring results with the 60-degree and gap wedges caused Milwaukee to look at Hard Way in a panic. *You dragged me out here for this?*

"Hit the Jack wedge," Hard Way said.

Milwaukee handed Riley the MacGregor pitching wedge, but not before doing a double take.

"Damn, we got these relics hanging in glass cases in the clubhouse grill room. Leather grips, too? Wullkotte do these?"

Hard Way nodded.

"And I guaran-damn-tee you that's a Don White grind." Milwaukee thumbed through the rest of MacGregors. "Damn, they all look like Don White grinds."

"They are," Hard Way said. "Show him what they can do, Joe."

For the next twenty minutes, Riley sent iron shot after iron shot to distances Milwaukee had never seen. Before long, several members of the Golf Services Building staff had come out to watch.

"With all due respect, Mr. Riley," Milwaukee said, "how does a swing speed that slow create a ball speed that fast?"

"I get that a lot," Riley said. "It's a mystery."

"You ever hit those irons, Hard Way? You've got a respectable move."

"Tried them once. They don't work for me. They don't work for anybody except Joe. Wait until he hits the woods."

Milwaukee pulled the 5-wood from the bag.

"These are some raggedy-ass head covers. Want me to get you some new wool ones from the shop?"

"They have sentimental value," Riley said. "Belonged to a family friend."

Riley hit a half dozen 5-woods, 3-woods, and drivers before the director of the facility sheepishly approached them with a request.

"I can't believe I'm saying this, but apparently your first two drives almost reached the plate-glass windows of the media center building," he said. "That's more than 400 yards away. They're asking if you can stand down on the driver until they figure out what to do."

Milwaukee whistled. "Mr. Riley, I believe I now understand why our wise and esteemed Chairman extended you an invitation."

"I can hit the hybrids instead," Riley said to the director.

"That would be appreciated," he said, relieved.

Riley flushed, relatively speaking, a few of the hybrids, but not enough to impress Milwaukee.

"From now on, let's leave those in the locker room," he said. "The way you hit those Jack irons, ain't no reason to mess around with a hybrid. First and second cuts here aren't usually thick enough to bother those things."

"We're only going to play the first nine today," Hard Way said, lapsing by habit into the Augusta National vernacular for front nine. "We'll bring 'em out and try a few, but you're probably right."

Milwaukee dropped his head. He had hoped to rid the bag of some poundage. But the nine holes was a smart move. No reason to short-circuit Riley's brain on the first day out.

Riley moved to the short game area to work on his chipping, pitching, and bunker play. Hard Way and Milwaukee watched from the side.

"Not the best hands I've seen, but not the worst," Milwaukee said.

"Nobody's gonna mistake him for Ray Floyd."

Riley stopped. "I'm right here, fellas."

"Oh, yeah, we know," Milwaukee said. "You doin' all right, though."

When Riley was done in the short-game area, Milwaukee dropped a half dozen balls on the putting green. "Let's roll a few here, just so you can get a little feel for the speed, and then we'll head to the first tee."

As instructed, he ignored Gordo's knockoff White Fang and handed Riley the newer putter with admiration. "The Newport is a Scotty classic," Milwaukee said. "Love the blade."

Riley knocked his first putt, a 10-footer, nearly 8 feet past the hole. His next putt went 6 feet past.

"What's the Stimp here, 50?"

"They don't discuss Stimp here," Milwaukee said. "They call it 'tournament speed.' And don't even try to measure the speed, the slope, or the firmness with any gadgets. Same goes for trying to map the greens. You'll be in the parking lot before you know it."

"What's your best guess?"

"Mr. Riley, there's fast, extra fast, and if it don't rain, there's Daytona 500 fast. This here is training-wheels fast. Barely moving."

"I hardly tapped that putt."

"If it stays dry next week—and it's supposed to—the greens will be like concrete with green peach fuzz."

"Separates the wanna's from the be's," Hard Way said.

"You got that right," Milwaukee said.

Without patrons, the course looked and felt so different. Compared to the U.S. Open and PGA Championship, the Masters had very few bleachers, only eleven scoreboards, and no corporate suites. It was the patrons who defined the shape of most of the holes as they lined the fairways and formed a half ring on the majority of the greens.

Riley walked to the first tee, glanced at the stately oak in front of the famed clubhouse, took a deep breath, and then looked at Milwaukee, who looked at Hard Way.

"You're the pilot today," Hard Way said to the veteran Augusta National caddie. "I've got my yardage book from last year. I'm going to take notes, update some things, but I can tell you already that his second-shot yardages are going to make my book obsolete. I want him to hear your voice for the next few days, not mine."

"That's what I was hoping you'd say," Milwaukee said. He turned his attention to Riley.

"OK, prepare your mind for the hardest tee shot in all of golf: No. 1 at Augusta National on a Masters Thursday. For every player in the field, it's going to be their first shot of the first major of the year. Or in your case, your first-ever shot in a major. Heart gonna be pounding. Sweat gonna be dripping. Hands gonna be quivering. And guess what: It happens to everyone, even the guys who have green jackets hanging in that Champions Locker Room. Go look at what Tiger has done here at No. 1 over the years. It gives him fits. So embrace the difficulty. Breathe it in. Run toward it, through it, not away from it. Understand?"

"Sort of," Riley said.

"You're gonna have at least ten-deep on each side of this tee box. They're gonna announce your name for everyone to hear. TV cameras gonna be pointed at you. Sphincter muscle gonna be tight."

"If you're trying to make me nervous, mission accomplished."

"That's good. Ready your senses for the moment. Once you do that, then you can concentrate on your line. On this hole, you can run out of room on the left side real fast and end up in those pines. So let's favor the left corner of the second half of that fairway bunker on the right."

Riley poked his tee and ball into the perennial ryegrass that covered the Bermuda in the early spring months. He stepped back, surveyed the 455-yard dogleg right, and then created an imaginary line just left of that fairway bunker filled, as all the bunkers were at Augusta National, with cloud-white Spruce Pine sand from the mining region in western North Carolina. He took a practice swing and then unleashed the hounds.

The ball covered the bunker and then some.

"I didn't see it land," Riley said. "Is it OK?"

"Got me, Mr. Riley," Milwaukee said, astounded by the sight. "I've never seen anyone thread the tree chute like that. For all I know, the damn thing rolled on the green."

They walked down the first fairway and then up the incline, past the bunker shaped like a figure eight, and finally to the ball. The television broadcasts never quite conveyed just how many changes in elevation there were at Augusta National. Riley got to the ball first, with Hard Way and Milwaukee, clubs clapping against each other in the bag, lagging a few yards behind.

"Well, I sure scared the shit out of him on the first tee, didn't I?" Milwaukee said.

"Yeah, you sure did," Hard Way said, jotting down the numbers in his yardage book. "He only pumped it 383 uphill on the exact line you wanted."

"Mr. Riley, you got—and I ain't never said this before on the second shot of this hole—72 to the middle. Aim middle of the green, carry the false front. You can almost never go wrong by playing the middle of every one of these greens and then putting to the corners."

Riley hit a half sand wedge to the middle . . . and then three-putted.

"You ain't the first or the last to do that," Milwaukee said as he replaced the flagstick in the hole. "Greens will firm up more next week, so this is good practice."

They made their way to the par-5, 575-yard second hole, this one a dogleg left. If No. 1 was one of the toughest holes on the course, then Pink Dogwood was one of the easiest. In Masters history, the field had always played it under par.

"You might have known this—I know Hard Way does—but Mr. Nicklaus himself said there's only six shots that can end your Masters. This tee shot is one of 'em."

"Trees on the left, trees on the right," Riley said.

"Trees on the left *no bueno* because there's a creek down there, too," Milwaukee said. "Mr. Nicklaus called it 'the airline ticket office.' We call it 'the Delta ticket counter,' 'cause you ain't making the cut if you find that creek or get caught in all those pines. Then it becomes the Land of 8's and you'll be headed to the Delta counter for a flight home."

"Aim a little left of that fairway bunker?"

"Exactly. It's all downhill, so let 'er rip."

Once again, Riley landed his drive in the perfect position. The diaper-shaped green, protected by bunkers on each side, was within easy reach on the second shot.

"You got . . . sweet Jesus, only 168 to the middle," Milwaukee said. "On Sunday, that pin will be far right, so you'll want to use the slope to feed it to the hole. Now let's favor the middle again. We don't want any part of that right bunker."

"Just smooth a pitching wedge, Joe," Hard Way said.

"These fellas ain't gonna know what to make of you when you pull wedge for your second shot on a par-5," Milwaukee said. "Ol' Bobby Jones spinning in his grave right now."

Riley knocked it on the green, but three-putted again.

He did the same after driving the 350-yard par-4 third with a 5-wood, and again on No. 4 after reaching the 240-yard hole with a 7-iron.

"Twelve putts in four holes," Riley said. "I might set a record."

"Last one is my bad, Mr. Riley," Milwaukee said. "From that upper deck to that lower pin position, that's tough for anyone to two-putt. I should have told you that it's extra spicy from up there 'cause you're putting toward No. 12. That's the lowest part of the golf course."

Riley did par the par-4, 495-yard fifth hole, reaching the green in regulation and, at last, having a stress-free two-putt.

"You've been to St. Andrews," Milwaukee said. "Look at this green. Remind you of anything?"

"Deep bunker on the left . . . false front . . . death if you go long left," Riley said, trying to find a match with the Old Course. "Well, it doesn't have a wall on the right, but it looks a little like the Road Hole green."

"Hard Way, this man got some chops," Milwaukee said. "Yes, sir, it has some Road Hole in it. You make four here, you run, not walk, off the green. You make four fours here, you're gonna pick up a stroke or two on the field."

On the downhill 180-yard par-3 sixth, Riley plopped a pitching wedge just to the right of the bunker and just short of the green.

"I thought I hit that better," Riley said. "You warned me about the wind."

"Yeah, there's a gap in the trees on the left where the wind can cause havoc. Everyone always talks about the wind at No. 12, but No. 6 ain't far behind. And you watch: They'll move this pin around from year to year on Sundays."

Riley chipped up, but two-putted for bogey. And on the 450-yard par-4 seventh, he chunked a 60-degree wedge from 45 yards out. Then he three-putted for a double bogey.

"You underread that first putt," Milwaukee said.

"I thought you were supposed to help me on that," Riley said, his voice full of frustration after another three-jack.

"I am helping you, Mr. Riley. You gotta learn some of these things on your own. A lot of players underread putts on this green. Now you know."

"You're right. Sorry."

"Nothing to be sorry about. This is just a nine-hole scouting mission today. You're shaking hands with the course, and it's introducing itself to you."

"Me and the course aren't getting along right now."

"The National can't be understood on a first date. You got to learn her nuances."

"OK, No. 8. Let me hear about the nuances."

"We're gonna blow by that bunker on the right of the fairway. This is a gettable par-5 for everybody, especially you. We're looking for birdie here."

But Riley had lost his confidence. He walked off the green with a three-putt par.

"Nothing wrong with a par, Mr. Riley," Milwaukee said, knowing better. No. 8 always played below par to the field.

"You're driving it beautifully," Hard Way said. "Don't get down on yourself. These greens are the main line of defense, especially this one on nine."

Riley reached the elevated green in two, but the ball settled on the upper tier. He almost putted it off the green and was lucky to salvage a bogey five on the hole.

"I want to go jump in Rae's Creek," Riley said of the famous creek that ran behind the 11th green and in front of the 12th and 13th greens at Augusta National.

"Been a crazy two weeks," Hard Way said. "You were bound to hit the wall at some point. Today was the wall—big deal. We'll get 'em tomorrow."

"What'd I shoot?"

"No idea. Wasn't even paying attention to your score. I was more focused on your yardages, clubs used, that sort of thing."

"What about you, Milwaukee?" Riley said. "You must have kept track of my putts."

"Not really," he said. "This quickie nine was about you getting a feel for the place."

"Why don't you go grab your stuff, and I'll meet you at the car," Hard Way said. "I'm buying dinner. Milwaukee, you're welcome to join us."

"'Preciate it, but I'll let you and Mr. Riley chop it up. See you here tomorrow at . . ."

"I'd say 10 A.M. That'll give my man a chance to sleep in."

Riley thanked Milwaukee for his work and then walked toward the locker-room entrance. Hard Way waited until Riley was out of earshot before asking, "How many putts?"

"I counted twenty-five," Milwaukee said.

"Me too," Hard Way said. "Brutal."

"Shot 42 with four pars, four bogeys, and a double."

"He's on fumes, Milwaukee. First-day impressions?"

"He don't belong here. This tournament is going to chew him up. I don't know if he'll break 90."

"He drove the hell out of it today. Hit some nice irons. Put it in the right places."

"He did, I'll give him that much. Thing is, you can hit all the 400-yard FrankenRiley drives you want, but we got a sayin' here at the National: 'If you can't putt, you ain't making the cut.' He had seven three-putts."

"We turn those three-putts into two-putts and he shoots 35," Hard Way said.

"And if I eat kale salads every day for the next six months, I'll have a size-34 waist. But that ain't gonna happen, either."

CHAPTER TWENTY-NINE

Doubt

It was slightly better on Wednesday, but not much.

Milwaukee told Riley about the speed slot on the left side of the fairway on the downhill par-4, 495-yard 10th hole, and how you had to be below the pin at all costs on the second shot.

He told him about the downhill par-4, 520-yard 11th and how avoiding the pond on your second shot was No. 2 on Nicklaus's list of potential Masters round-wreckers.

He told him that they ought to change the name of the par-3, 155-yard Golden Bell to "Scar Tissue," since the 12th hole was the place where so many tournament leads had gone to die. He told him to look at the highest point of the trees behind the green to gauge the swirling winds, to never aim right of the front bunker (trouble spot No. 3 on the Nicklaus list), and that if they gave you three pars and a bogey there during that week, take it and run (Michael Greller's rule).

He told him that the drive on the par-5, 545-yard 13th (trouble spot No. 4 on the Nicklaus list) and clearing the water on your second or third shot (trouble spot No. 5) were more difficult because of the hole redesign.

He told him that the par-4, 440-yard 14th was the one hole where hitting it to the middle of the green wasn't necessarily an advantage.

He told him that reaching the par-5 15th in two wouldn't be an issue, but they'd have to be careful about having too much spin on the second shot or they'd end up in the pond (the final trouble spot for Nicklaus).

He told him middle of the green worked just fine for the par-3, 170-yard 16th.

He told him that the par-4, 440-yard 17th required a drive right down the pipes.

And he told him that a cut tee shot, starting at the right edge of the far bunker, was an absolute must on the par-4, 465-yard 18th hole.

He told him all of this, and Riley still shot 41 and had twenty-three putts, including five three-putts. Add the twenty-five putts from the previous nine, and Riley was at forty-eight putts—abysmal by any standard.

"Fellas, I apologize," Riley said as they walked off the 18th green. "I can't get the feel of these greens."

"Hey, you lowered your nine-hole score by a stroke and your putts by two," Hard Way said. "I like the way you're trending."

"You're not saying much, Milwaukee," Riley noticed.

"Not much to say, Mr. Riley. You hit some real good shots, and a few we'd like back. We just gotta get that flat stick going."

"Let's try this tomorrow: We'll meet in the morning and walk eighteen with just a wedge and putter," Hard Way said. "We can chip and putt around the greens, see if we can solve some things. Then we'll play the first nine. And after the Women's Am players finish their practice rounds on Friday, we'll start on the second nine."

That night, Riley called Laurel, and Hard Way called Sargent.

"How's he's doing?" Sargent said.

"We're making some progress," Hard Way said. "Still have some time."

"This is Sarge you're talking to. I'll ask again: How's he doing?"

"I think he might need to withdraw."

In the other room, Riley told his wife the same thing.

CHAPTER THIRTY

Panic Attack

Nothing worked.

The walkaround with wedges and putter seemed like a good idea at the time. But Riley's usually reliable short game was jagged, and his putting remained erratic. Augusta National's greens had become permanent residents inside his head.

Thursday's practice nine was more of the same, and on Friday, Riley started out birdie-birdie on Nos. 10 and 11 but fell apart on the remaining seven holes. He four-putted on No. 14 and nearly did the same on No. 15.

Milwaukee and Hard Way did what they could. They checked Riley's stance, his takeaway and follow-through, his clubface position at impact. They read putts for him. They made Riley read putts. They analyzed video. They did drills. But for whatever reason—psychological, physical, the diabolical nature of those greens, or all three—Riley had the putting yips.

The Scottish golfing legend Tommy Armour is said to have invented the word decades ago. So prevalent is the condition that the famed Mayo Clinic defines it as "involuntary wrist spasms" and says the yips sometimes can be tied to a neurological malfunction known as "focal dystonia."

The yips tormented Ben Hogan and Sam Snead in their later competitive years. At the 2016 Masters, four-time majors winner Ernie Els six-putted from 6 feet on the first hole. The next day, he three-putted on the same green. He later said that the yips "can cause snakes in your head." The snakes had made their home in Riley's head, too.

"Maybe I should watch the kids on Sunday during the Drive, Chip and Putt," Riley said.

Milwaukee started to laugh until he realized Riley was serious.

At Friday's end, Hard Way and Riley were on their own. Milwaukee had gotten a call from one of the amateurs who had qualified for the Masters. The amateur wanted to hire him.

"We'll see you out there next week," Hard Way said, slipping Milwaukee a palm full of cash.

"Much appreciated," Milwaukee said, not bothering to look at the amount. He knew Hard Way would do him right. Then he walked over to Riley and surprised him with a hug.

"What's that for?" Riley said.

"Mr. Riley, there's been all sorts of players who have made it to a Masters. Ain't been nobody like you, though. I gotta lot of respect for anyone who steps onto that first tee box. No matter what happens next week, you remember what you accomplished. Don't let anybody ruin that for you. Don't let anybody take that away from you. Understand?"

"I might not be here long, Milwaukee," Riley said.

"All that matters is that you're here now. I know you'll make the most of it, however long it lasts."

Hard Way and Riley drove back to the rental house in silence. Once there, Hard Way cracked open a pair of Shiners and announced that Saturday was an off day for Riley.

"I'm going to do some recon work during and after the Women's Am," he said. "You sleep in. Go see a movie. Read a book. Get a pizza at Mellow Mushroom. I don't care what you do as long as it doesn't involve golf. Turn your brain off. Recharge. We'll start fresh on Sunday. Sarge will be on-site that afternoon. He'll be on the range, and then he's going to walk a few holes with us on the first nine."

After a long pause, Riley said, "You'd tell me if I didn't belong here, right? If nothing else, you'd be honest about that."

"I would."

"So, do I belong here? Because I don't feel like I do."

Hard Way looked down, paused, and then looked Riley right in the eyes. "Right now? At this moment? No, you don't."

"Then maybe I should pull the plug."

"Why would you do that?"

"My family is going to be here Wednesday. I don't want to embarrass them. I don't want to embarrass you. I don't want to embarrass this club, this tournament."

"Milwaukee is right, you know? What you've accomplished is beyond belief. You made it to the Masters. Let's at least play in the damn thing. Whatever happens, happens."

Riley thought about it for a few moments.

"If Sarge can't fix me on Sunday, I'm pulling out of the tournament," he said.

"The Chairman took a gamble on you, Joe. You'd be embarrassing him if you quit before hitting a shot."

"He'll live. Maybe I'll come down with an elbow injury, a tweaked back. I've seen guys do it all the time."

"What about that speech you gave to Rinello in Houston about honoring the little guys, about not wasting a spot in the field?" Hard Way said, his voice rising. "Or was that just bullshit? If you're going to WD, then have the balls to say you weren't up to it. 'Cause if anybody asks me why you bailed, I'm going to tell them the truth."

Riley had been challenged. He walked toward Hard Way.

"You're all about the truth, eh?"

"I'm an open spigot of honesty."

"I heard you on the phone last night with Sarge. Your door was cracked open. Heard you tell him the truth: that I should withdraw."

Hard Way moved within inches of Riley. Any closer and their foreheads would touch.

"You little shit. Get your facts straight. I said you *might* have to withdraw. I know you're scared. I just didn't know you were a coward."

"Says the guy too afraid to stand up to the player who fired him."

As soon as the words left his mouth, Riley regretted it.

Hard Way stared at him. "Go eff yourself! You haven't hit a shot yet and you've already lost." And with that, he turned and walked to his bedroom, Riley walked to his, and their doors slammed shut in unison.

Riley looked at the clock on the bedside table. It read 5:53 A.M. *Who the hell is pounding on the front door this early on a Sunday morning?*

Riley walked downstairs, peered through the peephole, and took a step back.

"Oh, crap."

He unlocked the door and opened it. Sargent walked in without waiting for an invitation.

"I understand you're thinking of going home today?" Sargent said, more a declaration than a question.

"I don't know what Hard Way told you—"

"You listen to me." Sargent's voice was powerful enough to cause Riley to step back in involuntary fear. "I don't care if you shoot 101 on Thursday and 102 on Friday, you're not quitting. I don't care if your femur is sticking out of your skin, or you pump ten balls into Rae's Creek, or if every patron laughs their ass off at you."

"I'm not sure that's your decision, Sarge," said Riley.

Sargent glared at the challenge. Hard Way stumbled into the room.

"What time is it?" he said sleepily. "Whattya doing here, Sarge?"

"I'll tell you what time it is: It's grow-a-pair o'clock."

"Don't bother," Hard Way said. "It's no use."

Sarge turned to Riley.

"What are you afraid of? Failing?"

"Not just failing, but becoming a punchline. How do I ever get another job? How do I explain to Laurel that my stupidity made us a laughingstock? What do I tell my sons when they get mocked at school?"

"Joe, there are eighty-nine players in the field," Sarge said. "At least thirty-five of them are going to be gone by the weekend. A handful of them—elite pros, the best in the world—are going to struggle to break 80. It always happens at this place."

"Exactly," Riley said. "They're elite pros. They move on to the next Tour stop. You move on to your next $2,000 lesson. Hard Way moves on to—"

Hard Way crossed his arms in amusement.

"This ought to be good," he said.

"I don't know what Hard Way moves on to," Riley said, momentarily flummoxed. "So, yeah, I'm scared of failing. I'm scared of what those clubs could do to my life. I've always had a plan. I always knew how to get from point A to point B."

"Then you got fired by AGN," Sargent said.

"And I didn't have a plan for that," Riley said. "I let myself believe that trying to play in a major was a plan. I left my family when I should have been looking for a job. My wife is holding off the monthly bills with a whip and a chair. And I'm not supposed to know this, but she sold my car to pay for Buddy's tuition. So yeah, I'm scared."

"Sold your car?" Hard Way said.

"Nothing gets by Chet," Riley said.

"I didn't know it was that bad," Hard Way said. "If it makes you feel any better, the bank gave me until the end of the month before it forecloses on my range. I'm way over my skis."

"Aren't we a pair?" Riley said. "Poor and poorer."

Sargent tenderly put his beefy arm around Riley's neck. He smiled sympathetically.

"Can I tell you something?" Sargent said.

Riley nodded.

"That's the biggest crock of crap I've ever heard," Sargent said. "You can't plan life. How'd you meet your wife?"

"Like, meet her for the first time?"

"You're as sharp as a marble. Yes, the first time! How'd you meet her? Was it planned?"

"Blind date," Riley said sheepishly. "Sox game. I knew I wanted to marry her when she brought her own pencil to keep score."

"See?" Sargent said. "Did you know what time your kids would be born? That you'd have two boys? That you'd end up on TV?"

Riley said nothing.

"No. Wanna know why? Because life is arbitrary. There's no flowchart to it. This is where you're meant to be. In this place. At this time."

"My journey is *my* journey," Riley said, as if it all suddenly made sense.

"Now you're finally getting it," Sargent said. "And not for nothing, but Hard Way here has believed in you from the very beginning. This is his last chance. So it's not just your journey; it's his too."

Riley looked over at Hard Way and then Sargent.

"I'll see you on the range at one-thirty," Riley said, his tone determined and enthusiastic. "Don't be late!"

His work done, a satisfied Sargent departed.

"So I guess we're not returning the courtesy car today," Hard Way said, sticking out his hand.

"It's even worse than that," Riley said in mid-handshake. "I'm going to officially register. We're in it now, pal."

Hard Way and Riley arrived at the course just as the Drive, Chip and Putt competition ended. As the patrons poured out of the property, it seemed each one had a Masters gnome box tucked under their arm or in a Masters bag. Riley was convinced that more patrons were interested in shopping than watching golf.

Riley registered for the tournament and was given his player's badge, which was the size of a squared-off poker chip. He was the thirty-third player to register that day, which meant Hard Way's caddie jumpsuit would feature a green No. 33 patch sewed onto the left breast pocket. Most of the players in the field would arrive that night and register on Monday. The caddie for the defending champion was always issued the No. 1 patch.

Sargent was waiting for Riley and Hard Way on the range of the eighteen-acre practice facility.

"You two make up?" he asked, but before either Hard Way or Riley could reply, he said, "Good. Let's get to work."

Riley hit a dozen non-Jack wedges before Sargent stopped him and slightly adjusted his stance and reminded him to turn his chest through the swing. The results were immediate.

"Joe, you're going to succeed or fail because of two things: your wedge play and your putting. You hit the ball so damn far that you're not going to need all the clubs in your bag. But you're going to need to be precise from 100 yards in, and you're going to need to sink some downhill 6-footers."

"I'd be happy to sink an uphill 1-footer. I'm clueless out there."

"We'll get to it."

They worked their way through the bag, saving the driver for last.

"What the hell is that out there?" Sargent said, squinting at something in the far distance.

"It's a net, Sarge," Hard Way said.

"A net? For what?"

"For him," Hard Way said, nodding toward Riley.

"He can reach the media center?"

"Pretty close. The range is 400 yards long, but we're hitting into the prevailing wind. I don't think they want to take any chances. The netting is white so it blends into the building paint color."

"Well, Joe, Augusta National just paid you a compliment," Sargent said. "At least someone is worried about you."

"I was hoping nobody would notice."

"Joe, you're not a secret anymore. *Everybody* notices you now."

Hard Way brought a couple of bags of balls to the short-game area, where a few other players were chipping and hitting bunker shots. When they saw Riley, they silently picked up their gear and moved to the other green complex.

"Something I did?" Riley said.

"Yeah, you got an invitation," Hard Way said.

Riley's bunker shots didn't feature the thumping sound that an accomplished player made when hitting out of the sand. But Riley got out and usually put the ball at a workable distance from the hole. His chipping and short pitches also were amateur level (no skip-and-bite shots), but they were dependable enough—and that's all that mattered to Sargent. The Masters wasn't the place to teach Riley radical new techniques.

"Let me see you putt," he told Riley.

Riley's body language instantly changed. He dropped three balls on the green, picked out a hole 12 feet away, and sent the first putt 7 feet past it. The second putt was 4 feet short, and the third putt 2 feet wide right.

"Quit screwing around," Sargent said.

"Sarge, he isn't," Hard Way said. "We weren't kidding about his putting."

"For chrissakes, what happened? You're a better putter than this. I've seen it."

"The greens are too fast," Riley said.

"You're putting into the grain. It's early afternoon, so they've had the whole day to grow. And you ain't seen fast until Thursday gets here."

Riley stared at his shoes.

Sargent's voice softened. "Don't worry, Joe. I've fixed worse than you."

Despite Sargent's best efforts on the practice green, Riley kept overcompensating. He was either too long or too short. Sargent looked at Hard Way. For the first time in his distinguished career, Sargent didn't have an answer.

With Sargent walking alongside the fairway and outside the ropes (at the Masters, instructors weren't allowed inside the ropes or on the fairways and greens during practice rounds), Riley played the first four holes at 3-over, and that included a birdie at No. 2. After yet another three-putt, this time on the sixth hole, Sargent had seen enough. He was waiting for them as they began to walk to the seventh tee box.

"Let me see that putter for a second," Sargent said, casually.

Riley handed him his beloved Scotty. Sargent snapped the shaft over his knee, and then tossed the two pieces to Hard Way.

"I don't want to see that putter again," Sargent said.

"Sarge!" Riley was in disbelief. "That's my baby!"

"Not anymore. It's taking a sabbatical."

"Whatta I use now?"

"A crowbar. A toilet plunger. A cane. But you need to change the mojo."

"What about the fake White Fang?" Hard Way said, pulling the ancient replica putter, a complete afterthought by this point, from the bag. "Milwaukee left it in here."

"I can't use that thing," Riley said. "It looks like somebody spray-painted it at a Putt-Putt."

"You're 4-over after six," Sargent said. "If a center-shafted putter was good enough for Jack, this old thing is good enough for you. Anyway, you can't putt any worse with it."

Riley's second shot on the par-4 seventh left him with an 18-footer. Hard Way pulled the pin and half closed his eyes in fear. Who knew where the putt would end up.

Riley took a few practice strokes and then stepped away.

"I can't putt with this. It looks ridiculous."

"Hard Way gave you the line," said Sargent, stationed on the outer rim of the green at the rope line. "Just stuff it in the hole."

Riley took the putter head back and hoped. Hard Way hoped, and Sargent hoped. And then it happened.

The ball rolled into the center of the cup.

Hard Way jumped into the air. Riley kissed the White Fang as if a priest had just pronounced them man and wife.

"Will you quit it with the theatrics?" Sargent said. "It was one putt. We didn't win the damn green jacket, for chrissakes."

Hard Way pulled the ball out of the cup and tossed it to Riley. Sargent was already walking ahead to the eighth tee, a wide smile on his face.

Riley eagled the par-5 eighth with a 25-footer and then birdied No. 9 with a downhill 20-footer from the top to second tier to finish at even-par.

"I just shot a 36 at Augusta National," Riley said, beaming. "How did you know the putter change would work?"

"It was three holes, Joe," Sargent said.

"Don't be a Debbie Downer, Sarge," Hard Way said. "You weren't here earlier in the week when he couldn't sink a tap-in."

"Perspective, gentlemen. Perspective."

"Have you ever thought of becoming a positive reinforcement coach, Sarge?" Riley said.

Even Sargent laughed at that one. His shock tactic with the putter had been a last resort. In Riley's case, the goal was to convince him that the painted putter was the reason for his sudden success when, in fact, it was nothing more than a placebo. Sargent had used the same tactic several times in the past with other players, but Riley's response had exceeded all expectations.

"Look, I want to start early tomorrow, before the gates open to the public," Sargent said. "Short warm-up at 7, then be on the 10th tee by 7:45. If I know these guys, there's no way you're going to be in a marquee group on Thursday or Friday. You're a novelty, but TV is going to want the big names going off in the ten o'clock hour and in the 1-to-2 P.M. tee window. I figure you'll be off just after Jack, Gary, and Tom do the honorary starters thing."

"We're flying low," Hard Way said. "That's OK with me."

"Another thing: You're going to get media requests."

"I already saw the interview room schedule," Riley said. "I'm not on the sheet, thank goodness."

"Flash area?" Hard Way said.

The outdoor flash area was located between the scorer's room and the oak tree. The leaders of the tournament would be brought to the main media center for formal interviews after their rounds. As for the rest of the field, reporters could ask tournament officials to bring a certain player to the roped-off flash area for a quick interview. Most players agreed to the requests, but it wasn't uncommon for a player to decline the ask.

"I didn't think about that," Riley said. "A lot of those reporters and producers are my friends."

"Do the interviews, don't do them, I don't care," Sargent said. "But we're not here to talk, and we're not here to make friends."

Sargent left to meet with another player. Hard Way turned to Riley.

"Speaking of talking, did you and the Chairman have a chat?"

"Not in person, but I left a note with his assistant."

"They're going to take a look?"

"I hope so. That's what I asked him to do."

"Then you've done all you can, Joe."

There was a trio of players and caddies on the 10th tee first thing Monday morning.

"Gentlemen, how we doing on this fine day?" Hard Way said amiably as he and Riley walked up. "Mind if we join you?"

The players turned around, revealing themselves to be Jensen Pruitt, a four-time winner on Tour and a perennial whiner; Lars Svensson, a young Swedish player who had won several months earlier at Pebble and was duller than a Volvo owner's manual; and Hard Way's former man.

Hard Way's smile disappeared.

"Look who's here," Pruitt said. "It's the two cheaters. And no, you can't join us—we've already got a threesome."

Pruitt sneered at Riley, while Svensson stared at him with Nordic indifference. Then they turned away, leaving their caddies to pretend to clean the same clubs they had already cleaned before leaving the practice range.

Hard Way began to say something, but Riley stopped him.

"Max, it's not worth it. Let it go."

The threesome teed off, and Pruitt and Svensson began to walk down the dew-moistened fairway. Hard Way's former man started to join them, hesitated, and then gestured for his caddie to walk ahead. He turned to Hard Way.

"Can I talk to you for a second?"

"Nothing to talk about."

"It's important," he said softly.

Hard Way was surprised by the gentle tone. They met on the other side of the tee box, away from Riley and out of earshot of the patrons.

"You've got sixty seconds," Hard Way said.

"First of all, I'm sorry about Jensen. He shouldn't have said that."

Hard Way blinked in disbelief. *An apology? From him?*

"I know you and Joe are getting beat up a bit this week, but that's just because these guys are looking out for me. I wish they wouldn't do it."

Hard Way's former guy's attitude was contrite and even humble, but Hard Way knew that as good as he was at golf, he was even better at acting.

"If you really mean that—and I doubt that you do—thanks. But why do I keep checking my back pocket to see if you stole my wallet?"

"Max, this isn't easy for me. I was going to try to find you later today or tomorrow, but since you're here, you should know that Kat and I are getting back together. I've been working on becoming a better person, and we're going to make a fresh start."

At first, the revelation jolted Hard Way. Then he remembered whom he was talking to.

"Don't you ever get tired of lying?" Hard Way said.

"I probably deserve that," his former man said, his voice even more remorseful. "I've made mistakes in my life. I hope I can make amends for them all. I bought Kat a new ring for a new beginning, and the ceremony is booked in Dana Point for May twenty-eighth."

He patted Hard Way on the shoulder, as if to console him.

"I thought you should hear it from me first." Then he turned and started jogging down the fairway.

Hard Way suddenly looked lost, his equilibrium disrupted. He thought he could read his former man as easily as an uphill 2-inch putt. He had heard him twist and ignore the truth so many times that he instantly assumed this was the latest and most outrageous of the lies. But it wouldn't be unlike him to make a grandstand ring purchase out of desperation, or to plead for a final chance, or to invoke his daughters' names and play to Kat's strong sense of family. When framed in those terms, reconciliation seemed plausible. And the *way* his former man spoke about the wedding plans, with a specific date.

Riley walked up to Hard Way. "What was that about?" he asked.

"Nothing."

"Didn't look like nothing."

"It was nothing," he said, in a tone that made it clear the subject was closed. "Time to go to work."

It took longer than usual to play the nine holes, mostly because Svensson and Pruitt were moving at a glacial pace and doing so for no other reason than to be annoying. A Green Jacket, made aware of the bottleneck, eventually arrived on 14th hole to hurry the offending threesome along.

By then, the patrons were on the course, but all of them were following the more popular and famous players in the field. As Sargent walked outside the ropes, he overheard a conversation between a man and his young son.

"Who's that, Daddy?"

"That's the TV reporter. See his name on the back of the caddie's uniform?"

"He any good?"

"He can hit it from here to Aiken."

"Can he win?"

"The only way he gets a green jacket is if he spray-paints one of his own sport coats."

The father and son didn't stay to see Riley make nearly every putt he attempted. And when Hard Way dropped small discs on the greens to show the likely hole locations for the first two rounds, Riley's putts tracked directly to them. The difference in his accuracy and confidence from twenty-four hours earlier was astounding. Had he kept score of his first ball hit on each hole, Riley would have shot 34.

"What is going on with you?" Sargent said, amazed by the transformation.

Riley broke into his best imitation of Drew Fetting, one of the interviewees from the Whisper Rock shoot.

"Son, I was just tarred of missing," he said in a dreadful Southern accent. "I finally just told my own self, 'Joe, don't think. Just do.' So I'm doin'. Just like my mama taught me.'"

"That's the worst drawl I've ever heard," Sargent said, laughing.

"But some of the best putting I've seen," Hard Way said.

The walk back to the clubhouse was punctuated by more laughter and something new: hope.

On Tuesday morning, Riley shot a first-ball 34 on the first nine, sank a dizzying number of putts, and even received a rare compliment from Sargent.

"You keep playing like this, you're going to be a problem for everybody else," he said.

"No way," Riley said.

"Son, if you and that fake Fang keep dropping putts, you're not only going to make the cut, you're going to turn this place upside down."

"What happened to perspective? It's only been a few practice nines."

"You're right. And maybe you'll crumble come Thursday. But Milwaukee and Hard Way have done you proud. And you've done yourself proud. I'll stick to my prediction."

"You noticed that I wasn't invited to join the twosome in front of us today," Riley said. "They hate me."

"It's not you," Sargent said. "It's the *idea* of you. They don't think you're legitimate."

"I didn't invite myself; the Masters invited me."

"The pros don't like special invitations unless a pro gets one. Hell, they're probably pissed that the U.S. Am runner-up gets an automatic spot. And Hard Way's former guy isn't helping the situation."

The former guy had put Hard Way into an emotional spin cycle. Hard Way had debated whether to call Kat. She was scheduled to fly in Wednesday night from Orange County, but that had been arranged before this latest news of a mulligan marriage with her ex. Laurel and Chet would be there in time for the Par 3 Contest at noon on Wednesday, with Buddy flying in Thursday night after his last class at Madison.

Hard Way had been uncharacteristically quiet since the Monday confrontation. Even during the Tuesday round and a brief return to the practice area to work on his distance wedges, Hard Way said the minimum. When they were done early that afternoon, Riley told Hard Way to head back to the rental house without him.

"One of the Green Jackets asked if I would do five minutes at the flash area," Riley said.

"I'll wait."

"No, go ahead. It never takes just five minutes. Plus, I want to say hello to some of the AGN folks."

"You sure?"

"Yeah. I can get someone at the club to help me bum a ride back to the house."

Hard Way took Riley's clubs to the secure storage room in the Golf Services Building. The Masters, for all its quirks, was the only tournament where Hard Way made an exception to his rule of keeping the clubs himself. It helped that Augusta National was something of a golf fortress, that the caddie room director and his staff personally attended to the clubs, and that you couldn't swing a 5-iron without hitting a security guard, state trooper, or local police officer.

Riley ducked into the locker room to change his shoes and as had become the custom during the last few days, the other pros either ignored him or scattered when he sat down. On his brass nameplate on the shared locker, someone had scribbled "Fraud."

Riley had received similar treatment in the clubhouse restaurant. He had asked if he could join several pros for lunch at their table. He had had a good working relationship with them while at AGN.

"Have a seat," said David Krafty, whom Riley had covered since the NCAA champion had joined the Tour five years earlier.

When Riley sat down, Krafty and the others grabbed their plates and moved to an open table across the room. Riley ate his meal alone.

Now he stared at the desecrated nameplate, shook his head, but said nothing as he put on a dry pair of socks and his well-worn Cole Hahn loafers.

"Not right what they're doing to you, mate," said a voice from the corner.

Riley hadn't noticed the young man until now. He was no older than twenty-one or twenty-two, and when he stood to introduce himself, he was at least six-foot-three, but as thin as a bag strap.

"Derrin Brown," he said, his Aussie accent instantly recognizable. "Disappointing to see a fellow competitor treated with such disrespect."

"You won the Asia-Pacific Am," Riley said. "Congrats on that."

"Thanks, mate. Thrill of a lifetime. Good on ya to get here too."

"I think you're in the minority on that one."

"I might be, but know that you have at least one supporter in the room. Well, me and the Chairman."

"That won't earn you many friends, but thank you."

"No worries. My caddie and a few mates are going to meet up for dinner and some coldies, if you'd like to join us. A place called TBonz?"

"I know it well. It's a Masters-week institution. If I get over there, I'll look for you. You staying near the course?"

"You could say that."

"Where?"

"Upstairs, mate. I'm in the Crow's Nest for a couple of nights."

The Crow's Nest was on the third floor of the historic clubhouse. Riley and an AGN camera crew had been granted access to the room several years earlier for a feature story. It was part hidden fort and part youth hostel.

To get there, you walked up a winding staircase to the second level, where the library, dining area, and Champions Locker Room were located. In an alcove between a pair of bookshelves was a white door with two vertical glass panels and a bronze placard that read "Telephone." The door led to a small hallway, which led to another door and a fifteen-step stairway that was as steep as El Capitan. At the top of the green-carpeted steps, you were greeted by a black-and-white photo of a young Bobby Jones and transported back in time.

The room was decorated in early Mamie Eisenhower. White walls, white wood beams, white sheets, white pillowcases, white bedcovers, black-and-white bathroom tile, white sinks, white shower stalls and curtains, white washcloths, white bath towels, and white bathrobes with the Augusta National logo. White partitions separated the sleeping areas. In the sitting area was a green couch, a patterned wingback chair, a few wooden tables and lamps, a handful of throw pillows, and a pair of fire extinguishers that dated back to the early 1930s. It was your grandparents' guest bedroom, but without the doilies.

Only the amateurs in the Masters field were allowed to stay in the Crow's Nest. Tiger had slept there as an amateur. So had Nicklaus, Mickelson, Crenshaw, and Tom Watson, among other amateurs who had gone on to win the green jacket.

There were five twin beds, but only one TV for the entire room. The monitor was the size of a dinner menu.

But what the Crow's Nest lacked in creature comforts, it made up for in location. Late at night, when the clubhouse and grounds were deserted, you could sneak down to the Champions Locker Room. As for the morning commute, the amateurs had just two flights of stairs.

"I'm jealous," Riley said.

"I've heard that some of the other amateurs prefer their rental houses or hotel rooms, but I couldn't pass this up," Brown said.

"Their mistake."

Brown closed the door to his locker and stuffed his cell phone into his back pocket. "If you can't make dinner, I'll see you Thursday morning on the first tee. We're playing together."

"I completely forgot about the pairings. What time? Who's our third?"

"We're Group 2, 8:12 A.M. local, 9:12 P.M. in my hometown of Perth. Then 10:48 on Friday morning. And our third is Cedrick Harrison."

"Oh, gawd. So much for flying under the radar."

"I heard he's . . . colorful."

"That's an understatement."

A Green Jacket approached, causing the Aussie to give a quick wave and excuse himself.

"Joe," the Augusta member said, "can we head out now?"

As they turned to leave, the Green Jacket noticed the defiled nameplate. His face turned red with anger.

"This will not stand," the Green Jacket said, motioning for a locker-room attendant, who immediately unscrewed the offending nameplate from the wood door. "Such behavior is unacceptable."

"I don't take it personally," Riley said.

"I do," the Green Jacket said. He turned to the attendant. "Mr. Fetting is sharing a locker with one of our amateur contestants. Please move the amateur's belongings here, and Mr. Riley's belongings—and a new nameplate—to Mr. Fetting's locker."

"Is Drew OK with that?" Riley said.

"Both he and Mr. Lippon made these offers at the beginning of the week. They both spoke highly of your professionalism at the interview session in Arizona."

"They did?"

"You have more supporters here than you realize, Mr. Riley. Now let's go speak with your former colleagues."

Over the years, Riley had spent many a post-round standing with other reporters in the flash area pen, waiting . . . hoping that a player would see fit to give them a few minutes of their time. In most cases, the players would agree to the requests. After all, the setting was casual and convenient, and the number of reporters usually small and manageable. If the player was of a certain stature, the Green Jackets would have the reporters on a hard pitch count. More than a few times in the past, a Green Jacket had warned that Woods would answer three questions, and no more. Invariably, a certain rally-killer national radio reporter, dreaded by all because of his ability to get a player's attention before anyone else could speak, would waste one of the precious questions by trying to show off.

"Tiger, it sounded as if you hit your second shot on 14 a few grooves high on the clubface. Did I hear right?"

Woods, thrilled that he was one step closer to escaping the media scrum, would happily and quickly say, "No. I actually flushed it."

Two questions left.

Afterward, an enraged newspaper columnist from New Jersey had told the radio reporter, "Do that again and your microphone is going to be interviewing your rectum."

There would be no pitch count for Riley, mostly because he didn't expect the session to last very long. Only a half dozen media members were waiting, which made sense since Tuesdays were when the Green Jackets brought the remainder of the top-ranked players to the velvet coffin.

Riley recognized some of the faces as he stepped onto the riser at one of the roped-off flash area positions, including AGN producer Jan Chaffin.

"You guys must be desperate," Riley said. He was self-conscious, almost embarrassed to be there.

Chaffin spoke first.

"Joe, if I'm not mistaken, it appeared you caught your approach shot on No. 9 a few grooves low," she said, smiling.

Riley laughed and relaxed a tiny bit.

"Joe, this is a little bit strange for all of us," she continued, looking at the handful of reporters, "but how do you make sense of where you're at and what you're about to do, which is play in a Masters?"

"There's no point in trying to make sense of it," Riley said. "I'd have a better chance of solving a Rubik's Cube in the dark. All I know is that I'm humbled and grateful to be here, that I'm going to do my best and try to savor every moment of it."

Before Chaffin could follow up, a reporter for a golf website known for its smart-ass ways and its commitment to creating controversy said,

"That was a heartwarming answer, but I've talked to a dozen or so pros who think it's a joke that you're in the field. One player called you a 'buffoon.' You've got a fired caddie who can't count clubs. You're a 1,500-to-1 longshot. And you finished tied for thirty-seventh in the only tournament you've ever played."

"Is there a question someplace in there?" Riley asked, no longer smiling.

"You know what I mean," said the reporter, who had three days' worth of stubble on his face and wore a "How do you like me now?" T-shirt. "Do you think you cheapen the Masters?"

"I know I'm a controversial choice," Riley said.

"And an unpopular one," another reporter added.

"And apparently that too," Riley said. "But how about judging me by my play? That will answer everything. If I stink it up, rip away."

The session had gone sideways fast.

A columnist from the Augusta paper began to ask a question, but the T-shirt reporter interrupted him. It was time to reveal his inside information.

"I wouldn't be doing my job if I didn't ask about persistent rumors that your caddie has or had a relationship with the then-wife of his former player," said the T-shirt reporter, who had been pulled aside by Hard Way's former man after the practice round and offered a deal: a few spicy details about Riley's caddie in exchange for anonymity. "Are you comfortable with hiring someone who would do that?"

A Green Jacket stepped in.

"I think the subject matter is inappropriate for this setting," he said. "We're going to end this here."

The Green Jacket tugged at Riley's elbow as he led him off the riser.

"Hold on," Riley said as he returned to the rope line and the T-shirt guy. "Have you ever talked to Max?"

"Uh . . ."

"Ever introduced yourself to him, walked some holes with him, stood out on the range with him? Ever made an effort to earn his trust, or let him earn yours?"

"I don't need to be his best friend to ask the question," T-shirt guy said, suddenly defensive. "The rumors are out there."

"Rumors."

"Actually, I've been told that it's fact."

"You wanted to know if I'm comfortable with Max as my caddie? No, I'm not comfortable with it."

The reporter, now joined by others, scribbled furiously in his notebook. Riley waited for him to look up.

"I'm not comfortable with it," Riley said, "I'm *honored* by it. I wouldn't want anybody *but* Max on the bag. And that isn't a rumor, that's a fact. You get all that?"

"I did," the reporter said smugly.

The Green Jacket escorted Riley away.

"Damn," Chaffin said to her cameraman. "Did *you* get all that?"

"Every word," he said.

Hard Way pulled the Mercedes into the driveway but didn't get out. He stared at the thin coat of green pollen on the car, which was an annual spring occurrence in Augusta as the pines and flowers turned the town into the allergy capital of the South. Pharmacies and car washes did huge business the week of the Masters.

There was no way around it: Hard Way was in a funk. Destiny had determined that he couldn't escape the serpent shadow of his former guy. He had been all but blackballed on Tour because of him, forced to work opposite shifts at Whisper Rock because of him, and now lost Kat to him.

Hard Way sat in the car, the air-conditioning at full force, and decided to call her.

She answered on the first ring.

"I was waiting for this call," she said, sounding nervous.

"I'm going to make this easy on both of us," he said. "I wish you the best. You deserve whatever type of happiness you can find."

"I appreciate that," she said softly. "Now get in the damn house before Joe gets back."

"What?"

"Get. In. The. House."

The call abruptly ended.

Hard Way heard the faint sound of music as he entered the mini-mansion. He walked up the sweeping staircase. There were two unused bedrooms in front of him, with Riley's suite down a long hallway to the right, and his room down a long hallway to the left.

The music took him toward his bedroom, where the door was cracked open and a black thong hung from the glass doorknob. A handwritten sign was taped to the door: PLEASE DISTURB!

Hard Way nudged the door open. The white window shutters had been closed, and candles on the dresser and nightstands flickered. A red scarf covered the top of one of the small lamps, giving the room a hazy glow. It was as if Annie Savoy had done the decorating. From a Bluetooth speaker on a bookshelf came what Hard Way now recognized as "Augusta," the Dave Loggins song that had long been the soundtrack of the Masters broadcasts. The arrangement was unmistakable. And sitting with her bare back against the tufted headboard of the king-sized bed was Kat. Next to the bed was a stainless steel bucket filled with ice and a bottle of what looked to be Dom Pérignon.

"Hello, friend, and welcome to a bedroom unlike any other," she said in a horrific imitation of Jim Nantz.

A dumbfounded Hard Way could only manage, "What are you doing here?"

"I heard you had low-self-esteem issues, so I decided a surprise was in order."

"I got my surprise Monday when I saw your ex. Or former ex? I'm confused."

"Hold on." Kat reached over and turned off the music from her iPhone. "A woman can only take so much piano and guitar weeping."

"Riley told you what happened?" Hard Way said.

"He called me that day," Kat said.

"Is it true?"

"Yes, it's true that the ex wants to become the ex-ex. It's also true that I told him I'd rather eat greenflies than be married to him again. He didn't like that answer, so he took it out on you."

"He said he bought you a new ring."

"He did." Kat held up her left hand. It was ringless. "Hope he kept the receipt."

"And the ceremony he booked in Dana Point?"

"He did that too. He'll be going stag."

"So you're not getting back together with him?" Hard Way said.

"You're in Augusta. He's in Augusta. I'm in Augusta with you. That answer your question?"

Hard Way softly banged his head against the bedroom wall, the light thumps eventually causing a small framed painting to tilt.

"I can't believe I fell for it," he said. "That guy should be in the Screen Actors Guild. I'm so stupid."

"It's his gift. And how do you think I feel?" Kat said. "I *married* him."

"I'm a wreck."

"Well, maybe this will help," she said, pulling him toward the bed. "You don't happen to have that Masters jumpsuit with you, do you? I find onesies incredibly sexy."

"You probably say that to all the caddies working for former TV golf reporters."

"Go take a quick shower. I'll pop open the champagne. We'll compare yardage books."

Hard Way all but sprinted to the shower. Kat uncorked the bottle and poured two glasses. Then she found a pen, opened the bedroom door, and for Riley's benefit, crossed out the word *Please* on the sign and replaced it with *Don't*.

CHAPTER THIRTY-ONE

Anticipation

The USGA Head of Equipment Standards was escorted to the club storage room shortly before 5 A.M.

Still bleary-eyed and without his usual coffee starter, he was surprised to see a pair of members of the Masters Competition Committee, a representative of the R&A, a representative of the PGA Tour, and the Chairman himself all waiting for him outside the storage room.

"We apologize for the early hour and the surprise request," said the Chairman, who was wearing his club-issued green jacket, as were the Masters committee members. He gestured for the group to enter the room. The door was pulled shut, and a Georgia State Trooper was stationed outside to prevent any unwanted interruptions.

"We have a situation that requires both your expertise and your discretion," the Chairman said.

The Chairman pointed to a golf bag positioned next to a worktable.

"These are the clubs," he said.

The USGA official removed a laptop and a $175 scanner from their padded carrying cases, set them side by side on the small table, and readied them for the GrooveScan testing process.

One by one, a putty-like compound was administered to each of the twelve clubfaces selected for the tests: driver, 3-wood, 5-wood, and 3-iron through sand wedge. Once the compound cured, the casting was sliced from a club and spread across the flatbed scanner, which had a resolution of 3/20,000th of an inch.

If, say, the width of any groove exceeded 35,000th of an inch or the depth exceeded 20,000th of an inch, the club would be ruled nonconforming and ineligible for play.

When he was done, the USGA official explained the data to the group. The Chairman asked him to conduct the tests again.

"The results are accurate," the equipment expert said.

"I'm sure they are," the Chairman said. "But there's a reason why there are five witnesses here, and a reason why I want the tests done twice. The integrity of the Masters is at risk."

The testing process was repeated. The results were exactly the same, and the data was downlinked to secure Masters, USGA, and R&A servers.

Joe Riley's golf bag and clubs were then returned to their original place in the storage room. An attendant wiped down each clubface to make sure no remnants of the compound remained.

At exactly 11 A.M., as was tradition on the day before the tournament began, the Chairman took his seat in front of the assembled reporters. The press center auditorium fell silent.

Reading from a prepared statement, the Chairman spent the next fifteen minutes providing Augusta National's views on the successes of the Masters Foundation, expanded hospitality services, an initiative to improve local public courses, the possible future lengthening of holes at Augusta National, and the latest additions to the Masters qualification categories. He did so in a tone so somber that you would have thought he was reading the names of those lost at Gettysburg.

"With that, I'd be delighted to take a few questions," he said, sounding entirely undelighted about the prospect.

There were several ponderous inquiries about ball rollback (*zzzzz*), about the chances of a women's Masters (slim to none), and, of course, about the gnomes—a tournament merchandising sensation (cha-ching).

Fredericka Toney, a national newspaper columnist known for her pointed inquiries involving topics that Augusta National would have preferred to ignore, raised her hand. The moderator reluctantly called her name and activated her microphone.

"Roy"—she refused to call him "Chairman"; it wasn't the politburo—"all of us in the media center are fond of Joe Riley, but how can you possibly justify his inclusion in the Masters field?"

The Chairman stiffened.

"That's quite a blunt remark," he said. "Are you asking me or telling me?"

"I'm respectfully asking how you can invite someone with no standing on the PGA Tour, who has competed in exactly one Tour event, didn't finish in the top 35, and has no real golf pedigree," she said, not backing down.

The Chairman cleared his throat and then took a small sip of water from a plastic bottle with a Masters label.

"We are an invitational," he said. "With that designation comes certain advantages, including, at our discretion, the use of rare but not unprecedented special invitations."

"I think we all understand *how* you invited him. What we don't understand is *why*."

The Chairman had verbally sparred with Toney in the past. He always thought she would have made a formidable litigator.

"In our view, Joe Riley's circumstances and standing are the epitome of the word *special*. And thus, we chose to extend an invitation that reflects his unique situation and qualities."

"But should he be in the field?" Toney persisted.

"That is a question for which the expiration date has passed," the Chairman said unsparingly. "He is in the field. And no matter how hard you might wish otherwise, that fact will not change between now and tomorrow."

The moderator quickly clicked off Toney's microphone and pointed at the first raised hand he saw. He would soon wish he hadn't.

It was the T-shirt reporter.

"Since nobody else in this room has the balls to ask the question," the reporter said self-righteously, "I'll do it myself. Why haven't you tested Riley's clubs to see if he's cheating? Is it because you're hiding something?"

The Chairman remained quiet for several moments, his face impassive as he decided how best to deal with the impertinent little man. He had hoped to escape the question, but he had been expecting it nonetheless.

"As I assume you're aware, there were no formal requests for Mr. Riley's clubs to be tested at the Houston event," the Chairman said. "There have been no formal requests made by any of his fellow competitors this week, either."

"Well, *I'm* requesting it," said the reporter, who had been encouraged by Hard Way's former man to confront the Chairman in a public setting. "And if it turns out that you invited a cheater, will you resign as chairman of the club?"

The Chairman covered his microphone and leaned toward the moderator, who also placed his palm over his mic. They had a brief conversation. The moderator motioned to a Masters media official, who was given a set of instructions and then disappeared.

"Such tests aren't conducted on a whim," the Chairman said, returning to the reporter. "What evidence do you have of any wrongdoing? A man's reputation has been called into question."

"You'll read about it soon enough," the reporter lied.

"I see." The Chairman collected himself. "To answer your original question, if there is any credible proof that Mr. Riley is using illegal clubs, I will resign as chairman."

There was an instant clamor in the room.

"But," said the Chairman, now aiming his punishing gaze at the reporter, "if no such proof exists, I'm sure we can count on you to publicly retract any such accusations of alleged cheating and hold yourself accountable to the same standards you've demanded of me."

"You mean leave?" said the T-shirt reporter.

"If you insist, sir," the Chairman said, closing the trap. He motioned toward the back of the room, where closed-circuit TV cameras and a stenotype operator recorded the exchange for posterity. "It's quite honorable of you to say so on the record."

"Hold on a second!" said the reporter as he searched nervously around the room for allies. There were none.

Just then, a half dozen Masters employees entered the room and started distributing stacks of freshly printed media releases, still warm to the touch. The Chairman put on his reading glasses leaned toward the microphone, and recited the statement.

"Earlier today, at the direction of Chairman Jewell—and at the express request of Mr. Joe Riley—Mr. Riley's clubs underwent a series of rigorous and industry-standard conformance tests. The tests were conducted on-site by a USGA equipment expert and witnessed by representatives of the R&A, the PGA Tour, and the Masters Competition Committee, as well as the Chairman.

"The results of those tests are included below. According to the USGA's Head of Equipment Standards, Mr. Riley's clubs 'conform to all established Rules of Golf and violate no existing equipment regulations.'

"The Masters accepts these independent results and thanks Mr. Riley for his utmost integrity related to this matter. There will be no further comment."

The Chairman then looked out at the room of stunned reporters. "Thank you, ladies and gentlemen," he said. "A pleasant day to all of you." And then he stood up and left.

The T-shirt reporter was given several minutes to post his online retraction before being escorted out of the building. His ban, merciful by Masters standards, would extend only for the duration of this tournament.

Laurel and Chet made it to the Par 3 Contest just before the noon start time (Buddy would arrive from Madison on Thursday). A Masters onesie and green caddie ball cap were waiting for Riley's younger son. The jumpsuit pant legs were too long, so Laurel rolled them up over his ankles.

"You can call me 'Short Way,'" Chet said to his dad. "Get it? Hard Way . . . Short Way."

Riley knew the history: Since the Par 3 Contest began in 1960, no Contest winner had ever gone on to claim the Masters championship that same week. There were nine holes, ranging from 70 to 155 yards, which meant Chet would only have to carry two Jack wedges, a non-Jack 60-degree, a non-Jack gap wedge, and the fake White Fang in the thin, lightweight Sunday bag Riley had bought in the Masters pro shop.

"Dad, look at all these people," Chet said on the first tee.

The people. Riley hadn't truly noticed them until that very moment. They were everywhere, covering every available slope and walking path. This wouldn't be like his practice rounds, where he played in relative obscurity.

The Par 3 Contest was meant as an afternoon of fun, the last lighthearted experience the players would have before the grind of the actual tournament began. Players often had a family member as a caddie. And it wasn't uncommon for there to be multiple holes in one during the day. Throughout the history of the Contest, there had been more than 110 in all.

Riley didn't feel lighthearted. He could sense his breath quicken and his armpits moisten. Not even the news of his club tests had eased his anxiousness. He had entered the Par 3 Contest at Sargent's suggestion. It would be a way, Sargent said, to become accustomed to the crowds and work on his wedge game in a friendly, semi-competitive way.

It all sounded like a logical idea at the time. But as Riley stood on the first tee, he was gripped by anxiety.

If I'm this nervous now, what about Thursday? he thought.

"Dad, why are you wearing a glove on your right hand?"

Riley looked down. Overwhelmed by the jitters, he had shoehorned his upside-down left glove onto his right hand.

There would be no danger of Riley winning the Par 3. His tee shots found the water on Nos. 1, 3, 5, 6, and 8. Riley had laughed off the first couple of mishit wedges, as had the patrons, who thought maybe he was splashing shots on purpose to avoid the Par 3 jinx. But it was clear that Riley had no feel for any shot.

Chet could hear the murmurs and even the occasional mocking comments as they walked from the green to the next tee box.

When they got to the final hole, someone in the crowd shouted, "Let the boy hit one! He can't do any worse than you!"

There was a mixture of laughter and some scolding "Shhhhs," but Riley knew the man was right. He handed Chet the longest club in the bag, the Jack-pitching wedge.

"Go ahead, son."

"I'm gonna shut that guy up, Dad."

The hole was 130 yards long. There was no possible way that Chet, who was still a month away from his ninth birthday and small for his age, could clear the water with a wedge. Back home at the Cantigny Youth Links, Chet would have hit driver from that distance.

Chet teed up the ball (the last one remaining from two sleeves) and took two practice swings. He looked at Riley, winked and smiled, and then swung with all his might.

He skulled the shot, but it carried far enough from the downhill tee box to skip hard against the mirrored waters of the pond and hydroplane all the way to the grass bank, where, at the last moment, it popped onto the green and rolled, and rolled, and rolled toward the flagstick . . . and directly into the cup.

The patrons, including Laurel and the man who had mockingly suggested that Chet hit the ball, erupted. Chet jumped into Riley's arms. A Green Jacket threw his white Masters bucket hat into the air in celebration. Father and son could have floated across the pond to retrieve the hole in one.

When it was done, Laurel hugged both of them. Photos were taken by a Masters rep. A patron asked for Chet's autograph. It didn't matter that Riley had registered NS—No Score—in the field.

"Wait until I tell Buddy," Chet said.

"Oh, he'll know about it," Laurel said. "That's going to be on AGN's Top Ten."

That night at the rental house, after Hard Way and Riley had made spaghetti for Laurel, Chet, Kat, and Sargent, they watched replays of the ace on AGN. Chet still wore his caddie jumpsuit, though it now had specks of spaghetti sauce on the front.

The doorbell rang. Riley looked at Laurel.

"Expecting someone?"

"Not me."

Riley opened the door. A young woman, no older than Buddy, stood on the porch holding a medium-sized box. An Audi SUV purred near the end of the driveway.

"I'm so sorry to bother you, but my grandfather asked that I deliver this to you personally," she said, handing him the gift-wrapped package.

"Uh, OK," Riley said. "Who's your grandfather? And how did you know where we were staying?"

"He wouldn't want me to say," she said, glancing back at the vehicle.

Riley noticed someone sitting in the driver's seat, but the glare from the headlights prevented him from seeing any detail.

"Well, thank you. And please thank your grandfather—whoever he is—for whatever this is."

"My pleasure. And he asked that this gift remain private."

"Promise."

The woman started back down the driveway and stopped.

"Oh, I forgot: Good luck tomorrow," she said.

Riley waved and went back inside the house. Through the entry foyer windows, he saw the SUV work its way past the other cars in the circular driveway as it exited. The light from the porch illuminated the left side of the car and the man driving it.

He was wearing a white Masters bucket hat.

"Who was it?" Laurel said.

"I'm not sure," Riley said. "But the envelope has Chet's name on it."

"For me?" Chet said.

"It's heavy," Riley said.

Chet opened the envelope and read the note to the table.

This will be our Masters secret. Display it proudly, young man.

Chet tore open the green and pink wrapping paper, tugged free the strip of tape at the seam of the box, and then, with both hands, struggled to lift the Bubble-Wrapped contents.

"I'll help you," Sargent said, pulling the gift out with a grunt.

The bubble wrap fell away to reveal a Masters crystal vase.

"What is it?" Chet said.

"It's a hole-in-one vase," Hard Way said. "These are for making an ace at the Par 3 Contest. But I've never seen them give one to a non-player."

"We're not supposed to say anything about it," Riley said.

"Then don't," Hard Way said. "But this is an incredible gesture. Chet, you're a very lucky kid."

Chet received a round of applause.

"You know what this means," he said, looking at Hard Way and his dad. "It's your turn to get some swag."

CHAPTER THIRTY-TWO

Thursday, Round One

Masters Thursday morning began as it always does.

At precisely 7:40 A.M., the Chairman introduced the honorary starters, with Gary Player hitting first, then Jack Nicklaus, then Tom Watson. From there, the three players were escorted to the media center, where the first question was directed at Nicklaus.

"In only a few minutes," the well-respected Brit writer Alistair Knight began, "a former golf reporter with no credible playing credentials will compete in the same storied tournament you've won six times, and he'll do so, by all accounts, with clubs once made for you decades ago. I'm curious if you think, as many in the field do, that his presence compromises the integrity of this historic major. I ask because you're not only a champion of this event but also a member of the club."

Nicklaus leaned back in his chair, deciding whether to engage. He had known Knight for years and trusted his intentions. But this was tricky territory.

"Alistair, I'm going to respect the decision of the Chairman," Nicklaus said in his distinctive high-pitched voice, the Ohio accent still prominent. "He made his feelings known yesterday. Special invitations are his prerogative. We've done the same at the Memorial."

"A trio of quick follow-ups, if I might," the reporter said before the moderator could turn off his mic. "You're being quite coy, which isn't your nature, Jack. At the Champions Dinner on Tuesday evening, did you and the past winners discuss Riley's inclusion in the field, and do you plan to stay and watch him play these next two days?"

Nicklaus leaned forward.

"The conversations at the Champions Dinner are private, and I'm going to keep them that way," he said with a terse, thin smile. "To answer your second question, I'm leaving later this morning and will be on a fishing boat off the Keys. I wish Joe, and all the players, the very best. And it doesn't matter if I think he belongs in the field. The quality of his play will answer that. It always does."

Nicklaus, ever the gentleman, then said, "You had a third follow-up, Alistair?"

"Yes. Right. Thank you. Have you had a chance to actually see the clubs purported to be yours?"

"I've been assured by Leeds Sargent that the clubs match my exact specs, and like you, I read the Masters statement saying they've been cleared for competitive play. I also saw some footage of Joe hitting them on the range. Does that answer your question?"

"Not entirely. So you haven't had the opportunity to personally examine them?"

"Alistair, does Joe Riley hit those clubs farther than anyone you've ever seen?"

"Why, yes, he certainly does."

Nicklaus broke into a grin. "Then they're definitely mine."

The room erupted in laughter. Knight gave Nicklaus an exaggerated salute of admiration.

Riley stood at the back of the first tee box, waiting nervously to be introduced. On a table shaded by a green and white umbrella were green Masters pencils, packets of sunscreen, and white tees. A stack of grouping sheets was held in place by an Augusta National drink coaster. Fist-sized brown stones sat atop the rules sheets and hole locations charts. The stones, stored away during the year until Masters week, had been retrieved decades earlier from Rae's Creek to serve as paperweights.

At exactly 8:12 A.M., Riley was called forward. Hard Way handed him his driver, pointed one more time at the preferred line, and said, "We're going to have a blast today."

A Green Jacket addressed the patrons who had gathered in a semicircle around the tee box, some as close as several feet from the players. The introduction, to be repeated with different names throughout the day, was six words long.

"Fore, please. Joe Riley now driving."

There was polite applause, but certainly no roars. Riley gave an awkward wave to the patrons, took several practice swings, and then stood over the ball. He looked down the fairway and, as Milwaukee had predicted the previous week, the sight was overpowering. A spasm of nausea caused him to step away.

"Joe, you OK?" Hard Way said.

"I think so."

He gripped and regripped the club, did a quick waggle, and then let whatever muscle memory he had take control of his swing.

When he hit the ball, it took the patrons several moments to process its flight, as if their emotions were on tape delay. Had there been a freeze-frame of the patrons moments after impact, it would have resembled a portrait of disbelief.

But after the freeze came the thaw. First there were the gaping mouths and gasps. Next, the momentary silence tiptoed to an uneven cheer and then, like a tropical storm strengthens into a hurricane, so did this into a baby roar.

"I can't see it," a wife said to her husband.

"That's all right," the husband said. "Maybe NASA can."

The ball flew the right two fairway bunkers and bounded forward after landing. From white tee to green fairway, the ball traveled 402 yards. Even the starter, who had seen his share of wondrous shots at Augusta National, sneaked a fist bump with a patron.

"Thanks for nothing, mate," the young Aussie told Riley as Riley stepped to the side after his shot. "I've got to follow *that*."

Brown slightly pulled his drive, but it landed safely and avoided the trees.

Next up: seventy-five-year-old Cedrick Harrison, a former Masters champion known for his outrageous attire, controversial opinions, and insistence on playing in the major despite having missed his last fifteen cuts at Augusta National and not having broken 80 in his last eighteen tournament rounds there. Rather than gracefully step aside, as then sixty-three-year-old Ben Crenshaw had done after the 2015 Masters ("We're all two-down to Father Time," Crenshaw had told the late writer John Feinstein at the time. "I was out of presses."), Harrison had declared that he would take full advantage of his lifetime exemption until "the Great Starter in the Sky" called him heavenward.

Earlier in the week, Harrison had told reporters, "Joe Riley belongs here like a dance pole belongs in Butler Cabin."

His remarks became news. So, of course, the cameras were there on the first tee, where Harrison not only declined to shake Riley's hand but refused to even acknowledge him.

When his own name was announced, Harrison received spirited applause from the patrons.

"You're a truth teller!" a patron yelled.

Harrison's drive was more than respectable for his age—it split the fairway and covered about 210 yards. He pinched the bill of his silver-sequined ivy cap to the cheering throng, stuffed his tee back into the right front pocket of his pink-and-purple-striped bell-bottom pants, and then began the walk toward his ball. As he walked, he flipped up the back collar of his pink golf shirt.

It would be the last time that anyone noticed he was in the group.

Riley walked up the first fairway and heard a faraway voice. Standing on a metal riser tucked hard against the trees right of the walking path for patrons was Star Sports's Portia Pendersmith. She was about to do a live report for the network but had just enough time to wave to her friend.

"Birdie the bloody hole!" she yelled to Riley, before a producer began counting her down for her TV hit.

Riley did exactly that, sinking a 7-footer for birdie. His eagle on No. 2 took him to three-under and to the top of the leaderboard. He drove the third hole and recorded another birdie. He parred the next three holes but birdied Nos. 7, 8, and 9 for a first-nine score of 29.

The AGN broadcast window had begun at 10 A.M., when the feature groups were scheduled to tee off. But Riley's remarkable start had changed the dynamic.

"Good morning from Augusta National and the first round of the Masters, where a 1,500-to-1 betting long shot is leading his first-ever major, and doing so in unfathomable fashion," Neil Lassiter said as he welcomed in the viewing audience to a live shot of Riley walking to the 10th tee box. "His name is Joe Riley. If you watch our network, you know Riley from his previous work with us as a reporter. But you might also know him because of his recent stunning performance in Houston with an extraordinary and controversial set of vintage Jack Nicklaus clubs, and because of the surprising and much-debated decision by the Masters chairman to offer him a special invitation. This man and those clubs, along with a caddie who has his own compelling backstory, just played the first nine in a record-breaking twenty-nine strokes. Riley leads by four shots."

Lassiter appeared on a split screen as Riley teed up his ball on the par-4 10th.

"I'm Neil Lassiter, and I'm joined by two-time U.S. Open champion Andrew Hallmark. Andrew, there are Cinderella stories, and then there is this: Our former colleague Joe Riley, who could generously be described as a recreational player, is leading the Masters after nine holes. No bogeys. One eagle. Five birdies. You've competed and won at the highest level and covered this game for decades. How is this happening?"

"This is how," Hallmark said as Riley sent his drive down the speed slot on the left side of the 10th fairway. "Look at the distance: 416 yards! He has less than 80 to the pin. I'm here watching it in person and I still can't comprehend what I'm seeing."

"Let's take a close look at his swing with our FrameZoom technology."

"The setup and takeaway are fine," said Hallmark as the slo-mo replay of Riley's drive appeared on the monitor. "Sarge—that's Leeds Sargent Jr., maybe the best instructor in golf—has cleaned that up. The arc is wide, the swing path is solid, the impact point—my gosh, look at the compression of that ball—is incredible. It is an amateur's swing with superhero results. Nobody should be able to hit a ball that far with that low of swing-speed numbers."

"You've played with him before."

Hallmark laughed. "He was the epitome of a weekend golfer. To see this metamorphosis, this golf miracle, is hard for me to understand. They've been playing this tournament since 1934, and nobody has ever shot an opening 29. I'm sure every player in this field is thinking three things: Who is Joe Riley? How did he just shoot 29? And when will he wake up and collapse?"

"We have to emphasize that Riley has only played in one professional tournament prior to the Masters, where he made the cut and finished tied for thirty-seventh," Lassiter said. "This is obviously his first-ever major. He has been questioned, even ridiculed, about his presence here."

"I was one of those who questioned the invitation," Hallmark said as the cameras showed Riley hit his approach shot. "I felt that—oh, my, look at that, to 3 feet—a special invitation could have been better used. But Joe and Chairman Jewell are proving me wrong, at least through these first ten holes."

The camera panned to the first tee box, which normally would be ten to fifteen deep with patrons as the game's biggest names teed off in the prime morning slot. Instead, many of those patrons had begun to follow Riley's group.

"We have company," Hard Way said, glancing at the swelling crowds. Kat, Laurel, and Chet waved from the fairway ropes.

"I'm trying to stay focused," Riley said.

"That's a good thing," Hard Way said. "But it doesn't hurt to finally have some people rooting for us."

Hard Way's read on the 3-footer was spot-on, and Riley made the birdie putt. He parred the 11th hole and arrived at the famous par-3 12th hole just as the wind kicked up. The Aussie amateur had the honors after a long birdie putt on No. 11. His 9-iron on the 12th flew short and into the front bunker.

"Whattya think?" Riley asked.

"Let's take a little something off the wedge," Hard Way said. He ignored what the flag was doing on the 11th green and gave only a quick look at the top of the pines behind the 12th. For the moment, he was more interested in what he felt standing on the tee box. "The pin is fourteen paces on, nine over. Let's wait until we get the wind we want here. Just be ready to go when it settles down. Target line is left-middle of the front bunker."

Riley did as he was told, and when the wind paused for a moment, he sent the three-quarter wedge exactly on line. It landed just over the bunker, rolled toward the hole, and stopped a half inch short of becoming only the fourth ace Golden Bell had ever given up in Masters history. The cheers of the patrons echoed all the way back to the clubhouse.

Even with no cell phones allowed on the course, word spread of Riley's round, especially with the birdie on 12, followed by an eagle on the par-5 13th.

"I can't believe I'm invoking his name in the same sentence as Joe Riley's, but what we're seeing right now is Tiger-esque," Lassiter said.

"What we're seeing," Hallmark said, "could be *better* than Tiger-esque. Riley has a legitimate chance to break the Masters record for lowest round, and—how nuts is this—he could break 60!"

"You really think that's possible?"

"I'm beginning to believe anything is possible with this guy."

Riley parred No. 14 and then birdied the par-5 15th to move to a minus-12. He needed one birdie and no bogeys in his last three holes to shoot 59.

By now, almost all the patrons at Augusta National seemed to be following Riley's group. It was as if forty thousand people were moving as one, as if they might cause the entire property to tilt down like a playground seesaw. Laurel, Kat, and Chet squeezed into a small opening near the green.

"A few months ago, he was snowblowing our driveway and picking up dog poop in the backyard," Laurel said.

"Now he's leading the Masters," Kat said. "The *eff-ing* Masters."

Laurel covered her mouth in mock horror. Then she covered Chet's ears. "You didn't hear that, Chet."

"I eff-ing did!"

On the tee box, Hard Way tried to convey a businesslike demeanor. But it was a façade. His hands trembled slightly as he pulled out his yardage book. *Get it together, Max. If you're calm, maybe he'll be calm.*

"Pin is thirty-six on, six from the right," Hard Way said in a forced monotone. "Just a touch of wind coming from two o'clock. You could take something off the 9-iron or hit a full Jack wedge. I like the wedge. Let's just get it back there."

"I serve at the pleasure of Hard Way," Riley said. Hard Way handed him the wedge. "And Max, I'm OK. It's like someone else is hitting these shots."

As soon as the ball left the club, Hard Way knew it was going to be close. It landed, bounced, rolled, and then settled 10 inches from the cup. It wasn't the same as when Tiger had chipped in on the same hole in 2005 and Verne Lundquist had told the TV audience, "In your life have you seen anything like that?!" But there was a similar kind of seismic disturbance, the same kind of feeling that comes while witnessing history. The patrons thundered. Photographers pressed hard on the buttons of their motorized cameras.

"Mate," Brown said, "I've never had so much fun watching someone else play golf in my life. That was a corker of a shot."

The nudge-in birdie dropped Riley to minus-13. Chet yelled loud enough to attract the attention of Riley as he left the green. Riley looked at his son and made a heart sign with his hands, and later that day, a photograph of that moment would be featured in most sports pages across the world.

The par-4 17th always gave Hard Way the heebie-jeebies. A lot could go wrong if the tee shot leaked to the right and the ball trickled into the trees and pine straw.

"I know you've been pounding driver all day, but let's just get something in the middle of the fairway," he told Riley. "I'm thinking 3-iron right through the pipes. Plus, it leaves us a nice distance for the second shot."

Riley wasn't going to wave off his catcher in the middle of a no-hitter. Without even thinking, he flushed the 3-iron 323 yards to center cut. In the broadcast tower, Hallmark threw his research notes in the air.

"There are no adjectives left," he said.

"Well, maybe we just admit that we're witnessing the greatest round in golf history," Lassiter said.

The pin was fifteen on, eight from the left. Bunkers guarding the front of the green. No wind of consequence.

"The Jack sand wedge to the middle," Hard Way said. "A two-putt par is just fine here."

And that's what Riley did, though his birdie putt caught the right edge of the hole and just spun out.

One hole remaining: the 465-yard par-4 18th. Hard Way handed Riley a 3-wood.

"No driver?" Riley said.

"Not today. We just want a baby cut, which you usually do with the 3-wood. You hit it far enough to give us a good chance of finding a flatter lie."

The ball flew nearly 370 yards, and almost on the exact line favored by Hard Way. But on his second shot, Riley took too much off the Jack sand wedge and pushed the ball into the right greenside bunker. With the pin on the back right, he had short-sided himself.

"I haven't hit a bunker shot all day," Riley said nervously.

"The sand is as soft as a Waikiki beach," Hard Way said. "Just drop it anywhere on the back section and we'll take our chances with that putter."

With half the state of Georgia forming a three-quarter ring around the green, and viewers from two hundred countries and territories watching around the world, Riley used his 60-degree wedge and a mid-handicapper's technique to escape the sand. Players such as bunker savant Justin Rose would have had no problem juicing the ball with enough spin to make it stick and stop. But Riley's bunker shot tumbled out of the sand and rolled past the hole. It finally settled just short of the fringe, nearly 20 feet from the cup.

"The math is simple," Lassiter said. "A one-putt equals 59."

Hard Way and Riley settled on the line. As he moved away, Hard Way said, "You got this, pro."

The putt tracked toward the left outside edge of the hole, enough to make Hard Way think he had misread the line. But during the last few feet, the ball broke ever so slightly and caught the inside edge, spinning completely around before it fell exhausted into the darkness.

Hallmark started to speak, but Lassiter reached across and put a hand on his wrist. This wasn't a time for words. "Lay out," he mouthed to Hallmark—broadcast shorthand for "Let the moment do all the talking."

There was a spiritual quality to the roar. Strangers hugged. Laurel and Kat cried. Chet told anyone who would or could listen, "That's my dad!" And inside the private office of the Chairman, there was a muffled yell of celebration.

Riley pulled the ball from the cup and raised it over his head as if it were Simba. The tens of thousands who had witnessed the 59 in person shared in the moment. It was theirs as much as it was his.

Hard Way stood with the flagstick in his hand, speechless at first, but then awash in pure joy. He didn't hear the patrons. He just watched Riley—his man—bask in the moment.

When they embraced, Hard Way said, "Fake White Fang, my ass."

"That was Gordo's spirit. It had to be."

Brown still had a 2-foot par putt for 71, which he made after Hard Way and Brown's caddie politely asked the crowd for quiet. Harrison tapped in a 10-inch putt for bogey and a round of 81.

Brown, Riley, and the caddies met near the hole. Hats were taken off, handshakes exchanged.

"Mate, thank you," Brown said to Riley. "When I have kids, I have something to tell them."

As Riley made his way up the corridor behind the green, he felt a tap on his shoulder. It was Harrison, hat off, his hand reaching for Riley's.

"I misjudged you," Harrison said. "I hope you'll accept my profound apology. I was—who am I kidding?—I *am* a blustering, bloviating bagpipe of nonsense, and my behavior was a reflection of my own weaknesses. Had you shot 79 rather than 59 I would have said the same thing. You conducted yourself in a manner that I should aspire to. Today you were, as Trevino once said of Seve, 'A touch of class, baby.' "

"Mr. Harrison," Riley said, "can I buy you a beer in the clubhouse?"

"No, you cannot," he said, putting his arm around Riley, "but I'll buy you one. And bring the lad with the funny accent with you."

Buddy arrived that night. He walked in the door of the rental house, dropped his bag, and found everyone outside on the patio. His father had a six-stroke lead after the first round of the Masters.

He looked at the group and said with a huge smile, "Did I miss anything?"

CHAPTER THIRTY-THREE

Friday, Round Two

The Miracle at the Masters was on.

Riley extended his lead to ten strokes, doubling the previous Masters record after thirty-six holes. His 9-under-par 63 on Friday was now tied for the second-lowest round in Masters history, but only because he had shot 59 on Thursday. There were comparisons to John Daly and his out-of-nowhere victory at the 1991 PGA Championship, and even to Francis Ouimet, the twenty-year-old amateur who beat such distinguished pros as Ted Ray and Harry Vardon to win the 1913 U.S. Open.

In the post-round press conference, Riley was visibly uncomfortable addressing such comparisons. For so many years, he had sat in that media center interview room asking questions rather than answering them. The whole idea of sitting on the interview stage next to a Green Jacket moderator and going through his eagles (Nos. 2 and 13), birdies (Nos. 3, 6, 8, 15, 16), and pars (there were no bogeys) remained surreal to him.

As the moderator paused to choose the next questioner, Riley glanced at a large screen across the room with an updated leaderboard. He couldn't help but notice that Hard Way's former man was tied for tenth.

When Riley returned to the locker room, Derrin Brown was waiting for him. The Aussie had made the cut with a second-round 71 and was low amateur after two rounds. As expected, Harrison had failed to advance to Saturday's play.

"We won't be paired together during the weekend, but all the best to you, mate," he said. "I'll be pulling for you."

"You'll be one of the few."

Brown glanced behind his shoulder and smiled. "I'm not so sure about that."

Brown stepped to the side to reveal Gary Lippon. Behind Lippon were about a dozen other players. Riley felt a lump form in the back of his throat.

"Is this where the Joe Riley Fan Club meets?" Lippon said, waving the others forward. "You have some converts." One by one, the other players came and shook his hand and wished him luck. Unsurprisingly, Hard Way's man was not among them.

At dinner that night, Buddy sat next to Hard Way and peppered him with questions about the course. The quality of the questions was what caught Hard Way's attention: prevailing winds, where to miss, hole locations, slope differentials, best angles, putting strategy, and a half dozen other nuanced inquiries that even some professional caddies failed to consider. Buddy had gotten to the course early Friday and walked nine holes before his dad's midmorning tee time, walked all eighteen with his dad's group, and then walked the back nine with the last threesomes of the day.

He had taken his own notes during those thirty-six holes and now wanted to compare his observations with Hard Ways'.

"I'm getting ready to go over my yardage book for tomorrow," Hard Way said. "Bring what you wrote and I'll walk you through each hole."

"Really?"

"Sure. It'll be a good way for me to prep. I'll get the pin sheet tomorrow, but I already have a decent idea where they'll be."

"This should be framed and hung on a wall," Buddy said.

Buddy was amazed by Hard Way's attention to detail in his yardage book. There were notations, numbers, wind directions, slopes, breaks, carries, specific tree locations . . . everything. The illustrations were as precise as an architect's blueprint, and the lettering and notes as perfect as in a Bible copied by a medieval monk.

"I get carried away," Hard Way said. "Every caddie has their own style and system. Your dad's distance made my old books obsolete. And there have been some changes to the course. They always tinker here."

The two of them then spent nearly forty-five minutes going through Hard Way's book and Buddy's notes. As a friendly test, Hard Way asked Buddy if he'd noticed anything about the putts on the No. 4 green. Buddy flipped through the pages of his notepad.

"Hold on, I wrote down something. Here it is, No. 4:

> Bamboo on right side . . . left hole location is death . . .
> take par and run . . . putts from back to front super quick,
> everything funnels toward 12th hole, low point of A.N."

"Mind if I look?" Hard Way said, palm open. Buddy handed him the notepad.

"You *were* paying attention," Hard Way said as he thumbed through the pages.

"Beginner's luck," Buddy said.

Hard Way shook his head.

"I think you know that's not true," he said. "I gotta tell your old man about this."

"No!" Buddy said, grabbing the notepad from Hard Way. "Please. This is just between you and me."

"But why? You're a sponge. You're a natural."

"You've got to promise me you won't say anything," Buddy pleaded.

"He's in a zone. If you mention me and caddies, it's not going to end well."

"I think you and your dad need—"

"To talk? Maybe. But not now. Promise you won't tell him?"

Hard Way considered the request. "I don't understand you Rileys. But you've got my word. I won't tell him."

Later, Hard Way made his way to the fridge for bottled water. Laurel was in the kitchen scooping grounds into a paper filter for the coffee maker.

"Habit," she said as Hard Way walked in. "Last thing I do before going to bed: set up the coffee machine."

"Nectar of the morning." He pulled out two bottles of water, one for him, one for Kat, and turned to walk back to their room. "Good night."

"I noticed that you and Buddy disappeared after dinner."

Hard Way stopped and turned around.

"Oh, yeah . . . that. We were just, uh, watching the wrap-up show on AGN."

"In that upstairs den?"

"Yeah, the den."

"There's no TV in there," Laurel said innocuously.

"I meant, in my room."

Laurel tapped the last scoop of grounds into the filter. Hard Way, hopeful that he had squirmed his way out of the lie, again turned to leave.

"Buddy loves his dad. He just can't figure out how to show it. Joe's the same way."

Hard Way stopped but said nothing.

"Buddy showed you his golf course notes."

"Uh . . ."

"It's not a question, Max. I saw him taking notes today during Joe's round. Moms and teachers see everything. I'm both."

Hard Way turned around to face her. "Your kid knows golf. Like, *really* knows it. He took better notes than most of the caddies out there who have been doing this for twenty years. I didn't have to tell him anything twice."

"Knows it. Loves it," Laurel said as she poured water into the coffee maker and shut the lid. "But something is broken between him and Joe and I can't fix it."

"Give it time."

"Time. They've already wasted so much time." She wiped up a few granules of coffee and drops of water with a paper towel. "There's a quote I once saw. Something about how twenty years from now, the only people who will remember you worked late are your children."

"You can't blame a man for working hard," Hard Way said.

"Oh, yes I can." She tossed the paper towel into a plastic bin under the sink and walked out, leaving Hard Way in the empty kitchen holding two bottles of water and trying to figure out which was more impossible—Riley actually winning the Masters or winning back his son.

CHAPTER THIRTY-FOUR

Saturday, Round Three

Rain and wind swept through Augusta beginning at midmorning and lasted through much of the afternoon. While almost the entire remaining field struggled to break par, Riley shot a 65 as his distance off the tee became an even bigger advantage in the poor conditions. When he didn't hit the persimmon driver or fairway woods, he flighted the Jack irons with pinpoint accuracy.

His playing partner that afternoon was the Irishman Sean McCaffrey, who told reporters afterward in an accent that was occasionally allergic to the letter *h*, "You tink you've got quite a round going—I mean, a 72 in Celtic Sea conditions is a point of pride. But it was lovely what my fellow honorary Irishman did today. He hit tree-arn [3-iron] farther than I hit a tree-wood [3-wood]. I tink I played with the next Masters champion."

Rounds of 59-63-65 put Riley at an astounding 29-under par and an astonishing eighteen shots ahead of four other players at minus-11. His 187-stroke total was thirteen shots lower than the previous low for the first fifty-four holes of the Masters. The record for the low seventy-two-hole Masters score (268) was laughably within reach. Riley could shoot a final-round 80 and still set the record.

The clubbies in the locker room joked with Riley after his round.

"Won't see you in here ever again," one of the old-timers said. "You'll be upstairs in the Champions Locker Room by Sunday night. No more slumming with us common folk."

Riley laughed with them, but his mind wandered to places where it shouldn't have. Then he caught himself. *Stop! What did Nick Saban call it? "Rat poison." Win the damn tournament first.*

As Riley closed the door to his locker, a clubbie came over and picked up his golf shoes for cleaning.

"Hey, did you see who you're paired with tomorrow?"

"I heard four guys are at 11-under, but I didn't look at the names yet. Hard Way ordered me not to look at the leaderboard during the round."

"You'll know one of them."

"Don't tell me."

"Yep. He got in before the other three. It's you and him in the last group."

Him.

Hard Way's former man.

CHAPTER THIRTY-FIVE

Sunday Morning

Golf was a cold, cruel, solitary game, especially on the final day of a major. A player couldn't take a time-out, call his swing coach from the gallery to help solve a flaw, have a relief golfer come in for him. It was the player and his caddie vs. the elements, the pressure, the course, the crowd, the field, and their own self-doubts. For Riley and Hard Way, there would be an additional foe: the unknown.

Hard Way had never caddied for a player who entered the final round of a major with the lead. He certainly had never caddied for someone such as Riley. Nobody had. To pretend this would be just another round with just another player would have been to pretend there weren't pines at Augusta National. In the history of golf, there had never been a Sunday scenario like this.

It would be up to Hard Way to determine when his man needed a hand on the shoulder, an encouraging word, silence, or to be told a story that distracted him from the pressure at hand. Maybe he needed to be read the riot act, have a couple of F-bombs dropped on him, be grabbed by the balls in a figurative sense. Everything was about timing and professionalism. Hard Way would have to be like a big-league catcher trying to get his rookie starting pitcher through the game. It was easy when your man had his good stuff. The trick was to get him through the days when he had nothing.

It was a daunting task to win on Tour. Nicklaus won about 13 percent of his Tour starts and yet was considered the greatest champion in the game. Woods, who shared the record for most Tour victories (82), won 22 percent of the time. There were veteran players ranked in the top 100 in the world who had earned millions in prize money but had never won a Tour event.

But nothing was harder than winning a major, especially this major. Even with a supposedly insurmountable lead, Hard Way understood the laws of golf.

As he had done on Saturday, Hard Way drove to the course early Sunday morning to quickly walk each hole and mark the latest pin positions for himself. The walk also gave him a chance to get a feel for the day's wind and how it might change. Buddy walked with him just outside the ropes.

When they were done, Hard Way arranged for one of the caddie shack volunteers to shuttle Buddy back to the rental house. Hard Way still had work to do.

Riley had mentioned after Saturday's round that the leather grips had lost some of their tack. In the past, Hard Way had used lukewarm water and a mild soap to help remove the dirt and grime that had built up during play. Because these grips were decades old, he had used neat's-foot oil to soften the leather. It was the same oil that baseball players used to help break in their gloves.

Hard Way walked into the storage room and pulled the driver from the bag.

There was a problem.

There were large gaps in the leather wrapping of the grip. The underlisting, which was made out of crepe paper, was completely exposed. Whatever adhesive Wullkotte had used years ago had chosen the Sunday morning of the Masters to give up the ghost. One by one,

Hard Way checked the other Jack clubs; the leather was in various stages of unfurling from the shafts. *This can't be happening,* he thought, his disbelief surpassed only by the rate of his heartbeat.

Hard Way speed-walked to the courtesy car in the lot and pulled his cell phone from the center console. He called an equipment guy still on-site who specialized in grips and explained the situation. There was a long silence on the line.

"Hard Way, I think you're screwed," the equipment expert said. "A few of the European and Aussie players use leather grips, but I haven't seen crepe paper underlisting for years. Maybe moisture built up over time and compromised the paper and the adhesive, which back then might have been tar. Maybe it was the rain and humidity we had yesterday. Or the air-conditioning in the storage area. It's hard to say for sure. How's the leather look?"

"It's good, but Joe said it was losing some of its tackiness. Can you help us?"

"I'll try. We've still got a Sprinter van here for emergency repairs. We'll make something work."

"I'll be there in ten minutes."

Hard Way collected the bag and drove across Washington Road to where the equipment trailers had been parked during the week. Only a few remained.

The grip expert examined the MacGregors.

"You're right; the leather is in good shape for being so old. Just think if they'd come apart in the middle of the round."

"No, thank you," Hard Way said. "Can you MacGyver these things back to health?"

"I think so."

The equipment man carefully removed the grips and placed them next to the club they came from. He used a rubber-tube underlisting, wrapped it with a thin layer of double-sided tape, and then wrapped the original leather around it.

"Well?" Hard Way said.

"Because of the rubber, they're going to feel softer and a little thicker than the grip you had," he said. "But under the circumstances, this is the best I can do."

"What do I owe you?"

"Just mention me during the awards ceremony," he said, smiling.

Hard Way drove back to the rental house and found Riley, Laurel, Buddy, Chet, and Kat, as well as Gallagher and Sargent, sitting around the dining room table picking at cinnamon rolls, a fruit plate, and biscuits.

"Welcome back," Kat said, giving Hard Way a peck on the cheek. "How'd the scouting mission go?"

"That went fine," he said. "But there was something wrong with the Jack club grips."

"I knew it," Riley said. "I could feel the grip on the sand wedge give and slip a little bit on 18 yesterday."

"You pushed that shot into the right trap," Sargent said.

Riley nodded.

"So how big of a problem?" Buddy asked.

"There was separation on the grip of every Jack club," Hard Way said. "My equipment guy performed some reconstructive surgery on them."

Riley pulled the driver from the bag.

"Looks the same," he said.

"Same leather strapping, but it's spongier," Hard Way said.

"Rubber underlisting?" Sargent said.

"Yeah; the paper and adhesive were toast."

Riley gripped the driver and took a quarter swing. "It feels a little different, but nothing crazy. This will work." Buddy looked like he was going to be sick. Laurel noticed him slip out of the room.

Hard Way glanced at his watch. It was 10:40—four hours to the minute before they teed off as the final group.

"Leave here at 12:30?" he said. "By the time we get there and get situated, you'll have about ninety minutes to warm up. That's been the schedule all week."

"Man, Scheffler wasn't kidding about the long wait on a Masters Sunday," Riley said.

"It beats teeing off with the first group at 10:10," Sargent said.

Laurel checked on Buddy, who was sitting by himself in the living room.

"Honey, you OK?"

"I have a bad feeling."

"We're all nervous. Your dad was tossing and turning all night. He needs to know we believe in him."

"It's not that, Mom. It's something Gordo told me that day at the garage sale. I didn't think about it until just now."

"What did he say?"

"It's going to sound crazy."

"Your dad plays with magic clubs. Nothing is going to sound crazier than that."

"He said the clubs shouldn't be changed. He said they were 'unalterable.' That was the word he used."

"But Buddy, the grips were coming apart. You heard Max. They had to do *something*."

"I guess. I'm just antsy, too."

Laurel sensed that someone else was in the room. She turned to find Gallagher standing near a corner just out of view.

"My apologies," he said, stepping in. "I left my reading glasses in here." He retrieved the glasses and hurriedly excused himself.

"Honey, today is going to be a day we'll never forget," she said after Gallagher had left.

"That's what I'm afraid of, Mom."

"You nervous?" Riley said to Hard Way as they drove to the course.

"Not nervous. Excited. You?"

"Focused."

"That's what I like to hear. And with apologies to the Cliché Police, one shot, one hole at a time today."

"Exactly. And since it's just you and me in the car, are we gonna talk about the elephant in the Masters?"

Hard Way shook his head. He didn't want to acknowledge or discuss his former guy.

"It's you, me, and Augusta National today," Hard Way said. "Nothing else exists."

"Well, he's going to be standing right there on the first tee. I'm going to have to shake his hand."

"Better you than me," Hard Way said.

"Max."

"I'm fine, really. But listen to me: He's going to do everything he can to knock us off our game. No matter what, just ignore him. He wants you to react. He wants to know he's getting to you. It's the only chance he has."

Hard Way turned into the players' entrance, drove down Magnolia Lane, and parked the car in the clubhouse lot. He hesitated and then turned to Riley. There was a sheen on his eyes.

"Are you crying?" Riley said.

"Not officially."

"I don't understand."

"Let me just get through this," Hard Way said. "Whatever happens this afternoon, thank you."

"For what?"

"For today. For this week. For all of it."

CHAPTER THIRTY-SIX

Sunday, Round Four

Mike McMullins pressed the talkback button to the AGN talent on the ground and in the booth towers.

"Sixty seconds to air, forty-one minutes until our leader tees off," he said evenly, trying to mask his own excitement. "Our traffic: Open with Neil, Neil hands off to Maury and Andrew, Maury tosses to Rinello at the range, then back to Neil, and then to the action. The story is going to tell itself today, so nobody needs to help it along. Everybody have a good show."

Left unsaid was that one of their own was on the brink of an unimaginable victory, that sports history was going to be made on their watch. But that was McMullins—understated, composed, concise.

At exactly 2 P.M., AGN came on the air with the sound of violins, an undercurrent of percussion, and an occasional cymbal to add a bit of thunder to the intro theme. Lassiter began to speak over the music and the accompanying images provided by a drone as it swept across the pines and expanse of Augusta National.

"The Masters and this famed course have given us more than just moments over the years," he said as B-roll of Jones, Sarazen, Snead, Hogan, and Palmer filled the screen. "They have given us history." And with that came announcer SOT of Nicklaus's sixth and unlikeliest

Masters victory in 1986, of Larry Mize's chip-in to win the 1987 Masters, of young Tiger's record-setting victory in 1997, and of oldish Tiger's win in 2019. "But today it will give us the greatest underdog story in golf and, perhaps, sports history. Or it will give us the greatest comeback ever to be seen."

The director cut to a shot of the main Masters scoreboard, where Riley's name sat at the top.

"And for all of this we can thank Joe Riley, a forty-three-year-old former reporter for this network who has done what no other player has ever done on this grassy stage: render Augusta National completely defenseless with his longest club, a persimmon driver, and with his shortest club, an elderly putter."

Lassiter appeared on camera.

"Welcome to a Masters filled with the impossible and incomprehensible. I'm Neil Lassiter, along with Maury Walsh and two-time U.S. Open champion Andrew Hallmark."

The producer cut to a three-shot of the announcers in the booth of the 18th tower. Lassiter continued.

"Going into today's final round, Riley is already 29-under par and eighteen shots ahead of his nearest competitors. And we thought nobody would ever surpass Tiger Woods' 12-shot margin of victory here in 1997. There are no sure things in sports, but Maury, it certainly feels as if Riley has spelled the first three letters: *s-u-r*. All that's missing is the final *e*."

"That letter . . . and the final round," Walsh said. "Barring a playoff—and that seems equally impossible given how well Riley has performed—only eighteen holes separate this golf nobody from leaving here with the most prized wardrobe addition in sports: a green jacket. A matter of months ago, he had never played in an amateur or professional tournament, never mind a Masters. But thanks to a much-debated special invitation and set of clubs, he comes here and shoots the lowest round in majors history. After three rounds, he has lapped the field and become the patron saint of underdogs. It would take an equally historic collapse to undo what seems inevitable and incredible: a Riley victory."

For all his eccentricities—and there were many—Walsh could turn a phrase and frame a moment like few could. It was a fact not lost on Lassiter.

"Certainly there is no precedent for what he has done through fifty-four holes, and no precedent for a comeback by anyone in the field," Lassiter said. "The largest comeback in majors history is ten strokes—that was at the Open Championship in 1999—and eight strokes at the Masters."

"Or to put it in perspective," Hallmark said, "Riley could shoot a 4-over-par 76 today, and one of the four players in second place would have to shoot 58 just to tie! At the beginning of the week, I gave Riley no chance whatsoever. I thought it was a wasted special invitation—a travesty, if I'm being completely honest. But I owe both Riley and the Chairman an apology."

McMullins pressed his talkback to Lassiter as Hallmark finished up. "Let's go to Rinello at the range."

"Our Tim Rinello is at the range monitoring the beginning of Riley's warm-up session," Lassiter said. "Tim?"

"Thank you, Neil," Rinello said. "Riley arrived here only a few minutes ago, along with his caddie, Max Mitchell, and swing instructor, Leeds Sargent Jr. Those two have been instrumental in helping Riley navigate these unusual times. And, of course, there is the subplot involving Mitchell—known to everyone out here as 'Hard Way'—who was fired unceremoniously and very publicly by the same player who will join Riley in the final group. Mitchell's career as a Tour caddie was all but over until he joined forces with Riley.

"As for Riley's preparation for this final round, it's the same as the previous three days. He is starting with some easy swings with his 60-degree wedge—one of only three clubs in his bag that aren't part of the original collection made for Jack Nicklaus. The two other non-'Jack' clubs are a less-lofted wedge and a secondhand putter that resembles the original White Fang Nicklaus used in the past."

"Do you notice any difference in demeanor or routine, Tim?" Lassiter said.

"None. When he walked by our position here at the corner of the range, he smiled, said hello, and seemed entirely comfortable with his extraordinary situation. Part of that is obviously his familiarity and friendship with many of us at AGN. Then again, you might be relaxed, too, if you held an eighteen-shot lead. But as always, we'll see how the pressures of a Masters Sunday manifest themselves as the afternoon unfolds."

"We'll check back with Tim as we get closer to 2:40 P.M.," Lassiter said. "In the meantime, let's go to No. 12 and catch up with some of our earlier groups."

Rinello stayed put until his cameraman took off his own headphones. "You're cleared," the cameraman said.

Rinello handed the mic to the audio tech but kept his IFB in and kept the remote audio box hooked to his belt so he could listen to the broadcast. Rinello watched as Riley hit about a half dozen shots with each of the two non-Jack wedges. Nothing unusual there.

"Can you see what club he's hitting next?" Rinello asked his shooter. The cameraman zoomed in on the bag.

"Looks like maybe a 9-iron," he told Rinello. "But it's definitely one of the MacGregors. I can tell by the grips."

Rinello would know soon enough. He had been charting Riley's club distances with a range finder and knew that he usually hit the sand wedge about 135 yards, the wedge about 175, and the 9-iron about 210.

Riley's first shot failed to reach a marker that was no more than 100 yards away. He cocked his head, looked at Sargent with a smile, said something that caused them to laugh—Rinello was too far away to hear—and dragged another ball from the pile with the club. He swung again. This one squirted to the right. Sargent stepped in, said something to Riley, patted him on the back, and then stepped away. The third shot was shorter than the first.

Rinello turned to the cameraman. "Tell the truck that I'm in position and they need to come to me as soon as possible. Riley can't hit the ball."

"Max?" Riley said after the third try with his sand wedge traveled just 70 yards—nearly half its usual distance. "What's going on?"

"No worries," Hard Way said, doing his best to hide his own sense of panic. "Let's give the sand wedge a rest. Just hit a few smooth 8-irons. I don't think you've missed the center of that club all week."

As Hard Way had predicted, Riley flushed the shot. The problem: It flew only 140 yards, 90 yards shorter than usual.

The patrons assembled in the viewing area behind the range had begun to notice Riley's difficulties, as had a half dozen other players on the range, including Hard Way's former man.

"You watching what I'm watching?" he said to his caddie. "Either he's screwing with us, or we might have a chance to make today interesting."

Hard Way handed Riley iron after iron, but the results were similar. No matter how solid the contact, the distances were drastically shorter.

"Give him the driver," Sargent said.

Rinello and the patrons didn't need a camera to see that Hard Way had handed Riley the persimmon driver. Nor was it difficult to follow the low screamer that traveled, at most, 200 yards.

"Coming to you in ten," a voice said from the truck.

Rinello did a quick thumbs-up to the camera, fluffed his pocket square, and waited for Lassiter to tee him up.

"Rinello with a developing story," McMullins told Lassiter on talkback.

"Let's break away from the golf for a few moments and head back to the range for an update from Tim Rinello, who has some developing news," Lassiter said.

"Thanks, Neil. As you can see behind me," Rinello said as he stepped to the side to allow a direct line to the range, "our tournament leader, Joe Riley, his caddie, and his swing instructor have been huddled for the last several minutes. Neil, we've watched Riley hit about thirty shots with those much-discussed MacGregor clubs during this warm-up session, and to put it bluntly, it's been a disaster."

Walsh interrupted.

"By 'disaster,' you mean what exactly?" he said. "In the past, we've seen some shaky warm-ups by great players followed by championship-quality golf."

"I agree, Maury, but this is far different and far more troubling. I think we have some B-roll of a few of Riley's earlier shots on the range." Rinello looked at the small monitor perched on a folding table as a handful of Riley's range swings were shown. "In some cases, such as this series of shots with his driver, Riley was hitting it barely 200 yards, less than half the distance of his usual 400-yard-plus drives. It was that way with every club we've observed so far."

"Tim, this is Neil. Any idea what they could be discussing?"

"Leeds Sargent, and Max Mitchell are certainly veterans out on Tour, but they've never encountered anything like this. Given the circumstances, I would be reluctant to speculate."

"Keep us updated," Lassiter said. "Andrew? Maury? Your thoughts?"

"A few minutes ago, I said I couldn't imagine a scenario where Riley could lose an 18-shot lead," Hallmark said. "Well, there's one now."

Maury jumped in. "Like all of us, I expected a coronation today. He now has, what, less than thirty minutes to solve this sudden mystery. If he doesn't, this final round is reduced to a simple question: How long can Joe Riley hang on?"

Buddy sat on a metal bleacher in the patron viewing area behind the range. Laurel, Kat, and Gallagher had walked to the roped-off short-game area, where Riley, Hard Way, and Sargent had gone. Chet had stayed behind with his brother.

"Buddy, what's wrong with Dad?" Chet said.

"It isn't Dad. It's the new grips."

"Whattya mean?"

"When I first got the clubs, Gordo—you remember him from the garage sale?"

Chet nodded.

"Well, he basically said there was some kind of cosmic bond between those clubs and Dad. When they fixed the grips this morning, it must have disrupted the connection, or something like that."

"But aren't they the same grips?"

"Same leather, but underneath it's different."

"So Dad is going to lose?"

"I don't know, little dude. He has a big lead."

"That's good," Chet said optimistically.

"But he's back to being an 18-handicapper."

"That's bad."

"Very bad," Buddy said.

Riley's short game was unaffected, but the same couldn't be said of his putting. Riley missed a half dozen 5-footers at the practice green before one finally dropped. His putter, whose grip also had been updated, suddenly provided no refuge.

"You're not thinking what I'm thinking, are you?" Hard Way said.

"That all along Gordo had a real White Fang but didn't know it?" Riley said. "I don't know what to believe anymore."

"This is all my fault. I should have just glued the damn grips back on."

Riley lowered his voice, but the desperation could be heard louder than ever. "What am I gonna do, Max? Nothing is working."

"Sarge and me were talking about it," Hard Way said as Sargent squeezed toward the entrance of the green. "One of the four guys tied for second is going to shoot at least 2-under today, maybe lower."

"So all you need to shoot is an 87 or so," Sargent said. "That gives you a real chance to hold on."

"Oh, that's all?" Riley said.

"We've played enough practice rounds and tournament rounds to have a working knowledge of the course," Hard Way said. "Your short game is decent. You're not a bad putter."

"We just need to avoid the crooked numbers," Sargent said. "The goal is to play bogey golf on the par-4s and 5s, and not lose any ground on the par-3s."

"Did you see me on the range?" Riley said as he began pacing. "Did you see me on the green?"

"OK, so it's not going to be easy," Hard Way said. "If it were easy, everybody would have a green jacket."

"We thought about having the equipment guys swap out the Jacks and put together a regular set for you, but there wasn't time," Sargent said.

Riley leaned the putter against the bag and stared blankly at the sky.

Watching from 30 yards away was Laurel.

"Uh-oh," Laurel said to Kat.

"'Uh-oh'?" Kat said. "You mean there's something worse than that warm-up?"

"I know that look. Joe is a having a moment—a bad one. He stares when he doesn't know what to do."

At 2:30 P.M., Riley and Hard Way walked down the roped-off path from the practice green to the first tee. It was Augusta National's version of an HOV lane. By now, word had spread throughout the course: Joe Riley had lost his golf superpowers.

A few of the patrons reached out for fist bumps, but Riley buried his hands in his pockets. There were shouts of encouragement, but Riley could think only about his impending doom. He didn't even notice the half dozen college students dressed as Nicklaus from his final round at the 1986 Masters: beltless blue-and-brown plaid pants with a bell-bottom flare, yellow short-sleeved shirts with Golden Bear logos over the left-breast pockets and opened two buttons deep, white golf shoes, and, in this case, blond wigs parted on the left as was Nicklaus's hair back then. The students called themselves "the Jacks."

Three Green Jackets greeted Riley at the back of the tee box and shook his hand. One of them handed him a scorecard. Hard Way's former guy soon approached.

"Good luck today," he said with faux sincerity. "Looked like you were having a rough time on the range. You'll probably shake that off."

Riley could manage no response. Instead, he quietly joined Hard Way on the right side of the tee marker of the par-4, 455-yard hole. Hard Way quickly counted the clubs in the bag. As he did so, his former guy looked at the crowd and gestured toward Hard Way.

"*Now* he counts them," he said, smiling, but loud enough for everyone on both sides of the tee box to hear. There was laughter from the patrons.

Hard Way followed his own advice and ignored the dig.

Riley had the honors. Hard Way handed him his driver.

"We're a team, pal," Hard Way said. "Just put a smooth, easy swing on it. Let's keep it simple: middle of the fairway, middle of the greens. That's our motto today."

The enormity of the moment became too much. Milwaukee's words became prophecy.

Heart gonna be pounding. Sweat gonna be dripping. Hands gonna be quivering.

Riley teed up the ball and then stepped back.

"Fore, please!" boomed the Green Jacket. "Now driving, Joe Riley!"

Riley gave a half wave, took a practice swing, and then tried to concentrate. It was no use. He was lost.

Hard Way walked casually to Riley, took out his yardage book, and showed him a page.

"Max, isn't that the seventh hole?"

"Yeah. I was just trying to buy you some time."

"I'm scared."

"Milwaukee, right?"

"Yeah."

"Remember, he gave you the antidote."

Riley thought about it for a moment. Then he and Hard Way recited it together, like two people singing the chorus of a song.

"Embrace the difficulty," they said as one. "Breathe it in. Run toward it, through it, not away from it."

Hard Way leaned in.

"Breathe, baby, breathe. Smooth swing, and we'll figure it out from there."

Riley hit the ball solidly, but it barely managed to reach the incline of the first fairway, some 215 yards away. The patrons offered a combination of stunned murmurs and polite applause.

Head down, Riley dropped the driver in the bag.

"Hey, right down the middle," Hard Way said. "Good job."

Hard Way's former guy pinched the bill of his cap after his introduction and then piped his drive almost 100 yards past Riley's. The roles were now reversed, with Riley the short hitter. But there was another problem: Riley and Hard Way were flying blind when it came to the yardages.

Hard Way had done his best to jot down the numbers as Riley went through his bag on the range. They were guesses more than anything. There was no time to do a detailed distance check of each Jack club.

In his yardage book, Hard Way had inserted a piece of paper with the new persimmon and Jack irons estimates next to the old numbers. He also included the non-Jack 60-degree wedge.

> New: Dr—210, 3W—194, 5W—185, 3i—175, 4i—168, 5i—161, 6i—154, 7i—147, 8i—141, 9i—129, PW—116, SW—76, 60-degree—68
>
> Old: Dr—407, 3W—368, 5W—351, 3i—320, 4i—299, 5i—280, 6i—265, 7i—250, 8i—228, 9i—210, PW—177, SW—136, 60-degree—68

It took Riley three shots to reach the first green, followed by three putts for a double bogey. His lead was now sixteen strokes.

He bogeyed the par-5 second hole while Hard Way's former man sank a short birdie putt to move into sole possession of second place. Fourteen strokes.

Riley parred the short par-4 third hole, good enough not to lose ground. Fourteen strokes.

Riley never had a chance on the 240-yard par-3 fourth. He had to scramble for bogey and dropped another shot. Thirteen strokes.

A bogey on the par-4 fifth cost him another shot. Twelve strokes.

He parred the par-3 sixth, but so did the former guy. Twelve strokes.

He lost two more shots when the former guy sank a 25-foot birdie putt on the par-4 seventh and Riley bogeyed the hole. Ten strokes.

Riley reached the par-5 eighth in regulation, but three-putted while the former guy got there in two and two-putted for birdie. Eight strokes.

A bogey at the par-4 ninth was bettered by a routine par. Seven strokes headed to the turn.

"He made up eleven strokes in nine holes," Riley said to Hard Way as they walked to the 10th tee box.

"You're doing great, Joe," Hard Way said. "You shot 44 on the front, so you're on track for an 88 or lower. I love how you've handled this."

"Don't know if you noticed, but he shot 33," Riley said, glancing at the giant scoreboard

"One shot, one hole at a time. Remember? Anyway, the back nine is easier."

"But isn't it easier for him, too?" Riley said, nodding toward Hard Way's former man.

"I know him and how he thinks. He's going to get cocky and make a mistake. He always does."

"I'd be cocky, too, if I'd made up eleven shots in nine holes."

"Concentrate on making good swings. I love our position and the way you've handled this so far. You need to keep up the good attitude."

"What I really need is a tourniquet."

CHAPTER THIRTY-SEVEN

The Finish

Once again, the Masters revealed an eternal truth about itself, a truth that the great golf writer Dan Jenkins had first observed while covering the tournament in 1975: that the final round didn't truly begin until the second nine at Augusta National.

With no other player making a run at the lead, almost the entire Sunday crowd was following the final group. The patrons were rooting for so many things that Augusta National had become a petri dish of conflicted feelings. There was the underdog story that was Riley, the comeback story that was Hard Way's former man, and the backstory of Hard Way and his former man. The patrons had come to see history—Riley setting new records—but now they were witnessing the unexpected: the prospect of golf carnage.

Laurel, Chet, Buddy, Kat, Sargent, and Gallagher traveled around the course as a pack. At the turn, they were joined by Milwaukee. With the enormous crowd, they could only catch glimpses of Riley and Hard Way. But they could see the scoreboards, and the news wasn't encouraging.

Knowing that the AGN cameras were following the group's every move, Hard Way's former man made a grand gesture on the 10th tee box by taking off his hat and walking toward Riley and Hard Way.

"If you're conceding, I accept," Riley said.

"No, but that's a good one," he said. "I know this is your first time under this kind of pressure, but I just wanted to say I'm proud to share the moment with you and may the best man win."

"As long as that's you, right?" Riley said through a smile.

"Well, if the green jacket fits, if you know what I mean."

"I know what you mean," Riley said, noting the change of tone. "You've got the honors."

"I do, don't I?" he said of hitting first. "I seem to be having the honors a lot."

Augusta National officially opened in January 1933, and during its first two years, the first hole was what is now the 10th hole. Riley looked admiringly at the long stretch of fairway on the downhill 495-yard par-4, which historically ranked as the hardest hole on the course.

Riley's drive was his best of the day. It caught part of the speed slot on the left side of the fairway, but was still 75 yards shorter than his competitor's bomb. He had a tricky downhill lie for his second shot, but he caught it perfectly and the ball bounced to the left of the right bunker and onto the green in regulation. He matched pars and stayed seven shots ahead.

The par-4 11th, the second-hardest hole, was the beginning of Amen Corner.

"We're going to play this as a par-5," Hard Way said. "Bogey is a good score for us here."

"I thought you said the second nine was easier," Riley said.

"I lied."

"Again."

Riley got his bogey and for the first time during the round—just as Hard Way had predicted—his opponent made a careless mistake. His second shot trickled into the pond on the left of the hole. He got up and down for bogey, but had failed to gain any ground. Riley was still up by seven strokes with seven holes remaining.

On the par-3 12th, Hard Way's former guy hit a 9-iron to the middle of the green. It was a safe play, what with the pin in the traditional Sunday location: four paces from the back right edge of the 3,200-square-foot diagonally positioned green, nearly half the size of the average Augusta National green.

"Smart," Hard Way admitted. "We want to go exactly where he did. Just take it over the middle of the bunker."

The tee shot at No. 12 was as close to a hit-and-hope moment as there was in golf. Years earlier, *The New York Times* reported that a Johns Hopkins University aerodynamics expert had tried to accurately predict the flight of the ball at No. 12. The professor told the reporter that trying to solve all the mysteries and secrets of that sublime hole might be "a fool's errand."

Hard Way and Riley needed to solve two mysteries of their own: what the wind was doing, and what club to hit. Riley's new reality meant new distances. A 7-iron wouldn't be enough. A 6-iron, if unaffected by the devious winds, could work. A 5-iron might be too long. All of it was an educated guess at this point.

"I like the 6 here," Hard Way said, looking at the top of pines behind the 12th green for a clue to the swirling breezes.

"We're sort of in between clubs?" Riley said.

Hard Way didn't want to create doubt. He wanted his man confident.

"No, the 6 is the way to go. It's a good club. Commit and hit. It's perfect for you."

And the shot *was* perfect, until a gust of wind chose that exact moment to stir above those nearly hundred-foot pines. Riley's ball hung in the air and was pushed by the wind toward the right side of the front bunker. It caught the outside edge of the bunker, caromed right, and rolled without hesitation into Rae's Creek.

Golden Bell had claimed another victim.

The thousands of patrons assembled behind the 12th tee box moaned in unison. Meanwhile, Hard Way's former man did a poor job of hiding a small smile.

"You put a helluva swing on it, Joe," Hard Way said. "Wind kicked up at the worst time."

Out of range of the microphones, Hard Way's former man walked by as Riley and Hard Way headed toward the drop zone.

"See you guys up there at some point," he said before veering off to cross the Hogan Bridge.

The remark was ignored. There was work to be done.

"What's the best play here?" Riley asked.

"Let's get a nice yardage, about 60 yards from the pin. That way you can take an easy three-quarter swing with the sand wedge."

But Riley caught the shot fat and his ball plopped again into the murky water. Counting the penalties, his fifth shot finally cleared Rae's Creek and came to rest on the back fringe of the green. A rattled Riley three-putted for an eight.

"There's no nice way of saying it," Lassiter told the viewers. "This is excruciating to watch. You almost want to turn away."

"He isn't the first player to leave No. 12 with that number here," Hallmark said. "I hate to say it, but I think he's done. It's only a matter of time now."

Riley's lead was down to two strokes.

As they walked to the 13th tee box, Hard Way's former guy said, "Well, at least you beat Tiger's ten in 2020."

Hard Way began to respond, but Riley waved him off.

"He's not worth the effort," Riley said.

It took Riley three textbook shots and two well-executed putts to par the par-5 13th, but he still lost another shot to a chip-in birdie. And despite a scrambling bogey on the par-4 14th, Riley dropped another stroke.

"An eighteen-shot lead is gone," Lassiter said. "We now have a tie with four holes remaining."

The advantage had swung wildly toward Hard Way's former guy, especially with the 550-yard par-5 15th up next. Riley couldn't reach the green in two, but his opponent could.

Instead, Riley had to play position golf, hitting driver and then 3-wood, still leaving him, according to Hard Way's yardage book, with

100 yards to cover the pond, and another 15 to 20 yards to reach the back portion of the green.

As expected, Hard Way's former man went for the green in two, the ball coming to a stop just 15 feet from the hole. He twirled the club in his hand and acknowledged the cheers from the patrons.

"Crap. He's putting for eagle," Riley said.

"He's hamming it up for your benefit," Hard Way said, almost bored with the display. "Now he'll look our way, cross his arms, and tap his foot. He wants you to know that everyone is waiting on you. I've seen him pull this act before."

Hard Way's former man turned toward Riley, crossed his arms, and tapped his foot.

"He's doing it!" Riley said.

"Told you," Hard Way said, returning to his yardage book—the whole time hoping that his nonchalance would calm his player.

In the booth, Hallmark also noticed the body language.

"I'm not a fan of this kind of behavior, but it can be effective," Hallmark told the audience.

"What about Riley's third shot?" Lassiter asked. "Only 100 yards."

"Yeah, but there's nothing easy about it. The fairway is tilted. It's a downhill lie. You're hitting over water. You're hitting into the grain. And the front right part of that green is steeper than you think. It's treacherous."

"So if you're Max Mitchell, what are you telling Riley right now?"

"I'm not telling him any of that. Just keep it simple."

Hard Way put away his yardage book, looked one last time at the pin, pulled the pitching wedge from the bag, and handed it to Riley. The message was indeed simple.

"Whattya say we stick this close and wipe that stupid smirk off that guy's face?"

"With pleasure," Riley said.

The shot never left the pin. It bounced and then stuck the landing like Simone Biles. It stopped less than 2 feet from the hole. Cheers erupted among the patrons, including the Riley entourage, which did an impromptu group hug. Riley and Hard Way had sent a message of their own: They were going to fight to the finish. Rather than celebrate, they did a modest fist bump and then snuck a look at Hard Way's former man. The smirk was gone.

"That was a *professional* golf shot right there, boys," Milwaukee said to Chet and Buddy. "You remember that. Your dad done you proud."

Unnerved by Riley's shot, Hard Way's former man missed a 15-footer for eagle and a 3-footer for birdie, and almost missed the 10-inch putt for par. After the disappointing par, his face was the same shade as a bright pink azalea. It took on a red hue when Riley sank his birdie putt and moved ahead by one shot with three holes to play.

"I told you he'd get overconfident and make a mistake," Hard Way said as he slung the bag straps on his shoulders.

"I think you've got a real future in this business," said Riley, patting his caddie on the back as they began to make the walk from the 15th green to the tee box at No. 16.

Riley was a few steps ahead of Hard Way when he heard a howl, followed by the sound of clubs crashing against the ground. Riley swiveled around to find Hard Way on his back writhing in pain, the golf bag at his side, a half dozen clubs strewn on the grass. Riley rushed back and gently pulled the bag straps from Hard Way's shoulders and arms.

"You OK, Max? What happened?"

Hard Way lifted his left leg and pulled his knee toward his chest.

"I wasn't paying attention, and I stepped on the inside edge of that sprinkler," he said.

Riley looked back to his right. The hole was about 10 inches wide, with the sprinkler inset 3 to 4 inches below the surface. You could still see the imprint of Hard Way's Hoka. It was like falling off the side of a short curb.

A Green Jacket arrived.

"How can I help?" he said.

"Twisted the hell out of my ankle," Hard Way said. "Just give me a couple of minutes."

Hard Way's former guy walked by, not even pausing to look or offer assistance.

Another golf cart arrived, this one with two local EMTs.

"Heard you took a tumble," said the older of the pair.

"I'll be all right."

The other EMT rolled up the leg of Hard Way's white pants.

"It won't swell right away. Let's see if you can put any weight on it."

"Just help me up," Hard Way said. "I'm good to go."

The two EMTs slowly pulled Hard Way from the ground. When he pressed on his left foot, he almost crumpled to the turf again.

"Can you tape it up?" Hard Way said.

"We can," said the first EMT, "but I'm not sure it's going to help much. That's probably a grade 3 sprain—torn ligaments in there. You've got, what, three holes left? That's close to three-quarters of a mile of walking, and you're carrying that bag?"

The younger EMT wrapped the ankle, but Hard Way could barely get his shoe back on. When he tried to walk, he did so gingerly. Each step caused a shiver of pain.

"How about if I carry the clubs?" Riley said.

"That's not your job," Hard Way said.

"It is now. We're finishing this thing together."

Riley slung the bag over his shoulder. Hard Way used a 3-iron as a cane, but it was no use. He essentially hopped on one leg to the No. 16 tee box.

"I can't do it, Joe. I'm so sorry."

The Green Jacket approached.

"Gentlemen, I'm afraid a decision has to be made."

Hard Way looked over the Green Jacket's shoulder and caught a glimpse of Sargent as the patrons made room for the instructor at the front of the rope line. Sargent waved for someone to join him. It was Milwaukee.

Sargent caught Hard Way's eye, pointed at Milwaukee, and mouthed, "If you can't go . . ."

Behind Sargent, Hard Way could see Laurel, Kat, and the others.

"Joe, Milwaukee's here."

"He is?"

"Been with us since the turn. Came out to support us."

"I didn't know."

"It's a lucky break. He can take you in, but—"

"But what?"

"Nothing against Milwaukee," Hard Way said as he balanced his weight on the 3-iron, "but I've got somebody better for you."

Hard Way looked past Sargent and Milwaukee and yelled, "Buddy!"

Buddy ducked under the ropes with a course marshal in hot pursuit. He fast-walked to Hard Way and Riley.

"He's with us," Hard Way said to the marshal, who immediately looked at the Green Jacket.

"Mr. Riley, we would prefer you not use a patron to carry your bag. I see that Mr. Joyner is available. Or we'll send for one of our other club caddies to join us on the 17th tee."

"This is my son," Riley said, turning toward Buddy, his voice resolute, "and he's my caddie."

"This is highly unusual."

"Sir, *everything* about this week for me has been highly unusual. I have three holes left. I'm trying to win your tournament with every odd against me. If I can't walk in with my caddie, at least let me walk in with my son."

"For real, Dad?"

"Absolutely," he said, putting his arm around Buddy. He looked at Hard Way. "I just wish I had thought of it myself."

Hard Way feigned ignorance, and turned his attention to the Green Jacket.

"You won't regret it," Hard Way said to him.

A handful of patrons who had overheard the conversation began chiming in.

"Let the boy carry the bag."

"Give him a chance."

"Have a heart."

The Green Jacket, who had a teenage son of his own, made a decision.

"What are you wearing underneath the jumpsuit?" he asked Hard Way.

"A pair of cargo shorts, boxers, and a Tennessee T-shirt."

"Take off the jumpsuit and give it to—what's your name, son?"

"Buddy."

"Give it to Buddy." He turned to Buddy. "Son, we expect you to uphold the protocol and conduct of the Masters. Now let's play on."

"Yes, sir," Buddy said.

Their eyes met for a moment. "Good luck to you, son."

Hard Way unzippered the front of the onesie and, with the help of the EMTs, slipped out of it with minimal trouble. It was two sizes too large for Buddy, so Riley rolled up the sleeves and the pant legs.

Riley gave Hard Way a hug. Buddy picked up the bag.

"You're going to need this," Hard Way said, handing Buddy his yardage book. "You know these holes. You know my book and my notes. I scribbled down the new club distances. Pin sheet is in there."

"Thanks," Buddy said. "But are you sure you don't want Milwaukee?" Hard Way grinned and shook his head.

"Oh, and one more thing." Hard Way took off his Masters-issued green caddie cap and placed it on Buddy's head. "You bring him home."

The EMTs made room for Hard Way in the front of their cart.

"Let's get you out of here," said the older EMT. "We'll put an ice wrap on the ankle, get it elevated, and find you a TV."

"I know just the place," Hard Way said.

As the players waited for the cart to drive down the path and past the hole, Riley approached Hard Way's former man.

"He's going to be OK."

"Like I give a shit," he said dismissively, unaware that a nearby microphone was picking up the exchange. "I thought I was going to die of old age waiting for you guys. You're up."

He was feeling the pressure. The momentum had turned once more.

"We apologize for the salty language," Lassiter said to his viewers. "But there is a Masters at stake, and tensions are running high."

"The correct term," Walsh said, "is 'game on.'"

Buddy flipped open the yardage book, did a quick check of the wind, and then suddenly realized how many patrons were gathered around the width and length of the 170-yard hole. It had to be fifty deep with people just left of the green.

"How about this for a Take Your Child to Work Day?" Riley said playfully.

"Dad, concentrate. You've got a hint of wind in your face. Pin is four paces off the left edge. I like the 3-iron here."

Riley kept looking at the flagstick. He shook his head.

"I think I can get there with the 4-iron," he said as he reached for the club.

Buddy blocked his hand. Riley tried to reach for it again.

"Dad, I'm using a caddie veto. Hard Way said he had two of them left. Hit the 3-iron."

Riley began to argue, but he stopped when he saw the determined look on Buddy's face.

"Right half of the green?" Riley said.

Buddy double-checked Hard Way's notes and pencil drawings. Everything would funnel to that pin position.

"If you get it on that side of the green, it's gonna break toward the flag."

As he had done all day—all week, actually—Riley pretended he was about to do a live TV hit. He had survived the Arjun Atwal debacle in front of a national audience. If he could come back from that, he could handle hitting a 3-iron.

Riley didn't hit it perfectly, but it was on the right line. With the lower trajectory, it bounced hard, bounded forward, and then began to take a left-hand turn toward the pin. For a moment, it looked as if it was tracking directly at the cup. Instead, it settled 3 feet below the hole.

Buddy took the 3-iron from his dad and wiped down the clubface.

"Nice veto," Riley said.

"Nice shot," Buddy said. "I'm still not giving you strokes when we play."

When we play. Riley had given up hope of Buddy ever wanting to play again—and especially with him. But now this.

Hard Way's former man hit 7-iron, but it carried too long. He would have a challenging downhill 30-foot putt.

The EMTs and Hard Way had just arrived at the caddie facility when they heard a roar in the distance.

"Somebody did something," said the younger EMT.

Hard Way slapped his hand against his thigh. "I bet you that 18-handicapper just made birdie! Let's get inside and watch this thing!"

Thanks partly to Hard Way's notes, Buddy's read, and Riley's nerve, the putt had curled directly into the cup. Meanwhile, Hard Way's former man had done well to two-putt for par, but he still lost a stroke. Riley was up by two shots with two holes remaining.

"We thought he would crumble after the eight on No. 12, the bogey on 13, and losing his caddie after the 15th hole," Lassiter said. "But somehow Riley clings to a lead. He has willed himself into this position."

"I've been doing this for a long time, Neil," Walsh said. "It's the most extraordinary round I've ever seen—more extraordinary than the 59 he shot on Day One. Think about it: Whatever mysterious, enchanted connection he had with those Nicklaus clubs evaporated before today's round began. He lost his caddie to injury, and we're now told that the patron carrying his bag is actually his older son, Buddy. Can you think of a more unlikely pair to be leading the Masters?"

"The answer is no," Hallmark said. "Not now. Not ever. Fellas, I'll be damned—this is something."

The par-4 17th required one thing: a straight tee shot. With his drastically reduced length, it would be difficult for Riley to reach the plateau on the fairway. Hard Way, his ankle wrapped and propped on a chair, watched in the caddie dining area. He had invited the EMTs to stay.

"OK, Buddy, the right side of the fairway is not your friend here," he said, talking to the big-screen TV.

"How come?" the younger EMT said.

"Because the ball tends to kick right and into those trees. You've got a little more margin for error on the left side."

On the tee box, Buddy was thinking the very same thing.

"Dad, let's favor the left center on the drive." He pointed to the line. "It's perfect for you."

The swing was good, but the ball was curving slightly right.

"That needs to grow claws," Lassiter said. "Will it end up in the trees?"

It ended up in the trees.

Hard Way's former man had a driver in his hand, but as he watched Riley's ball bounce into trouble, he switched to a 3-wood. What he lost in distance, he gained in accuracy as his drive landed safely in the middle of the fairway.

An AGN cameraman was the first to arrive at Riley's ball. It was sitting atop a collection of tousled pine straw. A marshal shooed him away to an area that obscured his clear view. The cameraman, who had been covering the tournament for years, knew better than to argue.

"We only got a quick look at the ball, which appeared to be perched nicely," Lassiter said. "But does he have a clear view of the green, or even an open shot to the fairway?"

"Hard to tell right now," Hallmark said. "I've been in that pine straw a few times here. You can catch a good lie, but you have to be careful."

"Careful about what?" Lassiter said.

"Moving the ball."

Riley and Buddy walked up several minutes later. Buddy noticed immediately that they had options. There was a wide enough opening for a safe escape, and the ball was just far enough away from a tree trunk that Riley could make a full swing.

"The ball's sitting up," Riley said. "I think I could run a 5-wood down the fairway."

The AGN director in the truck asked the cameraman to maneuver for a better angle. Viewers could see Riley and Buddy as they considered the second shot, but the ball was still hidden. The cameraman took one step closer before the marshal raised a palm to stop him.

"Dammit," Hard Way said as he watched the marshal step in. "But it looks like they've got an opening. Not the time for a hero shot, Buddy."

Riley began to pull the 5-wood from the bag.

"Dad, the 5-wood is a good thought, but whattya think about punching a 6-iron into the middle of the fairway? Less risk, and we really don't lose a lot. Going to be a three-shot hole anyway."

"I could get this near the green if I flush it."

"You could. But let's just lay it up, get a good number, and stick it close on the third shot."

"Good plan," Riley said, dropping the 5-wood and grabbing the 6-iron.

Riley took a practice swing and walked toward the ball. He tested his stance in the pine straw. It was solid. He took one last look at the opening and carefully positioned the iron above and behind the ball. As he did, the heel of the club barely nicked the end of a strand of pine straw, causing several other strands to give way. The ball tumbled ever so slightly, settling no more than a quarter inch to the right.

Riley froze. Buddy, standing only a few feet away, knew immediately what had happened. But the patrons and viewers had no idea why the ball hadn't emerged yet from the cluster of pines. Their views were blocked.

"He's certainly taking his time," Lassiter said as their monitor showed an overhead shot and then an obstructed view from the camera on the ground.

For a split second, Buddy considered pretending he hadn't seen a thing. The movement had been so imperceptible that maybe he hadn't, he told himself. But he knew. Just as he had known that day as a caddie at Chicago Golf Club.

"Dad?"

"You were watching?"

Buddy took a deep breath. "I was. The ball moved."

"I thought it did, too, but I wasn't completely sure."

Riley took several steps back and then waved for the rules official.

"This looks ominous," Walsh said to the audience.

"We couldn't see for sure, but my guess is that the ball moved at address," Hallmark said. "But if it moved in the pine straw and didn't change positions—in other words, if it oscillated but remained in its original spot—then there's no penalty. Otherwise, he's going to get dinged a stroke. You want to talk about honor. This is why golf is unlike any other sport."

The rules official inspected the lie and turned to Riley.

"You say you think it moved?"

"It did move."

"Is there a chance it rolled back?"

"It happened so fast, I can't say for sure. I wish I could."

The official turned to Buddy.

"Could you tell?"

"Yes, sir. It barely moved to the right—and stayed there."

"You're sure."

"I was staring at it the whole time. My dad didn't even ground the club. It was an accident."

The official put his hands on his hips, looked at the pine straw, and delivered the ruling.

"Joe, based on what you and your caddie are telling me, your contact with the pine straw—and I know it was accidental—caused the ball to change positions. You violated Rule 9.4 (a) and you'll incur a one-stroke penalty. Return the ball to its original spot."

Riley did as instructed.

"The ball is now in play," the official said. "You'll be hitting three from there."

The official walked away. Riley dropped his head.

"Dad, I'm sorry," Buddy said, near tears.

"Buddy, don't ever be sorry for doing the right thing."

"You're not mad?"

Riley could hear the pain in his son's voice.

"Mad? I've never been prouder of you."

With that, Buddy's face broke into a relieved grin.

A few moments later, Riley's ball flew from the trees on a line and bounced down the fairway.

"After a long delay, Riley obviously chose to punch out and—wait, we now have been told that was actually Riley's *third* shot," Lassiter said. "Just as you had mentioned earlier, Andrew, Riley must have summoned the rules official for that very reason."

"I wish I had been wrong," Hallmark said. "That's a shame."

"I wish you had been wrong too!" Hard Way yelled at the screen.

Riley reached the green in four, nearly made his 12-foot bogey putt, but left with a double. Hard Way's former man two-putted for par. They were tied.

"And so it comes down to this," Lassiter told his audience. "On a day when drama has walked every hole with this final group, it only seems appropriate that a winner be decided on the final hole."

Hard Way's former man was up first. He had parred the hole each of the first three days by doing what you're supposed to do on the par-4 18th at Augusta National: start the drive at the right edge of the second of the two fairway bunkers and let it cut softly to the fairway. As soon as he hit it, though, he knew he might be in trouble.

"Don't do it to me, you no-good piece of crap!" he yelled as the ball flew toward the bunker.

"C'mon, baby!" his caddie joined in. "Start cutting!"

The ball landed inches from the right edge of the near bunker and kicked right and into the fairway.

"Whew," his caddie said.

"Keep your mouth off my ball," Hard Way's former man said.

The caddie turned away, embarrassed to be reprimanded by his man, and in front of the TV cameras and mic.

Riley didn't have to worry about reaching the fairway bunkers. He was more concerned about threading the pines that stood at attention on each side of the long tee box and beyond. So was Hard Way.

"C'mon, Buddy, build up his confidence. He needs you now."

Buddy began to pull the yardage book out of his back pocket but changed his mind. Numbers didn't matter at that moment.

"Dad, if I had told you at the beginning of the week that you'd be standing on the 18th tee on Sunday tied for the Masters lead, how would you have felt?" He looked up at his father. "Let's just get it on the short grass with the drive."

"OK, let's give it a go."

The drive made it through the chute but leaked right.

"We'll be fine, Dad."

They found the ball, but Riley's options were limited. Blocked by trees ahead on the right, Riley curled a 5-iron over the fairway bunkers and left himself with about a 100-yard shot to the green.

"All you could do there, Dad. We're still in this."

Hard Way's former man had no such issues, but his nerves were in disarray. He barked at a TV camerawoman who was 30 yards behind him and out of his sight line. He demanded that a young mother and her four-year-old son be escorted off the course because "the little peckerwood has a cough-y thing." He was paralyzed by indecision and the pressure.

When he airmailed his iron shot to the back second tier of the green, someone had to be blamed—and it wasn't going to be him. He flung the iron in disgust at the feet of his caddie.

"Nice pull," he said sarcastically, even though the caddie had suggested hitting one less club.

Meanwhile, Riley had to fly a bunker guarding the left front of the green. The pin, Buddy informed him, was nine paces on and five from the left.

"Take a little bit off the pitching wedge?" Riley said.

"Wouldn't mind that at all," Buddy said.

But Riley caught the ball too flush and it flew not only the first bunker but also the green and landed in the right greenside bunker.

In the caddie room, Hard Way buried his head in his hands.

Hard Way's former man had the longer of the two shots, so he went first. The long, slippery downhill putt from the upper to lower tier would not be easy. He waved away his caddie and instead studied the line by himself. He took several practice strokes (speed would be everything) and then punched lightly at the ball. It fell slowly down the slope, gained speed, and came to a stop no more than a foot below the cup. It was an impressive lag.

Rather than wait and test his nerves again, he tapped the putt in for par, then punched at the air.

Riley's turn.

"So Riley knows exactly what he has to do," Lassiter said. "Hole it for par and we move to a playoff, this time at the 10th hole. Miss, and he becomes part of a complicated legacy: the man who lost an eighteen-stroke lead at the Masters."

"Neil, I want to remind our viewers of a Masters Sunday in 2022, when Rory McIlroy holed a bunker shot from almost the exact same spot where Riley is. And McIlroy's shot was followed by another hole-out by playing partner Collin Morikawa from that same bunker."

Riley pulled the 60-degree wedge from the bag.

"Rory made this shot," he said to Buddy. "I was there."

"I know you were, Dad. All you've got to do is drop it about 5 to 6 feet past that fringe and gravity will do the rest."

Riley settled into the sand, aimed slightly to his right, and concentrated on just popping the ball onto the green. Sargent had worked with him on the technique dozens of times.

He took about a three-quarter swing. The ball floated out of the sand, landed, as the players like to say, "as softly as a butterfly with sore feet"—and almost exactly where Buddy had pointed—fell down the fault line of the green, and began to curl like a question mark toward the cup.

"It's going in! It's going in!" Hard Way yelled as the EMTs began to cheer with him.

Kat, Laurel, Chet, Sargent, Gallagher, and Milwaukee raised their hands in anticipation.

Hard Way's former man dropped to his knees in disbelief.

Thousands of patrons, assembled on the grass amphitheater like the world's largest church choir, prepared to unleash their loudest roar of the day.

Lassiter, Hallmark, and Walsh stood in the booth, transfixed by the moment.

As the ball tracked toward the heart of the cup, it hit a nub of raised grass created by the tiniest of spike marks from the previous twosome. The ball was redirected to the right edge, and like a stock car on a banked turn at Talladega, ran high around the entire hole but refused to fall in. Instead, it spun out and came to rest 18 inches away.

The crowd was speechless, as if it needed time to process and grieve. The only sound heard was that of Hard Way's former man yelling in triumph. He threw his hat into the air and tried slapping hands with patrons as he ran around the back of the green. A Green Jacket politely but sternly told him to be still so Riley could finish out.

Riley sank the bogey putt for a final round 88. He removed his hat to congratulate the winner, but received only a fly-by handshake. Instead, Hard Way's former man ignored his own caddie's attempt at a hug and made a beeline toward the roped-off lane leading from the 18th green to the scorer's area. That's where he saw Kat standing next to Laurel.

"You could have been the wife of a Masters champion!" he said, mocking her.

Before Kat could respond, a woman in her mid-twenties wearing a sundress shorter than the first cut at Augusta National darted under the ropes and jumped into the winner's outstretched arms. She pressed against him as if drawn by static cling. They kissed for what seemed like minutes and then they were gone, escorted by security guards to the clubhouse area, from which, presumably, winner and woman were eventually destined for a hotel room. His caddie, carrying the flagstick and flag from the 18th green, sprinted after them.

"Excuse me, dear," an elderly woman said to Kat as the winner moved out of sight. "Do you know that crass man?"

"I knew a better version of him, but that was a very long time ago."

"Yes, indeed. A *very* long time ago. If I were his mother, I'd beat him with a good stick."

Riley and Buddy rounded the corner a few moments later.

"I was rooting for you, young man," said the woman.

"So was I," Riley said.

Laurel leaned forward and gave him a kiss.

"You were amazing. Both of you were," she said, pulling Buddy toward her.

"Everybody's getting a kiss except me," Kat said.

"And me," the elderly woman said.

Riley pecked the woman on the cheek.

"Thank you for putting a smile on an old lady's face. I can tell people that I got a kiss from the real champion."

She waved goodbye.

"Where do you want us to meet you?" Laurel said.

"Got to do some bookkeeping and take care of a few other things. We'll see you outside the clubhouse in a few minutes."

Laurel took Kat by the arm.

"Let's go find your clumsy boyfriend."

CHAPTER THIRTY-EIGHT

Scores Settled

Riley and Buddy stood on the near-empty 18th green. A lone security guard discreetly positioned himself off to the side.

"I thought I'd made the shot," Riley said.

"I did, too, Dad. Everybody did."

They looked down the 18th fairway, the shadows lengthening as the sun dipped toward the horizon.

"I never knew I had a crush on this place until just this moment," Riley said. "I think I've always looked for its worst qualities instead of appreciating its best traits. I owe it an apology. I'm going to miss it."

"But, Dad, you get to play in the Masters next year. The top 12 and ties are in."

"Nah, I'm done. The Jack clubs called it quits. Now it's my turn. But it was the grips, wasn't it?"

Buddy nodded. "It's not like you had a choice. They were coming apart."

"And I came apart with them."

"You just shot 88 under the craziest of pressure. Remember what Gordo wrote in that note? 'With or without those clubs, the game will test you.' "

" 'And you will be the better for it,' " Riley said, reciting the next sentence. "I remember."

"You were tested, Dad. Gordo would have been proud of you."

"He would have been proud of you, too—just like I am. I owe him a lot. But I owe you more. Those clubs you gave me brought us back together. And they brought you back to golf."

"But because of me, you lost the Masters. And you lost it to . . . *that* guy. He gets the green jacket, the trophy, the Champions Locker Room. He gets it all."

"In his case, he has everything and yet he has nothing. I didn't lose; I won. So did Hard Way."

"Dad, you're getting mushy."

"You're right. That's why I need to do this."

Riley turned and hugged his son long and hard. After a moment's hesitation, Buddy hugged him back.

"Hard Way says you're a natural caddie. And ten times the player I am."

Buddy wiped his eyes. "I'm still not giving you strokes, Dad."

"Let's head back. I'm sure they're waiting for us in the scorer's area."

"One second, Dad."

Buddy spotted a Masters plastic cup left under a folding chair near the green. He grabbed it and walked to the same bunker that Riley had been in. The security guard saw Buddy reach down with the cup. Buddy hesitated, but the guard looked both ways, smiled, and said, "I never saw a thing." Buddy took a scoop of sand and put the cup in his right front pocket.

"What was that for?" Riley said.

"A friend," Buddy said.

Buddy pulled the bag over his shoulder. Father and son walked off the green, and just as they passed the TV tower on their left, they heard cheers. For a moment, Riley assumed the awards ceremony had already begun. When he looked up, he realized the assembled patrons were there for him, and for what they had witnessed. The church choir was singing its chorus.

The patrons formed a human chain from the TV tower to the left edge of the ninth green, across the first tee, and finally to the clubhouse and scorer's area. Riley saw their faces as they reached out for handshakes, fist bumps, and backslaps. One of the college Jacks tried to hand him a blond wig. As he neared the clubhouse, the line included Green Jackets—Ivan Johnson and Richard Nielsen, the member with the white bucket hat (and his granddaughter), the member who had allowed Buddy to caddie—locker-room attendants, practice range workers, clubhouse waiters, and other caddies, including Milwaukee, Bang Bang, and Sand Man. Bang Bang and Kat had helped Hard Way outside, and Hard Way raised an aluminum crutch in salute. The Aussie Brown, who had finished as low amateur, was there to pay his respects, too, as were at least a dozen other players, including Harrison and a handful of past champions. Chaffin was there with an AGN crew, as was Portia Pendersmith with her cameraperson. Laurel and Chet were flanked by Sargent and Gallagher. And for a fleeting second, Riley swore he saw Nicklaus himself in the background.

Riley signed his scorecard and emerged from the room for a group hug with his family and friends. A Green Jacket asked if he would make a brief appearance at the media center before the winner arrived. Riley asked if his small group could join him. The Green Jacket assured him they could watch on a monitor from a nearby room.

The golf carts took them to the side of the building, with Buddy holding the bag between his legs. Before Riley walked in, he reached into a side pouch and pulled out his iPhone.

"I didn't see you put that in," Hard Way said.

"Sneaked it in when we first got here today," Riley said.

"Gonna take some photos?" Hard Way said.

"Better," Riley said.

The Green Jacket who served as the moderator was kind with his praise, and gentle when explaining that Riley would be replaced by the winner in a few minutes. Hands shot up.

"We're all sitting here trying to understand what happened today," said Harrick, whom Riley had known for years. "Can you explain it to us?"

Riley pulled the thin black mic toward him.

"Vicar, I lost. I lost fair and square. I lost an eighteen-stroke lead, which almost seems impossible to do. But my whole journey here has been impossible. So congratulations to our new Masters champion."

He paused. "But I won, too. I don't want to go all '*Golf in the Kingdom*' on you, but those clubs were a part of me, and I was part of those clubs. When Max came to the course this morning, he saw that the grips on the MacGregors and my putter had peeled from the shafts. When we regripped them, we basically disconnected their powers—and mine."

"So it was the clubs all along?" Harrick said.

"That's what I always thought," Riley said. "I know better now. The man who gave the clubs to my son always knew it. And my son did, too."

"Is this the same son who carried the bag for you after Max's injury?"

"He *caddied* for me. And he carried me those last three holes."

In the side room, Chet tugged at his brother's shirt after the exchange.

"Yeah, little dude?"

"I'm proud you're my older brother."

There were a handful of other questions before the moderator ended the session, to exasperated groans from the reporters. The winner had just arrived and was waiting outside the door. Riley stopped him before he made his way to the stage.

"Is it possible to have quick private moment with our champion?" Riley said cheerfully to the winner.

"Excuse me," a nearby Green Jacket said. "We are on a schedule."

"It will only take a minute," Riley said.

He looked at Hard Way's former man for approval.

"Hell, I'd rather do anything than talk to those hyenas," the new champion said, tilting his head toward the interview room. "They can wait."

Riley took him to a nearby office and closed the door.

"I need you to do a small favor for me," Riley said.

"You did one for me—you blew an eighteen-shot lead—so I guess I can help you out," he said. "You want me to sign a Masters flag or something?"

"I need you to go out there and tell everyone that Hard Way is one of the best caddies on Tour, that he didn't miscount your clubs back at the Memorial, and that you were responsible for the extra club in the bag."

"Sure. You want my green jacket too? Maybe the hottie I have parked outside?"

Riley continued. "After you tell them it was your fault at the Memorial, I need you to tell everyone that Hard Way wasn't responsible for the breakup of your marriage, and that you apologize for accusing him of any wrongdoing. While you're at it, I want you to wish him and Kat the very best."

Hard Way's former man burst out laughing.

"Did you suffer some sort of head trauma? Did that choke job of yours cut off the oxygen to your brain? I'm outta here."

He moved toward the door.

"I wouldn't do that."

"Who's going to stop me?"

"You."

Riley pressed the Play icon on the voice memo in his phone.

"You stuffed that 7-iron in the bag so I wouldn't see it."

It was Hard Way's voice from his locker-room confrontation with his man at the Memorial the previous season. Riley pressed Pause. By then, Hard Way's former man had turned ashen.

"Where'd you get that?"

"Does it matter? Want to hear the whole thing?"

The details of what had been said—and recorded!—that day caused Hard Way's former man to find the closest chair and sit down. It all came pouring back to him. He didn't need Riley's iPhone to recite it to him. He remembered every word.

HARD WAY: "So you're doing this to spite me?"

HIM: "No. I'm doing it to spite her. I'm doing it to *ruin* you."

HARD WAY: "Why? I didn't know she was your wife. She said she was splitting up with her husband."

HIM: "That's rich. I was getting ready to put *her* on injured reserve."

HARD WAY: "You stuffed that 7-iron in the bag so I wouldn't see it."

HIM: "Framed you like a painting."

Hard Way's former man stiffened. "This is blackmail."

"Whatever it is, it's more humane than what you did to Hard Way and Kat."

"I'm not doing it," he said defiantly. "I apologize for nothing."

"No problem. "I'm walking back into that packed room right now and I'm going to play the entire conversation for every one of those reporters and cameras. I'm giving you a chance to make things right. If you don't, I will."

There was a knock on the door. A Green Jacket opened it and stuck his head in the room.

"Gentlemen, I'm afraid we've kept the press waiting long enough," he said.

"Well?" Riley said.

There was a long pause. The new champion knew he had been cornered.

"I'll do it on one condition: you delete that recording."

"You have my word—after I hear the apologies."

Hard Way's former man walked out to the reporters, but instead of exuding the air of a new champion, he looked like he was about to get his gums scraped.

Riley stayed for the winner's opening statement.

"Before I answer any questions, I wanted to take a moment to right a couple of wrongs," the champion said, his tone soft and confessional, as if he was revealing a secret to old friends. "When you win a Masters, you realize you're representing not only yourself but also this great club and tournament."

Riley had to give the man credit; he was laying it on thick.

"Last year, in a moment of confusion and anger, I lashed out at my then caddie, Max Mitchell. I said some awful things and blamed him for an incident that, upon reflection, wasn't his fault. It was mine."

He stopped and pretended to compose himself. The reporters bought it.

"I want to make it clear that Max is a fantastic caddie. We all saw that this week. Any player would be lucky to have him."

A roomful of reporters raised their hands.

"I'm almost done, fellas. Just bear with me a few more moments."

He took a deep, theatrical breath.

"I also made some mistakes in my personal life, and for those I apologize to my ex-wife. Her and Max have become very close friends, and I think that's great."

He nearly choked on the final few words—not out of emotion, but out of disdain. Stunned by the revelations and by his unexpected tone of humility and remorse, those in the room suddenly felt empathy for the flawed champion.

There was a smattering of applause from several club officials standing in the back, and the Green Jacket moderator reached over and gave him a gentle pat of support on the arm. Realizing that the apology, disingenuous as it was, had worked, Hard Way's former man brightened.

"Now let's talk about me winning the damn Masters!"

When Riley returned to the holding room, Buddy was still in the borrowed Masters jumpsuit. Chet was trying to flirt with the Augusta National intern who was serving as their post-round chaperone. Laurel, Kat, Sargent, Gallagher, and Hard Way were drinking beers pirated from the open bar on the second floor of the media center. Kat handed one to Riley and raised a plastic cup.

"A toast to four days that will be remembered forever, and to whatever the hell you said to my ex."

"Son, I know that two-faced SOB wouldn't have said any of that to the media unless he didn't have a choice," Sargent said. "Whatever it was, it worked,"

"Whatever it was, it was on that phone," Hard Way said, pointing toward Riley's iPhone. "Right, Joe?"

Riley turned to the chaperone and asked for privacy. She quickly departed, happy to be rid of the feisty eight-year-old. Lowering his voice, Riley explained his actions.

"A few weeks after the Memorial, one of the locker-room guys there sent me a link to a voice memo," Riley said. "He wasn't a fan of Max's former guy, so when he heard the two of them arguing, he decided to tape it."

"You mean, you could have exposed him last year?" Hard Way said.

"No. The locker-room guy didn't get in there until after you guys were halfway through your argument. He was so nervous he'd get caught that he fumbled and dropped his phone after ten seconds of recording."

"So *he* was the person we heard in the locker room that day," Hard Way said.

"Yep. He grabbed the phone from the floor and bolted out of there. The only thing you hear on the voice memo is Max asking if his guy had hidden the fifteenth club in the bag. He didn't get the whole conversation."

"And?" Sargent said.

"And that was it," Riley said.

"But my ex didn't know that, did he?" Kat said. "He thought you had everything on tape."

Riley shrugged his shoulders.

"So you fooled him with the one sentence you did have," Laurel said.

Riley nodded.

"That's quite a bluff," Gallagher said. "Remind me to pay your entrance fee for the World Series of Poker."

"I owe you," Hard Way said, putting his arm around Riley. "That's twice this week you've stood up for me."

"I owe you, too," Kat said.

"Let's get out of here," Riley said.

"My friends," Gallagher said, "I must bid you farewell here. My plane is waiting at the airport. I'm flying back to Vegas tonight. The house is yours until 5 P.M. tomorrow. I left a note on the dining room table for you, Joe." He shook Riley's hand. "I want to thank you for everything," he said.

"Thank me? I didn't win it for you."

"A win can have many meanings. You did more than you realize."

It was dark by the time Riley returned to his locker and gathered his things. Hard Way was waiting in the courtesy car, while Laurel, the kids, Kat, and Sargent had already returned to the rental house.

Riley handed the locker-room manager an envelope with a tip for him and his crew. Hard Way had suggested a generous number, and Riley had doubled it.

"Mr. Riley, we enjoyed having you here," he said. "Wish it woulda turned out differently for you."

"I appreciate that."

"Anything else we can do for you?"

Riley began to say no, but then reconsidered.

"You know, there is one last thing, if you don't mind."

The locker-room manager returned ten minutes later.

"Everything will be shipped to your house by Tuesday," he said.

Riley walked out to the oak tree and looked into the darkness. The lights from the clubhouse illuminated a sliver of the first tee box but little else. What was it that Bobby Jones had written about the once virgin, undeveloped terrain? "It seemed that this land had been lying here for years just waiting for someone to lay a golf course upon it."

Riley thought about plucking a few blades from the ground and bringing them home with him. But Augusta National deserved better than that. In the spirit of Hideki Matsuyama's caddie, he gave the place a curt bow, walked to the players' parking lot, nodded to Hard Way in the passenger seat, and drove away knowing he'd never be back.

CHAPTER THIRTY-NINE

We'll Always Have Augusta

Riley held the door open as Hard Way maneuvered into the house on his crutches. They heard laughter and the unmistakable pop of a cork breaking free of a champagne bottle. Everyone was gathered around the massive island in the kitchen.

"So much for the grieving process," Hard Way said as he took his place on a leather barstool.

"Boys," Sargent said, raising his glass to Riley, Hard Way, and Buddy, "I've been doing this for a long time. You didn't win, but you sure as hell didn't lose."

There was a clinking of glasses, then Chet raised his cup of ginger ale and said, "Plus, Dad, you got almost $2.3 million for finishing second! I just saw it online."

Riley looked at Laurel. "The prize money!" he said.

"We're making bank!" Chet said.

"Not bad for an 18-handicapper," Hard Way said.

After several Door Dash deliveries of food and more champagne, the party came to an end shortly after midnight. An Uber took Sargent back to his hotel. Kat and Hard Way said their goodnights. Buddy carried a sleeping Chet back to the little dude's bedroom.

Alone with Laurel finally, Riley poured what was left of the one remaining bottle of bubbly into their glasses.

"Here's to the wife who took the leap of faith with me back then . . . and now," Riley said.

"And here's to the husband who wasn't afraid to jump. But it's been a long day. You need to get some sleep."

"I'll be up in a minute."

Riley did his best to clean up the kitchen quietly. Then he wrote a note of thanks to the homeowners and placed it in front of a floral arrangement on the dining room table. That's when he saw the envelope left by Gallagher.

Forgot all about you, he thought.

Too tired to read anything, he stuffed it in the pouch of his backpack.

During the Monday afternoon limo ride from O'Hare to their house, Laurel had been unusually quiet, even nervous as she sat in the middle of the second-row bench seat with the boys. Riley, who sat in front with the driver, knew why. He had been dreading it as much as Laurel had.

As the black SUV pulled into the driveway, Buddy and Chet spilled out of the back seat and raced to the front door with the house keys. Laurel helped Riley and the driver place their luggage on the stoop.

"What about the golf case?" the driver said.

"Just put it in front of the garage, please," Riley said.

As the driver drove off, Riley flipped open the plastic shield of the garage keypad. As he punched in the code, Laurel appeared next to him.

"I need to tell you something," she said as the garage door lurched upward. "It's about the Beemer."

Riley turned toward her, his back facing the garage.

"Chet already told me," he said as he watched Laurel's eyes widen. "He said the Beemer is—"

"The Beemer is here!"

Riley turned to see the white minivan and the blue BMW parked next to it.

"I thought you sold it for Buddy's tuition?"

"I did—and you weren't supposed to know that! Then I tried to buy it back with your Houston winnings, but the dealer wouldn't sell it. Said he had another buyer. I have no idea how this got here."

Riley noticed a sheet of paper under the left windshield wiper.

It was the car title. In Riley's name.

Early Tuesday morning Riley received the package from the Augusta National locker-room manager. He went up to his attic office and spread the contents out on his desk. He reached into a drawer for a Sharpie, but there were none. He remembered he had a marker in his backpack.

Riley unzippered the first pouch, where the Sharpie—and Gallagher's envelope—were stored. He opened the envelope. Inside was a two-page handwritten note.

Joe,

I have great admiration for those with a moral code, and even greater respect for those who take care of their friends, as you did for Max and Sarge the day of our match.

With that in mind, I hope you'll forgive me for taking care of you.

Shortly after the announcement of your surprise inclusion in the Masters field, I placed a $30,000 wager on you to win at 1,500:1 odds. Only one sportsbook would take the bet. The others declined—and rightfully so—because of the financial exposure should you have miraculously won.

Obviously, your odds plummeted exponentially as you built a seemingly invincible lead entering the final round. Conversely, the odds of your nearest challengers, such as they were, increased exponentially.

Early Sunday morning, I accidentally overheard a conversation between Laurel and Buddy about the possibility of your clubs no longer possessing their special powers. Information, not luck, is what wins in my business.

I made the decision to contact the manager of the sportsbook who had taken my original wager. I sent him a screenshot of my bet slip that confirmed my $30,000 wager, the 1,500:1 odds, and the $45,750,000 payout. I asked if his company would be interested in negotiating a buyout of what everyone, including the sportsbook manager, assumed would be a winning ticket. Given your chances of victory (which were in the 95 to 99 percent range), they offered a buyout figure that was unsatisfactory. I made a counteroffer, which they rejected. I said I would keep my slip and collect the full amount after you won. Just as I was about to end the call, another voice came on the line. It was the owner of the sportsbook, who overruled his manager and made one final offer: an 80 percent payoff of the final figure. I accepted and the money was wired to my account before you reached the course.

In the meantime, I placed a series of hedge wagers on your four closest pursuers. Needless to say, the bet paid off handsomely for me.

At your convenience, contact my assistant, who will ensure that your winnings are wired to the financial institution of your choice.

I deducted a small percentage from your winnings (consider it a commission of sorts), but I'm confident you'll be satisfied with the final figure. And if you're curious about the amount of the original wager, that figure—$30,000—was the exact amount you returned to me after our match in Vegas. As I said, respect.

And now, the numbers:

The negotiated buyout: $36,624,400
My fee: $1,098,732
Your winnings: $35,525,668

As an added token of appreciation, I arranged for the return of your BMW, which should have been delivered by now.

For this, you can thank your little dude. He offered to trade his Par 3 crystal—a rare collector's piece, to be sure—in exchange for me purchasing the car from the dealer. That sort of love needs to be rewarded.

In return, I ask only that you not reveal the details of this transaction to anyone. It seems I have a heart after all. And if that were made public, it would be bad for business.

Best wishes,
Gimme

Riley stared at the eight digits and accompanying commas for several minutes before allowing himself to believe they were real. As for Chet's gesture, it only confirmed what Riley had already decided to do.

Late that morning, Riley drove to the downtown branch of his bank, where he informed the manager that his assistance would be required for a deposit. Once the routing and account numbers were exchanged with Gallagher's assistant, the wire transfer was initiated. The bank manager's eyes widened when he saw the figure.

"I assume we'll get free checking from now on?" Riley said.

The manager laughed. "We'll even throw in a Bears calendar. And since the tranfer comes from our sister bank, this should clear within 15 minutes."

Once the transfer was confirmed and the funds deposited into Riley's account, the manager, at his client's instructions, arranged for cashier's checks to be sent via secure courier to a pair of out-of-state addresses. Riley then drove to a nearby shipping office and sent two packages and two boxes for next-day delivery. Then he went home and waited for Laurel and Chet to return from an after-school grocery run. Buddy was in the living room watching TV.

"Honey, you here?" Laurel shouted as she walked in the house. "I could use some help with these bags."

"I can't carry them all, Dad!" Chet yelled. "I'm little!"

Buddy ran out to help. A few moments later, Riley came downstairs. His face was solemn.

"What's wrong?" Laurel said.

"I think I accidentally bounced a check," he said.

"Really? Don't we have the Masters prize money in there?"

"I thought we did, but they said it could take a few days to process."

"Let me get this food in the fridge and I'll take a look," she said.

"I'll take care of the groceries. You go change, relax, and we'll figure it out later."

"No, let me take care of it now," she said, annoyed by the inconvenience. "Goodness, Joe, you've got to be the last person in America who actually writes a check. I'm surprised we don't have kerosene lamps. Why didn't you just put whatever it was for on our credit card?"

"Yeah, I messed that up," Riley said.

Riley heard Laurel at her built-in desk next to the mudroom, her fingers tapping on the keyboard of the laptop as she entered the bank password.

A few moments later, there was a scream that could be heard down the length of West Street. Laurel had just seen their checking balance. There was a little more than $30 million in their joint account.

Riley waited in the kitchen. Laurel walked in, pulled two Old Styles from the fridge, popped the caps, handed one to her husband, clinked the bottles, took a swig, and said evenly, "I looked at our account. I think we're covered."

The box was waiting on the Chairman's desk when he walked into his office late the next morning. He had allowed himself the luxury of sleeping in.

"There's no name or return address?" he said to his administrative assistant.

"I wondered the same thing, sir. Would you like our security team to look at it first?"

"No, that won't be necessary."

He tugged at the perforated pull-away strip on the side of the long package. Dark Bubble Wrap surrounded the enclosed item. There was a note taped to it.

> Chairman Jewell,
>
> Tradition dictates that the newest Masters champion donates a club from his bag to be placed in the grill room display cases. As for the runner-up, perhaps you can find a suitable place for this in your office? Feel free to take it for a spin once in a while. It liked Augusta National.
>
> With appreciation,
> Joe Riley

The Chairman peeled away the Bubble Wrap.

It was the MacGregor driver.

Mike McMullins was sitting in his dimly lit office when an AGN mailroom employee knocked on the door.

"Yes?" McMullins said without looking up.

"This just arrived."

McMullins sighed. "Whatever it is, just put it on the desk."

The mailroom guy, only a few weeks on the job, had been warned not to bother McMullins more than necessary. He placed the squat, well-wrapped box on the corner of the desk and then returned to his delivery cart in the hallway. It wasn't until a half hour later that McMullins finished reading his production spreadsheets and at last noticed the eighteen-inch-high package. He looked for a return address, but there was none. His interest was piqued.

When he opened the box, the most un-McMullins thing happened: He laughed, and didn't stop laughing for several minutes.

The box contained a white-bearded Masters gnome dressed in a Masters-green shirt, yellow bucket hat, and khaki pants. But this gnome had been customized to include him holding a stick mic. The note read:

> Mike,
>
> You put me in a position to succeed. Thank you for believing in me when others wouldn't.
>
> Gratefully,
> Atwal Arjun

Sargent pulled into the Esperanza Canyon parking lot and discovered two deliverymen from competing companies waiting at the locked door of his golf school facility.

"You guys work in pairs?" Sargent said as he pressed the code on the keypad.

The deliverymen looked at each other, confused. One of them had Sargent sign for the padded envelope, the other for a larger package.

Sargent checked his lessons calendar. He had three scheduled for the day, including with the Aussie Derrin Brown, who had turned pro after earning the Silver Cup as the Masters' low amateur. The promising young player was looking for a caddie. Sargent knew exactly whom to recommend.

He tore open the top of the package. Out spilled a note, as well as a yellow Masters flag wrapped tightly with a rubber band.

Sarge,

You have countless signed flags of champions on your golf school walls. Though I didn't win the Masters, I am allowed to autograph the flagstick flag outside the confines of the club's U.S. logo. I hope the testimonial has meaning to your more skeptical students.

Best,
Joe

P.S.—I looked it up. You and the Chairman played on the same Walker Cup team. You're the one who called him, didn't you? Life isn't so arbitrary after all . . .

Sargent unfurled the flag. There in the bottom left corner was Riley's signature and a printed message.

To all of Sarge's students,

If you're reading this, that means you asked the question.
Trust me, he's sure.

Sargent immediately walked over to a wall and replaced one of the first-place flags with Riley's flag.

He stepped back to admire it.

"Perfect," he said.

Then Sargent turned his attention to the envelope. He used a letter opener presented to him by the captain of the Honourable Company of Edinburgh Golfers at Muirfield. The opener sliced through the paper, revealing the cashier's check. Sargent removed it.

Pay to the Order of Leeds Sargent Jr.
Two Million Dollars and 00 Cents

Sargent stared at the check. Almost in a whisper, he said, "You're damn right I called him."

Kat and Hard Way had just returned with her two teenage daughters, Hailey and Zoe, from an unsuccessful house-hunting tour with a Mission Viejo real estate agent. Kat had decided it was time to sell the home she had purchased years ago with her ex. She deserved a fresh start. The girls deserved it. Hard Way deserved it.

She would have to split the proceeds with her ex, which, given the tight Orange County housing market, didn't leave many purchasing options.

"See anything interesting?" said Kat's mom, Carol, from the kitchen, where she was making her famed meat ravioli and red sauce from scratch. She was a daily visitor at the house, what with her apartment being only a mile or so away.

"Our agent must have thought I was a member of the Getty family," Kat said as she and the girls hugged Carol and then observed the cooking master at work from the kitchen counter stools. Hard Way leaned against the refrigerator. "She showed us a $4.4 million place on the lake and said if we put $1 million down, our mortgage would *only* be $28,000 a month, plus the HOA and the $35,000-a-year property taxes."

"Your father and I bought our first house in Huntington Beach for $24,000," Carol said, winking at Hard Way.

"And that's why nobody likes my mother," Kat said.

The doorbell rang.

"I'll get it," Hard Way said.

Waiting outside was a courier holding a digital tablet with one hand and balancing an envelope and an oversized package with the other.

"I'm looking for a"—the courier double-checked the name—"Max Mitchell?"

"That's me."

The courier handed him the tablet and asked him to sign.

How did anyone know I was here? thought Hard Way as he scribbled his name on the screen with his forefinger. *And 'Hard Way,' not 'Max'?*

Hard Way brought the envelope and package into the kitchen, where Kat was thumbing through a magazine.

"You can't stay off Amazon, can you?" Kat said playfully. "What'd you order this time? More bikini briefs?"

"Ewww," said Hailey and Zoe.

Hard Way frowned at Kat. "I'm not paying for their therapy."

"You're right," Kat said. "Girls, they weren't briefs. More like thongs."

"Double ewww," came the response.

"Thanks," Hard Way said.

"Anything for my man," Kat said. "So seriously, what'd you order?"

"Nothing," Hard Way said. "Swear."

"You see this?" Kat said.

She held up the latest issue of *Golf Monthly*. Inside was a two-page ad for a stupidly expensive cologne. A woman in full lioness body paint, her legs as long as a fire hose, stood over her prey. She held a small black bottle of the cologne, a single drop falling toward the open palm of a muscular, bare-chested man, his chiseled, expressionless face framed by his thick sun-bleached hair.

"Nothing says 'golf' like a lioness," he said.

"Recognize anyone?"

He looked again.

"That's not who I think it is?"

"It's Bang Bang. Ooh la la. Why am I wasting my time on you?"

"That's easy," Hard Way said. "I'm presently unemployed and can name all fifty state capitals. Can Gerald say that?"

"I love him, but I'm not sure Bang Bang can name all fifty states, much less the capitals," Kat said. "But I can see why the lioness likes him."

Hailey, Zoe, and Carol leaned over to look.

"You know that man?" Carol said.

"I thought I did," Hard Way said.

"Can I get his number?" Carol said.

"Whatcha got in the package?" Zoe said, ignoring her grandmother's comment.

Hard Way tugged at the pull tab. His Masters jumpsuit tumbled out like biscuit dough from a container, along with a note. He read it out loud for everyone to hear.

Max,

Buddy wanted to make sure you got this back. He said he was "permanently borrowing it" from Augusta on your behalf.

One day, when your new man wins, you're going to leave Augusta National with a flagstick and flag. I just know it.

I couldn't have done any of this without your help. To get me from where we started to where we ended was, to use your phrase, "all carry."

You'll soon receive an envelope with two items.

Kat waved the envelope from the counter.

Hard Way began reading again.

The first item is meant to help establish a scholarship fund for the children of Augusta National caddies. Perhaps you and Milwaukee can coordinate the initial effort?

If it's OK with you, I'd like to name it in honor of Cemetery, the former Masters caddie you said you met years ago. It's my hope that Augusta National will agree to match our initial contribution and any subsequent donations. Laurel and I are going to make an annual commitment.

The second item is for you.

I owed you for caddie fees.

Your friend,

Joe

Kat handed the envelope to Hard Way, who opened it and pulled out the contents one by one.

On top was a check for $525,000. He handed it to Kat.

"That's way more than the 7 percent you said caddies get for a top-10 finish," she said.

"I know!" Hard Way said. "This is way too generous. I can't believe he did that."

"Wait, I'm confused," Kat said. "Didn't he say the first check was for the scholarship fund and the second item was for you?"

Hard Way pulled out a second check.

"You're turning whiter than the jumpsuit," Kat said. "Is everything OK?"

"That's not the word I would use."

Kat, Carol, and the girls huddled around him. He dropped the check on the counter. There were gasps.

The check was for $5 million.

"Babe," he said to Kat, "Cemetery is getting a scholarship named after him. To the Linksland is getting a mortgage paid off."

He dropped to a knee on the salmon-colored pavers.

"And if the four of you will have me, we're getting an engagement ring and a new house."

Kat hugged Hard Way and then turned to Carol and the girls for final approval. They nodded yes, but then Hailey approached Hard Way and whispered something in his ear.

"And I've just learned there's one small amendment to the proposal," he said, smiling at a proud Hailey, "which I think is an inspired idea."

"Are you going to tell the rest of us?" Kat said.

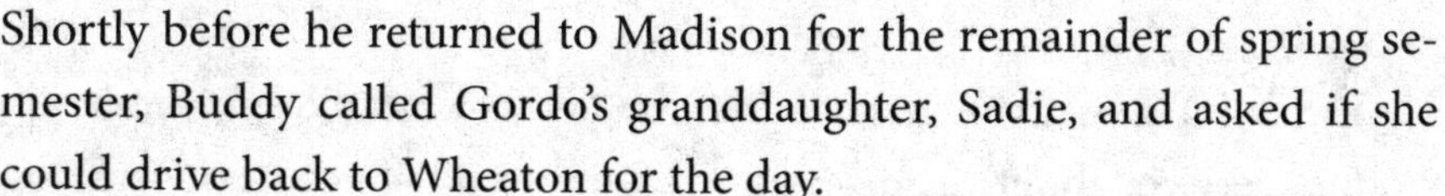

Shortly before he returned to Madison for the remainder of spring semester, Buddy called Gordo's granddaughter, Sadie, and asked if she could drive back to Wheaton for the day.

"For what?" she said.

"A ceremony," Buddy said.

"What kind of ceremony?"

"The kind worth driving home for. I'll text you the street address."

"You're killing me, Smalls," she said. "I'll see you at noon tomorrow."

The next day, Buddy was waiting in his car when Sadie pulled into the entrance of 1109 Warrenville Road.

St. Michael's Cemetery.

Sadie rolled down her driver's-side window. A light rain was falling on the raw April afternoon. The drops began to dot the armrest.

"Buddy, what's going on?"

"Your granddad is buried here."

"I know, I was here for his funeral," she said sarcastically. "How did you know?"

"I looked it up online. Every so often, I come here to pay my respects."

"You do?" Her expression instantly softened.

"Whenever I'm back home. C'mon, follow me."

They drove slowly through the cemetery and parked their cars near Gordo's gravestone. Buddy pulled a small paper grocery bag out of the back seat.

The grave marker was modest, but the grass surrounding it had been recently edged and mowed. Buddy swept away bits of dirt and grass blades off the flat marker with the back of his hand.

"What's in the bag?" Sadie said.

"Something I think he'd appreciate," Buddy said.

He pulled an envelope from the bag and handed it to Sadie.

"It's from my dad," Buddy said as she opened the letter.

Sadie,

I wish I had met your grandfather. Buddy told me about his military service, about his devotion to family, and about his love of all things golf.

Somehow, he knew that the true power of those Nicklaus clubs had more to do with what happened off a golf course than on it. I thought the clubs' gift was their ability to hit a ball a great distance. Instead, their real magic was to reduce the distance between me and Buddy. For that, I am forever indebted to Gordo.

Buddy mentioned that your grandfather thought highly of the Evans Scholars Foundation. At Buddy's suggestion, I've endowed a full Evans scholarship in the name of Standish Gordon Jennings. The scholarship is fully funded in perpetuity.

In addition, I've contacted the law school at Madison. I've arranged, if you'll allow me, to pay off your student loans and cover all costs related to your final year there.

With gratitude,
Joe Riley

She folded the rain-dotted letter and returned it to the envelope before looking up.

"This was your idea?" she said, her voice as soft as the rain.

"I guess I'm good at spending my dad's money," he said. "He always says, 'Live life going forward. Understand life looking back.' Gordo helped me do both."

"This would mean everything to SG. When he died, people told me, 'He's in a better place.' And I always wanted to say, 'It's a better place because he's in it.' I miss him so much."

She reached out for Buddy's hand. "Thank you."

"There's one more thing," Buddy said.

"More? How can there be more?"

He took a small jar from the bag and held it up for Sadie to see.

"I don't understand," she said. "You brought beach sand?"

"I brought it from the 18th hole at Augusta National. The sand is from a greenside bunker."

Tears began to stream down her face.

"When I was a kid, my granddad and I used to watch the Masters. It was his favorite week of the year."

Buddy unscrewed the top of the jar and handed it to her.

"He would love you for this," she said. "I know I do."

"Go ahead," he said.

Sadie held the jar at knee level, as if she were taking a free drop, and began tapping the side of the jelly jar. The white sand spilled out in a steady stream as she poured it in front of the gravestone. The sand nestled into the grass. The rain did the rest.

When classes at Madison ended in early May, Buddy returned home, only to find Hard Way sitting in the living room with his parents.

"Please tell me you didn't . . ." Buddy said.

"Get fired again?" Hard Way said. "No, the Aussie has skills. Sarge helped us get a couple of sponsor exemptions, and we've made a little noise, cashed a few medium-sized checks. We're having fun."

"With Sarge as his coach and you on his bag, that's no surprise," Buddy said. "How long you here?"

"I flew in this morning, out tonight to meet Derrin in Myrtle Beach for a tournament," Hard Way said. "Just wanted to check on To the Linksland and stop by and say hello to your mom and your old man. I'm hoping I can convince all of you to come out for the wedding in late September." He turned to Riley. "I need a best man."

"Me?"

"I think you qualify."

"I'd be honored."

Hard Way glanced around the living room. On the wall behind the couch was a framed strip of brass. He stood and examined it more closely.

It was Riley's nameplate with "Fraud" written on it—the one that the Green Jacket had ordered be removed. On the white border, it read A REMINDER OF WHAT YOU OVERCAME. It was signed by the Green Jacket and the locker-room manager.

"Very nice," Hard Way said.

"I heard you did a very nice thing for Kat's mom," Laurel said. "I talked to your fiancée."

Hard Way was caught by surprise.

"Yeah, we don't have to talk about that," he said, embarrassed by the topic.

"What'd he do?" Buddy said.

"He asked his mother-in-law to move in with the family," Laurel said. "What a sweet gesture."

"For a very sweet person, but I can't take credit for it," Hard Way said. "It was Hailey's idea. Our new place has a casita, so Carol has her own space. It's a win-win, especially with Kat traveling with me now and then. The girls are crazy about Carol, and so am I."

"I like the idea of a good deed," Buddy said.

"Like the bunker sand at Gordo's grave?" Hard Way said.

Buddy shot his dad a look. "That was supposed to be a secret, Dad."

"What can I say—I'm a proud father."

"That was a good deed," Hard Way said. "Now I need you to do one more."

By the time Hard Way left that day, Buddy had agreed to oversee the driving range for the summer. In return, Hard Way would give him a modest budget to make improvements at the range, as well as a 20 percent share of the profits, which, given To the Linksland's financial history, meant 20 percent of zero.

In late July, Hard Way returned to Chicago to attend the ceremony for the well-deserved and long-overdue induction of Sand Man into the Caddie Hall of Fame. Before driving downtown to the Peninsula Hotel for the Western Golf Association's Green Coat Gala, Hard Way decided to make a quick surprise visit to his driving range.

When he arrived, the parking lot was full of cars and customers, which was a first for To the Linksland. Instead of his original fifteen artificial mats, there were now twenty-five—and they were all new, and each was protected by covered hitting bays and featured cooling fans that gently stirred the humid July air. His beloved bent-grass hitting area had been expanded, too. Hard Way counted a dozen players working their way through their buckets, with another dozen players using an adjacent chipping and putting area. There were range finders at each hitting station, attached discreetly by a thin steel cable.

In the far distance, Hard Way could see several new signs on the range. He asked one of the customers if he could use a range finder.

"You're kidding me," Hard Way said as he read the first sign: 400 YARDS—JOE RILEY DISTANCE.

And then 50 yards beyond that: 450 YARDS—GORDO DISTANCE.

Positioned throughout the driving range hitting areas were a half dozen industrial-sized Yeti coolers, each filled with ice and free bottles of water. A sign outside the office read KIDS UNDER 12 HIT FREE FROM 3 TO 4 EACH WEEKDAY.

"Free?" Hard Way said.

Then he noticed a new addition to the office shack. The green neon OPEN sign in the window was still there, but now above the front door was another neon sign, this one declaring the new name of the range.

No. 33.

Hard Way hadn't noticed it when the Uber pulled in, but his small To the Linksland sign in the parking lot had been replaced too. Buddy had changed the name of the range—HARD WAY'S RANGE!—in honor of Larry Bird's Boston Celtics jersey number?

Hard Way marched into the shack. A high schooler was working the counter.

"Is Buddy here?" Hard Way said, not bothering to hide the anger in his voice.

"He's out driving the picker," she said, unfazed by the display. "He'll be done soon."

Hard Way glanced at the walls. There were framed photos of Joe Riley and Hard Way from the pre-qualifier in Houston, as well as from the tournament itself. There were dozens of photos from Augusta

National: the Par 3 Contest and each of the four rounds of Masters play, including Riley's greenside bunker shot on the 18th hole on Sunday. There was a group shot from the rental house, and a picture of Hard Way and Riley hugging outside the clubhouse after Sunday's round. Hard Way stared at each photo as the memories returned.

The sound of an engine interrupted the nostalgia tour. It was Buddy. He was done picking the range of balls.

Hard Way stepped outside and was greeted with another shocking site. On each side of the metal cage of the picker was a steel cutout of Hard Way's former man's face. Above the smarmy, smug mug shot was a message: HIT HIM AND GET A FREE BUCKET.

"Hard Way!" Buddy said as he bounded out of the picker cage and shook Max's hand. "I thought you guys were playing in the Twin Cities this coming week."

"Mechanical problems with the plane on my connection through O'Hare. Had an afternoon to kill." He gestured toward the range facility. "Buddy, what's going on here?"

"Isn't it great? We've made a few changes."

"A few?! You changed the name of the place without asking me."

"You guys were at Royal Melbourne and then Singapore. Dad said not to bother you. Said that you'd trust my judgment."

"Larry eff-in Bird's jersey number?"

"What?"

"The name of the place."

"No . . . what? Larry Bird? Come here."

Buddy opened the door to the shack and pointed to a framed photo of Hard Way and Riley on the first tee at Augusta National.

"Thirty-three is for this," Buddy said, tapping at the image of Hard Way.

Hard Way leaned in and then understood.

"I'm an idiot," Hard Way said, instantly recognizing the green patch on the front of his white jumpsuit.

There it was, No. 33—their Masters registration number.

"The customers love it," Buddy said. "They love the story behind it.

They feel connected to it . . . to you and Dad. Nothing against To the Linksland, but they didn't get it."

"The mats expansion? The extra turf? The covered bays? The range finders? Free balls for kids? Free waters? How much is this costing me?"

"Costing you? It's *making* you money. A lot of money. The ROI is at 15 percent and climbing. You saw the parking lot."

"But how?"

"What you and Dad did at the Masters made a difference. The creature comforts help separate us from a lot of the public ranges. I switched us to Pro V1s, upgraded the mats, and added more bent grass. I raised our bucket prices by 25 cents, which helps defer the costs of those gawd-awful range balls you were using here. The free buckets for the kids brings in the parents, who almost always buy a bucket for themselves. And the range finders are a huge hit."

"And the new range signs?"

"An homage to Gordo and dad."

"And what's with my former guy?"

"We're telling a story, Hard Way. The customers love it."

"Buddy, it's all amazing. I'm almost as surprised as the first time I saw your dad hit that Jack driver. But do me one favor: Let's take the high road on my former guy. I've seen him a few times on Tour. He's actually been civil. I'd like to keep it that way."

"I didn't know that. I'll take the faces off today. And by the way, you should have all the monthly financials in a doc file. Plus, I've got a good transition team ready to go when I head back to school."

Buddy extended his hand, but Hard Way pulled him in for a hug.

"I've got to head back to O'Hare, but I'll check back in a few weeks."

"Depending on which week, I'm taking three days off, but I'll be around."

"Hmmm. You and the law school student?"

"Not exactly. Me and Dad."

Riley donated the remaining MacGregor clubs and the Masters scorecard from the record-setting round of 59 to the Jack Nicklaus Museum in Columbus. Riley thought the museum curator was going to cry when he told him the news.

Several networks, including AGN, offered Riley a job, and at triple his previous salary. He told them he had family commitments.

Publishers tried to convince Riley and Hard Way to write about the green jacket that almost was. The book advances began at $1 million. Several movie production companies asked if they would be interested in selling their life stories. These offers also were substantial.

Hard Way told them it would violate his personal caddie code: *Thou shalt not go public.* Riley also declined all offers. After all, Gordo had entrusted him with his secret and those clubs. He wasn't going to violate that trust for money.

But there was another reason Riley said no. The golf club he had recently joined frowned on its members drawing attention to themselves.

The good news?

Buddy and Riley finished fourth in their flight at the Chicago Golf Club Father/Son tournament.

Acknowledgments

I've never done the exact math, but I probably covered between sixty and seventy-five majors and at least the same number of PGA Tour events during my sports reporting life. If you throw in a handful of Ryder Cups, a few LPGA and amateur events, the occasional U.S. Open qualifier, and countless practice rounds, it's a respectable figure. It doesn't come close to the number of majors covered by the late and legendary Dan Jenkins (230 plus), or by present-day golf writers such as Bob Harig, Doug Ferguson, Jim McCabe, Ron Green Jr., Geoff Shackelford, and Rex Hoggard, but I'm OK with that.

I wasn't there when Jack Nicklaus won the Masters—and his eighteenth career major—in 1986. But in 2005, I saw him play in his final Masters and, later that summer, the final major of his career: the Open Championship at St. Andrews. I still have a commemorative five-pound note featuring Nicklaus issued by the Bank of Scotland, but damn if I can find it. I've interviewed Nicklaus more than a few times, including several sessions at his guesthouse in North Palm Beach, Florida, where the walls are covered with animals that met unfortunate hunting ends.

I walked I don't know how many practice and tournament holes with Tiger Woods during the prime and twilight of his astonishing career. I've kneeled or crouched at rope's edge of a tee box, fairway, or green and watched in wonderment as Woods did what we previously thought impossible. But most of all—and it was part of my to-do list in every tournament Woods played—I used to love watching him on the range or at the short-game area. You could see his mind at work. You could see the pursuit of perfection. And maybe I'm wrong, but even when he was inside the ropes and that protective cocoon, there were moments when his eyes would dart here and there, as if he was aware of everything but acknowledging nothing.

I traveled to Holywood, Northern Ireland, the hometown of a then teenage Rory McIlroy, at a time when no golf hat could fully contain his exploding curly hair, and no course could intimidate him. The local bakery sold cookies with his face in icing, and a tattoo shop would happily put McIlroy's visage on the body part of your choice. Years later, the hair is tamer, but he still bends the knee to no course.

I saw Tom Watson almost win the Open Championship at age fifty-nine, only to lose in a playoff. And the next day there was an electrical fire on my flight to the States and we had to dump fuel and brace for impact during the final emergency approach into Reykjavík, Iceland. Flight attendants stuffed passports down their pants and tops. Passengers attempted to call loved ones. And there's still a small and perverse part of me that thinks Watson had a tougher day than we did.

I was almost tossed from covering a Masters because I committed the sin of parking in the wrong space in the media lot. I was summoned to the on-site trailer of local law enforcement, where a police commander poked his beefy finger at my chest and in a slow, menacing drawl threatened to expel me from the premises himself.

After covering an Open Championship at Royal St. George's, I realized the next morning that I had left my newly purchased and expensive rainsuit in the media center. After several frantic calls, I located the one remaining person still at work there—a lovely American press conference stenographer who was just moments away from loading her equipment into her rental car. She kindly agreed to bring the rainsuit back to the States, where I would arrange shipping. A few days later, she left a voicemail, which I unknowingly played just as my wife entered my home office. It began, "Hi, Gene. This is Sandra. I have your pants."

This is all a wordy prelude to simply say I've seen and heard some golf stuff. The guts of this novel are based loosely on what I've witnessed and experienced while wading in the waters of that addictive sport. The rest of it is how I imagined it could be.

There was no major I covered more often than the Masters. I remain in awe of the Augusta National members, staff, and volunteers who make that tournament singular in every way. I loved it and loathed it but always respected the idea of it, and in recent years I've respected it more because of the club's willingness to evolve.

During my last several years at the Masters, I was one of several reporters assigned to conduct a short TV interview with the newest champion in the clubhouse grill area. By the time we would finish, the grounds were deserted and the course covered in rich darkness, save for the beams of light filtering from the clubhouse windows and the small spotlights aimed at the famed Big Oak Tree. I would stand under the tree, stare out toward holes shrouded by the night—Nos. 10, 18, 9, and 1—and think of those players and caddies who had walked the same grounds over the previous 90-plus years. It was the one time I had the place to myself.

No book is written by the author alone. At least this one wasn't. It is built around a fantastical premise, but covered, I hope, in layers of golf authenticity. I developed a good working relationship with dozens of professional players, but it was their caddies who became my favorites. It is unavoidable. Caddies have blue in their collars and not in their blood. They have a spectrum of odd and lovely backstories, a catalog of wonderful nicknames, and a patience and giving nature that I always appreciated. If you earned a caddie's trust, you usually earned a friend at the same time.

For the purposes of this book, I owe considerable thanks to such renowned caddies as Jim "Bones" Mackay, Michael Greller, Joe LaCava, Joe Skovron, Joe Greiner, Mike "Fluff" Cowan, Billy Foster, Paul Tesori, and Steve Williams.

Jim is one of the very best and most honorable people I've ever known, and Michael, despite an incident involving a cheerleader's megaphone and a sideline pass I arranged for him at a Michigan game, is a close second, tied with the great LaCava. The others have helped me in ways they probably don't even realize. I took bits and pieces of interviews and conversations I had with them over the years and wove their insights and perspective into these pages.

I also drew on the expertise of those I met and worked with during my time as a minor widget in ESPN's golf broadcast coverage machine. By osmosis, you became smarter and better by being in the same studio, greenroom, rental house, or production meeting with Scott Van Pelt, Andy North, David Duval, Michael Eaves, Matt Barrie, Jeff Sluman, Sean McDonough, Bob Wischusen, Curtis Strange, Dave Flemming, Billy Kratzert, Chris Fallica, Steve Coughlin, and Marty Smith. Scott, Andy, and Curtis deserve a special mention for their assistance with this project, as do Aaron Katzman and Jen Chafitz. And I never would have been part of that world had it not been for Mike McQuade and Lee Fitting.

The gifted Dottie Pepper of CBS Sports, whose career playing achievements are worthy of the World Golf Hall of Fame (and overdue), provided me with invaluable information, context, and support, while valued friends Harig, Ian O'Connor, Tom Rinaldi, Joe Wojciechowski, John Marvel, Tom Young, and Ivan Maisel gave their time and feedback during the formative years of the manuscript. The spirits of Jenkins, Steve DiMeglio, Jeff Babineau, and Ron Green Sr. are also present in this book.

I owe much to Whisper Rock Golf Club founder and owner Gregg Tryhus and general manager Trent Rathbun. The Rock is golf heaven.

I feel similarly about Chicago Golf Club in my hometown of Wheaton, Illinois. The excellent and invaluable books *The Prairie Raynor* by John Moran and Rand Jerris, and *Chicago Golf Club 1892–1992,* by Ross Goodner, have many dog-eared pages from my research. I drive by the club at least once a week and wish.

Jim Yachinich, a respected golf-club maker and tech adviser, walked me through all things related to the creation of vintage clubs, while

Steve Auch, the curator for the Jack Nicklaus Museum in Columbus, Ohio, gave me many insights into the Golden Bear and the clubs he used.

The good people of the United States Golf Association, specifically those in the Equipment Standards office, provided me with invaluable and patient explanations of club technology and testing protocol. Weirdly enough, it was fascinating.

This book never would have reached critical mass without the remarkable Amy Einhorn, senior vice president and publisher at Crown. Her support, belief, and good humor were a constant comfort, and her brilliant notes, suggestions, and editing made the book better. Much better. I owe her more than she'll ever know.

Thanks also to the indispensable Lori Kusatzky, an associate editor at Crown, and to the production, editing, and design teams there.

Literary agent David Black and tag-team partner Mark Tavani didn't laugh when I first pitched the idea of this novel. Instead, they went to work, which is what they always do. They encouraged me. They fought for me. I couldn't ask for better teammates and advocates.

As always, T. L. Mann provided his customary inspiration and strength. And the exploits of the Tornadoes—Tommy Chuck and Owen—are sprinkled throughout these pages.

I save my most sincere gratitude for my wife and book widow, Cheryl Coffey. These are time-consuming projects, but Cheryl, as she always does, shared the journey with me.

About the Author

Gene Wojciechowski is a *New York Times* bestselling author who has written or co-written thirteen books, including *The Last Great Game: Duke vs. Kentucky and the 2.1 Seconds That Changed Basketball* and Kirk Herbstreit's memoir, *Out of the Pocket: Football, Fatherhood, and* College GameDay *Saturdays.* He spent nearly twenty-six years at ESPN as a columnist and reporter, winning multiple Sports Emmys and Edward R. Murrow Awards for his features work. He lives in Wheaton, Illinois, with his wife.